STORM

Originally published in Germany
under the title "Sturm"
by Heyne, in January 2018.

Published in the United States in 2024
by Auguste Crime, an imprint of

CLEVO BOOKS

530 Euclid Ave #45
Cleveland, Oh 44115
www.clevobooks.com

Library of Congress Control Number: 2023951562
ISBN: 978-1-68577-009-9
E-book ISBN: 978-1-68577-010-5
Printed in the USA

Translator: Steve Anderson
English language layout: Ron Kretsch
English language editing: Martin Schneider
Author Photo: Marion Laub Photography

First American Edition

STORM

UWE LAUB

TRANSLATED BY
STEVE ANDERSON

AUGUSTE

For my father
Thank you for everything

"They should be ashamed, all those who benefit from the wonders of science and technology and yet never bother to comprehend them any better than a cow does the botany of the plants it devours with such total complacency."

—Albert Einstein

1

Berlin, Olympic Stadium

DANIEL BENDER SHUT HIS EYES AND WISHED HE WERE anywhere but here. A half hour ago he was feeling great, fired up, ready to take on the world. But now his Saturday afternoon was turning into a nightmare, and it wasn't just the weather that was getting worse. He kept one eye on the thunderclouds rapidly swelling above Olympic Stadium, but the true horror was playing out on the soccer field. FC Bayern Munich had just made it 3–0, and it was only halftime. Daniel glanced at his buddy Ben standing next to him, his Hertha Berlin scarf wrapped around his eyes and ears, suffering like a dog. He gave Ben a reassuring pat on the shoulder. "It's not over till it's over."

Ben yanked down his scarf. "Save the sound bites for your viewers." He glared at Daniel and stared up at the sky as if praying.

Daniel didn't push it. Ben would calm down after the game, over a cold beer. Instead Daniel tugged at his Hertha jersey, which kept sticking to him. He wasn't used to such muggy weather this time of year. It had been like this for days. The tabloids were calling it a "heat wave"—embellishing as usual. Daniel took a more level-headed view of things. He knew that the high-pressure system they were currently experiencing was caused by a pattern meteorologists called a block. This happened when a stable high pressure system in the upper troposphere drove away neighboring low-pressure systems, creating a large pocket of good weather that could extend more than 1,200 miles across Europe. It was actually a good thing. Yet like most people, Daniel was hoping for a little cooling. Copying Ben's example, he looked up.

The mass of clouds had formed an imposing column that towered high into the sky. It was a cumulonimbus cloud with a pronounced anvil shape, and that did not bode well. Daniel could only frown at that. Then, right on cue, they heard a rumble of thunder, dull and prolonged, swelling with such intensity that it drowned out the singing of the fans in the stands.

Daniel looked across the oval of the stadium toward the gap in the roof above the Marathon Gate. There stood the Bell Tower, about five hundred feet outside the stadium at the end of a vast lawn, the Maifeld. From his position in the East Curve, Daniel could easily make out the upper section of the 250-foot tower. His mouth hung open as he stared at the black mass of clouds that suddenly lowered from the underside of the thundercloud, soon hovering so close to the ground they were practically scraping the tip of the tower.

A wall cloud, he thought. *But that's not possible.*

A bright flash of lightning streaked down from the sky, followed immediately by a cracking thunderstrike. The grandstand shuddered.

"Wow," Ben said.

No one was watching the game anymore. Everyone was staring upward. Many pointed at the cloud wall hovering right over the Bell Tower, while others filmed the event with their phones. Daniel pulled out his phone too. Over the next few minutes, he was sure he could capture some great footage for his next program.

It started to pour. Lightning lit up the sky, each flash brighter than the last. Thunderclaps cracked the air like fighter jets breaking the sound barrier. A bolt of lightning struck the tip of the Bell Tower right where the Olympic Bell was located, and for a second Daniel thought he saw the four-and-a-half-ton bell glow red hot against the pitch-black sky.

The wind picked up. Daniel watched with growing concern as the clouds above them started to rotate. They were rapidly crystallizing into the rounded form of a thunderstorm cell, a form so massive it could cover all of Berlin's Westend district. It started rotating faster. If Daniel wasn't mistaken, the air now carried a chorine-like smell. His first thought: *ozone*.

The game continued but was sure to be stopped at any moment. Right as Daniel pondered seeking out an exit, a bolt of lightning struck the floodlights in the roof across the stadium. Sparks flew; metal and glass fragments rained down on the crowd. People were screaming. Then all the floodlights went out, and the whole stadium was plunged into darkness. The players now fled to the locker rooms. But Daniel kept his focus on the West Curve across from them, where panic was now setting in.

The thousands of people in the stadium suddenly had the same exact thought: *I am getting the hell out of here!* The crowds rushed for the exits. Some fans probably thought themselves lucky to have seats near the exits, but many of them failed to beat the relentlessly charging throngs past the barriers and were soon crushed against those same barriers. Piercing cries could be heard over the screaming. And with horrifying clarity, Daniel now grasped that people would die here today. He stopped recording and stuffed his phone into his pants pocket.

"That can't be!" shouted Ben, nudging Daniel in the ribs and gesturing toward the Bell Tower.

Daniel forced himself to look away from the surging masses in the West Curve. But he forgot all that once he saw the reason for Ben's distress.

"Holy Mother of God. . ." Daniel muttered. He stood mesmerized, unable to move as he watched the events play out around the Bell Tower.

The low hovering cloud wall was changing shape, forming a gigantic funnel. The narrow end of the funnel cloud began elongating and soon resembled an elephant's trunk, heading straight for the ground below. Daniel gasped. He'd never witnessed the birth of a tornado from such a close distance, not even on his semester abroad at the University of Oklahoma's School of Meteorology. He never could have imagined experiencing it right here in the middle of Germany.

The trunk kept getting closer and closer to the Maifeld. It finally touched down, made contact. Grass, earth, and everything else on the lawn swirled up and was sucked aloft mercilessly, the raging tornado convulsing and booming as it cut a devastating swath through the field.

At first it seemed that it would take a hard right and veer off toward the stadium, but instead it changed course and spun toward the Bell Tower. The narrow structure was no match for such primal fury. It burst into a thousand pieces under the force of the violent winds—

concrete, bricks, and chunks of masonry were hurled in all directions. The larger debris struck earth while smaller fragments were carried high upward, only to be spat back out like cannon shots. The massive bell plunged down, crashing through the roof of Langemarck Hall directly below. Daniel had no time to worry if the bell crushed anyone because the tornado was now heading for the stadium.

Many fans were still in the stands, but that changed once everyone saw they were in grave danger. In a matter of moments all of the exits became jammed. No one could get out.

It had grown dark, as if night had fallen instantly. Hard rain mixed with hail pelted down on everyone. Daniel threw up his arms to protect himself. All his instincts urged him to flee, but one look at the jammed exits told him that any attempt to get out was hopeless. One thing was clear, however: if the tornado stuck to its current path, it would get him and Ben.

Everywhere people were frantically trying to reach safety. Men heading toward the supposed shelter of the stadium tunnels shoved women and children aside, only to discover they had no hope of penetrating the human walls. The tornado reached the stadium and grazed a column of the Marathon Gate. It crumbled as if made of sand, spewing concrete and mortar in all directions. People dropped, struck by the jagged shards. Yet the true horror was just beginning. The tornado grabbed its first victims. They were sucked in, were whirled up into the air screaming, and then were spat back out. From many meters up they plunged back to the ground, where they lay lifeless.

The tornado's roar swelled to an infernal screech, reminding Daniel of a freight train barreling at him with full brakes on. He curled up in the fetal position, keeping his hands above his head to block the hail.

He wasn't sure how long he stayed in that position, but the monstrosity eventually pulled away from the stands and headed for the now-abandoned soccer pitch, where the deadly winds dismantled a goal as if it were made of Tinkertoys. The tornado's trunk swayed back and forth and seemed to seek out new prey. The rain and hail pummeled down on Daniel, but he hardly noticed. He was like a deer in headlights, unable to turn his gaze from his gruesome fate.

The tornado hovered over the midfield line as if deciding which direction to take next. Then it made a 90-degree angle, heading right for the main grandstand. The glass VIP boxes above offered no protection at all, their full-length panes promptly exploding. Shards and splinters dumped onto the main stand below, followed by tables and chairs from inside the boxes. The VIPs inside had had ample time to flee, yet to Daniel's amazement many had stayed behind. Did they really believe they would be spared inside their golden cages? Such a lethal fallacy now cost many of them their lives.

A few moments later, the tornado tore through the stadium's outer walls and finally pulled away. Trembling, Daniel watched the upper reaches of the funnel cloud recede. Its roar weakened, and the wind, rain, and hail ceased as abruptly as they had begun. The grounds outside the Marathon Gate looked like the target of an air raid. Inside the stadium, corpses and severed limbs covered the stands, the blue running track, and the pitch.

Daniel looked up, his eyes filled with tears. Up in the roof's framework of beams and floodlights, he could see more bodies still. Hurtled upward by the tornado, the bodies had gotten caught in the iron and steel girders. Daniel pulled Ben close, hugged him as tight as he could, and together they sobbed like they never had before.

2

Yakutsk, Far Eastern Federal District, Russia

EVER SINCE LUNCHTIME, THE RUMOR HAD BEEN MAKING the rounds that something strange was happening up at ground level, yet no one knew exactly what was up. Yevgeny Sorokin watched his co-workers' faces and saw that same helplessness he'd been feeling for the last half hour after the announcement that their shift was ending early. Yevgeny had been extracting diamonds from deep in the tunnels of the ALROSA Mines since the 1970s, and the conditions had always been life-threatening. But this situation was a new one even for him.

The only thing good about it, he figured, was that he would soon find out what was going on.

He opened his locker, stuffed his work shoes and gloves inside, and pulled out the boots, winter gloves, fur cap, and face mask he'd stowed before his shift. He slipped into his unty moon boots, the world's warmest boots, and carried the rest—as a rule, he usually waited until right before the ride above before putting them on. Winter was a few weeks late, yet the temperature at ground level was already hovering around –22 degrees Fahrenheit. Yevgeny wasn't really bothered, though. Like all Yakuts, he didn't know otherwise. He was born in the coldest city in the world and had grown up dealing with temperatures of –50 degrees from a very early age.

Yevgeny stepped into the elevator, the iron cage lumbered into motion, and he rode up to ground level along with his fellow mine workers. The mood remained tense. The rattling and grating of the elevator had never sounded so loud to Yevgeny as it did today.

"This must have something to do with that green light," said an older miner with a beard.

"What kind of light?" Yevgeny asked.

"My brother-in-law Alexey saw it last night. He couldn't sleep and was looking out his window. That's when he spotted it."

"What did he see?"

"Alexey swears that the whole sky was lit up green."

"The northern lights?"

The other miner shook his head. "According to Alexey, it looked like a pulsating green ball."

Yevgeny eyed his bearded coworker skeptically. Tales like these had always circulated among the older and frequently superstitious locals. He was about to comment when he noticed something odd. With irritation he looked down at himself. It felt as if a layer of thick, heavy air was wrapping around him like a cocoon, pressing in on his chest. The alarmed faces of his fellow miners told him that they felt it too.

As they ascended toward ground level, Yevgeny became more uneasy. His breathing became more difficult, and he wiped a film of sweat from his forehead with the back of his hand. He looked up at the bright strip of daylight marking their exit. Did it smell different, too? And just where was all this warmth coming from? He wiped again at his damp forehead.

The elevator stopped, and the doors opened. A blaze of light blinded Yevgeny. He squinted, shielded his eyes with his hand, and tried to make out what was in front of him. A mild breeze brushed his sweat-covered face. Damn it, why is it so warm up here? It should be ice cold right now.

Someone commanded him to step out. With deliberation, Yevgeny obeyed, stepping into a world that was nothing like the one he remembered from a few hours earlier.

Strong beams of sunlight penetrated his clothes, warming his body. He shuffled away from the elevator, blinking and squinting again. The ground beneath his feet was so soft that it gave way under his weight. Yevgeny stepped into a puddle, righted himself, and instantly stepped into a second puddle. He eyed its oily streaks and wondered why the water was not frozen. He looked around, his eyes gradually adjusting to the brightness. People were standing around alone or in groups and observing the inconceivable: the ground, which without exception remained completely frozen from September to April in all of Yakutia, was thawing out at an astonishing pace.

Massive puddles were forming all over the compound. The ground resembled delicate sand. Not far from Yevgeny was a truck. The tires on the driver's side rested on firm ground, but those on the passenger side were submerged in water up to the hubs. Two workers were rushing to unload the boxes threatening to slide off its increasingly canted cargo bed. A short distance away, a tall pole with heavy floodlights attached to the top also began to tilt dangerously.

Nine hours earlier, Yevgeny had left his home at first light to head to work as always. The thermometer was still showing −44 degrees Fahrenheit, which was routine for Yevgeny, who had never left Yakutsk in his whole life. Now the sun was beaming down with an intensity he had never thought possible. After barely five minutes, his skin was itching on his face and the backs of his hands, and he stared helplessly at his jacket, fur cap, gloves, and face mask he was still carrying. The temperature surely had to be over freezing now—if not in the 40s! How was this possible?

A deafening noise jolted Yevgeny from his thoughts—the floodlight pole had fallen over. All at once, Yevgeny recognized the full magnitude of what was now happening. If all the earth at ground level thawed out, it would dissolve into the brittle soil that Yevgeny's untys were already sinking into, up to his ankles. In most countries, no one would consider building on such a problematic foundation, but in Yakutsk they had no choice. All their buildings stood on stilts—for each individual stilt, they had to bore a hole deep into the rock-hard ground. In the summer, the ground thawed to a depth of only thirteen feet maximum.

But that rule was obviously not holding true anymore—as the fallen pole had just revealed.

The realization made Yevgeny sick to his stomach. If the ground kept thawing at this rate, there was a real threat that whole residential areas would sink into the earth—after all, Yakutsk was literally built on sand.

O bozhe moy!—my God! Yevgeny now remembered his own little home. And his wife Irina and his son Dimitry, who both were waiting at home for him, probably feeling as anxious and helpless as he did. He had to get to them immediately.

He couldn't leave the fenced-off and alarm-secured compound before first undergoing the usual inspection, which the mining firm declined to waive even on this unusual day—with the purpose of preventing any diamonds from being smuggled out of the mine.

Yevgeny was led into an unfurnished room, where he had to disrobe down to his underwear. An employee wearing powdered latex gloves waved him over and submitted him to a full-body search that spared no orifice. Yevgeny closed his eyes, always hating this part of his daily routine. Next, he had to pull on all the clothes he'd been wearing and step up to the X-ray machine. The whole exit procedure seemed to be taking more time than usual. He impatiently rubbed at the stubble on his face, and he started pulling his jacket and sweater back off even before he had been allowed to leave through the airlock doors. The heat outside was unbearable.

At the nearby bus stop, a rusting shelter with a corrugated roof full of holes, the buses came at a high frequency during the shift change of a normal workday. But nothing was normal today.

"Buses stopped coming," said a fellow miner who had apparently come to work on foot. Like Yevgeny, he was carrying his sweater and jacket, his face red and sweaty.

"They're not getting through?" Yevgeny asked. "Are things that bad?"

The miner started to answer, then just shook his head and continued on his way.

Yevgeny didn't hesitate either—he started off on foot for the five-mile trek home.

At daybreak, the cars and buses had been spinning their wheels on the icy main road as usual, but now everything was mud. It stank of rotten eggs; permafrost ground, Yevgeny knew, contained methane and other fermentation gasses, and now it was all being released.

The sun stung like fire on his skin. To shield his face, he pulled his fur cap over his head and folded down his earflaps. The heat under the cap immediately became unbearable, but it was more critical to protect his skin from the stinging sunlight. His undershirt stuck to his chest and back, and his feet were baking inside his thick untys, lined as they were with reindeer fur.

After a half hour, Yevgeny reached a long bend in the road. It led to a deep depression in the ground. Now he understood why buses weren't getting through to the mines—a stretch of earth about a hundred feet wide was submerged in a deep pool of water right where the road ran through. The surrounding meltwater was obviously collecting here, and in the middle of it sat a bus with the water up to its windows. Three more buses stood idling on the far side. Their drivers stood together, smoking and debating the situation, looking equally helpless.

Yevgeny knelt at the edge of the water, scooped some up with both hands and splashed his face with it. It was a blessed relief. He removed his cap, pushed back his hair with his wet hands. Then, following the example of other miners, he skirted the small lake by keeping to the rise along the right side.

He eventually reached Yakutsk this way.

What he found there surpassed his worst fears. Nearly all the homes on the edge of town had sunk into a brown sludge; some were already starting to pitch to one side. Frantic activity filled the streets. Men were arguing loudly and gesturing violently at one another, while others rushed to save whatever belongings they could from their homes. Women young and old wailed and prayed as they watched. One building was on fire, the flames shooting out of the ground floor. The fire department was on the scene at least and was starting to put out the flames, which must have been caused by the building's gas line breaking as it sank. If that were true, then the same danger threatened hundreds of homes in the area—all Yakutsk would be transformed into a flaming hell if this damned thaw didn't stop soon.

Yevgeny crossed himself. He thought of his little home on the Lena River over on the eastern edge of town. A horrific thought struck him: if certain riverbank areas were sinking, wasn't it also possible that the river's course could change? What if the Lena overran its banks and flooded his whole neighborhood? The powerful current would take everything with it—cars, houses, people. Irina and Dimitry's very lives might be in danger. Yevgeny picked up his pace.

He passed by a market where yesterday the various stands had offered frozen milk by the slab and the frozen fish had poked straight up out of the vendors' buckets. Now the fish hung their heads, and white stains on the ground revealed the fate of all that milk. An old market woman grabbed Yevgeny by the arm, wailing and rambling about spoiled goods and her business being ruined. He pushed her aside, hating himself for it all the while, but there was no time. He just needed to reach his family. He heard a dull explosion from somewhere near the city center, and the howl of sirens. Another gas line? As best as he could, he tried to block out the panic and commotion around him. Yakutsk had just under 270,000 residents, and all of them seemed to be out on the streets.

He soon reached his neighborhood. The large multi-family homes were submerged in sludge up to their doorsteps, but so were the little houses. Was that because of the river?

Was the Lena washing away the soil? Yevgeny's stomach tightened when he saw that his house was also affected. A watery, gurgling sludge was making its way through the opening of his cracked front door.

Yevgeny ripped open the door. "Irina! Dimitry!"

No answer.

O bozhe moy, he thought, when he noticed the smell of gas in the house.

3

Bredenstedt, Germany, near Hanover

THE LAST SUNDAY IN SEPTEMBER WAS A GORGEOUS DAY. The bright sun drove the temperature up to 85 degrees for probably the last time this year, and the organizers of Bredenstedt's annual town fair could not have asked for better weather. Laura Wagner sat on the edge of the circular fountain in the town square and observed it all through her sunglasses. She wore a cream-colored blouse with turquoise shorts; her mid-length brown hair was combed to one side and fastened with a barrette. The fountain bubbled away in the center of the square. The glittering spray of water floated in the air, and Laura enjoyed how it made her bare legs tingle. She dipped her hand into the water and dabbed the back of her neck with its coolness. Such a blessing. She promptly slid out of her strappy sandals, dipped her feet into the fountain, and wiggled her toes. A young couple in love sauntered by, holding hands. Laura watched them disappear into the crowd, sighed dreamily, and returned her attention to the other passersby.

The old town was closed to traffic just like every year on this day. Balloons floated outside shops, and there was even a flea market. Umpteen stalls and food trucks were offering all kinds of grub; the aromas of grilled sausages and cotton candy filled the air. Meanwhile the local music society was performing in the small main tent on the edge of town square.

There was no sign of the parade yet, so Laura raised her face to the sun. It was going to make all her freckles reappear, but she didn't care. As a teen she'd tried to cover up the light brown flecks with makeup, yet at some point she'd come to realize that her freckles simply belonged to her face—and besides, it wasn't as if there was currently a man in her life who had an opinion about them either way. For some years now, her world had only revolved around Robin, her eleven-year-old son. She could hardly wait to see him in his costume.

The sun disappeared behind a cloud. Laura removed her sunglasses and let her eyes wander. The people of Bredenstedt had been darting around to concerts, exhibitions, and other events all weekend long, but the high point, without a doubt, was always the parade that all the schools, kindergartens, and clubs performed in. Faint music now found its way to Laura from some ways away—muffled at first, then gradually louder and clearer. The spectators found their spots, quickly freeing up the parade route through town square. Laura stood on the edge of the fountain, where she could look over all their heads. Yet something was bothering her. She craned her head back and looked up into the sky.

A rare lone cloud had moved in front of the sun. It seemed odd to her, somehow. There was hardly any breeze, and yet the cloud was in motion and transforming rapidly. Laura could see it swelling up. It now resembled a gigantic cauliflower, with more and more bulges. More clouds formed out of nowhere, as if by magic. The sky was clouding over, bit by bit, the weather changing so quickly it took her breath away. *Please don't rain now,* she thought.

The first parade float finally rolled onto town square, a green tractor decorated with flowers and pumping out black exhaust. Right behind that came the first musical band, and spectators along the route started clapping to the beat. Robin's school class would be marching by soon, but she still saw no sign of them. Instead, she noticed something else that was odd: the pigeons that ordinarily flocked to the town square were nowhere to be seen. There was not a single creature. Where had they gone? And why?

When she glanced up again a few minutes later, things were looking even worse.

Low-lying clouds were rolling in from the east, glowing a muddy yellow. The humidity had turned oppressive all of a sudden, and Laura's blouse was sticking to her body. It was definitely looking like a storm now. Laura frowned. The parade was making slow progress, kept bogging down. Then, finally, here came the children.

And with them came the storm.

The menacing cloud front reached the center of town. Strong gusts swept across the square out of nowhere, and Laura had to swing her arms to keep from losing her balance on the edge of the fountain. Her barrette came loose; her hair was whipping all around. She pulled a scrunchy from the pocket of her shorts and tied a ponytail. Something struck the ground with a loud clink. Everyone was fighting the wind; paper plates and napkins were scattering all over. A jacket blew across the square, followed by its cursing owner.

At first Laura couldn't pick Robin out among the crowd of kids, as all the knights and princesses pretty much looked the same from a distance. Only when they got closer could she spot her son. He was marching with his friend Samuel, performing a little duel with his wooden sword. The changing weather didn't seem to bother any of the kids; they were so immersed in their roles that they'd forgotten the world around them. Laura longed for a time as carefree as the one those two boys knew right now. She called out Robin's name and waved to him, but of course he didn't see or hear her.

The rain started in. The first thick drops splashed down from the sky, and within seconds it turned into a downpour, the temperature sinking. It didn't take long for Laura's clothes to get soaked through. She started to shiver, wondering if she should go find cover somewhere, but something deep down stopped her from doing it. She believed in a maternal instinct. Her friends Andrea and Katrin always laughed at her when she brought it up, but Laura knew that it did indeed exist, and as she stood in the downpour getting soaked and freezing on the edge of this fountain, that instinct of hers spoke to her loud and clear.

She remembered those pigeons clearing out. Animals were supposed to have a sixth sense—that should have alerted her sooner. She nervously glanced up at those low-hanging clouds. They had turned black. Now lightning flashed on the edge of town. A dire need to get Robin to safety overcame Laura. He was still having his swordfight with Samuel, about a hundred feet away from her. She jumped off the fountain and ran to her son.

"Excuse me, excuse me," she called out as she cleared a path through the spectators, most of whom were not about to let a little rain and stormy weather spoil their big day.

She soon found herself out among all the children. She spotted Robin and bounded over to him. "Robin!"

"Mom? What are you doing here?" He too was dripping wet, his papier-mâché helmet and shield already warping and about to come apart.

"We're going," Laura said.

"Where?"

"Home."

"Right now? Why?"

"Come on, let's go." She grabbed him by the arm.

"No!" He yanked his arm away. "The others get to keep marching."

"I don't care."

She could tell she was attracting attention. People smirked at her, probably assuming she was being overanxious. Let them smirk, she thought. She pulled Robin to her, more determined than ever. "Now come on!"

"Did Robin do something wrong?" asked Samuel, standing in front of them. His paper helmet hung from his head in tatters.

"No," said Laura. "It's just that—"

Above their heads the thunder bellowed. Laura tensed up. Right then a hunk of ice struck the cobblestones in front of her, bursting into dozens of smaller chunks. She jumped back in shock. More ice came down, and the children let out startled cries. She could not believe her eyes—these hailstones were as big as baseballs.

Panic broke out on the square. A man who had been struck on the head fell to the ground right in front of Laura. Terrified children screamed and ran off in all directions; people sought shelter, but the cover available under the food stalls and in front of the cafes rapidly filled up.

But really, none of it offered any protection.

A hard blow to Laura's shoulder sent a stinging pain down her back; a hailstone had struck her. At the same moment she heard Robin cry out. He pressed his hands to his head and started crying as blood streamed out between his fingers. Laura's heart skipped a beat. This was her wake-up call. Her paralyzing shock vanished at once, and she peered around frantically. Hardly any shelter was left under the food stalls, and the fleeing crowds were now blocking the doorways of all nearby cafés.

She took Robin and Samuel by the hand and ran toward a tractor idling on the square a short distance away. The cab windshield was smashed; the driver was holding his bloodied face with both hands, likely wounded by the broken glass.

"Under the trailer!" shouted Laura. She pulled the two boys down; Robin and Samuel instantly understood and crawled under the trailer's cargo bed. She then got down on her knees and got underneath with them. Several adults and children followed their example until no room was left. Laura only hoped that the driver wouldn't suddenly decide to drive away. He had looked seriously wounded, and who knew what was going through his mind. Yet the alternative was far more dangerous, so they had no choice but to take the risk.

As the hail hammered the cargo bed above them, Laura inspected Robin's injury. She gently felt around his head, which made him cry out.

"Okay, okay," she told him. "I'll be careful." She parted his hair at a spot where she thought the wound was, but it was too dark to see much.

"My head hurts," moaned Robin.

"I know, sweetie. I'll patch you up just as soon as we're back home." She kissed him firmly on the cheek, hoping that he wouldn't notice how worried she was. As soon as this hail stopped, she'd have to take him to the hospital. But for now, they would just have to wait it out. Freezing and shaking, they watched the horrific scene play out on the town square.

The hailstones struck men, women, and children, knocking them down, many with open wounds. They held their arms over their heads for protection, curling up so that the ice chunks plummeting down had less target area. Children wandered across the square calling out for their lost parents while other parents rushed around desperately searching for their children. An older man stumbled across the square, stooping over. A heavy clod of hail struck him on the back of the neck; he slumped down to the ground motionless.

Laura spotted two little girls no more than six years old. They wore pink dresses, held each other's hands, and sobbed horribly. Where the hell were their parents? It broke her heart seeing those two girls so distraught. She couldn't just leave them there like that.

She was about to crawl out from under the tractor when Robin tugged at her shoulder in fear. "Mom, where you going?"

"I'll be right back."

"No," he cried, his eyes wide, one side of his face smeared with blood. "You can't go."

"You see those two girls? I'm just getting them to safety real quick."

"No! Don't leave me." Tears filled his eyes.

"You should listen to your son," said a man crouching next to her. "You're only putting yourself in danger."

"Someone has to help them," she said, undeterred. "You obviously aren't going to." The man warily peered out from under the trailer. "I don't see any girls," he grumbled.

Laura was about to tell him just how useless he was when she realized the girls had disappeared.

The hailstorm raged on. It destroyed windows, awnings, and car windows and smashed roofing tiles. It shredded balcony plants, the decorations on the buildings and parade floats, the parasols outside the cafés. A white blanket of hail was already covering the cobblestones. The worst part was seeing people stumbling across the square for cover where there was none to be had. Laura shut her eyes. She couldn't watch anymore.

And then, the nightmare suddenly ended. The pounding above them ebbed, and a ghostly silence reigned for a moment. The hail shower had only lasted a few minutes, yet it had been enough to plunge Bredenstedt into chaos.

The sounds drowned out by the hail now returned full force—the crying, the sobbing, the calls for help. Laura gave Robin and Samuel the signal, and together they crawled out from under the trailer.

The town square was no longer recognizable. Everything was buried under a layer of melting ice, steam was drifting across the square, and countless contorted bodies were strewn across the ground. Parents huddled with their children, treating their wounds the best they could.

"Mom, I don't feel well," said Robin. He looked white as a sheet. Blood was still seeping from the wound on his head.

Laura crouched down and hugged him. She wanted to say something to comfort him, but before she could, he lost consciousness and went limp in her arms.

4

Lake Alexandria, South Australia

They hadn't encountered another vehicle for miles, yet Riley Dohaney made sure to turn on his jeep's blinker before turning onto Poltalloch Road. The dusty dirt lane leading up to the lighthouse was so bumpy that Riley and his passenger, Steve Jenkins, were jolted along the whole way. Riley had a pendant hanging from his rearview mirror of Jesus on the cross, and it swayed back and forth. He had slowed to ten miles per hour, since a few minutes either way didn't matter. He had plenty of time nowadays, having gone into early retirement for health reasons. For him, every new day was a gift from God. He made the sign of the cross at the thought, and next to him, Steve rolled his eyes. Riley noticed but didn't say a word. One day Steve too would realize that the true meaning of life lay in having faith and not in hunkering down for hours in front of the TV set watching soccer and scarfing down donuts.

They reached their destination, Point Malcom Lighthouse, its 22-foot tower overlooking the little canal, which since 1878 had connected Lake Alexandria and Lake Albert. The Poltalloch Homestead Heritage Historical Preservation Society was responsible for upkeep, and Riley checked out the site twice a week as a volunteer. He switched off the engine, they climbed out, and the warm wind hit them. A dragonfly flew over and buzzed in front of Riley's head before attaching itself to the jeep's antenna.

"Didn't reckon it would get so hot today," Steve groaned. He did love to complain.

"Is rather warm." The thought made Riley pull on his wide-brim leather hat and tighten the chin strap just to be safe, since this wind was strong enough to carry his hat right over the short cliffs and into the lake.

Steve came waddling around the jeep, adjusting his Adelaide Crows cap. "Will this take long?"

"We'll be off quicker than you can shear a sheep." Riley gazed around the grounds.

Next to the bright white lighthouse stood the former keeper's cottage, its solid brick construction still in good condition thanks to regular renovation work. Apart from the dried-out grass, some knee-high bushes, and a solitary dead tree, there really wasn't much to see, though the barren landscape did possess an austere sort of charm. Riley took a walk around. Everything was fine with the lighthouse and the keeper's cottage, as usual. Yet something was bothering him. Somehow the place looked different.

A faraway shriek caught Riley's attention. High up in the sky, an eagle was flying in circles, releasing short, sharp cries. Below that, a good deal lower, four Australian pelicans were gliding over the lake. Riley couldn't see the lake itself from where he stood—he was too far back from the edge of the cliff. The eagle shrieked again.

"You done yet?" Steve asked. "You know Doc Flanner doesn't see patients when they're late."

"You won't miss your appointment," Riley said, starting to regret offering to take Steve into town today.

He turned around, and as he headed back to the jeep he noticed another dragonfly, on the hood. It lay on its back and wasn't moving. To his astonishment, he now spotted more dead dragonflies on the ground below. He pushed his hat back on his head and scanned the surrounding area. Dozens of dead dragonflies lay in the dust around the jeep.

"Holy shit," he heard Steve blurt. "You have to see this!"

Riley spun around. "How many times have I told you? Don't curse."

Steve was standing at the edge of the cliff, staring down. "You have to see this, mate," was all he said.

Riley walked up next to him.

Lake Alexandria was a shallow lake fed by several rivers originating from the eastern slopes of the southern-lying Mount Lofty Ranges. At Goolwa, a few miles southwest of Point Malcom, the mouth of the Murray River connected the lake and the ocean. In the past, this estuary was often blocked by a sandbank when the river's current was low—flooding and southwesterly storms would then cause large amounts of sea water to push into the lake. To avoid this, a bank of flood barriers was built across the channel and its islands. In the years since, the water levels and fresh water content of the lake had remained constant—a factor that was extremely important for the fish population, which mostly consisted of carp. But Riley couldn't believe what he was now seeing. The lake's water level had sunk by at least fifty feet overnight.

"The lake's disappearing," Steve muttered.

Riley stepped closer to the short cliffs so that he could check out the bank directly below them.

"It's just not possible," he said as he scanned the dark line running all around the lake, which he took to be the mark left by the original shoreline. The low water level had actually changed the lake's shape and dimensions. But how could such a thing happen overnight?

"Why's the water glittering like that?"

"How you reckon?" Riley looked closer. Only now did he see the lake's surface shining with a strange silvery sheen in the morning sun. Depending on the sun's position, the water usually shimmered a bright turquoise or a rich dark blue. But it had never glittered, not ever. It was as if someone had spread sheets of corrugated aluminum over everything.

The realization hit Riley like a punch to the gut. The eagle high above was circling again, but Riley took little notice. He just stared at the lake and made the sign of the cross. "Good Lord . . ."

He rushed over to the jeep, rummaged through the glove compartment for his binoculars, ran back to the cliffs, and raised the binoculars to his eyes. And then he saw it. His shoulders sagged.

"Mate, what's wrong?" asked Steve.

Staring blankly, Riley handed him the binoculars.

Steve soon let out a gasp. "Holy shit! Those are all fish. They're all dead."

This time Riley did not reprimand Steve for his crude choice of words. The lake had not only seemed to disappear before his eyes, it was now covered with countless thousands of dead fish, their stomachs turned upward. The sight left him paralyzed. *O Lord, what sins have we committed that you punish us so bitterly?*

"Muldjewangk," Steve said under his breath.

"What did you say?"

"It's that aboriginal tale, mate. They say a monster lives in Lake Alexandria. Muldjewangk. And this Muldjewangk, he reappears from time to time and claims new victims."

"Rubbish," Riley said. "Come on, we'll have to report this."

Behind them something crashed to the ground with full force, as if someone had dropped a bowling ball from a great height. Riley and Steve whirled around. Next to the jeep lay the eagle that had been circling up in the sky a few minutes earlier. A cloud of dust shrouded it; its neck was bent out of shape. Feathers swirled around them and were carried off by the wind.

Riley did not believe in the old aboriginal myths. He believed in God's power. It was clear to him that the Lord Almighty must have had a hand in this.

It was either He or the Devil.

5

LAURA PRESSED THE ACCELERATOR OF HER VW POLO to the floor and got as much speed out of the little old rustbucket as there was to get. The trees along the suburban highway flew by.

Robin lay unconscious on the back seat. Samuel sat next to him, frightened and upset. Laura had quickly decided to bring Samuel along and drop him off at home later. Her only goal right now was the Siloah Hospital in Hanover.

She drove like a madwoman, and when she saw her face in the rear-view mirror with her wet hair hanging down and her mascara running, she saw that that was exactly how she looked.

Ambulances with flashing blue lights headed in the opposite direction—Bredenstedt was in a state of emergency and needed all available help. Laura honked wildly to get a Mercedes out of her way and then passed it at a blind spot. Her growing concern for Robin propelled her onward, as his condition seemed to be getting worse. She stole another worried glance at him in the rear-view mirror and saw that the compression bandage she'd improvised with gauze from the first-aid kit was already staining red. She clenched her teeth and fought back tears.

They finally reached the hospital. Laura steered into the entrance, braking hard.

Apparently half of Bredenstedt had the same idea of driving to the next hospital over. Cars were parked in every direction outside the main entrance. Men with children in their arms rushed into the emergency room while injured adults made their way inside leaning on one another. Ambulances pulled up and rapidly dropped off the injured before speeding off again.

Sirens howled; the honking was nonstop. Laura looked around her, wondering what to do. Park the car here and carry Robin up to the entrance? But that would mean leaving Samuel by himself.

She made her decision—she slalomed past the cars and people all the way up to the main entrance, then parked halfway on a flowerbed so that the ambulances could get through. She leaped out of the car.

"Hey! You can't park there!" A male nurse came running up waving his arms. "Get that car out of here!"

"Help me. Please." She opened the rear door, pointed at Robin.

The nurse saw her boy, sighed, then carefully pulled Robin off the rear seat and lifted him. "What's his name?"

"Robin Wagner. I'm his—"

"I'll take care of him. Now go move that thing."

Laura nodded and watched the nurse disappear into the emergency room with her unconscious son in his arms. Once the door shut behind them, everything around Laura began to spin. She propped herself against her car with both hands and breathed deeply, in and out. The dizzy spell soon passed. She glanced at Samuel, got behind the wheel, and slowly drove over to the hospital parking lot.

The wait was taking forever. Samuel's mother had come to pick him up long ago, thanking Laura profusely for taking care of him. Laura was now left standing at Robin's hospital bed staring at her watch. She'd been waiting over two hours for a doctor to update her about Robin's condition. He was given a four-bed room, which was a lot better than so many others who had to spend the night in the hallways because of overcrowding. The three other beds were all men, one with a horrible rattle coming from his throat, and the smell of disinfectant stung Laura's nose. Robin was sleeping soundly. His head was wrapped in a white turban of gauze, and he was connected to pulse and heart rate monitors that beeped occasionally. She stroked Robin's hand, gazing at the sensor they had placed over his index finger.

"Frau Wagner?"

She started. Before her stood a man in a white doctor's coat, a stethoscope hanging from a side pocket. He was in his late thirties at most despite his completely gray hair, and he seemed somehow familiar to Laura.

"I'm Dr. Fund. I examined your son and stitched up his cut."

"How bad is it?"

"It required five stitches, but that's not the issue."

"Then what is?"

"Let's start with the good news. We x-rayed your son's head. There's nothing broken. The calvarium—the skullcap—is intact. The lamina externa and interna are also unharmed, which is really good."

"But?"

Dr. Fund placed a fatherly hand on her arm. "I'm sorry. I must be alarming you. That was not my intention." He eyed her. "Frau Wagner, you don't remember me, do you? Think back a few years. My hair was still dark back then." He added a smile.

Laura slapped her forehead. "Dr. Fund! Of course... Please excuse me. I'm a little shaken up."

"Completely understandable. Besides, it's not like I still look the same." He ran a hand through his hair.

"I'm still embarrassed, though. After all, you did save Robin's life," Laura said, adding in a lower voice, "and probably mine as well."

"Now you're exaggerating. Though I do have to admit the situation was pretty unusual."

Laura didn't comment.

"If I remember correctly, the media blew the whole thing up," the doctor added cautiously. "Did you know that when we got that emergency call I was basically right out of med school and—"

"I truly am grateful for all you did," Laura interjected, "but that's all behind me now."

"Of course." He nodded understandingly.

"So, about my son. You're saying there's bad news?"

"It's likely that Robin suffered a moderate concussion. I'll only know more once we've done more tests. I'd like to keep him here a few days so that we can keep an eye on him. Is that all right with you?"

"Do I have a choice?"

"He's in good hands here with us. Now go on home and get some sleep. We'll see each other tomorrow." He sent her on her way with a smile goodbye and hurried off.

Easy for him to say, she thought as she watched him go. How could she think of sleeping after what happened today? Now those dark memories she'd suppressed so long ago only added to her concern for Robin, all brought back by a doctor who was only trying to be friendly and had no idea what his words triggered inside her. That old anxiety of hers threatened to return.

The man in the bed opposite with the rattling throat had a coughing fit, and the nasty gurgle from his lungs snapped Laura back to the present. She pulled a plastic chair over, sat next to Robin's bed, held on to his hand, and waited for the past to fade again. It always did, sooner or later.

6

Gakona, Alaska

BRAD ELLISON WAS AMAZED, FOR ONCE. TOURISTS RARELY strayed into this snow-covered wasteland—maybe two or three motor homes in the summer months, beyond that a few local hunters or trappers during hunting season. He rarely saw much else. Ellison folded the corner of the page of the book he was reading, stood up from his chair, and pressed his nose to the fogged-up window of the guardhouse for a better look.

The motor home jolted along the grimy access road, swirling up dust. It reached the entrance to the facility and stopped. The sticker on the motor home's windshield revealed that it came from Fraserway RV, one of the largest RV rental agencies around. A man sat at the wheel; a woman was next to him in the passenger seat. The windshield was filthy, but Ellison could see her red hair. He wondered why the driver didn't use the wipers. The washer nozzles had probably frozen over, which often happened on those older models. But why were they stopping here? They'd probably mistaken this facility for the campground about seven miles farther down Glenn Highway. Ellison could only sigh.

He pulled on his parka, straightened his belt and holster, stepped out of the guardhouse, and planted himself at the gate. It was already light out despite the full blanket of clouds concealing the rising sun. Apart from the drone of the diesel generator powering the guardhouse, it was dead silent. Ellison looked through the gate's iron bars and waited. For a solid minute nothing happened. Then the driver's door opened, and the man climbed out. He had gray hair and a full beard and wore a thick, dark-blue down jacket. He carried a partly folded map in one hand. He alternated between looking at the map and the access road, and he kept talking to his wife and pointing toward the way they'd come.

Ellison couldn't help snickering. These two had definitely lost their way, and she was probably still blaming him for forgoing the navigation system just to save eight whole dollars a day. The real mystery to Ellison, though, was why the two would even bother leaving Glenn Highway.

The man was getting louder, his breath condensing in the chilly air. He hadn't seemed to notice Ellison at all. Ellison was now certain they were looking for the campground. And they were all the more confused by this totally fenced-in facility they'd pulled up to, since it wasn't on any of the tourist maps.

Ellison lost his patience. "Hey!" he shouted. The man raised his head, looked over at him.

"Come here!" Ellison shouted and waved him over.

The man shrugged and walked up to him, his walk oddly bouncy considering his chunky fur boots.

"You looking for the campground?" Ellison asked.

"You can probably spot a clueless tourist a mile away." The man smiled, holding up his map.

Ellison grinned, opened the fence gate, and stepped out. "You could probably say that, yeah—"

"Good," said the gray-haired man. Still smiling, he pulled a pistol out from behind the map and pointed it at Ellison's head. "That means it worked."

The grin on Ellison's face faded. He raised his hands without the man demanding that he do so. Despite his surprise, Ellison instantly recognized the pistol as a SIG Sauer P226, standard issue for the Navy Seals. The gray-haired man, who definitely no longer looked like a clueless tourist, took Ellison's weapon and stuck it into his jacket pocket.

"What's this all about?" Ellison asked.

"What's it look like? You're going to open that gate so we can get this vehicle off the road."

Ellison glanced at the motor home. The woman seemed more than intent on remaining inside the warm vehicle. "Do you two have any idea where you are?"

"At one of the worst-guarded military installations I've ever seen. Now open that gate!" He pressed the pistol to Ellison's temple and shoved him along in front of him.

They stepped into the guardhouse. Ellison activated the gate opener. The gray-haired man yanked him around by the shoulder and pressed the pistol into the small of his back. "Out!"

The man led Ellison over to the motor home's passenger door. Ellison could now see the woman through the filthy windshield. Why wasn't she moving? He got a queasy feeling in his stomach.

"Open it," ordered the gray-haired man.

Ellison pulled on the door handle. The woman's body slumped to the side and toppled out the door before he could get it open. Ellison gasped as he caught her, his muscles tensing up. Behind him, the gray-haired man laughed.

Ellison stared in bewilderment at the object in his arms. "A mannequin?"

"That red hair's not bad, huh?"

Ellison just stared at the mannequin. "What now?"

"Throw her in the ditch, then get behind the wheel."

Ellison did as he was ordered. The gray-haired man took the passenger seat, and they drove into the installation until they reached the facility's former dwellings. The low buildings had seen better days, if there ever had been such a thing. Many harsh winters had faded the exterior paint, large patches of which were peeling off. Some window blinds were shut, while others hung halfway down and crooked. Not far from a front door stood a bearproof trash receptacle.

The gray-haired man waved his SIG Sauer. "Get out."

"What could you possibly want here?" Ellison asked once they were standing back out in front of the motor home. "This facility was decommissioned two years ago. There's no one here besides me."

"I know. But if the facility really was decommissioned—then why keep *you* here?" Ellison opened his mouth, then realized that he didn't have an answer.

"See?" The gray-haired man snorted. "You're nothing more than a fucking puppet, obeying orders without question." With that, he grabbed his hair and yanked it off, revealing a polished bare head underneath his wig. Then he pulled off the false beard.

Ellison guessed the man standing before him was barely thirty years old, yet deep creases filled his face. He now opened the small door at the back of the motor home, tossed the wig and beard inside, and pointed at five small packages lying inside. "Get those out and set them on the ground."

The ocher-colored blocks had the consistency of modeling clay. They looked familiar to Ellison. "Are those what I think they are?"

"Soon they won't need anyone guarding this facility," the bald man said.

"I take it you have a reason for blowing up some obsolete computers and a few hundred antennas?"

"You can bet your life on that."

"I don't really care personally, to be honest." Ellison swallowed hard. "Just, please let me live."

"That depends on how well you cooperate."

Over the next few minutes, Ellison placed several of the C-4 explosive blocks out on the vast antenna field behind the buildings. The bald man told him where, keeping the SIG Sauer trained on him the whole time. Ellison wondered why the man wasn't doing the work himself—after all, he seemed to have a well-toned physique under those thick clothes of his. And yet, some of his movements did seem oddly halting. There was something different about this guy, but what was it?

After the work was done, the bald man led Ellison to the main building, which had a fully automated 4-4-2 fingerprint scanner mounted at the door. All of a sudden, Ellison realized why he was still alive. The print scanner used an infrared sensor to determine whether the finger pressing on it belonged to a living person or not. It wouldn't have done the bald-headed man any good to kill Ellison, hack off his hand, and place it on the sensor.

The door unbolted once the scanner confirmed him, and they entered a corridor that had more corridors branching off every few dozen feet. The old building wasn't heated. A musty odor of damp carpets and moldy walls hit them. Ellison had to position more of the explosives here too, inside several empty rooms. The tech room was the only place with a few of the old computers and monitors left, all sitting on a rack. Once Ellison had placed the last C-4 block next to the old main server, the bald man led him outside.

The man stopped out in front of the building. His eyes narrowed. "On your knees!" Ellison felt the blood drain from his face. His insides cramped up. "Sir, please, I—"

"Don't call me 'Sir'!" barked the man and raised the SIG Sauer to Ellison's temple.

Ellison got down. He felt the snowy ground penetrating his pants with the cold and wet. He had trouble keeping himself upright. His head was pounding. "Please, don't. I'm married."

"Everyone makes mistakes in life." The bald man pointed his gun at Ellison and pulled the trigger.

A violent blow to the chest propelled Ellison back. He could feel the red-hot projectile pass through his heart and tear it apart. He tipped over to one side.

Brad Ellison was dead before he even hit the ground.

7

THE MORNING AFTER THE HAILSTORM, LAURA DROVE TO the headquarters of Andra, Incorporated. The company she worked at was a worldwide leader in the field of high-frequency technologies. It occupied a modern industrial building in Tönniesberg Business Park, which was located in Bornum, on the eastern outskirts of Hanover. Out in front of the parking lot, on a well-manicured strip of grass, stood a flagpole with the German federal flag at half-mast. After the devastating tornado in Berlin, the whole country had been under a state of emergency. The terrifying catastrophe was all over the news, and in the face of such a tragedy hardly anyone was talking about all the hail that had gotten dumped on Hanover. That was just a side note.

Laura parked her VW Polo and climbed out. She had to squint—the sun shone bright as ever in the cloudless sky, as if nothing unusual had transpired over the weekend. She had lost her sunglasses during the hailstorm, she recalled—and she could really use them now after hardly sleeping at all last night. She smoothed out the skirt of her business suit and slammed the door shut. The paint was peeling off the door's edge, among other places, but that was barely noticeable now next to all the dents that the hail had left in the body of the little car. She tapped the roof twice as if giving a dear old friend a reassuring pat on the shoulder and then made her way to her office. Such frightening things had occurred over the weekend, yet life had to go on. The earth was still spinning, after all. And it was a Monday.

Work proceeded to take up all of Laura's morning, and for a time she forgot her worries. The office had received some good news: the upturn in Japan was continuing, and Hardenberg would be delighted. She checked her watch, a used Longines La Grande Classique, her pride and joy—last year at Christmas she had bought it on eBay for €48.22.

It was already after eleven a.m. Where was Hardenberg?

"How's the Far East? Business going well?" She looked up.

Henri Seigneur was leaning in the doorway smiling at her, his hands in his pockets.

He worked with their technical documents and hadn't been with the company long. "Sales are through the roof in Japan," she replied cheerfully. "Hardenberg will appreciate that."

"He sure will. He'll get the credit for it."

Henri pulled his hand from his pocket and scratched at his chin. "So why has he been in such a bad mood lately?"

"Has he been?"

"It's just that I've never gotten any feedback from him about our new prototype. How come, do you think?"

"I'm afraid you'll have to ask him that yourself." As Laura moved her chair back from her desk and crossed her legs, her skirt slid above her knee. She hadn't intended it to, but she saw that Henri had noticed. She liked Henri well enough, but she did not like the way he was eyeing her at the moment. She stood up. "Herr Hardenberg is probably just too busy right now."

"Maybe." Henri pushed away from the door frame and sauntered over to her. He stopped before her desk. He picked up a framed photo of Robin. Robin was clutching the bag of sweets and school supplies that every German child receives on the first day of school, his wide grin revealing three missing teeth. "Your son is going to break all the ladies' hearts."

Laura smiled. "Capturing just one heart will do fine. The right one."

Henri looked up. "He has your smile, you know."

"Is there something I can do for you, Henri?"

He placed the photo back in its spot. "It really is urgent that I speak to your boss about the prototype. According to the records I have, the last software update for the Diamond prototype isn't fully documented. There's data missing. It's a mystery to me how that could have happened."

"I understand. It's just that today's not a great day. Herr Hardenberg just returned from Beijing overnight." Laura took another glance at her watch. "He actually should have been back in the office a while ago. If you think he's been in a bad mood the last few weeks, wait till you see him after a long-distance flight. My advice is to stay patient for a day or two longer."

Henri nodded as if he had expected little more from the conversation. "Well, I need to get back to it," she told him.

"Sure." He went to the door, where he turned to her one last time. "But you'll put in a good word for me with the big man?"

"I promise."

Henri thanked her and left.

He was barely out the door before Laura checked her phone, then her emails on the company PC. Nothing. No messages from Hardenberg. She tried calling him, got his voicemail, and hung up without leaving a message. Once he saw that she had called, he would call back.

Her next call was about Robin, who had been sound asleep when she visited him at the hospital on the way to work in the morning. That was more than four hours ago. It took her a few minutes to get a nurse on the line, who told her that his condition had not changed. They were still waiting for the results of various tests. Laura thanked her and hung up, disappointed. She opened the top drawer of her desk, reached into a bag of gummi bears she stocked there in case of emergency, and stuffed a handful into her mouth. Then she returned to her work.

Two hours later, she ripped off her headset and flung it onto the desk in frustration. She leaned back in her chair, massaging her temples. Being on a call with the company's Asian partners always made her head feel as if she'd been out drinking the night before. Hardenberg really needed to show up. He still hadn't gotten in touch. He had been living alone since his divorce and had no children, only a few friends. How was anyone supposed to be reached if they didn't ever answer the phone? There was, however, one option that she had not yet tried.

Laura hesitated. She actually shouldn't be doing it. Hardenberg was sure to give her a reprimand, since she'd be disregarding one of those understandings they had. Well, she was just going to have to take that risk.

8

"KEEP MOVING LEFT . . ." DANIEL BENDER WAVED his interviewee toward the optimal spot as he eyed the screen of the Panasonic 4K camera behind the cameraman's shoulder. His friend Ben had given his consent for an on-camera eyewitness interview, and he now cautiously stepped into position. "Stop! Perfect. Right there." Daniel raised his head, checked the camera angle again.

From their location on the Maifeld, the southwest section of Berlin's Olympic Stadium loomed in the background like some ancient ruin. The tornado, officially classified as a Category F3 by the German Weather Service, had left nothing intact around the Marathon Gate. A few minutes earlier, Daniel had ducked under the stadium barriers and headed inside for a better view of the destruction. It was even more devastated than he remembered. The western grandstand looked like a demolition halted halfway through. Iron girders protruded from exposed concrete, plastic folding seats lay scattered all over, and only a few warped steel beams still suspended the rounded roof. There were 207 dead and over 400 injured so far, including dozens of severely injured who might not make it. The figures seemed shockingly high, yet Daniel knew it was a miracle more had not died, considering all the people he'd seen fully exposed to the tornado. The rubble lay scattered over a few hundred feet, blocking the access roads along with the fallen trees. Two days after the catastrophe, workers, bulldozers, and wheel loaders were only now starting to clean up in large numbers, and the dull clattering and pounding of the machines from across the Mayfield droned away in Daniel's ears. It was doubtful whether a soccer match would ever be held here again.

Daniel checked the camera angle one last time, then clapped his hands. "This shot works."

"Why didn't you just tell me you wanted the wrecked tower in the background?" said his cameraman, Yousef. "I would have set up here in the first place."

"You know how I am. I never know what I want." Daniel winked at Yousef, then put an arm around his shoulder and pointed at Ben in his Hertha Berlin soccer jersey about thirty feet away. "We'll start with a close shot of me and Ben. When I say 'the extent of the destruction is indescribable,' you go wide and pan over the stadium and the Mayfield and end at the destroyed clock tower. Make sure to get that bulldozer at the stadium gate. We'll grab a few isolated shots of the big clock later. Got all that?"

"Sure."

Armed with his mic, Daniel marched across the lawn to Ben. He needed to do a report live on location as soon as possible if his YouTube channel was going to keep up with all the networks and stations who had been doing nonstop broadcasts from Berlin just minutes after the tornado. After all, YouTube was all about speed and fresh content.

He had been forced to set his sights much lower after he'd gotten fired from Germany's popular Sat.1 network. And time is money, he now thought, another stinging reminder that he still owed Yousef for their last filming. He hesitated, then turned back around.

"Something wrong?" Yousef said.

"Listen, about that two-hundred and fifty euros . . ."

"You don't have it. I knew it."

"I've always made it clear to you that my finances might be a little, uh, tight at the moment."

Yousef gave him a sideways grin.

"You'll get your money, I promise. Last week I got seventy thousand hits?" Excitement filled Daniel's voice. "In three months? I'll reach over a hundred thousand subscribers. Things are looking up."

"Great. Does that mean you'll make any money from it?"

Daniel frowned. "Making money on YouTube isn't as easy as people think."

"Maybe you should think about going with another name." In an exaggerated register Yousef said, "*The Jet Stream Weather Channel* ... doesn't exactly roll off—"

"You don't think?"

Yousef shrugged. "Who knows why more people don't watch. After all, you're basically a B-list celebrity."

"Those days are over," Daniel grumbled with remorse. "Maybe I should try getting on *Celebrity Survivor*? It could raise my name recognition."

"How about you just nail this segment for now?"

"Yes. That's the plan." Daniel's eyes lit up. "Already have a teaser in mind: 'The Berlin Tornado: Random Chance, Act of God, or Is Something Else Behind It?'"

"Oh, man." Yousef rolled his eyes. "Don't get started on your conspiracy theories."

"They're not that, they're . . ." Daniel put his hands on his hips. "Look, manipulation of the weather is a real thing. Every day, all over the world, there are hundreds of attempts to control natural weather conditions. There's the Chinese, the Russians, the Americans, even we Germans are actively trying to manipulate the weather. It's just that no one can tell."

"All I'm saying is ... viewers need to be able to take you seriously."

"In China they even have a government agency for manipulating the weather."

"See?" Yousef sighed. "You just did it again."

"Don't go judging things you don't understand."

"Hey, take it easy."

"I can't help it. You know how sensitive I am about people calling me a crank."

"I have never, ever called you a crank."

"You know what Mark Twain once said? 'Everyone talks about the weather, but nobody does anything about it.'" Daniel snorted. "I'm telling you, my friend, plenty of people around the world are trying to do something about it."

"All right, man. I get it. Now let's focus on this interview, okay?"

Daniel took a deep breath. "I'm sorry. You'll see. After today's show? There will be tons of sponsors knocking at my door."

Yousef held up a finger. "Just remember to give me that money when you get it."

"You're the best." Daniel grinned and ran over to Ben. He positioned himself next to him, pulled a little pocket mirror from his back pocket and checked his hair. He put the mirror away and looked at Ben. "Ready?"

"For a half hour now. This'll cost you more than a beer, buddy."

Daniel laughed. "When was it ever just one?" He put his face through a few grimaces to relax his face muscles, then raised the mic and nodded to Yousef.

"On July 14, 1894, Germany's first officially documented hurricane tore through Upper Bavaria's Ebersberg Forest, causing two deaths and several injured and destroying two hundred major buildings. July 10, 1968: A tornado categorized F4 passed through Pforzheim in Baden-Württemberg, damaging more than 1,700 homes and taking two lives before continuing a path of destruction through neighboring forested areas that left traces for years. May 5, 2015: In Bützow, near Rostock, a Category F3 tornado destroyed sixteen homes, hurled cars more than two hundred feet into the air and injured thirty people. In the chaotic summer of 2016, several tornadoes tore through Schleswig-Holstein and Hamburg within the span of a few days. Fortunately, no one died. Many in this country think that tornadoes only happen in the USA. They are wrong." Daniel inserted a long and momentous pause. "Yesterday, Germany was struck by a natural catastrophe never before seen in the history of the Federal Republic." He then gave the camera a grave stare. "Welcome to the latest edition of *Jet Stream*. Today we're at the very site where the tragedy struck yesterday. Next to me is Ben, an eyewitness who looked death straight in the eye and barely escaped with his life." Daniel turned to his pal. "Ben, at what point Saturday did you first realize that this was not a typical storm?"

For the next several minutes, Daniel expertly interviewed his friend about how the disaster unfolded. He was completely back in his element in his *Jet Stream* persona. "Jet Smart," the press used to call him. That was back when all had been right in his world, when his career showed every sign of taking off for good. After the scandal hit, they would use less flattering terms for him. Nothing deteriorated faster in today's media-driven world than a reputation, which also meant, luckily, that a shitstorm was forgotten just as quickly. That was all months ago, anyway.

As Yousef panned around on their cue, Daniel saw something moving out of the corner of his eye. Off in the distance, a camera crew was running toward the destroyed Marathon Gate. A cluster of workers had gathered there and were standing around something.

"Cut," he shouted to Yousef and pointed at the crew, now setting up at the gate. "They're getting something."

Yousef knew the drill. He started packing up his gear. Daniel turned to Ben. "Thanks, buddy."

"Done already?"

"We are. We'll talk soon."

"All right."

Daniel patted him on the shoulder and took off.

He reached the Marathon Gate and started squeezing through the crowd of workers. A dry and mineral-like grit hung in the air, stinging his nostrils. He recognized the three-man camera crew as his former colleagues from Sat.1. Gerlach was there—*of all people.* Daniel gritted his teeth. With his scrawny build and poorly fitting suit, Karsten Gerlach looked more like a scarecrow than on-air talent. Daniel ignored his former crewmates and focused on the excitement at hand. Workers had discovered a man under a layer of rubble—just the guy's hand and arm sticking out, to be precise, the rest of his body buried under heavy chunks of concrete. The hand was not moving.

Daniel heard Gerlach's nasally voice. "Well, look who it is. Who let you in here?" He approached Daniel, a toothpick stuck between his teeth.

"Is the man still alive?" Daniel asked him.

"Dead as a doornail." Gerlach glanced over his shoulder as if to make sure the poor man's condition didn't suddenly contradict him. "Someone thought they'd found a survivor, but that was probably just a rumor. What are you doing here, Jet?"

"Take one guess."

Gerlach slid his hands into his pockets and gave him a smug smile, rolling the toothpick from one side of his mouth to the other. "So, how's it going?"

"As interested as ever in me and my work, I see. You going to steal my latest idea too?"

Gerlach's face darkened. "Don't blame me for your failures. You screwed things up all by yourself."

"You wanted my show from the very beginning."

"It's not *your* show anymore." Gerlach shook his head. "Man, you were about to get nominated for a German Television Award, too, but then you went pulling that shit—"

"Stay the hell out of my life!" Daniel pointed a finger at Gerlach and glared into his eyes. "You got that?" He grabbed the toothpick, flung it at the ground.

Some of the workers were watching now. Daniel pushed by Gerlach and found Yousef, who was packing up his equipment.

"They were right to get rid of you!" shouted Gerlach behind him. "You might have a screw loose."

"Fuck you," Daniel muttered. He had let Karsten Gerlach get under his skin once again, despite promising himself, over and over, that he would just ignore the loser next time.

"Was that Gerlach?" asked Yousef.

"Yes. We're done for the day."

"You need to mellow out. That guy's numbers are in the cellar. Plus, I hear he's screwed things up with Jeanette."

Daniel smiled at that. "Yeah, well, you know what we meteorologists say: Women or weather, we usually get it wrong."

Yousef laughed.

Daniel helped with two of his heavy bags. "Now, let's get those shots of the big clock and then take a look at the footage. The show needs to be edited in the next two hours."

9

LAURA HAD TEXTED HARDENBERG THEIR PREARRANGED code word, yet it was now past lunch hour and she was still waiting for him to call. She glanced through the door connecting their offices and could see all the files on his desk along with his unopened mail, the piles nearly taller than that goofy waving gold cat Hardenberg had brought back as a souvenir from his first trip to China years ago. Laura didn't have a good feeling about this. Something was not right.

She couldn't just keep waiting around doing nothing. She grabbed her car keys.

Outside she passed Henri Seigneur, who was smoking with a colleague near the front door of their building. Henri saw her, stubbed out his cigarette in the standing ashtray, and came up behind her. He smelled like cigarettes. "Calling it a day so soon?"

"I wish."

"You heard anything from Hardenberg?"

"You'll get that prototype info soon enough," she told him firmly but not in a cold way. She paused, eyeing him, and got an idea. "Do you have a little time? It'll take an hour at the most."

"Depends on what it is."

"We're going to drive over to Hardenberg's house."

"*To his house?* Why?"

A shrewd smile stretched across her face. "Do you want that info or not?"

"Definitely," shrugged Henri.

"Well, let's go then."

It took Laura two tries to get her car started. As they drove off, Henri pointed his thumb at the comic books on the rear seat. "Seriously? Superman and Batman?"

"They're for my son." She didn't tell him that Robin was in the hospital. She had no desire to discuss it with Henri.

He grinned. "Your son just happens to be named Robin?"

"Robin is a very common name."

"That why are you turning red all of a sudden?"

"Okay, maybe I do flip through them now and then," she said with a wink. As a kid she'd always preferred comics to playing with dolls, especially when the superheroes teamed up to fight the evil villains, and it had always stayed with her. She and Robin had shared the new issue every week ever since he'd been able to read. Sharing comics with him was twice the fun.

They drove out of the parking lot and turned into Nenndorfer Chaussee, which ran through the middle of the business park. Henri rolled the window down and stuck his hand out, wiggling his fingers in the wind.

"All right, Laura, why are we really driving over to Hardenberg's?"

"I'm worried about him."

"Just because he hasn't checked in? Maybe he's fighting jet lag and needed to crash."

"Maybe."

"Maybe? So, there *is* something else." He observed her profile. "Does this have something to do with how you keep checking your phone all the time?"

She sighed. "Nothing gets by you." He grinned.

She made a decision to confide in Henri. "Hardenberg and I, we had an agreement," she told him. "I'm only supposed to disturb him in meetings when it's an emergency. For situations like that I send a certain text message to his phone. He's always called me back right away."

"What's the text?"

"Reimpo."

"Reimpo?"

"Stands for 'really important.'"

"Very clever."

She shrugged. "It's always worked."

"I see," he said. "You sent him that urgent message, and you still haven't heard back."

"He always responds."

"You are really worried about him, aren't you?" Henri said.

"I hope I'm wrong."

He sat back in his seat. "All right, let's check it out."

Twenty minutes later, Laura parked in front of a single-story clinker brick house from the seventies, just like all the other homes in the neighborhood. Clean exterior, well-groomed front yard, precisely trimmed boxwood hedge. This was one of those peaceful areas of Hanover where all the neighbors knew each other, waved to one another, barbecued on weekends. Laura guessed Hardenberg was one of the few residents who didn't fit the mold, at least not after his divorce. He'd kept to himself ever since.

Henri was staring to look nervous. "You really think this is a good idea?"

Laura got out and looked the house over. "We have to try."

He followed her up the paved path to the front door. "I still don't get why you need me here."

She pressed the doorbell. "Relax, Henri."

No one opened, not even after several rings. Next to the house was a garage, with a backyard and patio in the back. When Hardenberg was still married, he and his wife once invited Laura to a garden party. She remembered there was a big panorama window facing the backyard that offered a clear view of the living room.

"Maybe we should drive back," Henri remarked. "It's probably nothing."

"Wait here." Laura went over to the garage and tested the door handle. Much to her surprise, the door wasn't locked. She pulled it open. Hardenberg's white BMW was in the garage. She placed a hand on the hood. "It's cold."

"That means he's been here," Henri said.

"Probably. But why didn't he check in?" A door at the rear of the garage led them to the backyard, where they followed a path of brown pavers to the patio.

"We should not be doing this," Henri whispered behind her.

"What if he fell in the bathtub and hit his head, and he's lying unconscious on the bathroom floor?" For an instant she saw Robin lying in his hospital bed with his eyes closed and that bandage around his head.

She stepped onto the patio, passing a wooden table with chairs and a folded-up sun umbrella. Roses climbed up a trellis along the back wall of the house. The living room curtains were cracked a couple inches, letting her see inside. She shielded her face with her hands and peered into the living room. It took her a moment to adjust to the different light. Then she saw the leg on the floor.

She pulled back. Her heart was pounding.

"What is it?" whispered Henri.

She took another look. "Hardenberg. He's . . ."

"What?"

She took one more look. "Oh, my god!"

Roland Hardenberg was lying on his stomach on the parquet floor. He was wearing slacks and a white shirt with the sleeves rolled up, his tie loosely knotted. His hands rested alongside his body with his palms facing up and his fingers all contorted, like claws grasping at air. A pool of blood spread out in a circle from his chest. His head was twisted to the side, his mouth wide open as if still trying to let out the one final scream stuck in his throat. His lifeless eyes stared straight through Laura.

10

THE VIKING DISCOVERED NOTHING NEW IN THE FRIDGE. His stocks were starting to run low, which was no surprise—he hadn't set foot outside for eleven days now. He slipped his hand under the waistband of his sweatpants, scratched at his crotch, and eyed the last of the canning jars filled with his homemade plum jam. They would only last him four more days, tops. He badly needed to replenish his supplies.

As he stood at the open fridge, he savored the cold air drifting out over his naked feet. He loved the cold. If he'd inherited anything from his grandparents—who'd left Iceland behind to try their luck in Germany more than thirty years ago—it was the love of the cold.

The refrigerator started chirping. The Viking pulled out a jar of his jam, gave the door a shove. He fished a used spoon out of the sink, went into the living room, and gazed neutrally at his sofa, covered as always with his crumpled-up sheets and stained bedding. He'd been sleeping here for two years. The top floor of the villa had three different bedrooms to choose from, but the Viking attached increasingly less importance to whatever memories they still held.

He sneezed and wiped the snot from his nose with the sleeve of his T-shirt. The sight of his sofa depressed him. He went into the den, dropped into his armchair, placed his naked feet on the desk, and unscrewed the lid of his canning jar. Lost in thought, he wiped the spoon on his sweats and unhurriedly spooned out the jam. As he did, he scanned the flickering wall of 27-inch hi-def monitors he'd mounted on the desk.

There were still no comments on the last blog entry he'd published ten minutes ago: "Are the Tornadoes and Hailstorms in Germany Connected to Extreme Weather on Other Continents? What's Really Behind It?"

The Viking calmly stuffed another spoonful of gooey jam into his mouth, knowing the comments would soon come. Over the past few years, his blog *The Viking Explains* had established itself as a forum for those German residents seeking truly critical analysis and independent thought. The Viking researched and wrote about any topic he deemed to be important and was sure to avoid using the usual propaganda regurgitated by the fully compliant mass media. As a rule, he covered politically motivated incidents around the world that had been swept under the rug or denied or distorted by official sources. 9/11, the *Charlie Hebdo* massacre, the terror attacks in Paris and Brussels—all revealed clear irregularities for the Viking to scrutinize. A few weeks ago, he started seeing clear confirmation that his theories were finally hitting a sore spot with certain authorities. This reminded him that he hadn't yet checked on Dobby today.

He shuffled over to the front door and peered out the little window, surveying the street outside. The dark-blue Passat that had been parked across the street day and night for several weeks was nowhere to be seen today. The Viking didn't know who the man sitting in that car worked for, but his guess was the highest levels of German intelligence, either national domestic intelligence (*Verfassungschutz*) or the agency dedicated to foreign and military intelligence (*Bundesnachrichtendienst*). He'd given his mysterious observer the name Dobby after the goofy house-elf from the Harry Potter books.

The Viking returned to his monitors. Obviously they had given up shadowing him for now. He told himself that the operation had been little more than a clumsy attempt at intimidation. They'd wanted to show him they knew his true identity and were probably hoping that he'd simply stop his investigations. He grinned at the thought. All they were doing was showing him that his theories were correct! Why else would anyone take such trouble to unmask his camouflage and track him down?

He glanced at the diploma he'd tacked up on the wall years ago. Taped underneath it was a photo from his college days showing him with one of his classmates. Was the Berlin tornado the opportunity he'd been waiting for? Should he finally make the call he'd been putting off for so long?

A black icon started blinking on one of the monitors. Instantly, the Viking cleared all his thoughts. Someone was waiting for him on the dark net. He only communicated with a handful of users there, in a special chatroom they'd set up. They were all extremely skilled in the latest technology, and they all valued the advantages of complete anonymity. The dark net kept them safe from the intelligence agencies' hackers and usual data phishing methods for the simple reason that, in contrast to the conventional Internet, the cyber agents didn't know where to find them. In order to safeguard their chatroom even further, they never accepted new members. Theirs was a small and secret society. The Viking clicked on the black icon and slipped inside the hidden web.

Rousseau was waiting for him in the chatroom. Rousseau was not his real name, of course; no one revealed their true identity on the dark net. Hardcore hackers and computer nerds exchanged info, materials, and data here—from banal bootlegs and illegal music downloads right up to top-secret government documents.

ROUSSEAU: Interesting article
VIKING: Which one?
ROUSSEAU: The most recent one. On extreme weather
VIKING: Thanks
ROUSSEAU: Your own findings or outside sources?
VIKING: I know more than most of the meteorologists on TV. What's up?
ROUSSEAU: Interested in info about the green light that always appears every time the weather goes crazy?
VIKING: In return for?
ROUSSEAU: Nothing. Just a friendly turn
VIKING: Degree of truth?
ROUSSEAU: High
VIKING: Source?
ROUSSEAU: Reliable
VIKING: Fire away
ROUSSEAU: A certain insider suspects artificially created balls of plasma in the ionosphere. Could easily be mistaken for the northern lights.

VIKING: What insider?

ROUSSEAU: As I said: Trusted

VIKING: Okay. Theory on how the plasma gets formed?

ROUSSEAU: Using extremely strong, pulsing radio waves

VIKING: Got proof?

ROUSSEAU: It's technologically feasible. Clearly documented. In Alaska, HAARP has already experimented with creating artificial northern lights

VIKING: HAARP was shut down in June 2014

ROUSSEAU: Since when do you believe everything you read on the Internet?

VIKING: Got proof?

ROUSSEAU: Official statements have the Air Force Research Laboratories running HAARP until August 2015, but was basically subordinate to the military the whole time. The civilian version of the program supposedly in place there ever since is likely just for show.

VIKING: So who's really behind it?

ROUSSEAU: DARPA. Defense Advanced Research Projects Agency. Its projects are directly subordinate to the U.S. Department of Defense. Annual budget 3 billion dollars

VIKING: DARPA as in the creator of Arpanet, precursor to the Internet?

ROUSSEAU: Exactly. Responsible for GPS, invisible cloaking tech etc. Now they're creating plasma spheres in the sky and nobody knows why. Some major shit is going down

VIKING: I need more

ROUSSEAU: Project "Nimbus" — I'm sending you a data packet.

VIKING: I'll need to verify

ROUSSEAU: Start here: U.S. Patent No. 4686605, August 1987, "Method and apparatus for altering a region in the earth's atmosphere, ionosphere, and/or magnetosphere"

VIKING: 1987?

ROUSSEAU: Now you understand just how long this shit's been going on

VIKING: Anything else?

ROUSSEAU: U.S. Patent 4999637, March 1991, "Creation of artificial ionization clouds above the earth"

VIKING: Okay. What else?

The cursor on the monitor blinked, standing by—Rousseau was still online but wasn't responding. For some reason he was hesitating. After nearly a minute, right as the Viking stopped counting on anything more, there was something.

ROUSSEAU: Andra
VIKING: Who or what is that?
ROUSSEAU: Corporation. Manufactures electrode guns. Should look into them
VIKING: Why?
ROUSSEAU: You'll see. Logging off now
VIKING: You have my attention. Will start digging at once

Rousseau disconnected. The Viking carefully read through the patent descriptions. The United States, he learned, had been researching ways to manipulate the ionosphere for over thirty years. The big question now was: could they have possibly achieved a breakthrough?

His eyes found that photo below his diploma again. That data packet Rousseau wanted to send might just give him the best chance to revive a certain lost friendship—and to settle old disputes at the same time.

A red triangle blinked in the lower left corner of his main monitor. WARNING! it read.

Infiltration. The Viking pursed his lips. Someone was trying to penetrate his network. "Well, well, my little friend," he muttered, "let's see what you got."

Over the next few minutes, the Viking neutralized the Trojan dropper someone was trying to slip in the back door. A dropper was malware that hackers deployed to install more Trojans and viruses. Sometimes, though, their true aim was to prevent other malware from being detected. A dropper could get pretty nasty, yet this one was relatively simple in nature. He took care of the issue in no time at all.

But something was bugging him. He ran his hands through his greasy hair. Was it simply coincidence that someone tried hacking him right after he'd heard from Rousseau? Had someone gotten wind of their secret chatroom and was listening in? Not likely. A dark net chatroom was always secure. Except maybe. . .

The Viking started. What if it were someone from his own group? Could one of them be violating their secret code?

The Viking stood up, reached for the open jar, and stuffed the last remnants of the gooey sweet jam into his mouth. He needed the sugar to get his brain firing on all cylinders. He needed to think. There might be a traitor among them.

And there was only one way to find out who it was.

11

THE SKY HAD TURNED COMPLETELY GRAY BY THE TIME Laura drove back to the office with Henri Seigneur. The color of the autumn leaves on the trees had been glowing in the midday sun but now were entirely without shimmer. They rode in silence. Laura tried to concentrate on driving, yet her thoughts kept returning to her dead boss. Right at this moment, the body of Roland Hardenberg was on its way to the Forensic Medicine Department of the university hospital in Hanover. The autopsy should better reveal how he was killed.

Laura was highly reluctant to return to the office, where an uncomfortable task awaited her. She looked at Henri, who was curled up in his seat, practically hiding. "Someone has to tell management about Hardenberg dying," she said.

"So?"

"I'm ... I *was* ... his secretary. I feel obligated to deliver the news." She sighed. "I'll inform Herr Leinemann. I could really use your support here, Henri."

"Please, don't take this the wrong way, but—"

"You trying to duck out?"

Beads of sweat glistened on Henri's brow. He mopped his forehead. "I'm not feeling so great. I mean ... with that body lying there, and all that blood, and then the police asking us questions—"

"Oh, and you think I'm doing any better?" She turned into the company parking lot.

"I'm sorry, Laura. If you want, we can tell Leinemann together tomorrow."

"By tomorrow all of Hanover will have read about it." She stopped at his car.

Henri placed his fingers on the door handle. After a moment, he wordlessly exited the vehicle.

You're all letting me down, Laura thought, eyeing him in the rearview mirror. Once again, she was left to act all on her own. It was apparently her fate in life.

The Chairman of the Board of Andra Inc., Johann Leinemann, PhD, and his deputy, Rüdiger Gauder, were both away at meetings. Laura instructed the chairman's office to contact her at once if either of the two men became available.

She walked the hallways of the main building, feeling numb, and stopped at a floor-to-ceiling plate-glass window. She could see across the roofs of the vast production building, to where a little stretch of woods began beyond. Dusk was setting in. It would soon be dark.

She had never seen a dead person before. She couldn't get the sight of Hardenberg's lifeless, waxen face out of her head. Who had done that to him? And why? Was it just a random act? Or premeditated murder? The latter option assumed the existence of enemies. Sure, Hardenberg was generally considered to be hard-nosed, the kind of person who always pushed his own agenda whatever the opposition. But Laura couldn't imagine him making any lethal enemies, not this way. And as far as his private life went, she simply didn't know enough to speculate.

The lights came on outside the company buildings and in the parking lot. It reminded her that she had wanted to call the hospital before the doctors on duty went home for the day.

Back in her office, she couldn't help staring at the connecting door to Hardenberg's office. Management would soon name his successor. What if that person brought their own secretary along? Laura bit at her lip worrying about it. She couldn't afford to lose her job.

She called Siloah Hospital, where the nurse on duty explained in a monotone voice that Dr. Fund had been called into the OP a few minutes before and that she didn't know when the doctor would become available. The exams planned for today had been rescheduled for the next morning as well. Laura, grinding her teeth, thanked the nurse for the info and ended the call.

What a day.

12

LAURA LAY AWAKE A LONG WHILE BEFORE FINALLY
checking the red digital numerals on her alarm clock. 5:25. Three
days after that terrible weekend and two days after she'd found
Hardenberg's body, and she was still sleeping poorly. She yawned,
flipped onto her other side, pulled the covers over her head. But
nothing helped. She dragged herself out of bed and padded barefoot
over to the window in her pajamas. A freezing draft was forcing its
way through the cracks of the old wooden window frame that had
warped over time—like most of the windows in her apartment. She
had long stopped believing the landlord's constant assurances that he
would start renovating her increasingly run-down apartment any day
now. She opened the rolling shutters up all the way.

A storm was brewing outside, as if early autumn wanted to show it
already had a few tricks up its sleeve. The tree branches were bending
in the wind, their fading leaves whirling through the air in a wild
dance. A huge gust made the window shake and pushed more freezing
air in through the cracks. Laura closed the curtains, resisted the urge
to climb back into her warm bed, shuffled instead into the bathroom,
and turned on the shower. She'd only finally gotten to sleep after
midnight, but she still intended to drive to the office earlier than usual
so that she could go see Robin at the hospital by early afternoon.
Dr. Fund said she might be able to take her son back home today—
provided all went well, as he put it.

After a quick breakfast with a cup of chamomile tea, she stood at the front door buttoning up her overcoat. She grabbed the car keys from the wall hook and left the apartment.

An icy wind hit her outside. She reluctantly stepped out onto the sidewalk, the wind whipping at her coat. She pulled her collar up high and straightened her shoulders. She glanced around in amazement. The storm was dumping white snowflakes all around her. She shook her head—late September and starting to snow! The weather had gone completely crazy this year.

Keeping her head lowered, she made her way to her VW Polo up the street. As usual, the engine needed a few tries before it finally kicked into gear. Now the driving snow was getting worse. She turned on the windshield wipers and drove off.

At this early hour, only a few vehicles were out on the roads. No one was driving faster than twenty miles per hour, since a uniform blanket of snow was already covering all. Headlights and flashing brake lights we're almost entirely smothered in the heavy snowfall, as were the traffic lights and signs. She clenched the steering wheel.

Laura barely cleared Bredenstedt before the first snowdrifts started rolling across the road. Her windshield wipers were doing their best, but visibility was getting worse and worse, and her front tires immediately started spinning when she pressed the accelerator. Her first thought: *black ice*.

Moving at a snail's pace, she finally reached the Hanover city limits indicator. All had gone well enough so far. But right before turning into Tönniesberg Business Park she saw a blue light flashing, either police or ambulance, she couldn't tell which. It had to be an accident.

All traffic came to a standstill; no one was moving. The blue light reminded her of the police vehicles outside Hardenberg's house, and the memory of Hardenberg's corpse brought on feelings of deep sadness. As expected, the news of his death had caused great distress at the company. Everyone looked shocked about such a profound tragedy, yet they were equally concerned about how the company would move forward. With one foot touching the brake, Laura got lost in all her thoughts as she watched the snow bury the world around her.

A good twenty minutes later, they still weren't moving. A snowplow thundered by just inches away, causing Laura to start, its front plow hurling a wave of snow against the driver's side of her little car. Her heart thumping, she watched the vehicle continue on, its blinking lights blurring everything orange as a device on its rear end sprinkled road salt.

She looked at the clock. If she sat here stuck any longer, she could forget about trying to slip out of the office early and get Robin. She simply couldn't wait. So she yanked on the wheel and followed in the snowplow's path.

As she figured, an accident was blocking the next intersection—a police officer was questioning the two drivers, and a heated debate had ensued. She didn't envy the cop all bundled up in thick gear. With the weather like this, she was glad she could do her job in warmth.

After five hundred feet, she steered off the plow's path and rolled onto the blanket of snow, which now had a glassy sheet of ice forming under it.

It had gotten colder in the car as a result of the lack of movement. She turned up the heat. She checked the outside temperature display and couldn't believe her eyes: –8 degrees! Was that even possible here in Germany?

The snowfall had meanwhile picked up along with the wind, apparently, since her car kept shuddering from it. She squinted and gripped the steering wheel harder. A massive gust sent her car sideways on the glossy slick lane, startling her. She steered against it and instantly realized she'd spun the steering wheel too far to the right.

The car swerved.

The rear of her car swung around forward and crossed the center of the road. She frantically spun the wheel on the icy surface and quickly realized her mistake. The world spun all around her. The driving snow, oncoming headlights, darkness ... headlights again, this time brighter, wild honking. A shadow darted by her just inches away. She screamed in terror. A ditch appeared out of nowhere, coming right at her, a wall of snow rising beyond it. She slammed on the brakes, but it did no good. She slid helplessly toward the ditch, which was a few feet deep. She closed her eyes.

The impact was brief and harsh. Her seatbelt pressed down on her, painfully digging into her chest. The engine died, and all was silent. She opened her eyes. The hood of her car was half buried in a snowbank, the headlights were out, and a thin layer of snow was already coating the windshield. She took a deep breath. It was lucky she had been driving so slowly.

The heater had stopped when the motor stalled. Laura tried starting the engine again but nothing happened apart from a steady clacking under the hood, barely audible in the howling storm. Headlights appeared in the rearview mirror, came closer, then slowly passed her by before disappearing into darkness. This was just not her day. She knew no one was going to stop and help her, not in this weather. From the road, no one could probably even tell there was a car in the ditch.

Now what was she supposed to do?

She was starting to shiver. Staying in the car wasn't an option—she'd be frozen stiff before anyone found her. Though everything inside her told her not to, she pulled up the collar of her overcoat, took a deep breath, and shoved the door open against the wind.

The snow whipped at her, robbing her of all visibility. She shielded her eyes with both hands. Not far from the road was a container yard, without a fence. She knew where she was now—the yard was about a mile and a quarter from Andra, Inc. That gave her some hope. She looked around but couldn't make out any headlights anywhere. Where the hell had all the cars gone? Hadn't there just been busy traffic? She felt her body cooling. Her teeth chattered. She'd instinctively put on her ankle boots this morning but not especially thick socks, and she hadn't even thought about a hat. She looked around again. There was no help anywhere in sight. She would just have to make it by foot somehow. She wrapped her arms around her body, braced herself against the wind, and marched off.

She made slow progress in the thick driving snow. Her head lowered, practically blinded, she followed the path of the road. Her face stung, her lungs too. The snowdrifts continued to rise along the road, leaving only the tips of bushes and shrubs showing. A sound startled her, a crackle high above her so deafening it drowned out even the howling wind.

The overhead power lines were completely covered in ice, she saw. The fact that they led to a nearby transformer gave her a nasty feeling, and she buried her face in her neck and stomped onward. Moments later came cracks as loud as massive fireworks.

She whirled around.

One of the power lines had ripped away and plummeted to the ground shooting sparks. The electricity discharged blue and crackled through the air as the cable hit the snowy road. A second crack indicated the snapping of another cable. They twisted and twirled on the road like hissing snakes. Laura turned to keep going, but a deep dull crunch made her halt. In the adjoining meadow stood the high-voltage tower the severed lines led to. It too was covered in a thick layer of ice, from top to bottom. And she couldn't believe her eyes—the steel colossus was leaning to one side. The noise was deafening. The many tons of ice were apparently too much for the transmission tower, and it buckled and crashed forward to the ground with full force, churning up a high crashing wave of snow. Laura recoiled. She needed to get to safety—now.

She kept fighting her way through the powdery hard snow boring into her face like so many icicles. Every breath burned her lungs, she couldn't feel her feet anymore, and her snot froze on her face. With short hasty steps she stomped along the seemingly endless abandoned road. She again wondered why no cars had passed through here since the accident. A panic started rising up in her. She was shivering uncontrollably, and her movements were becoming more agitated.

She stopped on a stretch of ice, slipped and fell, landed on her back in pain. Her attempt to get back on her feet caused her calf to cramp up. She moaned in discomfort. She tried to get to her feet again, but her cooling body was responding less and less. Another cramp set in, this time in her right thigh.

She began to whimper.

Headlights appeared from behind and locked on her. She could hear a powerful engine idling. She wanted to turn to the vehicle, but her muscles wouldn't let her. She felt trapped in a nightmare. She wanted to stand but couldn't. She closed her eyes, exhausted.

Then she heard crunching in the snow. Strong hands reached under her armpits and lifted her up. She was placed on the rear seat of a pickup truck and wrapped in a blanket. The truck rolled on, the warm air enveloping her.

Life soon returned to Laura's stiff limbs, and her vision became clearer. Two men sat in the front seats, the driver wearing a black wool stocking cap with thick black hair sticking out from under it. He stared forward, focused on the road. The other man shook the snow from his blond hair, turned to her, and observed her with concern. He looked familiar to Laura.

"Don't worry," he said. "We'll get you to a hospital."

"I don't need to." She coughed and sat up, all her bones aching.

"I'll be all right in a minute."

"Are you sure?"

"I think so. At the end of this road is a company called Andra. Can you just drop me off there, please?"

The man smiled. "That works out great. We're heading there too."

13

Greater Hinggan Range, China

HANDS CLASPED BEHIND HIS BACK, HUANG ZHEN STOOD on the balcony of his apartment, which took up the whole upper floor of the housing complex. From here Zhen had an unobstructed view of the Heilongjiang facility they had built in this inaccessible valley within the vast Greater Hinggan Range. He was the one who had made it all happen. He gazed in pride at the 3,600 antennas rising into the sky before him, all in neat rank and file and as tall as buildings. It had taken many months of constant persuading, along with bribes in obscene amounts, to convince his comrade party functionaries of the necessity of such a facility. In the end, the project only got approved because Zhen had so ruthlessly utilized each and every recourse available to him through his high-ranking office in the Ministry of State Security. Few men could afford to refuse doing a favor for the head of the Anhui province secret police. He had pulled all the right strings, gotten crucial party supporters and patrons on his side, and despite a couple failures over the last few weeks, was now about to see his plan completed. The Chinese People's Republic, thanks to him, would return to its former strength and shine in a glory greater than ever. A few minutes ago, Zhen had given orders to prepare everything for awaking the Black Dragon—earlier than planned, because the circumstances required it.

Just before sunrise, the temperature was still below freezing. Zhen hardly noticed the cold even though he was wearing nothing but a traditional thin silk hanfu. He relished these extraordinary few minutes right before the day broke, when wafts of fog drifted down from the mountainsides into the valley, when the dampness of night lingered in the air and the mating calls of black grouse echoed in the distance. At this hour, anything seemed possible. Karl Marx had said that the philosophers only interpreted the world in various ways; the point, however, was to actually change it. Zhen smoothed his narrow mustache with his thumb and forefinger, his expression darkening. That change would come, and none too soon.

He gazed once more at the fifty rows of antennas rising up into the air with their sturdy, stork-like legs. Beyond rose the thickly forested slopes of the Hinggan Range, stretching nearly nine hundred miles through Northern China and Inner Mongolia. This was one of the most important forestry regions of all China, with more than 35 billion cubic feet in timber reserves. Yet the nearest forest region was still far enough away for him to keep the Heilongjiang facility under wraps. No roads led here, and Zhen hadn't even ordered a supply route cut through the woods; all supplies, as well as transportation for the few hand-picked men working at the facility, had come by air using helicopters. No one was going to just run into this place. Despite all this, Zhen still had a high-voltage fence erected all around the compound. Nothing could be left to chance.

He scanned the far edges of the forest with his naked eye. He was seeing fewer pheasants, elk, and reindeer, almost no brown bears now, as the animals were quickly learning to keep away from the fence. He took one last deep breath and entered his dining room.

He walked up to his table set for breakfast, passing elaborate wall murals depicting the deities and scenes of Chinese mythology. There was also a colorful portrayal of the tree of life, whose principle of immortality greatly appealed to Zhen.

Awaiting him on his long table were the most delectable delicacies of the traditional Chinese breakfast, his only meal of the day and one he celebrated accordingly. One after the other, he served himself bowls of shenjianbao, xiaolongbao, and shaomai—dumplings filled with rice, soy sauce, meat, and mushrooms. After this, he enjoyed hot congee soup. The seductive scent of fresh baozi and youtiao wafted up his nose, and he stuffed two of the deep-fried sticks of dough into his mouth.

Then, like every morning, he devoted himself to the highlight of his breakfast. He cradled the warm balut in his hand. Balut were duck eggs boiled after incubation; they originally came from the Philippines, where they were said to increase potency. Zhen saw more in them. In the balut's magical powers he was convinced he had found the universal remedy for providing long life, as he had not once become sick since he started consuming a balut egg every day for breakfast.

Zhen carefully removed the upper third of the shell. The nineteen-day-old embryo inside was barely discernible. He sprinkled some salt over the egg and slurped out the fluid, then peeled the whole egg and spiced it with salt and soy sauce. The duckling's beak was now clearly visible. Zhen bit into the embryo with delight, the thick juice running down the corners of his mouth. The brownish meat was soft, the beak and feathers decidedly firmer to the bite. Zhen took his time, chewing slowly.

A half hour later, he made his way into his office. It was time to dispense with a most unpleasant matter.

He called for his cousin Xian Wang-Mei. He'd ordered him here from Beijing. As Zhen waited, he stroked the two dao sabers mounted crossways on the wall. He'd received them as a gift from a delegate of the Mongolian People's Party many years ago, but they did not serve simply as decoration. He fully knew how to use them. With their extremely sharp, widely forged blades tapering to a point, he could easily slice through a piece of paper falling to the floor. And it was highly likely that his cousin might just get a demonstration of their sharpness—in just a few minutes, Zhen would decide whether to grant Wang-Mei a reprieve or to deprive his cousin of living to see another New Year. It all depended on the Black Dragon.

"Enter!" shouted Zhen at Wang-Mei when his cousin appeared in the doorway—bigger and fatter than ever.

"May the Three Sublime Ones favor you, honorable cousin Zhen," Wang-Mei said, adding the traditional bow, his hands clasped on his plump stomach.

Zhen returned the gesture. He would have preferred to deny his cousin this greeting, but in an age when destructive Western influences were increasingly subverting the Chinese people's demeanor, it was important to preserve traditional customs.

"Your invitation was most unexpected," Wang-Mei said, looking around as if visiting this room for the first time. "I had nearly forgotten how magnificent these wall decorations are." He pointed at the depiction of a bearded man in only a hanfu riding a blue-and-gold dragon over massive waves. "A most wonderful depiction."

"The floods will tower up into the sky," Zhen said, reciting deluge mythology from the age of Emperor Yao, one of the Three Sublime Ones. "I did have an ulterior motive in choosing that image."

"A masterpiece." Wang-Mei turned to face Zhen. "I nearly forgot how difficult the journey here can be, flying by helicopter. And this horribly cold weather."

"You should have checked more often that all was in order here. It would have been more prudent of you."

"You are here and running the project with great vigilance and skill. Why should I—"

Zhen held up a hand to silence him. "Do you know why I called you here?"

"I heard that the obstacles delaying our project have been solved."

"Indeed. We are about to fulfill our goal. Soon China will shine with a new radiance. We shall increase our people's well-being—of this there is no doubt. And yet some exceptionally concerning and also depressing news has reached me from Beijing."

"From Beijing? What sort of news?"

"About you personally."

Wang-Mei assumed an expression of surprise. "Surely these are only rumors."

"Confucius says we may learn to act wisely in three ways. ... First, by reflection, which is noblest. Second, by imitation, which is easiest. And third by experience, which is the bitterest." Zhen planted himself before Wang-Mei. "I have never reproached you for your many failures, though I profoundly despise the way you squander your life. Constantly seeking diversions to amuse yourself. Alcohol, drugs, women. Look at yourself, cousin, at what's become of you." He eyed Wang-Mei disparagingly. "Just a fat pig, wallowing all day in mud and filth."

Wang-Mei turned red. "Who do think you—"

"Silence! You've gone too far this time. You put Heilongjiang in grave danger. You shall therefore come to know the third way—the bitterest one—and answer for your transgressions."

"Contain your anger, honorable cousin. I assure you that whatever has reached your ears is only rumors. Peasant talk."

"My verdicts, like my actions, are never based on rumors." Zhen stepped around his ornately decorated mahogany desk and lifted the handset of an antique telephone from its cradle. "You may enter," he said.

Zhen had barely hung up before the door to an adjoining room opened. A European entered; in his mid-twenties, he was tall and slender. He wore a brown tweed suit with a properly matching black-and-tan checkered cravat. His hair was combed with a precise part, his pale skin betraying that he seldom saw sunshine.

"I've asked Charles to join us," Zhen explained. "He can give us a firsthand report."

"I imagine he can," Wang-Mei blurted. The veins on his neck had swelled noticeably.

Charles St. Adams stepped before Zhen and added a hint of a bow, which Zhen returned. He ignored Wang-Mei.

"Let's begin," Zhen said.

"Of course." St. Adams pulled out a DVD and glared at Wang-Mei with contempt.

Zhen observed his cousin as St. Adams made his way over to the flat screen on the wall. His cousin's face had become a mask that could not quite conceal the traitorous flush in his cheeks. Zhen was having trouble hiding his own contempt. Men like Wang-Mei possessed neither honor nor pride, and yet Wang-Mei enjoyed a respected high-level role as director of the Chinese State Weather Modification Office. All of the lickspittles in Beijing constantly heaped flattery on him and told him what he wanted to hear. Inside the party, though, the verdict had been reached long ago—refilling Wang-Mei's seat would come in a matter of months. So Zhen needed to exploit the time left. After that, all the cards would be reshuffled.

St. Adams placed the DVD in the player. "Ready?" he said and pressed start on the remote without waiting for an answer.

Images from a surveillance camera appeared on the flat-screen TV. They showed a deluxe hotel suite with two men sitting across from each other in opulent armchairs, separated by a side table. On it stood a bottle of whisky—Chivas Regal—along with four half-full glasses. The two men were talking to each another. Two women, easily identified as prostitutes in cheap outfits and heavy makeup, sat next to each man and said nothing.

Zhen had already seen the footage. St. Adams had brought it to his attention two days ago. Instead of following the events on the screen, he focused on Wang-Mei, who had turned noticeably pale.

"So, just rumors, my dear cousin?"

Wang-Mei didn't reply. He stared at the screen as if paralyzed, the sweat running down from his temples. By this point, he had to concede that any chance of leaving this room alive was quickly fading away.

14

THE SLIDING DOORS AT THE MAIN ENTRANCE TO ANDRA
Inc. closed with a hiss, reducing the howling wind to a muffled drone.
Laura crossed the front lobby followed by the two men who had
probably just saved her life.

The blond man who looked familiar to Laura was still watching her
with concern. "You're shivering all over," he said. "Don't you think
we should call a doctor?"

"Thank you, but I'll be all right soon." Her limbs still stiff, she
lumbered toward the set of modern leather sofas in the waiting area
and dropped down into a matching leather chair.

The man followed her. "Are you sure? You look like a walking
corpse."

"You sure know how to flatter a woman, don't you?" The heat in
the lobby was helping. Waves of warmth flowed through her, and
her hands and feet began tingling and her face stung a little from it.

"Wait there . . ." The blond man went back over to his buddy,
and they exchanged a few words. Only now did Laura notice that
both men were wearing heavy winter clothing complete with lined
boots—clearly, the two were better prepared for the weather than
she had been. His buddy removed his jacket but left on his hat, then
shuffled over to the reception counter. The blond one came back
and sat across from Laura on the leather sofa. "The color is slowly
returning to your face."

Laura touched her stinging cheeks. "I must look like I'm wearing clown makeup."

"There is a certain similarity." He smiled, and pleasant little wrinkles formed in the corners of his eyes.

Laura tilted her head. "Tell me something. Do we know each other somehow?"

The man smiled again. "My name is Daniel Bender." He held out his hand.

They shook and his grip was so firm for a second she thought her stiff fingers might snap. "Laura Wagner. I'm an executive secretary here."

Daniel Bender took a good look at her. "You're still shivering. I'll be right back."

He sprang up and ran over to the lobby's beverage machine. Soon Laura was holding a steaming plastic cup up to her nose, breathing in the aroma of instant soup.

"Cup-a-soup isn't exactly a culinary revelation, but it's warm and will fortify you." Daniel nodded at her to start sipping.

She sipped the broth and made a face. "It's hot enough."

He smiled.

"I would like to thank you. The two of you were heaven-sent." She took another sip. "If only I'd bothered to turn the radio on before heading out."

"Almost no one could foresee such an abrupt change in the weather." Daniel's voice carried a hint of indignation, she noticed. "Most of my colleagues wouldn't acknowledge the weather situation, not even when the first storm gusts were blowing in from the north over Schleswig-Holstein. Believe me, I made a ton of calls about it, but no one wanted to listen. As usual."

"Well, who would expect such a thing happening this time of year?"

"Indeed. Good question." Daniel had an inscrutable expression on his face. He glanced at the other end of the lobby. His companion stood at the reception counter having a lively discussion with the concierge.

She took one last drink from her soup, which was gradually returning to life. "You're a meteorologist?"

"I guess you could say that," Daniel said thoughtfully.

"You guess?"

He was looking away from her now. "Leif and I, we both studied meteorology. Ages ago."

Laura's face brightened. "Hey, now I know how I know you—you're that Jet Stream guy."

Daniel grimaced. "I'm only that guy on YouTube. You can call me Daniel."

"Fair enough. I'm Laura. So, why YouTube? Didn't you used to have a show on RTL?"

"It was Sat.1, and it's been a while. I don't really want to talk about it."

"All right." Laura looked over at his companion, whom he'd called Leif. Apparently there was some kind of problem. Leif was gesturing frantically, even pounded his fist on the counter. The concierge shook his head vehemently and pointed at the exit.

"Leif!" Daniel signaled for his buddy to calm down. Leif rolled his eyes, took a deep breath, then continued his discussion in a calmer register.

It occurred to Laura that no one had entered the building the whole time she'd been sitting here. Nothing seemed to be happening out in the parking lot either, no headlights, no plows out on the road. "How come you two were the only ones out driving? There were still cars on the streets before I went and dumped mine in a ditch."

"It's because of a second accident, at that intersection back before the business park. All the streets are blocked." A sidelong grin stretched across Daniel's face. "That's never going to stop Leif. His pickup has four-wheel-drive. We made it around the accidents by taking a little hill."

"How come you two were the only ones who could see this cold spell coming?"

Daniel nodded. He only now seemed to notice he was still wearing his thick jacket. He pulled it off and tossed it on the chair next to him. "Conditions over Scandinavia changed incredibly quickly, leaving hardly any time to arrive at a reliable forecast. By the time it was clear to us where this was heading, two weather systems were already colliding. That's what led to this genuine blizzard we're having."

"A blizzard? I thought such things only happened in America."

Daniel shook his head. "People in Germany used to say the same thing about tornados. There absolutely are blizzards here in Europe, as we've seen, though they are less common. First thing that comes to my mind was that chaotic winter of 1978 to '79. In just a few hours, the temperature fell more than thirty degrees Fahrenheit. Then a snowstorm set in, and it lasted five days, with a wind factor of ten. It turned the whole country white."

Laura stared, her eyes wide. "Five days?"

Daniel nodded. "But you're right. True blizzards, according to definition, happen only in America. Here in Europe, we generally refer to 'blizzard-like conditions.'"

"So what's the difference?"

Daniel looked around. "I'd love to explain it to you. But first I'm going to need some coffee." He stood up. "You want one? Or some more soup?"

Laura laughed. "Please, no more soup. Tea would be nice, no sugar." Daniel was back soon with two steaming cups. He handed Laura her tea. She smiled. "I'm still listening . . ."

"Right." He leaned back on the sofa. "So, in our latitude, snowstorms are generally less harmful because the temperature differences are seldom large enough. The distribution of land and water masses in Europe plays a role there too, as does the location of the Alps."

"How do they factor in?"

"Mountain ranges present an obstacle for air masses flowing north-south, so polar air rarely collides directly with humid, subtropical air."

"But isn't that exactly what happened tonight?" Laura said.

Daniel nodded. "Above the Baltic Sea, a low-pressure system from over the Rhineland, Belgium, and parts of Eastern France collided with an extreme high-pressure system over Scandinavia. In northern Russia and northern Scandinavia, current temperatures are hovering around –22 Fahrenheit. Air from high-pressure systems generally streams toward regions with low pressure. We were already seeing a massive onset of cold weather. Though a few special factors are currently adding to it."

"Like what?"

"Are you really interested in this?" he asked.

"Of course. I nearly froze to death out there."

Daniel sipped at his coffee. "Around midnight, a strong air mass boundary suddenly built up over the southern Baltic Sea, and in record time, too. Temperatures from northern Sweden as low as minus forty ran into warm air from Central Europe with a high relative humidity of approximately 90 percent. That, along with the extreme differences in atmospheric pressure, is now causing northeasterly winds with the strength of a storm, which in turn brings these incredible amounts of snow."

"So why didn't anyone see that coming?" asked Laura, her hands wrapped around her plastic cup. "I mean, with all this technology we have today?"

Daniel glanced at his buddy Leif, then leaned forward to her and lowered his voice. "Here's where we get to the weird part of the story."

Laura automatically leaned forward too. "Which is?"

"This extreme high-pressure system over Scandinavia had built up within just a few hours. Nothing, I mean nothing, was pointing to that beforehand. Up until then, weather conditions were looking completely normal." Daniel sat up again, took a deep breath. "For no known reason, atmospheric pressure began rising steeply after midnight. Contrary to all forecasts. It was purely a fluke that Leif and I were able to follow this happening in real time using the programs we have. We just happened to be sitting there together, talking about the severe weather we were having in Berlin."

"I see . . ."

Daniel nodded. "But, what we saw next was simply unbelievable. As if a gigantic balloon of high pressure was created out of thin air all of a sudden. There's no exact terminology for this phenomenon, but I don't know how to describe it apart from a balloon of such intensity that it's even diverting the jet stream in the upper troposphere. And in a massive way. You see, when extreme high-pressure systems are created, extreme low-pressure systems will inevitably start developing elsewhere at the same time. This bubble has an enormous impact on overall weather conditions in the entire northern hemisphere. And that applies, like I said, all the way up to the jet stream."

"'Jet Stream.'" Laura smiled. "Like your name."

Daniel rolled his eyes. "Named after the official terminology, yes. That guy over there gave me the nickname during college." He pointed at Leif, still standing at the counter. He had a furious expression on his face and his arms crossed at his chest while the concierge talked to someone on the phone. Either Leif had achieved some partial success or the concierge was calling security to have the annoying guy in the stocking cap finally thrown out. The next few minutes would indicate which way it was going to go.

Laura gave Daniel an inquiring look. "What are you here for? Are you doing business with Andra?"

He pursed his lips. "Well, Leif and I, let's just say we're here on the trail of something. The whole thing's going to sound pretty wacky, but—"

"Wacky how?"

Daniel hesitated. Then, as if first fearing he'd already said too much, he steeled himself to continue. "It's possible that this blizzard was not produced by natural causes."

"What's that supposed to mean?"

"I've been keeping an eye on an increasing amount of baffling weather abnormalities happening all over the world. For two years now these phenomena have been occurring at ever shorter intervals, something that has been puzzling meteorologists on all continents. For most of these occurrences no one's been able to come up with a plausible explanation."

"Like this blizzard, for example."

Right then the fluorescent lights in the lobby started flickering. They went out a few seconds later, and darkness fell at once. The lighting outside in the snow-covered parking lots and along the paths went out too, and the coming dawn was still too weak to penetrate the thick clouds and the snowstorm. Daniel Bender was now just a black silhouette.

He sighed. "I was expecting that."

Laura recalled the power cable ripping away and the transmission tower falling. "It must have affected other towers too. I always assumed we had emergency power generators for situations like this."

"I'm betting on it," someone said—right next to her ear.

Laura cried out and whipped around as the lights flickered back on. Next to her stood Daniel's friend Leif. He held his stocking cap in one hand and pushed back his greasy black hair with the other. Overall he looked pretty unkempt, Laura thought, at least compared to his partner.

"Told you!" Leif said and clucked his tongue. "Me, I'm guessing at least two honking generators down in the basement."

"You always creep up to people like that?" Laura said.

"You always get so frightened?"

"Leif, please." Daniel waved his friend over to him. "This is Laura Wagner. She's an executive secretary here."

"Aha." Leif sized her up. "Maybe you can be of some help to us after all."

"That depends." Laura looked at the two of them.

"We're here to meet someone," Leif said and pointed toward the concierge, who glanced at him disapprovingly. "Unfortunately, that lackey you got there at reception is pretty stubborn."

"Do you have an appointment?" she said.

"No."

"Yeah, well . . ." Laura stared at him, annoyed now. His tongue kept flicking from one corner of his mouth to the other. The guy seemed like he might have a screw loose.

"You take care of it, Jet," he said to Daniel, plopping down into one of the armchairs. He hauled up a black backpack from the floor, ripped open the zipper, and pulled out a laptop. "Got things to do."

"What things?" Daniel said.

"Have to see about Rousseau." He flipped open the laptop. Without bothering to look at Laura, he asked, "You know the Wi-Fi password?"

"This isn't Starbucks."

"Never mind, just got in anyway." He started hammering away at the keys.

Laura was speechless, and Daniel rubbed at his neck with embarrassment. She finished her tea. It was time to go now. Leif showing up had changed the mood—she got an uneasy feeling around such a coarse guy. It was tough to imagine these two completely different types being old friends. She wanted to leave but couldn't just abandon Daniel sitting there. So she said, "Whom are you trying to see?"

"A Lars Windrup."

"He's in the IT department," Laura said. "I never have anything to do with IT. Did he make it in to work?"

Leif looked up. "No. Would be nice if that loser at reception had told me that sooner."

Laura shrugged.

"Okay, well," she said, turning to Daniel, "Thanks again, and best of luck with your research."

She headed for the stairway. She wasn't about to get into an elevator powered by an emergency generator.

She bounded up two stairs at a time. She had a ton of work waiting for her, and she needed to pick up the pace if she still hoped to get to Robin any earlier this afternoon.

Once she got to her office she started going through emails from the last couple days.

There were requests, complaints, offers, some spam that slipped through the firewall. She mechanically moved various emails to the appropriate folders.

She halted suddenly. Something was weird about the last email she'd absentmindedly marked as spam. She hadn't completely been paying attention, had barely glanced at the subject lines, but her unconscious told her something was urgent. She sat upright and opened the spam folder.

manekineko2008@hotmail.com

The name of the sender and free Hotmail address both pointed to spam. But then Laura read the subject. The hairs on her neck stood up. The subject contained six letters: *reimpo*.

She stared in disbelief. It was the very abbreviation she and Hardenberg had come up with over two years ago. Her stomach tightened up as she opened the email, holding her breath. This was no spam. The email was meant just for her. And it came from Hardenberg.

15

HUANG ZHEN STOOD IN HIS OFFICE WITH HIS COUSIN Wang-Mei and Charles St. Adams, following the events unfolding on the flat screen.

They watched Wang-Mei interact with Roland Hardenberg. The two men had just finished exchanging the usual pleasantries. The two Chinese women in armchairs on either side of them were dressed suggestively but looked bored, checking their fingernails. With a fat grin on his face, Wang-Mei pointed at the prostitutes and said in broken English, *"For later, when finish business."*

Hardenberg eyed the women up and down. They noticed they were being talked about, put on fake smiles, and shifted their bodies back and forth provocatively as if dancing to music only they could hear. Hardenberg nodded in acknowledgment. *"Then let's not waste any time."*

"You have what I asked for?"

Hardenberg reached into his jacket, pulled out a USB stick and handed it to Wang-Mei. *"The source code. This should solve your problems."*

"Should?" Wang-Mei turned the little flash drive over in his hands, examining it.

"I'm not a mathematician, nor an IT expert. I'm just the delivery man."

"An extremely well-paid delivery man," Wang-Mei reminded him. He pocketed the USB stick. *"You are aware, we need the final software update in four weeks at latest. Can you meet deadline?"*

"I'm confident of it."

"I would prefer a clear yes." Wang-Mei added a smile that became the friendly grimace of the negotiating table. It concealed a sharpened dagger, ready to stab when the other showed any weakness.

"Yes," Hardenberg said, obviously realizing Wang-Mei needed confirmation.

"It pleases me to hear that."

"Have I ever disappointed you, honorable Chang?"

Wang-Mei didn't bat an eyelash hearing the fake name he had given at their first meeting. *"You have already shown much proof of your trustworthiness."*

Hardenberg leaned back, crossing his legs. *"Your clients must be quite pleased."*

Wang-Mei pulled a briefcase from behind his armchair, placed it on the table, turned it with the locks facing Hardenberg, and leaned back as well. *"See for yourself how pleased we are."*

Hardenberg pulled the briefcase over to him and clicked open the locks. He lifted the lid carefully, almost reverently.

"The agreed-upon sum," Wang-Mei explained.

Hardenberg, looking quite pleased himself, snapped the briefcase shut. *"Our collaboration comes to a close with the next delivery. Nothing's changed, I assume?"*

"No. However, I would not wish to rule out maybe using your services at some point in future, Mr. Hardenberg."

Hardenberg reached for the half-full glass before him on the table. *"Let's drink to that."*

"Which brings us to our enchanting ladies here."

On the flat screen, Wang-Mei grinned and gave the prostitutes a wink.

St. Adams stopped the playback, freezing the image.

"Are you finished?" Wang-Mei said.

"No." St. Adams adjusted his cravat. "I, for one, am not sure just how much you recall from the rest of the evening. You might well be surprised."

St. Adams exchanged glances with Zhen. Installing the surveillance camera in Roland Hardenberg's hotel suite had been St. Adams's idea, as the Englishman had not trusted Wang-Mei for some time. He always proved to have a nose for such things.

"Continue!" ordered Zhen.

The image returned to life. The two Chinese girls went on their knees before the men and deftly unfastened the men's belts as Wang-Mei and Hardenberg toasted each other with satisfaction. But then something unexpected happened. As Wang-Mei rested his head against the chair and tipped back his Chivas Regal, Hardenberg poured the contents of his glass into the flowerpot of colorful fake plants next to his chair. Neither Wang-Mei nor the two prostitutes devoting themselves to their duties noticed a thing.

"I've procured a little something for us," Hardenberg said, setting down his glass. *"Honorable Chang, I'm afraid you'll have to attend to both ladies yourself for the moment."* He steered the Chinese girl at his feet toward Wang-Mei. She understood and moved on her knees to join her associate, who was now struggling with Wang-Mei's flaccid penis.

"How could I refuse such a request?" Wang-Mei chuckled and poured two more drinks. He again tipped back his glass in one go, and again Hardenberg poured his whisky into the flower pot next to him.

While the two prostitutes overindulged Wang-Mei with their tongues, Hardenberg produced a baggie from inside his jacket. He let the white powder inside spill onto the table and formed two lines with the nail of his pinky finger. He pulled a banknote from the briefcase, rolled it up, and held it out to Wang-Mei. *"This time we should celebrate even more than usual."*

Wang-Mei's eyes lit up. He pushed both prostitutes aside and bent over the table, which with his huge belly wasn't easy, then tore the banknote from Hardenberg's hand and took a noisy snort.

"This coke comes from Macao," Hardenberg explained. *"Top-shelf product."*

Wang-Mei rolled his head around, released a vague grunt, grabbed the two prostitutes by the hair and rammed their heads back into his crotch. Hardenberg meanwhile acted as if he were snorting up the remaining line of coke. But instead, he wiped it off the table top with the inside of his hand and sprinkled it onto the fluffy carpet.

"Another toot?"

Wang-Mie looked up. His pupils were dilated, his face flushed. Beads of sweat glistened on his forehead. *"These ladies are at our disposal the whole night long. I hope you brought enough supply for that, Mr. Hardenberg?"*

The German businessman in the video smiled. *"Come now, you think I don't know how this works?"*

16

LAURA STARED AT HER MONITOR. IT TOOK HER A MOMENT to grasp what she was looking at. Shortly before his death, Hardenberg had sent her an email.

Dear Laura,

My last business trip to Beijing has changed everything. I'm going to take some time off and can't be reached for a few days. If I haven't checked back in within two weeks, please take care of my cat for me. I know she will be in good hands with you.

R.H.

Laura read the email three times. She didn't understand. Why had Hardenberg used an anonymous email address? He must have known that the message would probably end up in her spam folder—it was a complete fluke that she'd noticed it. It said that she had received the message at 3:23 a.m. She let out a deep breath. One of the last things Roland Hardenberg had done in his life was send her an email, but why? What was this supposed to mean? She rubbed her knuckles anxiously. The police would be interested in this email for sure, and investigators might be able to better determine the time of death by checking the Internet provider's logs. The strangest part was that

Hardenberg had mentioned a cat. Laura didn't know much about her boss's private life, but she was sure of one thing: he didn't own a cat.

manekineko2008@hotmail.com. It sounded Japanese. Laura thought she'd heard the name somewhere. Maybe it was the name of someone they did business with? She logged into Hardenberg's appointment calendar and scanned the saved contacts but didn't see any similar entries. Then she searched the company database. Nothing came up.

She stepped over to the window to think about it. The snowstorm was still raging outside—a *blizzard*, she now knew. Out in front of the main entrance, one floor below her, she could see the head custodian. He had hauled the snow blower out from summer storage and was trying to clear the entrance pathway as best he could. As he looked around to check on things, he noticed her. He raised a mitten-clad hand and waved, then continued with his work. Laura returned the wave and kept watching him—and all of a sudden, she figured it out. She slapped at her forehead and rushed back into Hardenberg's office.

She found the gold-painted waving cat next to the pile of unopened mail. It had been there for as long as she could remember. She warily picked it up. It was plastic, with one moveable arm that waved. Maneki-nekos originally came from Japan but had become popular in China and Thailand as good-luck charms. Hardenberg had told her that once. He also said that golden cats were supposed to attract great wealth.

Laura turned it over. On the underside was a little lid, probably to a battery compartment for the waving mechanism. She opened it and caught her breath. Someone had removed the batteries and placed a silver USB stick in the space, fixing it in place with tape.

She loosened it and cautiously looked it over. Why would Hardenberg want her to find a flash drive? Why her of all people?

She swallowed hard. Whatever her former boss was involved in, he was now dragging her into it by leading her to this flash drive.

The door swung open. Laura started, dropped the cat.

A secretary, Doris, came striding in carrying a stack of files, back to sashaying through the offices like she used to after recovering from a hip operation. She stopped in her tracks. "Pardon, I thought no one was here."

"You startled me," Laura blurted. She stuffed the USB stick into the hip pocket of her pants, bent over, and picked up the cat.

"I'm sorry." Doris hugged her files tighter. "Is anything broken?"

"No, it's okay." Laura took a deep breath, closing her eyes a moment.

"Is everything all right, Frau Wagner? You look pale."

"I'm fine, but thank you." Laura set the cat back on the desk, then held out her hands. "Here, I'll take care of those for you." She took the files from Doris and placed them on Hardenberg's desk chair.

The secretary turned to leave. At the doorway, she turned around once more and gave Laura a smile. "You seem like you're working too hard, my dear," she said. "We're all upset about Herr Hardenberg's sudden passing. Still, just try and take things easier right now. Once the new boss comes? You'll probably have more overtime at first than you'd like."

"Do you know if they have found a replacement for Herr Hardenberg?"

Doris shook her head. "All I heard was, the board is already talking to potential candidates."

Once Doris left, Laura returned to thinking about that USB stick in her pocket. What, she wondered, could Hardenberg possibly have been trying to keep secret?

17

CHARLES ST. ADAMS HAD PUSHED FAST-FORWARD ON the DVD player. The three men silently watched a speeded-up version of events in Hardenberg's hotel suite.

Zhen stroked his mustache. Wang-Mei had done such a monstrous thing. Not only had his cousin fallen back into his old habits, he'd also let the German lead him astray like some stupid boy.

Cunning and tactics were not only crucial elements of the art of war—they were equally essential to performing any negotiation well. Every kid in China knew the text *San Shi Liu Ji*, the "Thirty-Six Stratagems" that ensured that one would remain victorious in war as well as in negotiating. As the video continued in fast motion, Zhen recalled the three stratagems that Hardenberg had instinctively applied. The first strategy was "Feign madness but never lose sight of the goal." The second, "The beauty trap," used a beautiful woman as diversion.

Wang-Mei originally had hired the two prostitutes for Hardenberg, but the German had simply returned the gift to Wang-Mei. This cunning trick also matched the third stratagem: "Make the host and the guest exchange roles." From a certain point on, it was Hardenberg, not Wang-Mei, who was determining the course of action that evening. Zhen couldn't help acknowledge his respect for the German, and again he considered his two dao sabers on the wall, just as he'd done many times this morning. Fine weapons might be indispensable in battle, yet were not necessarily decisive to the war's outcome.

"So. Now it gets even more interesting," St. Adams said, breaking the silence, and let the video run at normal speed.

Wang-Mei released a contemptuous snort yet didn't protest, which Zhen took as a first sign of resignation on the part of his cousin.

According to the timestamp, just over an hour had elapsed since Wang-Mei and Hardenberg emptied their first whiskies, each in their own way. Wang-Mei now looked spent in his chair, the alcohol and coke having taken their toll. Both of the prostitutes had withdrawn to the bathroom.

Hardenberg still sat upright. He observed his fat Chinese counterpart. *"Our business is completed,"* he said after a period of silence. *"Both sides are happy. Don't you think it's time to introduce me to your contact at Chenlong Industries?"*

Wang-Mei laughed out loud and snorted and nearly choked in the process. Hardenberg poured him another whisky.

"Thanks," Wang-Mei wheezed and tipped back the amber liquid.

"Why do you laugh at my suggestion?"

Wang-Mei buttoned up his slacks, his fat paunch swelling over his tight waistband. *"You know very well that Chenlong is only a shell company."*

"I thought so."

"So why ask?"

"Please, honorable Chang. I've proven that I'm trustworthy. And I'd like to continue doing business with you in future. I can only do so when I know who's behind things."

"Why now all of a sudden?"

"They're getting suspicious at Andra, and they're starting to ask questions. I need more background knowledge if I'm going to make this all sound plausible."

Wang-Mei smirked. He was clearly having trouble keeping the secret. *"Perhaps you will not like what you hear."*

Hardenberg patted the briefcase on the table in front of him. *"For me, all that matters is what's in here."*

Wang-Mei grinned and, ever the ludicrous conspirator, waved Hardenberg close to him. *"All right. I will reveal something to you. Because I can actually stand you."*

Hardenberg smiled. *"I feel honored."*

Wang-Mei glanced at the closed bathroom door before shifting forward in his chair. *"Charles St. Adams, that English pansy? He's not the harmless contact he made himself out to be that first time."*

Hardenberg looked surprised. *"I haven't thought about St. Adams for months. So, what role does he play?"*

"He is one of the two funders of the Black Dragon."

"The Black Dragon?"

Wang-Mei smirked. *"You probably believe that we intend to copy the prototype and sell it to the competition, yes?"*

"What else would you need the prototype for?"

"Let your imagination run wild! Who, more than anyone, is interested in new technology—especially that which is, shall we say, most deployable in flexible ways."

Hardenberg's eyebrows pinched. *"Are you talking about the Chinese military?"*

Wang-Mei held up a hand. *"No."* He enjoyed another swallow of the Chivas Regal and stared at Hardenberg. *"But you are in the right direction. We need the prototype for developing an all-new type of weapon."*

Hardenberg stared in horror. *"A weapon?"*

"Here in China, we have a saying: For the dragon to fly high, he must do so against the wind." Wang-Mei's eyes sparkled with excitement. *"Thanks to you, Mr. Hardenberg, we now control a dragon that will fly wherever we command it. This dragon will unleash a storm that will devour them whole."*

"I'm afraid I don't follow . . ."

Wang-Mei belched. *"The West still sees China as backwards. The USA above all refuses to recognize us as an equal trading partner. But behind the mask of diplomacy, it is war which prevails."*

"In what way?"

Wang-Mei's face darkened. *"In 2015, the USA established a free trade agreement with eleven countries—with Japan especially, our archenemy. This is an insult to China. Ratification of this agreement is still being debated in the U.S., yet this does not stop America from increasingly seeking to secure its influence over Asia and thereby rupturing China's powerful position. There is no doubt about this."*

"Don't you think that's a little one-sided?"

Wang-Mei pounded his fist on the tabletop. *"For years, Japan, Vietnam, Taiwan, and even the Philippines have been stealing islands and maritime regions from my country, all where enormous amounts of raw materials are found. America is attempting to use its might to hinder China's rise to economic superpower. On top of that, they accuse us of ratcheting up our armaments and military capabilities. The USA is the one who sends more and more warships toward East Asia, all to demonstrate their power!"*

His verbal outburst had sapped his strength. Exhausted, he leaned back in the armchair before continuing:

"In China, there is one political group that will not watch silently anymore while the diplomats ensure that our land remains stagnant. My cousin . . ."

He halted, as if realizing he'd said the wrong thing.

"Go on," Hardenberg urged him.

"There is nothing more to say. The ignorance of the United States of America shall be its downfall. The Black Dragon will strike upon that land and raze it to the ground."

Hardenberg eyed Wang-Mei with skepticism. *"You speak in riddles, Chang."*

"We will subdue the very earth itself," Wang-Mei continued. *"The earth is the mightiest weapon of all. He who controls the forces of nature is the true ruler of the world."*

"Are you talking about—geoengineering?"

Wang-Mei waved away the notion. He leaned forward again, lowering his voice. *"I'm speaking of storms, my friend. Massive storms of the kind that this world has never experienced. I'm speaking of rains that will put whole countries under water. I'm speaking of droughts that will unleash famines. We will make war against our enemies without losing a single warrior. The Black Dragon is the most powerful weapon in the history of mankind."*

As Zhen, St. Adams, and Wang-Mei watched, they could see that Hardenberg was feeling increasingly uneasy. The man before him was raving as if in ecstasy, and that ecstasy was not just the cocaine talking.

"You intend to control the weather?" Hardenberg said.

"We've already been doing it for years now." Wang-Mei belched again. *"Yet now we are approaching a new stage. By waking the Black Dragon, we will make the whole world experience just what we are truly capable of and in imposing fashion."*

"But you cannot be serious, Chang. You are joking."

"You asked." Wang-Mei pointed at Hardenberg. *"We are ready to go on November 22. The Black Dragon will launch massive winds*

and release devastating floods, and it will strike the United States of America and seal its downfall."

Now they could see the German pour his own whisky and drink it down this time—all in one gulp. His face displayed a blank horror.

St. Adams turned off the DVD player.

"I think that should suffice," he said and turned to Wang-Mei. "For your information: Shortly after you went to the toilet, Hardenberg went through your jacket and pulled out your wallet. He surely learned your true name that way. So honorable Zhen and I saw no other option but to eliminate the German."

"Unfortunately, there remains one problem," Zhen added. "Right after your little celebration, the German recorded a voice memo. We couldn't understand its wording, but we can only assume he was taking measures to endanger our project in case of his death."

"Hardenberg is *dead*?" Wang-Mei's voice was little more than a whisper.

"You should be more concerned about where that voice memo went," St. Adams said. "Our man in the field did not find the file on Hardenberg's smartphone, nor on his laptop."

Zhen had heard and certainly seen enough. He planted himself before his cousin, the veins on his neck throbbing. "You are a disgrace to our family and our people. How could you deceive me like this?"

Wang-Mai lowered his head. "Forgive me."

Zhen spat in his face. "On your knees!"

Wang-Mei obeyed. Beads of sweat glistened on his face. Zhen's spit ran from his left eye down to his nostril.

Zhen whipped around. He grabbed one of the dao sabers from the wall and held the blade to Wang-Mei's carotid artery. A thin line of blood appeared where the razor-sharp metal pressed into his flesh.

Wang-Mai squinted his eyes shut. "Please, have mercy ... I can still be of valuable service to you. My influence in Beijing continues. How will you manage to keep all those functionaries happy and sympathetic to our cause?"

"That's my concern and mine only," Zhen hissed. "It is better to stumble on a new path than to keep going nowhere on the same old one."

"Mercy, please!"

Zhen panted with rage and foamed at the corners of his mouth and it threatened to overwhelm him, yet he could not lose his composure now. The responsibility for passing sentence on Wang-Mei must lie with the Black Dragon alone—Zhen would merely be carrying it out. "I will never forgive you for your betrayal. Yet I am granting you a chance to prolong your pathetic life."

"Tell me what you demand of me, honorable cousin, and I will fulfill your wish."

"I will spare your life, but only after the Black Dragon has risen."

Wang-Mei opened his eyes, which showed a faint stirring of hope. "When is that?"

"On this very day."

"But that's not possible. We're not ready yet."

"I already gave the order to commence preparations. Two hours ago. Our systems are ready."

"But, it's still too early," Wang-Mei protested in despair, torn between trying to demonstrate his fidelity and the dire need to save his life. "We haven't done final testing. We must improve the precision of Diamond. We both know what may happen otherwise." He gazed up at Zhen, his expression pleading. "Think of Russia, of Australia. And now Europe... We've already attracted too much attention."

Zhen pressed the blade deeper. Wang-Mei winced; more blood flowed.

"That is why it's too risky to wait until November 22," Zhen hissed. "That is your fault and yours alone. So you make certain that the dragon does rise today, or you will die—right here, today."

"As you wish." Wang-Mei lowered his eyes in confirmation, since he didn't dare so much as nod.

18

LAURA INSERTED THE SILVER FLASH DRIVE INTO THE USB port on her PC. The usual hourglass appeared on screen, then a window opened showing the files on the USB stick. There were two: a voice memo labeled "laura_1" as well as a file titled "sup_diam_fin." Judging from the date and time, Hardenberg had recorded "laura_1" in Beijing. The date on the second file indicated that it had been saved to the flash drive three weeks ago. Laura snatched her headset next to the monitor, pulled it on, and played the voice memo.

She only heard labored breathing at first, then Hardenberg's deep baritone voice came over the headphones: *"What a complete idiot I've been . . ."* She trembled, realizing she was hearing the voice of a dead man. *"If I had any idea what the Chinese actually needed the prototype for, I never would have allowed myself to get involved. But I'm not looking for an excuse for what I've done, or for forgiveness. The money seduced me. Now I sit here and must face the madness that I so carelessly helped unleash."* A pause followed, during which all she heard was his breathing in fits and starts. *"I do hope to get control of the matter on my own, but I can't guarantee it. As soon as fatso is sober again tomorrow, it would not surprise me if he tries taking me out. In case he succeeds, I at least hope to clear the air by saying this, right here and now."* Hardenberg took a deep breath. *"A year ago, with me in charge, Andra delivered Diamond—the prototype of a new gyrotron, as you know—to a Chinese company named Chenlong Industries."*

Laura listened closely. She recalled the deal as well as that it had been done with the highest secrecy. Fewer than five people at Andra had been involved. They hadn't even let her in on the details, even though as Hardenberg's secretary she usually kept an eye on how such deals were implemented. Hardenberg had preferred to take this one all by himself, and she hadn't given it another thought. It had certainly happened before. So now she was all the more curious to hear just where Hardenberg's confession—or whatever this should be called—would lead.

"My first contact with Chenlong came around seven months before the actual deal was made. An Englishman contacted me, through whom I then met Chang, who handled the deal. Just a few minutes ago, by the way, I learned Chang's real name: Xian Wang-Mei." Hardenberg sighed. He appeared to drink something before continuing. *"I had always assumed that Chenlong was a front for a rival company eager for one of our patents. Had I known that the prototype was being used for a new form of weather weapon, I never would have done the deal. I know how crazy this must sound, but: if something terrible happens on November 22, I will be to blame. I think these people are planning a devastating attack for that date. Even though I have no clue how, or where . . ."*

Laura clicked on pause. Was she hearing this right? Roland Hardenberg, who always seemed the embodiment of sincerity and integrity to her, had committed industrial espionage? At least that was how she interpreted his words. And what was a weather weapon? Maybe the rest of the recording would explain that, she thought, clicking play. It buzzed and crackled a few seconds as if the recording was corrupted, then she heard the howling turbines of an airplane starting up in the background.

"Hello, Laura." Hearing her name startled her a second. *"I'm back in Hanover. Sitting on an airplane these last few hours has given me plenty of time to think about everything. I really screwed up, but that can't be helped now. Listen closely now, Laura, because this is important."* She heard Hardenberg take a deep breath. *"If anything should happen to me, you will have to make sure that the software for the prototype is destroyed. Thanks to me, Chenlong has access to the Andra Intranet. Wang-Mei's people are getting all relevant updates from there. Along with this voice memo, I'm giving you another file. This one contains a virus that will destroy the software*

for Diamond and render Chenlong's prototype useless. Laura, you need to make sure that this update gets put onto the Intranet—as a required update. Chenlong will jump at it." Another pause, then he continued distractedly. *"Talk to Lars Windrup in IT. He will know what to do. Under no condition should you take this to the police. It won't help at all. No one will believe you."* Laura made a mental note of the name Lars Windrup. *"Be careful, Laura! These men are dangerous. They are not just extremely powerful—they will do anything to, to ... well, to protect their interests. Do not take any risks. I'm aware of the burden I'm putting on you. I really would have liked to fix my mistake myself, believe me, but the way things are looking now, nothing would come of that, unfortunately."* The recording ended.

Laura took off her headset. Her heart beat quickly, and her neck had that old sensation of a headache setting in. She could hardly believe what she'd just heard. Yet wasn't Hardenberg's murder the best proof of what he'd just told her?

She pulled the USB stick from her PC and stared at it in the palm of her hand. Her first impulse was to give it to the police. Yet what if Hardenberg's warning was proven correct and the police didn't believe her? What if no one did anything, and actual people died on November 22? How could she live with that? She rubbed at her temples and silently cursed Hardenberg for letting himself get mixed up in shady dealings with the Chinese. And for putting the burden on her, of all people, to fix the whole thing.

She stood up. Hardenberg had mentioned Lars Windrup in IT. And what did it mean, exactly, that two meteorologists, of all people, needed to talk to the exact same person today? She couldn't make heads or tails of it. All she knew was, she had to get to Lars Windrup. She stuffed the USB stick into her pants pocket and left her office.

She went up one floor to the IT department, an open office. Normally around twenty people were here in front of monitors, but today the room was nearly empty. Only Marc Bauer, an overweight guy whom she ran into in the lunchroom once in a while, had made it into the office. She felt strangely out of place in the brightly lit, nearly empty open space.

Laura stepped up to Bauer's desk, which held two empty Coke bottles and a half-eaten chocolate bar next to the keyboard. Judging from the rings under Bauer's eyes, his wrinkled Commodore 64

T-shirt, and the odor of sweat coming off him, he had to be at the tail end of a night shift.

"I'm looking for Lars Windrup," she said.

Bauer made a show out of looking around him. He grunted. "You see anyone else here? I was hoping to get home long ago, but now it's looking like I'll have to hold the fort until this goddamn snowstorm lets up."

Laura got an idea. She held the USB stick up to Bauer's face. "There's a file on here that I can't open. Could you maybe take a look, see what's on it?"

Bauer rolled his eyes, stretched out a hand. "Give it here." Soon he was squinting at his monitor. "Where did you get this?"

She told the truth. "From Herr Hardenberg."

"What is this, exactly?"

"You tell me. All I know is that Hardenberg gave it the highest priority and wanted it uploaded today."

"The file doesn't have the necessary certificate. I can't see it without that."

"Please? It's very important."

"You don't have the authority, unfortunately." Bauer eyed her with suspicion. "There are good reasons for only allowing certain personnel to install files on the company network."

"I'm aware of that, but—"

"I'm sorry, but I would never go uploading just any old file. You come back with official approval, that's a different deal entirely."

"But it's urgent," Laura told him.

Bauer swiveled his office chair her way and gave her a hostile glare. "You should go now. I'll forget that this conversation ever took place."

Laura raised her hands to placate him. "Okay, I get it." She thanked Bauer for his patience and asked him to let Windrup know he should get in touch with her immediately if he ever turned up. Bauer muttered something unintelligible and turned back to his monitor.

Laura was mad at herself. It had been naïve of her to try doing it like this. Now she had no other option but to wait until Lars Windrup got here.

She returned to her office and stared out the window again. The blizzard raged on outside with unrelenting force, and the heavy snowfall didn't let her see farther than the nearest parking lot lights, their beams barely reaching the ground. The head custodian was back out fighting all the snow, that or he'd never left, but his blower wasn't up to the job. She spotted no new tire tracks anywhere on the parking lot, either. She drummed her fingers on the windowsill, going back over things, and thought of Daniel Bender and his companion again. That made her head over to her desk and call the number for the concierge.

"It's Laura Wagner here," she said once she got him on the line. "Hey, do you remember that man with the stocking cap this morning?"

"You're joking, right? That guy was really getting on my nerves."

"Did you happen to notice when he and the other guy with him left the building?"

"Who said they left? They're still hanging around. But what am I supposed to do? I can't just throw them out with conditions like this. Oh, you haven't heard? The authorities have issued a ban on driving."

"No. I didn't know that."

"It's tough even for emergency vehicles and police to get to where they're going. All public transport has completely broken down."

"Good Lord. I didn't know it was that bad."

"It's affecting all of northern Europe," the concierge continued. "Everything's buried under heavy snow, all the way to the mountains. In Eastern Europe, temps are all the way down to minus thirty—"

"Tell me something," Laura interrupted. "Where are those two right now?"

"Down here in the lobby, where else?"

"Thanks."

Laura hung up and rushed out of the office. When she reached the lobby, the first thing she saw was a filthy boot protruding from behind the back of a sofa—Daniel Bender was lying on the sofa with his eyes closed, his hands folded on his stomach. His friend Leif was hunkered down on the floor behind one of the armchairs, his legs crossed, his laptop riding on his thighs.

"Comfortable?" she asked.

Daniel opened his eyes. "I've slept in worse places."

"Have you heard what's happened with the road traffic?"

"Of course." He gave a big yawn and sat up. "Leif keeps me updated."

Laura sat across from him. "How long is this going to last?"

"Tough to say. Weather situation like this, could last a few days."

"Oh, no." Laura grimaced with dread. She thought about Robin. He was still expecting her to pick him up from the hospital today.

Daniel leaned his head back and moved it in a circle, cracking his neck. The sound was unsettling.

Laura, watching him, decided to just get right to the subject. "Hey, tell me about those unexplained weather phenomena you mentioned this morning."

He raised his eyebrows. "All over again?"

She shrugged. "Looks like we've got time."

"All right . . ." Daniel ran his fingers through his hair, scratched at his chin. "There are three main events attracting our attention. In northeastern Russia, vast permafrost regions recently thawed several yards deep, all within a single day. Houses were literally sinking into the mud. The next day, the usual minus temps were back. About the same time, in Australia? A vast lake disappeared within twenty-four hours."

"Disappeared?"

"The water supposedly dissipated from the effects of extreme heat."

Laura's eyes widened. "I have a question. What about that tornado in Berlin? And last weekend's hailstorm?"

"From a meteorological standpoint, both cases aren't all that bizarre. What's unusual is how quickly the weather changed. So judging from that, I'd say that ... yeah, both the tornado and the hailstorm could fall into the category of a 'weather anomaly.'"

"And this blizzard too, of course."

"Naturally."

"But you mentioned three main things."

"Right. At the beginning of August, in the Emirate of Abu Dhabi, heavy rains started coming down in the middle of the desert. At that time of year, practically no rain ever falls." He studied her a moment before continuing. "Someone had been helping this along. According to eyewitnesses, rain clouds had formed in the middle of a completely clear blue sky."

"'Helping'? What is that supposed to mean? Did anyone actually see it?"

"There are phone videos. You can find them on news sites or YouTube."

She leaned forward. "I don't quite understand. You can create rain?"

"Oh, sure. It's not such a big deal these days to make clouds release rainfall within a limited area. But this doesn't have to do with that."

"Then what?"

"We're talking about something far bigger here." Daniel studied her again, apparently trying to decide just how much to tell her. He eventually sat up straight and said, "It started in Iraq in 2015, with an unusually rare heat wave . . ."

19

Alderney, off the French Coast

FRED BISHOP SAT NAKED ON A WOODEN COT AND HELD his left leg in his hand.

The flickering glow of torches on the walls and columns made shadows dance on the vaulted ceiling. The starkly furnished cellar room was part of a larger property that, legend had it, had performed an inglorious role during the Second World War. Supposedly the Totenkopf Division of the German Waffen-SS had maintained a secret command center here during the occupation of France. Bishop didn't love the thought of that, but his client's hideout was nothing to scoff at otherwise. He had everything he needed here—a place to sleep, running water, and a roomy cabinet for his equipment.

Bishop dipped the washcloth in the mild soapy water again and rubbed at his prosthesis until the lightweight yet unbreakable matte black carbon fiber gleamed again. He had little time to care for his prosthesis during his side trips to Alaska and Germany over the last two days, so a little extra care couldn't hurt. He focused all his attention on the intricate multiaxial knee unit with hydraulics specially tuned to his body. The interplay between its various components and the computer chip embedded in the joint ensured a harmonious and dynamic gait pattern, even at varying speeds. It also let Bishop move astonishingly quickly when the situation required it. He never came close to anything like stumbling, not even on uneven terrain, and only the most skillful observer would notice that his gait had a slight spring to it. And not being noticed, as it happened, was one of the most important prerequisites for Fred Bishop's work.

He set the washcloth aside, picked up a clean towel, and removed any soap residue. It had taken him years to accept the prosthesis as a part of him. He had railed against his fate for many dark months, just like every one of his buddies who'd ever woken up in a field hospital to discover that they were missing a body part. *Why me, of all people?* The question had dogged him over those months. He'd thought about putting an end to his life more than once—especially after Heather left him for another guy, which only happened because he might have accidentally slapped her around a little while under the influence once or twice.

What a joke. He inspected his clean prosthesis, feeling lucky for the high-tech carbon fiber frames they had these days. It had helped him find a new way to live again.

Bishop gently set the prosthesis down so that it could fully dry. Then he devoted himself to his stump, yet another task now part of his daily routine ever since an anti-personnel blew his leg off just below the hip in that rocky goddamned desert back in Afghanistan. If he didn't regularly care for his scarred stump, it quickly started smelling like rotten eggs.

He first examined the skin for tender spots and red areas, as it was especially sensitive where the stump pressed against the stem of the prosthesis, using a little hand mirror so that he didn't miss a single spot. He took the washcloth, dunked it into a second pail of pH-neutral soap and washed the scarred tissue, pushing his dick to the side with the back of his hand so he could better reach the scars around his crotch. At least he still had his dick. He knew men who weren't so lucky and were now pissing through tubes into plastic bags.

After washing, he rinsed with clear, cold water and thoroughly patted his stump dry. Then, to keep the skin supple, he massaged in his homemade extract of chamomile blossoms and horse chestnut seeds, a tip from a buddy he'd met in injury rehab who in the service of Uncle Sam had lost both of his legs—and his goddamn dick on top of that. *Fuckin' Army*. Bishop spat.

A ringtone sounded from his gym bag, next to the cot. There was no reception down here, so it had to be a VoIP call coming through the secure Wi-Fi. Bishop pulled out one of his three smartphones, looked at the screen. The connection was encrypted, so he took the call.

"Yeah?"

He recognized his client's voice, telling him that yet another problem had cropped up.

He listened carefully. He then said, "I'll take care of it," and ended the call.

He stared straight ahead, feeling surly now. *Goddamn amateurs.*

A little while later, Bishop stood at the cabinet wearing his prosthesis and inconspicuous street clothes. The shelves held various other leg prostheses and all kinds of equipment, from spare joints to tools to diagnostics devices, everything he'd need for maintenance or potential repairs should he need to act independently. The nature of his work meant that he couldn't exactly go strolling into the nearest orthopedic workshop to get his prosthesis fixed. There was, for instance, that bullet hole in the stem thanks to a now former Navy officer—that alone could lead to some uncomfortable questions. That alone was more than enough reason for him to resolve any issues all on his own.

Lost in thought, Bishop ran his fingers over his completely shaved skull and focused on the shelf holding his personal weapons arsenal. His selection met every possible need, from small-caliber pistols to shotguns to the most modern precision rifles and fully automatic weapons and even a grenade launcher. After mulling it over a moment, he decided on a Beretta M9, checked its operation, and stowed it in his gym bag along with ammunition. For his next assignment, which, as he'd just learned by phone, was unexpectedly sending him back to Germany, a simple pistol should suffice. He cursed his client's carelessness. They should have kept that Hardenberg in check from the beginning. Now he was the one who had to fix what others had gone and fucked up yet again. They hadn't foreseen his side trip to Alaska coming either, and he had needed to improvise. He never did like their last-minute timelines, not at all. He'd flown halfway around the world in the last few days and was drained, yet the way things were going his body would need to keep coping with little sleep a while longer. He checked to see if he had any caffeine tablets and nodded thankfully that he did. *What an irony*—for years he hadn't been able to sleep, and whenever he did he suffered from too many nightmares. In injury rehab they had pumped him with tons of meds to get him to calm down even for a few hours, and now here he was throwing back pills just to keep himself awake.

His smartphone beeped, and a woman's face appeared on the screen. She had a nice smile and medium-length brown hair she'd combed to the side and pinned with a barrette. She was too young to die. Yet the decision had already been made.

Below the photo was a name.

Laura Wagner.

20

"IN BAGHDAD, THE SUMMER OF 2015," DANIEL BENDER told Laura, "the temperatures hit over 120 degrees and stayed there for weeks." He propped his elbows on his knees, placed his fingertips together, and gave Laura a grave look. "Then, in mid-November, a hailstorm lasting several days created a miles-long flowing river of ice-cold water right in the middle of the Iraqi desert."

"This is getting more and more bizarre," Laura said.

"You can find articles about it on the Internet. But that was only the beginning." Daniel looked around as if making sure no one was listening. "Something similar occurred in Eastern Australia—a rare cold spell brought heavy snowfall to Queensland and elsewhere.

Streets had to be closed, hurricane winds damaged homes even far into the interior."

"And you see a connection?"

"I do." He stared at her a long time before continuing. "It's likely that all this weather we've been getting for weeks is only just the beginning."

"The beginning of what?"

Daniel was searching for the right words. "I think the coming threat will hit us with far worse than any blizzard."

Laura glanced out the glass walled lobby at the snow-covered company parking lot, then fixed her gaze back on Daniel. "We are still talking about the weather, right?"

He nodded.

Laura's head started throbbing, right behind her forehead. She didn't like where this conversation was heading, not at all. First this man sitting before her was talking about a bizarre increase in weather anomalies, then he was claiming that rain could be created at will, then that something far worse was coming. She would have thought he was off his rocker if it had not been for Hardenberg—and that voice memo of his, his horrible death. She still didn't see any direct connection between Hardenberg and what this Daniel Bender was telling her, yet it couldn't be pure coincidence either.

She started over. "So, you're afraid something worse will happen. You think nature has somehow become unbalanced and now it's paying us humans back for all things we've been doing to it for centuries. That about right?"

"It's an interesting angle. But no." Daniel nervously rubbed at the back of his neck. "If I tell you what I really believe, you'd think I was crazy."

"To be honest, I have reason enough to think that already."

He hesitated.

"Don't worry," she added. "You can trust me."

A little vein pulsed at his temple. "All right, fine. In short, my theory is that someone is trying to actively control the weather."

Laura kept her gaze fixed on him. All she could think of was Hardenberg's voice memo. If this Daniel Bender was some wacko conspiracy theorist, then Roland Hardenberg had obviously been one too.

"I'm not joking," he said, sitting upright on the sofa, apparently taking her expression for skepticism. "Someone is trying to manipulate the weather, and these inexplicable phenomena around the world are the result. The big question is, what exact purpose is manipulating weather supposed to serve? In other words, who might be interested in . . ."

He cut himself off, probably because Laura kept staring with a blank expression.

"You don't believe me. You think I'm some crank."

"No, no—what makes you think that?"

"I can tell by your face. I know that look."

For a moment she entertained the thought of telling him about Hardenberg mentioning a "weather weapon." She decided against it.

She barely knew the man, after all. He did seem nice, but could she really trust him?

"I can't hold it against you for not believing me," Daniel continued. "But I can guarantee you that, on November 22, you will be reminded of what I'm telling you. And you'll realize that I knew what I was talking about."

Laura had winced as if from electric shock. "What did you just say? How did you arrive at that date? What's happening that day?"

He rumpled his brow, eyeing her with interest. "What do you know about the 22nd of November?"

"I'm asking you!" Laura said it louder than she had intended. She glanced around feeling guilty, but there still wasn't anyone around to take notice. Just Leif, and he was hunkered down with his laptop looking as if he'd completely forgotten the world around him.

"What are you and your friend doing here?" she asked Daniel. "What do you want from Andra of all places? Why did you want to talk to Lars Windrup?"

Daniel stood up. He gazed around the deserted lobby and then turned to her. "What do you think about going and sitting somewhere else? Where it's a bit more secluded than this airport terminal you got here? You can call me Daniel, by the way." He smiled.

Laura stared at him, puzzled, but then played along. She stood up. "Laura. Nice to meet you. Just, wait one second."

She went over to the concierge and had him issue two visitor passes. She then led Daniel and Leif up the stairs to the second floor and into the smallest of the four meeting rooms. The room had just enough space for a round conference table and six low-backed black leather chairs. Several glasses stood upside-down on the table next to bottles of mineral water, apple juice, and soda pop. A flip chart was in the corner. It was cold, so Laura turned the heat higher and crossed her arms at her chest.

"Well?" she said, staring at Daniel and Leif, who had sat down and were helping themselves to drinks.

"How much time do you have?" Daniel said.

She glanced out the window. "More than enough, the way it's looking."

"Where should I start?" He thought it over. "Having the ability to control the weather, it's one of the oldest dreams of mankind—"

"If you believe Plato," Leif interrupted, "the people of Atlantis were attempting to influence the weather using crystal energy. Maybe they overdid it and that's why Atlantis sank. Ever think about that?" He poured some Coke, then eagerly gulped it down.

Laura was thinking more about what it must be like inside the head of this pale and disheveled-looking man. And the way he clutched his already empty glass and stared at her with that piercing glare confirmed that he wasn't joking around.

"Let's stick to the facts," Daniel reminded Leif. "The American Indians' rain dance, for instance, wasn't just some superstitious ritual. They were clearly attempting to develop some kind of technique, yet they probably didn't even realize just what they were doing. Doesn't matter. What matters is that they were doing it." He took a sip of his drink.

Laura did him the favor of asking him to go on. "Doing what?"

"It always involved a camp fire, often quite large ones. The resulting smoke particles would rise into the atmosphere. Once up there, the smoke would, under the right conditions, transform into what we call condensation cores, which actually could lead to cloud formation and eventually to rainfall."

Laura pulled up a chair and sat. "Wait, what are condensation cores?"

"That's just what we call those tiny particles in the atmosphere that allow the available moisture in the air to condense. It could be natural particles such as dust, sand, or something similar. Nowadays there are also certain chemicals." Daniel noticed her confused look and added, "Simply put, any available humidity attaches itself to these particles, and from those tiny ultralight droplets you soon get large, heavy drops, which then fall to the ground as rain."

Laura nodded. She had heard something like this before. It just hadn't interested her up until now.

"This is important," Daniel said, "for understanding how we can artificially make clouds create rainfall."

"So, rainmaking really does work?"

"What century are you living in?" Leif asked, shaking his head. He opened his backpack and pulled out his laptop. "A hundred years ago people were already using airplanes to spread sand over clouds, hoping to generate rain. About 1935, the French built massive steam chimneys in an attempt to implement the Indians' technique of using camp fires."

"Neither method ever worked right, though," Daniel added. "The breakthrough only came in 1946. Irving Langmuir, a mere Nobel

Prize–winning chemist by trade, developed what's known as cloud seeding. He had air flow into a freezer and added some silver iodide. Shortly after, little ice crystals were dropping down out of nowhere."

"Okay, but what does any of this have to do with Andra?"

"We're getting to that," said Leif, now clutching the power cable to his laptop and frantically searching for a socket.

Laura rolled her eyes. "Under the table, in the floor."

While Leif crawled under the table, Daniel picked up the thread: "Manipulating the weather has become completely legal these days and is officially carried out all over the world."

Laura narrowed her eyes. "Don't tell me we're talking about chemtrails or any of that nonsense?"

"No, not at all." Daniel shook his head forcefully. "Here we're talking about more or less authorized activities. Weather is regularly being influenced mainly in China, Russia, and the USA. But countries such as Australia or Thailand are very active in this respect too."

"Wait, Thailand?"

"Yeah, not the first place you'd think of, right? But Thai King Bhumibol was one of the early pioneers in artificial rainfall. He was on a trip in the northeast of Thailand in 1956 when he realized that certain kinds of clouds simply didn't want to release rain. From then on, he made it his big goal to create rain."

"Did he ever manage to?"

Daniel shrugged. "Thirteen years later, Thai chemists working under Bhumibol developed a nontoxic chemical that actually did release artificial rain. Today the Thais have an official royal rainmaking project, with a fleet of planes. They do about a thousand air operations per year around the country."

"Sounds like science fiction."

"It's not, though." Leif had crawled back out from under the table, happy to see the LED on his laptop flashing.

Daniel continued: "In southern Germany, in Rosenheim, they were already doing hail suppression back in 1958. They were using rockets to shoot silver iodide into the clouds so that they would start raining before hailstones could form. Today, little prop planes make the trip up there as soon as a hailstorm is imminent. These hail planes, they spray silver iodide right into the clouds, which helps disperse the humidity to more condensation cores. This usually leads to a soft hail coming down before any dangerous hail can be formed."

Laura thought about Robin and about the many injured people, not to mention the massive damage caused by the hailstorm in Bredenstedt, her hand clenching into a fist. "So where were all those hail planes on Sunday?"

Daniel sighed. "They only operate in the big wine-growing areas of Baden-Württemberg, mostly."

"How come?"

"Because of money, as always." Leif looked up from his laptop. "I heard that Daimler is looking at financing several hail planes for the area around their Stuttgart HQ—supposedly to protect all those thousands of new Mercedes sitting out in the open."

Laura sniffed at that. "How nice for them. If we only had a huge automaker in Hanover, my son wouldn't be lying in the hospital with a severe concussion."

Daniel started with surprise. "What happened?"

"He got hit on the head with hail."

Leif shook his head. "Hail suppression wouldn't have helped. Even if they tried it, the storm simply came too fast. We found out that the usual German Weather Service warning only got issued minutes before the storm hit."

"How is that possible, with all our modern computer technology?" Laura asked. "I mean, aren't you meteorologists capable nowadays of predicting something like six days in advance as accurately as you used to predict, say, twenty-four hours?"

"We are." Daniel nodded. "Me, I'd argue that we meteorologists are very seldom to blame for the wrong forecast. No one can predict an unpredictable weather event—as is indicated by the word itself."

"So, you two think that incorrect weather forecasts are the result of the weather being manipulated?"

"Not all, of course, but definitely many of them."

"And it's happening more and more," Leif added. "In the U.S. and Russia alone, there are already dozens of companies fulfilling orders for artificial rain."

Laura pointed to the window. "What about this storm outside?"

Daniel hesitated. "It's our guess that this blizzard is the undesirable side effect of a weather experiment."

"Side effect?" Laura thought that one over. "So, wait. You're describing this blizzard out there as the side effect of someone interfering with a natural weather pattern? But at the same time, you're also claiming that the weather's been messed around with for decades. If that's the case, then why haven't there been phenomena like those in Siberia or Australia a lot earlier? Why just now?"

Daniel gave her a defiant stare. "Who ever said that there haven't been?"

Leif released a loud snort. "Unexplainable weather phenomena have been increasing for years, verifiably so. The real question is: why does the media show such conspicuously little interest in these stories? Why do you get only a handful of reports about it in the media even though it's been discussed for years in Internet forums? What do you yourself know, for instance, about green plasma balls in the sky?"

"Green plasma balls?"

"You see? You have no clue! Because it's all covered up by the centrally controlled, lying press—"

"Leif, cut it out," Daniel barked.

"It's all right," Laura said.

Daniel cleared his throat. "What Leif means is ... there's a general consensus that the increasing appearances of tornadoes in Germany are a direct result of climate change, and that in future we'll have to be increasingly prepared for those kinds of extreme weather events."

"Well, isn't that true?" Laura said.

"Beyond the buzzword 'climate change,' which all agree on, there are plenty of other scenarios playing out."

"Targeted weather manipulation leading to anomalies that can never, ever be explained using the premise of global warming," Leif explained. "It's always the same. Alternative points of view either get ignored or stigmatized as conspiracy theories by the dominant complex of mainstream finance, politics, media!"

"Calm down," Daniel said, giving Leif a harsh glare. "Laura, this stopped being about getting a few clouds to rain over a relatively manageable area a long, long time ago. We are talking about massive interventions in the global circulation of our atmosphere, which in turn can cause devastating effects all around the planet."

"But to what end?" She kept her gaze fixed on Daniel. "What does this have to do with November 22?"

Daniel took a deep breath. "We possess certain information that a devastating natural catastrophe is supposed to be created for November 22nd of this year."

"So, a kind of terror attack?"

"It looks like it, yes. And our earth itself is supposed to be used as the weapon."

21

HUANG ZHEN STOOD ATOP THE IMPOSING 10-FOOT-HIGH observation deck. The soundproof glass from floor to ceiling provided an ideal view of the control room at the Heilongjiang facility, and the gray concrete wall behind Zhen was decorated with large red flags and banners that were supposed to bring good luck. Filling the air was the aroma of incense sticks, burning away on a small side table.

Zhen wore a golden silk hanfu with a black dragon pattern that he'd had made just for this day. In his ancestors' times, only the emperor was allowed to wear a garment with a dragon pattern. By waking the Black Dragon, Zhen would now rise to a rank comparable only to that of emperor, and this garment symbolized the moment in suitable style.

Zhen cradled a cup of green tea and observed the massive control room monitor with growing satisfaction. It was the size of a drive-in movie screen, its various windows displaying relevant information about the mission now underway as blinking numbers, diagrams, and symbols. The current position and flight path of the Chenlong drone was a blinking diamond on an undulating curve moving across a world map. The drone carried the Diamond series prototype, which was controlled and monitored by a three-man team. Zhen sipped his tea with contentment. All was proceeding according to plan so far.

The control room held three semicircular rows of desks with about twenty technicians sitting before monitors, keyboards, control panels. Behind them, Xian Wang-Mei stood on a slightly raised platform barking commands into a headset. As if sensing Zhen's piercing gaze at his back, he turned and looked up. He raised his thumb, nodded. Zhen kept his expression blank and just stroked his thin mustache with his thumb and forefinger. Wang-Mei turned away and focused on his monitor.

Zhen took a moment to close his eyes and inhale the aroma of incense. His moment had finally arrived. He would bring the Black Dragon to life. In a few hours, he would unleash the most devastating acts of nature that man had ever seen.

Charles St. Adams set foot on the observation deck. He wore a brown tweed suit with matching vest as usual, except today he'd selected an orange-and-blue checked cravat.

"Diamond exceeds our wildest dreams," he said.

Zhen gave him a thin smile. "A long road is behind us. All our efforts will finally be crowned with success."

"Indeed. There has been more than one failure."

"Failures were always calculated into it."

"I assume you've learned what's happening in Europe?" St. Adams asked.

"Snow is causing chaos? This does not interest me. A cup of tea?" He signaled for St. Adams to sit in one of the two armchairs by the low table holding the incense.

"The leaves for this tea come from my home province of Anhui," Zhen explained as he poured from a bulbous porcelain teapot. "This variety is distinguished by the fact that only the leaves of the tea plant are used. No buds, no stems."

"First-rate," St. Adams proclaimed after trying it. "I taste no bitterness. That tells me this must be the second infusion?"

"You have learned much of my people's culture and customs in the last few months," Zhen said kindly. "You already were exhibiting a distinct feel for foreign cultures back in Switzerland. A rare trait for a Briton."

St. Adams laughed politely.

"I'm serious," Zhen told him. "It distinguished you from the other snobs. No one else but you would have been considered as a partner for Heilongjiang."

"I am honored."

Zhen leaned back in his chair. "When we met again two years ago, I was, I'll be honest, not quite sure if you still had the same convictions.

The days when we stayed up all night philosophizing about politics are so long ago."

"What convinced you?"

"Convinced me that you had earned my trust?"

"Yes."

"I'm a good judge of people. I can see who's lying and who's trying to fool me."

"I don't doubt it. Sometimes I forget that I'm not only speaking with a good friend but also a high-ranking official of the Chinese Ministry of State Security." St. Adams sipped at his tea. "How's Wang-Mei holding up?"

"He can sense what's awaiting him, should he fail."

"And if we succeed?"

"I gave him my word that I would spare his life."

"You are a most decent man. Together you will accomplish so much for your people."

"Only no one will ever learn of it." Zhen gazed through St. Adams, as if an actual vision of that promising future had revealed itself behind him. "The next generation of my people will cultivate Chinese farmland where today the barren and infertile soil still deteriorates into desert. Our rain will wash away the dust and dirt of centuries. No one will remember how tough it was to farm those barren wastelands once the fertile soil is producing so much food, all reborn with the help of the life-giving rain that Heilongjiang will deliver us."

"A grand goal, without a doubt." St. Adams tugged his cravat into place. "It is clear to you, I assume, that all told, your country's considerable intervention in weather patterns will have substantial repercussions far beyond China. Just take a look at the images coming out of northern Europe."

"What do I care about that? The only matter relevant to me is that my people do not starve." Zhen's expression darkened. "Rejecting the One Child Policy was a grave mistake on the part of the Central Committee. My country is seeing a population explosion. If the birth rate triples as expected, Chinese agriculture will not be able to feed its own people in ten years' time at the latest. Our food imports are steadily increasing already. We need to prepare the groundwork for our future starting now."

"Isn't that a matter for the Central Committee to decide?"

"It's quite obvious that none of them are able to think outside the box. I neither debate nor do deals with party bigwigs who only have their own well-being in mind." Zhen balled a fist. "I act. For the sake of China. Many party comrades stand behind me."

"I understand you loud and clear," St. Adams said. "There does remain the possibility that certain questions might be raised."

"In future, we will only dispatch the Black Dragon when it becomes absolutely necessary. On top of that, I don't foresee that our various measures will prove of much importance globally. We would simply be making it rain a little more than usual."

An almost imperceptible smile curled the corners of St. Adam's mouth. "You are far too intelligent to be drawing such simple conclusions. You will be depriving your neighboring countries of their water this way."

Zhen's jaw muscles twitched. "The fact that we'd be making China's clouds artificially rain does not automatically mean that some of the water will not fall on foreign territory. Everyday clouds in the sky could also release rainfall across our land without any extra help on our part." Zhen smiled coldly. "Who could prove otherwise?"

"Governments don't need proof to start wars."

Zhen sprang up and aimed a finger at the control room below. "This is exactly why I'm dispatching the Black Dragon. You know my reasons. The U.S. continues to mobilize right at our front door. This is an assault on China's ascendancy in the Pacific region. We're only defending ourselves."

"The Central Committee should have prevented that," St. Adams said in agreement. "China is being weakened."

"Which is why we must demonstrate our power. All attempts at a diplomatic solution have been unsuccessful. It's crucial for us to put the USA in its place—of that there is no doubt." Zhen was working himself into a rage. "It's the only language that nation understands. Are we going to keep tolerating more and more warships in our territorial waters? The Black Dragon will remind that self-righteous world police force that there are powers out there stronger than the works of men."

"But will the United States even understand the message?"

Zhen aimed a piercing stare at St. Adams. "They will have to learn how to understand."

"But what if they do not?"

Zhen brought his fist down on his teacup. The precious porcelain shattered; hot tea sprayed. Tiny splinters had cut into Zhen's flesh, but he took no notice. "To scare the snake, you must stomp on the grass. America will learn. The first lesson is about to take place, and if necessary, more will be sure to follow."

22

LAURA JUMPED TO HER FEET, PACED BACK AND FORTH anxiously, and kept glancing out the window. The snowpack was still piling up out on the parking lot, and she was starting to doubt she'd ever get to see Lars Windrup today. She turned to Daniel. "The two of you really believe that someone is capable of using our planet as a weapon?"

"We do, yes." Daniel's expression darkened. "People have been dreaming of this for a long time. Back in 1957, the American President's Advisory Committee strongly warned that weather control could become a more significant weapon than atomic bombs."

"So, has anyone actually tried it?" Laura asked.

"In what way do you mean?" Daniel said.

"Just like you said, using the weather as a weapon . . ."

Daniel nodded. "During the Vietnam War the Americans tried to artificially prolong the monsoon season by cloud-seeding massive amounts of silver iodide. That was in 1967, as part of something called Operation Popeye. The goal was to increase the amount of mud on the Ho Chi Minh Trail, which the enemy was using to link troops and supplies."

"Did it work?"

"The general consensus among scientists is that the amount of rain tripled during that period."

"Military forces usually keep a real tight lid on such operations," Leif added. "But we do know that the German Bundeswehr's own planning office first started looking at geoengineering and weather manipulation in 2012. They concluded that weather modification should be used more frequently and more extensively in the future."

"All right," Laura said, "but do you two have any actual proof?"

Daniel nodded. "You could say that, yes. We know of experiments going on in the desert of the Al-Ain region in the Emirate of Abu Dhabi. They've built vast fields there holding numerous air ionizers that are 35 feet high. These ionizers emit electromagnetic waves from negatively charged particles, which then rise into the lower layers of the atmosphere, where they attract dust particles."

He stood up, went over to the flip chart, and grabbed the red felt marker from the tray. He drew a long vertical line, then he added four shorter lines to its top end pointing downward at acute angles. Then he added a line across to connect them all.

"The antennas, they resemble something like this."

"They look like cocktail umbrellas," Laura said.

Daniel now drew dotted lines leading upward from the top of the antennas, and a cloud above that. "The dots represent dust particles. Moisture condenses in the immediate vicinity of these electrically charged particles. Clouds form. Once a sufficiently high degree of condensation is reached, the clouds start raining." He drew raindrops under the cloud and looked to Laura.

"Here," Leif added, "so you see that we're not just making all this up."

His fingers flew across his laptop keyboard, and a window opened onscreen. Laura stepped behind him to better see the details, but Leif's pronounced body odor caused her to pull back in disgust.

"This is the official website for a Swiss firm called MetoSys," he explained. "They completed that project in the Al-Ain region Daniel mentioned. MetoSys is currently working on five other projects like it." He clicked like wildfire through the website until a collage of photos from various desert regions appeared. Laura could see vast grounds with antennas. On the tops of individual antennas, four bars each branched off slanting downwards in all directions.

"MetoSys has developed a technology they're calling WetTec," Leif continued. "When the geographical conditions are right, WetTec provides a significantly higher probability of rain than conventional cloud seeding. And that's without any chemicals."

"So what's the catch?" Laura asked.

Daniel sat back down at the table. "The catch is that during the summer of 2010, in the exact same time period when the project in Al-Ain was being completed, the strongest monsoon rainfall in more than eighty years started coming down only a couple hundred miles away in Pakistan. The country was faced with flooding on a large scale."

"Officially, more than fourteen million people were affected," Leif added, his expression somber. "More than seventeen hundred people lost their lives. Almost 1.8 million homes were damaged."

"You suspect a direct connection?"

"What have we been talking about this whole time?" Leif thrust his hands up, then let them drop as if powerless. "Those two regions are so close geographically there is no way the weather could not have been affected."

"I'm still not clear about what all this has to do with Andra."

Leif nodded while he pulled up another website. "The Al-Ain project alone has swallowed up over ten million euros so far. Which begs the question of who is financing it." He turned his laptop in her direction. "Take a look."

Laura saw a mass of Chinese characters. "What's that mean?"

"It's the website for a firm from Singapore. It became the majority shareholder of MetoSys in 2009 and eventually took over the whole company after the successful trials in Al-Ain." Leif grinned. "But you won't find that anywhere on the Internet."

"I thought you were on the Internet."

"You've never heard of a little thing called the dark net?" Leif asked in disbelief, shaking his head. "In any case, this firm from Singapore is doing all it can to conceal its connection to MetoSys by way of shell companies in Panama and various trusts and foundations."

"And they're going to all this trouble," Daniel said, "despite the fact that WetTec already works in principle. They could be making billions from completely legitimate deals. Which begs the question: why aren't they?"

Laura glanced back and forth at them for an answer. "Well?"

Daniel let out a sigh. "We still don't know the answer to that. But does a company named Chenlong ring any bells?"

Laura nodded. "Andra did a large deal with them."

Daniel nodded in return. "About the same time that Chenlong acquired MetoSys."

Laura grabbed a chair and sat back down. "How do you two know that? Everything we did with Chenlong here was subject to utmost secrecy."

"Leif is good at those kinds of things," Daniel said, smiling. "How much do you know?"

Laura stared back. "What makes you think I would know anything? My boss, Herr Hardenberg, was dealing with the Chinese on his own."

"So, this Herr Hardenberg . . ." Daniel eyed Laura expectantly. "Do you think we could talk to him?"

Laura stared at the floor. She was trying to maintain composure. She shook her head eventually.

"Herr Hardenberg was murdered," she said, her voice breaking.

"Murdered?" Daniel stared in disbelief. "When?"

She cleared her throat. "His body was found on Monday. Herr Hardenberg was the one who initiated the sale of the prototype to Chenlong and finalized it."

Leif's eyes widened. "What sort of prototype? What does it do? What is it capable of?"

"I'm not sure. Andra develops and manufactures all kinds of equipment and devices—oscillators, high-frequency cathodes, electron accelerators. I'm not sure what particular purpose each piece of equipment serves. They get used in all kinds of fields."

"We tried finding out what this deal was all about," Daniel said, "but we kept running into walls. According to its listing in Chinese company registers, Chenlong was founded in 2009. The sole owner is supposedly a Chinese lawyer."

"Supposedly?"

"The man is ninety-three years old. At least that's what the listing says."

"Can't a person own a company at ninety-three?"

"In principle, sure, but this guy just showed up out of thin air."

"He has no past," Leif added. "Or at least we couldn't find anything on him. An elderly lawyer and entrepreneur must have some kind of past. But there's nothing—zero hits."

"One of the executives is even more interesting," Daniel said. "An Englishman. Stinking rich."

"Speaking of executives . . ." Leif side-eyed Laura. "Who apart from your former boss was involved in managing this particular deal?"

"The board handled it all themselves."

"How well do you know the board members?"

"Hardly at all. How come?"

Leif pondered a second, then waved a hand dismissively. "That part can wait. There's something I need to check out first."

Laura said, "So you two believe that Chenlong is not only wheeling and dealing illegally, they're looking to control the weather for use as a weapon? Why would they do that, exactly?"

Daniel glanced at Leif before answering. "No nation is as obsessed with controlling the weather as China. They're the only country on earth with a weather modification agency run by the state and they've had it quite a few years now. Its mission is to provide rain but also nice weather for holidays and large events such as the 2008 Olympics. But they don't need a special occasion—they're always firing stuff into the air to break up the Beijing smog."

"They haven't been content with the usual methods for some time now," Leif said before gulping down another glass of Coke. "On December 17, 2014, the National Development and Reform Commission teamed up with China's weather service to propose a development plan for national weather modification through 2020. China wants to trigger more than fifteen billion gallons of rainfall artificially, for an area over two hundred thousand square miles." He stretched out his arms. "We're talking about a surface area bigger than Germany, Austria, and Switzerland combined. They even created a special budget equaling about twenty million euros."

Silence fell over the room. Laura wondered if Hardenberg knew about all this when he finalized the deal with Chenlong. She pointed at the picture of the satellite with its antennas. "So the Chinese are working with WetTec?"

Daniel nodded. "Their research is heading the same direction, at least. But the fact is, the Swiss don't yet have a fully developed technology. So WetTec couldn't have been responsible for these weather anomalies happening over the last few months."

"There must be some new factor that we don't know about yet," Leif said. He and Daniel stared at Laura.

"The Andra prototype," she said.

Daniel nodded. "Exactly."

Laura stood, stepped over to the window, and observed the ice patterns forming on the glass, deep in thought. "This all sounds pretty scary."

"You want to know just how scary all this can be?"

She turned around and faced him, her eyes filled with curiosity.

"In 1952, the English village of Lynmouth experienced some of the most disastrous flooding in British history," Daniel said. "Torrential rains hit the area for days on end. Thirty-five people drowned, four hundred and twenty were left homeless. In the days before that, the Royal Air Force had been seeding massive clouds as part of something called Project Cumulus, which was testing military uses for generating rain." He rose and stepped beside her. "In 1972, not far from Rapid City, South Dakota, the clouds over the Black Hills released downpours for days as scientists from the nearby Institute of Atmospheric Sciences tested ways of triggering rain artificially. That episode resulted in flooding, which in turn forced the dam of a mountain lake to break. Two hundred and thirty-eight people died."

"How terrible." Laura's voice was now barely a whisper.

Leif resumed the narrative: "The Chinese, by the way, got what they deserve at least once for manipulating their weather so recklessly. In 2009 the Weather Modification Office sprayed massive chemicals into the air in hopes of ending a drought near Beijing. They didn't get the desired result this time. A fierce snowstorm plunged Beijing into chaos for three days, bringing sixteen million tons of snow. The power grids collapsed, and all flights and train connections were cancelled. Similar to what's going on here."

"There are many other incidents," Daniel said, frowning with concern. "There are simply too many research projects going on these days that might be influencing circulation of the earth's atmosphere." He went back to Leif's laptop, dropped into a chair, downloaded a few photos off the Internet, then turned the display in Laura's direction. "This is the Americans' High Frequency Archive Auroral Research Program—HAARP for short."

Laura scooted over next to him and took in his aftershave as she leaned over, a blend of lemon and fresh grasses. He smelled so much better than Leif.

The photo onscreen showed a rectangular, fenced-off compound in the middle of dense woods. A road ran along the fence with several low, flat-roofed structures next to it and a larger two-story building off on its own. Farther off, in a main compound, stood strange poles lined up all in neat rows.

"Are those crosses?" she asked.

"The resolution is pretty crappy, unfortunately," Daniel said. "Not many actual photos of this facility exist."

"What do you mean by 'actual'?"

"There are several versions of this aerial photo. Most have been altered one way or another. The U.S. government kept this facility a secret for a very long time. These days you can find it on Google Maps, but you used to see only dense forest where this spot is."

Laura moved in closer. "Why put a research facility way out in the middle of nowhere?"

Daniel held up a finger. "Great question, if you ask me."

"I see what you mean," she said. "So what do they do there?"

He pointed at the poles. "Those things you called crosses are actually active phased array antennas, and there are a hundred and eighty of them total." He zoomed in on the photo, but the resolution turned poor so quickly that they couldn't make out any more details. "By positioning and intersecting the individual antennas together, you can increase the radiation that is transmitted in a desired direction."

She leaned back in her chair. "But what's it all for? The purpose, I mean."

"Officially, they're examining the ionosphere by using pulsing radio waves. The ionosphere is one part of our atmosphere, reaching from about forty to six-hundred miles in altitude." He held up hands to demonstrate. "But no one can ever say exactly, since the dimensions of the ionosphere are constantly changing, sometimes by as much as a couple hundred miles. This is the layer that produces the northern lights, by the way."

"What is so important about up there?"

"Well, for one, the ionosphere is where the short waves of our global radio communications get bounced around."

"Which is also one of the reasons why the facility is funded by the U.S. military," Leif added. "Though that's officially disputed, of course."

Laura was getting frustrated. "Okay, but what do radio waves have to do with the weather?" she asked.

Daniel turned around and pointed to his drawing on the flip chart. "According to some theories, it's possible to direct very strong pulses of radiation in a way that has a direct influence on the weather."

"Theories?" Leif stared at Daniel as if he'd just claimed the earth didn't revolve around the sun. "These are facts. There are even patents for it, which you very well know."

"The problem is," Daniel shot back, "there's almost never proof of it actually happening."

Leif shook his head in defiance. "No one disputes that you can use high-frequency pinpoint radiation to create artificial polar lights anymore either, not to mention plasma balls."

"Those are the green lights in the sky you two were talking about?"

Daniel nodded. "What's intriguing is that reports from nearly every unexplained weather phenomenon worldwide over the last few weeks all say the same thing—a green glow appeared in the sky beforehand."

Laura considered that a moment. "The patents Leif mentioned—what are those about?"

"Years ago I used to spend a lot of time and energy on this very topic." Daniel smiled as if recalling the good old days. "I'll give you an example. You could—provided you had the right technology—manipulate the jet stream in targeted ways. Say, strong winds on earth somewhere, at an altitude of thirteen thousand feet. By doing that, you could actively manipulate certain high- and low-pressure systems."

"Wow . . ." Laura automatically looked toward the window. Wind gusts kept pounding at the window, shaking the panes. "You two think that HAARP is responsible for this blizzard?"

"No," Daniel said. "HAARP isn't powerful enough for this. Plus, the facility was officially closed in June of 2014."

Leif laughed. "My ass it was. They haven't taken down a single antenna, even though they originally announced that was exactly the plan."

Daniel shrugged. "If you believe the rumors, the U.S. military research agency DARPA continues to operate the facility."

"Rumors? Hardly," Leif said. "In 1994, a firm named E-Systems bought the patents for the technology that HAARP is based on. E-Systems has been shown to be working closely with the CIA and the military. Altogether, these so-called covert projects add up to more than 800 million dollars of business. Not even the U.S. Congress gets informed about what this money goes toward."

"So, what do intelligence services want with weather experiments?" Laura asked them.

"E-Systems has its fingers in many pots," Leif explained. "The Doomsday Plan is just one project the firm is responsible for."

"What's that?"

"A program that would enable the U.S. president to launch a fully automated nuclear war if America was ever incapacitated by a cyberattack. DARPA played a big part in that, too." Leif scowled at Laura and Daniel. "Just one year after E-Systems took over HAARP? The company was bought by Raytheon, one of the main suppliers to the U.S. Department of Defense."

Daniel scratched at his head, deep in thought. "Which begs the question, what could a maker of weapons and military technology want from such an acquisition?"

"Damn right!" cried Leif. "And it gets even better. Because DARPA then took over control of HAARP. 'Temporarily,' according to statements. Well, 'temporarily' has been going on for some years now. DARPA gets a yearly budget in the double-digit millions for doing what's officially just called 'experiments relating to physics.' Call me crazy."

"Business as usual," Daniel said. "But I'm pretty sure that we'll need to look elsewhere."

"How come?" Laura said.

"Like I said, HAARP wouldn't have nearly enough power to make such an impact."

"If you believe the bullshit from the official press, that is," Leif said, getting worked up now. "There's a well-known physicist, Richard Williams, who's firmly convinced that there's a second top-secret operation inside HAARP that could deliver considerably more energy into the ionosphere. That would lead to substantial disturbances in the earth's atmosphere, ones that could continue distributing their effects for years."

"Even so," Daniel said. "A facility capable of causing this would have to be many times larger and more powerful than HAARP."

"How do you know so much about this topic?" Laura asked him.

He just shook his head. An odd gloss showed in his eyes. "It's a long story."

She decided not to push it. Instead she asked, "So, is there such a facility?"

"There are many. Facilities similar to HAARP have been springing up like mushrooms for years all over the world. Here in Germany too. Though now we're talking about relatively small sites that are intended for research alone."

"Not so in Norway," Leif said. "There will soon be a facility in Tromsø that will put HAARP to shame—EISCAT 3D will have fifty thousand antennas total." He snorted at the thought. "Insane. If you can generate plasma up in the sky using HAARP's hundred and eighty antennas, I hate to even think what a facility with fifty thousand is capable of."

Laura considered that information. "But you're saying that this EISCAT 3D isn't operational yet. That means there must be another facility this big. Right?"

"You got it." Leif nodded. Then he sat upright and recited theatrically, *"For in seven days, I will cause it to rain upon the earth forty days and forty nights, and every living substance that I have made I will destroy from the face of the earth . . ."*

Laura and Daniel stared at him, baffled.

Leif slumped back down in his chair, grinning. "First book of Moses, chapter 7, verse 4."

Daniel sighed. "Laura, listen to me. Someone at Andra has a hand in this. We have it from a reliable source that—"

Right then the door flew open.

A tanned, white-haired man in a tailored suit and angular, equally expensive glasses appeared in the doorway. He eyed them all with a surly expression.

"In my office, Frau Wagner," he snarled.

Laura swallowed hard. This didn't bode well. She rarely had to deal with Herr Johann Leinemann, PhD and Chairman of the Board, but those few times had been enough for her.

"We'll be finished in one minute," she told him.

Herr Leinemann removed his glasses and gave her a stern look. "Not 'in one minute'—right now."

"Of course."

Laura stood as confidently as she could, and Daniel and Leif rose as well. She moved to leave, but Leif stepped in her way. He looked like he was going to hug her, as if to say goodbye. He whispered something in her ear. His stench still disgusted her, but that was not why the hairs on her neck stood up on end. It was his words. They struck her like the lash of a whip.

Leif let go and got out of her way.

Laura stepped past Herr Leinemann out into the hallway. He closed the meeting room door after her. As they walked down the hallway in silence, Leif's words echoed in her ears like a constant mantra:

He's in on it.

23

HERR JOHANN LEINEMANN'S OFFICE WAS ON THE TOP
floor of the Andra building. On nice days it offered a lovely view of
the nearby woods, but the snowstorm had swallowed up the scenery
beyond a couple dozen feet. His furnishings were upscale but plain
and dominated by a large glass desk holding a silver MacBook and a
company telephone.

Leinemann sat in his dark-brown leather office chair and gestured
brusquely at the cantilever visitor's chair. "Terrible, this Hardenberg
business."

Laura sat down. "Yes."

"Must have been a nasty sight. How are you doing?"

"Well, I have to say, it's been—"

"I always had a funny feeling about Hardenberg," Leinemann said,
folding his hands over his chest. "I could sense that something just
wasn't right with him. We never cared for each other much. The two of
you, however, always had a tight bond. Is that the right way to put it?"

"I'm not sure what you mean by that," Laura replied carefully.

"Yes, you do. Everyone knows you were one of the few female
colleagues who socialized with him outside of the office."

Laura could see where this was going. "Any bond we may have had
was of a purely professional nature."

"That so?"

"He invited me to his home one time, and that was years ago. He
was also still married then."

Leinemann removed his glasses, pulled a cloth from his jacket, and started wiping the lenses. "In principle, I don't care what my staff does in their free time. Although I can't say that I'd approve of my executives having affairs with secretaries."

"Herr Hardenberg and I have never had an affair."

"Whatever you say." Leinemann's tone made clear he didn't believe her. "What do you know about any connections Hardenberg had to a company named Chenlong?"

The sudden change of subject caught Laura off guard. Her first thought was to tell Leinemann about the USB stick. But she remembered Leif's words and hesitated. Her heart beat faster.

"I don't know very much about that," she said. "Only what everyone else knows. Chenlong bought the Diamond series prototype."

"Did Hardenberg ever talk to you about this subject—in private, shall we say?"

"No. Why should he? That client was subject to a special nondisclosure policy."

Leinemann pursed his lips, held his lenses up to the light, then put his glasses back on. "What kind of meeting was that?"

"What meeting?"

"Those two men in the meeting room."

"Oh, that . . ." Laura made herself smile. "Those are just two guys who helped get me out of a jam this morning. I'd gotten my car stuck in the snowstorm. Now they're stuck here."

"So those two aren't staff?"

"No."

Leinemann leaned forward and reached for the phone. "Send someone from security to the meeting room," he barked into the receiver. "The two men in there are not to leave the room without my authorization."

As Leinemann listened to the reply, he looked Laura in the eye. "I don't care that only two security staff made it to work," he continued. "Someone needs to get over there right away. Why have security watch over production in weather like this anyway? The damned machines aren't even running." He hung up.

"That's not necessary," Laura said and stood. "I'll escort them down to the lobby if you'd like."

"We're not done here!"

Laura slowly sank back down into her chair.

"Who are these men? What do they want here?" Leinemann's glare cut right through her.

"They helped me. I nearly froze to death, and—"

"Do not take me for a fool, Frau Wagner." Leinemann slapped at the surface of his desk. "I saw you looking at a laptop with them. I also happened to notice that drawing on the flipchart." He glared again. "What's going on down there? The truth, this time."

"I wanted to thank them somehow for their help, so I offered them something to drink and a warm room to wait in," she explained, hoping her voice wasn't shaking too much. "I thought it was the least I could do."

"What about the laptop?"

"We were looking at the weather. Those two have been trapped here for hours."

"And the drawing?"

"That was already there—from the previous meeting, I'm guessing."

Leinemann set a finger to his lips and thought a moment. The next few seconds took an agonizingly long time. Eventually, he nodded. "I'm going to be frank, Frau Wagner. I lost a lot of trust in Hardenberg over the last few months."

"Can I ask why?"

Leinemann hesitated. His stern expression relaxed a little, and he looked almost kind for the first time. "What I'm about to tell you remains between us. Do you understand? Not a word to anyone, or you can start looking for a new job."

"Of course." Laura's fingertips felt prickly. She wondered where Leinemann was going with this.

"I'm convinced that Hardenberg was involved in shady business dealings. It would not surprise me if his death, as tragic as it may be, was a direct result of these dealings."

Laura stared, stone-faced. Her heart was thumping.

"We on the company board have suspected, for some time now, that Hardenberg was abusing his position for his own benefit," Leinemann continued. "We've never really known what he was doing on his business trips these last few months. The only thing consistent was his horrendously high expenses. His expense reports have become increasingly incoherent and, apart from the Chenlong deal, he hasn't been pursuing any new business in Asia."

"I'm afraid I'm not following you," Laura replied warily.

"I'm talking about giving away company secrets for money, Frau Wagner," Leinemann said, pointing gruffly at her to erase any ambiguity.

"You're accusing Herr Hardenberg of industrial espionage?"

"I am, and I'd like you to find proof of it."

Laura stared at the board chairman. Her thoughts collided. She could feel Hardenberg's USB stick in her pocket. If she handed Leinemann the flash drive now and reported the truth to him about all that she'd learned in the last few hours, there was a good chance she could keep her job. She needed to think about herself as well. She was relying on this job. "What do you want me to do?"

"You have access to Hardenberg's personal files. First, check his expenses for any irregularities. You'll receive further instructions after that."

She stared, helpless. "How would I know if—"

"You'll be able to tell if there are irregularities."

Laura mustered her courage and said, "I'm not sure that I'm capable."

Leinemann cocked an eyebrow. "I, on the other hand, am certain that you are."

Laura's thoughts were racing now. If Leinemann actually were conspiring with the Chinese, why would he ask a lowly secretary to find proof of Hardenberg's secret dealings? Didn't that instead point to Leinemann not knowing? Either that or the two of them had teamed up, and Leinemann was now cleverly exploiting Hardenberg's death to pin all the blame on Hardenberg. Laura bit at her lower lip, not sure whom to trust. Daniel and Leif, whom she'd only just met a few hours ago? Or Herr Leinemann, a worthy member of the Andra board who had committed himself to transforming the company into an international market leader over the last few years? She then thought about Robin. The idea of having to explain to her boy that his mom was out of a job was simply unbearable.

Laura looked up and nodded. "Very well," she said.

24

National Hurricane Center (NHC), Miami

"SO WHAT'S THE CRAZY EX DO THEN?" EMILIO SANCHEZ said and gazed around the room before supplying the answer. "She grins at me with those fake teeth of hers, that I myself paid for, and she gives me the middle finger."

Sanchez's pulse had risen to dizzying heights, as it always did when he trashed his former wife. He flailed his arms around, forgetting the paper cup in his hand—lukewarm coffee splashed onto the linoleum floor of the NHC break room, just inches from the feet of Selma Cooper.

"Shit, shit," Sanchez muttered.

"Didn't get me," Selma Cooper said after a quick check of her loafers and dark-blue pantsuit.

Brandon LaHaye grinned. "Mellow out, Emilio. You get a heart attack, that ex of yours will take the whole pot."

"I'd never do her the favor. My ticker's working flawlessly." Sanchez patted at his chest.

Selma set her coffee cup on the counter. "I need to get back to my desk. That low-pressure system in the South Pacific could continue moving toward Baja California, and I want to stay on top of it."

"Go for it," Sanchez said.

"Brandon's right," Selma told him. "You need to take it easy." She added a wink. "See you around, boys."

The two men watched her go, and Sanchez's lips curled into a smile. "You think I should ask her for a date?"

"Keep dreaming." LaHaye took a gulp from a plastic water bottle.

"What? I'm not even forty yet and totally still fit."

LaHaye eyed him up and down. "You could be her father. Plus, you've been in better shape." He smiled and patted Sanchez's slight paunch.

Sanchez's smartphone rang. He took the call and listened intently. "I'm on my way."

"What's wrong?" LaHaye said.

"That was the new guy, can't remember his name. Something's gone wrong with a data buoy, south of Bermuda."

LaHaye nodded. "Right, break over."

Sanchez emptied his coffee in one gulp, threw the paper cup into the trash can. They exited the break room and headed into the HSU Center—the Hurricane Specialist Unit of the NHC, which in turn is subordinate to NOAA, the National Ocean and Atmosphere Administration of the United States. The goal of the NHC was to predict and monitor tropical hurricanes in the Atlantic and Pacific Oceans. Despite being a U.S. government agency, the NHC was officially recognized by the independent World Meteorological Organization as the main information center for this region. To carry out its diverse missions, the NHC was divided into several independent units that all worked closely together. Sanchez and his staff carried great responsibility. Their work was so important, it literally meant life or death to millions of Americans living along the coastline.

Sanchez and LaHaye parted ways where the hallway branched off. Brandon LaHaye turned left for the Storm Surge Unit, which determined emergency evacuation procedures, while Sanchez went right and then entered the main HSU office.

Selma Cooper and the new guy were staring at the largest of the seven monitors. They looked baffled. Sanchez snatched a clipboard with the latest weather data and approached them.

Sanchez had been running the Hurricane Specialist Unit for about a year. The HSU observed weather conditions in the hurricane-endangered regions of the eastern North Atlantic and North Pacific basin round the clock. Every few hours, they created detailed forecasts of the weather developing over the coming five days. They started sending their forecasts to more possible outlets once the Internet took hold—almost anyone anywhere could now receive expert weather info that was updated every few minutes. The NHC also uploaded satellite photos, forecasts, and warnings to Facebook several times a day. There was one thing people could always rely on: as soon as a tropical low developed into a hurricane, Sanchez and his team kept their eyes glued on the storm system until it dispersed again. Normally, this was only a few hours, but sometimes it took days.

"NDBC Buoy 41049 South Bermuda reporting extreme increases in air and water temperature," Selma said as Sanchez stepped up between her and the new guy. She pointed to one of the monitors. Dozens of yellow arrows blinked in the center of a satellite image for the North American basin. But one arrow was blinking red.

"What was the exact message?" Sanchez said.

Selma shrugged. "It must be some kind of malfunction. Sea surface temperature 79.88 Fahrenheit—and rising. ... Now it's 80.6. Much too warm, plus—"

"What?"

"Surrounding air temperature is also too high." She looked at him. "It can't be right."

"What's it transmitting?"

Selma stepped closer to the monitor. "112.46 Fahrenheit."

"Bullshit." Sanchez frowned and squinted to better make out the tiny symbols on the monitor. The NDBC data buoy belonged to an early warning system made up of several dozen such buoys in the Atlantic and Gulf of Mexico. Anchored firmly to the ocean floor at fixed coordinates, they delivered data such as air and water temps, wind speeds, ocean currents, wave heights, and much more. The buoys were serviced every two years. Yet the financial situation at NOAA had been tight for some time, which particularly affected the buoys' extremely costly maintenance and repair. More than half of the fifty-five buoys had malfunctioned since 2012. The situation off the East Coast had been better in this regard, but it now looked like they were facing another breakdown.

"There's something else," Selma said. "You're not gonna like it."

"Spit it out."

"41049 South Bermuda is also reporting an extreme drop in atmospheric pressure. Last reported at 976 millibars, 1012 prior to that. Plus wind speeds of 85 miles per hour." Selma held a computer printout to this face. "Wave heights are increasing as well."

"This supposed to be some kind of joke?" Sanchez scanned the columns of figures. "41049 South Bermuda is 295 nautical miles southeast of Bermuda. What's the latest GOES sat image of that area?"

"Don't detect anything unusual," replied the new guy. Sanchez suddenly remembered his name: Zachary Haffernan. "Light clouds with density increasing in the last few hours, otherwise nothing conspicuous."

"Last update?"

"Twelve minutes ago."

"Okay, then we'll know a whole lot more once the latest images come in." Sanchez tossed the printouts onto the desk.

A shrill siren startled everyone in the room.

"What's that?" shouted Sanchez.

"It's not good." Haffernan sat at his desk and tapped frantically at his keyboard until the siren ceased. "I'll put it on the main screen."

Sanchez whirled around. Another red arrow was blinking on the NBDC monitor.

"41421 North St. Thomas also reporting extreme rise in air and water temps." Haffernan called out the buoy's latest data. "Atmospheric pressure 974 millibars, dropping rapidly. Wind speed 88 miles per hour. Ocean 80.24 degrees and rising, air temp . . ." He stared at Sanchez. "115.34 and rising."

"What the hell?" Sanchez rubbed his neck.

"Two malfunctions in such a short time?" Selma said. "Not very likely, is it?"

Sanchez shook his head. He scanned the computer printouts again yet the data still made no sense. He knew of no circumstances where the sea's surface temperature could heat up so rapidly in just a few hours. Then there was the rapidly dropping air pressure, which could prove realistic enough under certain circumstances. Yet the prerequisite for that would be a strong tropical low—a situation they saw no sign of anywhere. He glanced at the latest infrared GOES satellite images as well as the current isobar diagram but saw no indications of any tropical depression or any storm.

A strange sense of unease took hold of Sanchez. He couldn't trust his own data.

"What do you think?" Selma asked.

"I'm thinking of Wilma. October 2005. Wilma formed within just a few hours and did it faster than any hurricane ever observed in the North Atlantic."

"What are you saying?"

"Maybe we're dealing with a similar phenomenon here."

"But the region would first need a tropical low." Selma pointed at the satellite images. "You see any sign anywhere here of—"

The shrill alarm sounded again. Sanchez's heart skipped a beat. He stared at the main monitor.

"Now it's 41420 North Santo Domingo too," Haffernan said. "Surrounding temp 120.38 Fahrenheit—and rising!"

"Someone trying to fuck with us?" Sanchez growled. "Tell me there's a hidden camera."

Haffernan stared back, dumbfounded. "Atmospheric pressure 965 millibars, dropping rapidly. Windspeed 115 miles per hour."

Sanchez cursed under his breath.

Another alarm sounded despite Haffernan having just turned off the previous one.

"41046 East Bahamas!" Selma pointed at the screen. "What is going on?"

"I really wish I knew," Sanchez growled. "But whatever it is, it's getting closer."

Right then, the 15-minute update for the GOES satellite came on screen. Sanchez's eyebrows pressed together. "What the hell is that?"

Up until a few minutes ago, Emilio Sanchez thought his divorce was his biggest problem. He was clearly wrong by a mile.

25

LAURA STOOD AT HER OFFICE WINDOW AND WATCHED the custodian. He'd reappeared outside to continue his hopeless battle against nature, all bundled up and armed with his snow blower. The snow had long ago completely covered the few cars in the parking lot. She thought about Robin, who had sounded sad on the telephone because she couldn't come pick up him today as promised. She missed him terribly. She rotated her head, rubbed at her neck.

Someone knocked on the door. Marc Bauer from the IT department stuck his head in, panting like he'd just been mountain hiking. "The authorities have extended the driving ban. It's going to continue overnight, supposedly. We're setting up temporary beds in the large conference room."

Laura let out a low sigh. "Thanks for letting me know."

Bauer glanced at the door connecting to Hardenberg's office, still left open. "Did you ever get approval for your data upload?"

Laura shook her head. "I haven't been able to get to it."

Bauer gave her his suspicious look again.

"I'll be in touch about it," she added, keeping it casual, still hoping to resolve the awkward situation as gracefully as possible.

"All right." Bauer started pulling the door shut.

"Did Lars Windrup ever show up?" blurted Laura.

"Didn't you hear me? No one's going anywhere out there." Bauer rolled his eyes, then moved on.

Laura returned to her desk, where mountains of expense accounts and various other documents from Hardenberg's business trips were piled up—his personal files had ended up on her desk barely ten minutes after she left Leinemann's office. Searching for abnormalities in his statements was not only idiotic but boring, especially since she had no idea what she was supposed to be looking for. She picked up a receipt. It was from one of his countless restaurant visits, this time at some fashionable yacht club in Hamburg, part of yet another dull expense report for a meeting with someone named Maria von der See, one of so many names that told Laura nothing. 687 euros, for a business meal for two—the red wine alone had cost 190 euros per bottle, and two were billed. Hardenberg obviously thought little of frugality. Or maybe such sums were normal for dinner in his circles? Laura had no idea. Tired now, she massaged the bridge of her nose. She had not been able to spot one single conspicuous shred of paper so far. On top of that, all his expenses had been signed off by management. She just didn't see what Leinemann was hoping to gain from this.

687 euros for dinner. She couldn't get the total out of her head. She and Robin could buy food for a whole month with that, and it made her realize just how different her and Hardenberg's worlds were. Lobster in Shanghai, oysters in Beijing, champagne in Seoul, sinfully expensive whiskies in hotel bars throughout all of Asia. Hardenberg hadn't ever once skimped on his expenses.

The letters and numbers eventually blurred before her overtired eyes. She needed a break, so she stood up, stretched, and imagined what it would be like to hold Robin in her arms soon. Hopefully the authorities will have lifted the driving ban by tomorrow. She checked the Internet, but opinions differed. She wondered what Daniel Bender would say.

She decided to pay him a visit, since he was still holed up in the meeting room with Leif. She hadn't seen either of them since she'd left Leinemann's office.

A security guard was hunkered down on a chair outside the door to the meeting room. He had his legs stretched out, his hands folded over his beer belly and his chin resting on his chest, and he appeared to be sleeping. Yet his eyes popped open when Laura stood before him.

"Those two still in there?" she asked him.

"Uh, yep." The security guard stuck a finger in his ear and scratched.

Laura gave him a friendly smile. "I'll just pop in and ask if there's anything they need." She added a wink and stepped inside.

Daniel had pulled off his shoes and propped his feet on the table and was looking at his phone. Across from him was Leif, huddled with his laptop.

Daniel's face lit up. "I thought maybe all our boring stories had put you off."

"Herr Leinemann dumped a bunch of work on me. You two need anything? Something to drink, eat?"

"We're okay."

"That goon still out there?" Leif said, bitter as ever.

"He is. I'm sorry. But it's better than getting tossed out, right?" She was trying to sound optimistic.

Daniel brushed it off. "It's fine. If we weren't stuck here, it would just be somewhere else."

"So, did you guys find anything out?"

Daniel removed his feet from the table, sat upright, and gave her a cautious stare.

"What, what do you have?" Laura glanced back and forth between them.

"Can we trust you?" Daniel said.

"Why would you ask such a thing?" She sat down next to him.

"I need to know if I can count on your silence."

Laura held up a hand. "I'm not sure what you're thinking, but I promise not to pass on anything you tell me."

Daniel nodded. "We think that Hardenberg might have had backing from the very top when he was doing that deal with Chenlong."

"Herr Leinemann?"

He nodded. "Leinemann has skeletons in his closet. That's why he's always so suspicious." He looked to Leif. "Show her the contract."

"Still waiting for Rousseau," Leif grunted. He was pale and grumpy. "We were supposed to meet in a chat an hour ago already. Shit. The guy's fallen off the face of the earth as of yesterday."

"He'll turn up at some point," Daniel said. "Show her the contract."

Leif moved the cursor, clicked around noisily, and turned the screen to her. A copy of a written document appeared. Leif scrolled down to the last page. "This is Leinemann's signature for the contract with Chenlong. Now for the countersign . . ." He pointed at an ornate signature. "There's a certain Hao Chang. At least that's his name underneath."

The name Hao Chang made Laura sit up. Hardenberg, as she'd just learned, had a contact person named Xian Wang-Mei. They had to be the same person.

"Leinemann knew all along," Daniel told her.

"This doesn't prove anything," she said. "A deal this big is always done with the board's general knowledge." She took another look at the flipchart, at Daniel's drawing of WetTec antennas and raining clouds.

"What are you thinking?" he asked her.

"Why would Leinemann make me sift through meaningless receipts and reports if he was already in the loop? It doesn't make sense."

"Two possibilities. One, he's scared that Hardenberg could have been a whistleblower and left behind some kind of clue, so he's using you to find that out. Two, he wants to keep you clear of us in order to divert you."

She thought a moment. "Or maybe you're just seeing ghosts."

The security guard's head appeared in the doorway. "Herr Leinemann wants to talk to you."

"I'm coming," Laura said.

The security guard nodded and closed the door again.

Daniel's expression had darkened. "You're only here a couple minutes before he sends in that goon. You really think any of this is coincidence?"

Laura felt the pressure of a headache coming on. She rubbed at her temples. "I'll be back."

She stood and went toward the door but then hesitated, turned, and asked them, "Could you two get me something on a person named Xian Wang-Mei?"

26

EMILIO SANCHEZ STARED AT THE SATELLITE IMAGE OF the northern Caribbean Sea, now showing five arrows blinking red. A few minutes before, another NDBC buoy, this one 41047 Northeast Bahamas, had reported yet another extreme rise in temperature. The sweat gathered on Sanchez's forehead despite the air conditioning running full blast. 41047 Northeast Bahamas was situated much closer to the east coast of Florida than the other buoys.

Sanchez went through the data once more, studying the satellite images and checking and comparing columns and columns of figures, yet nothing was helping. Trying to come up with a plausible explanation for this absurd weather only led to dead ends. The NHC systems couldn't make heads or tails of such unconventional data as it didn't follow any set pattern.

Selma Cooper stepped next to him and pointed at a satellite image showing an unusually rapid increase in cloud accumulation over the previous few hours. "What's going on there?"

Instead of answering, Sanchez turned around and shouted to the room, "When are we getting updated sat images?"

"NOAA 19's transmitting right now," Zachary Haffernan reported from his desk. "Putting it on the main monitor."

Sanchez nodded. Their antiquated NOAA weather satellites simply weren't on a par with the GOES sat images; their only advantage was better resolution. Sanchez watched the main monitor up on the concrete wall. An infrared image of the North American basin faded to a high-resolution image of the region around Florida. Four images in a row appeared, each taken over a period of a few minutes. He let out a low whistle.

He stepped closer to the monitor, planted his hands on his hips, and eyed the first signs of a spiral-shaped cloud formation. Nothing a few hours earlier remotely pointed to anything like this developing. "I've never seen such a thing in my whole life. Whatever's going on out there—it's happening really fast."

Sanchez turned to Haffernan. "Send out the Hurricane Hunters. I need reliable data, images."

"On it." Haffernan reached for the phone.

Sanchez allowed himself a gulp of water and closed his eyes. He only wished that their new Global Hawk, which had been specially built for NOAA, was finally ready for action. The 46-foot-long, auto-flying drone could have gotten them real-time images of the scene faster than their Hurricane Hunters squadron and in better resolution, too, but the Hawk was still in its test phase, so it unfortunately could not yet replace manned flights into hurricanes. They would have to wait for that.

While Haffernan got the Hunters operation going, Sanchez recalled a special directive he had once received but that had never applied to him, not in all his years with NHC. He sighed at the thought. The way things were looking, he would probably need to consider the directive at some point today, whether he wanted to or not.

Haffernan gave a thumbs-up. "Clearance granted for the Hunters. Estimating four hours for the P-3s to take off and reach the target area."

"Look." Selma showed Sanchez a printout. "The latest GOES images corroborate the NOAA 19 data. Emilio, I don't think those buoys are malfunctioning."

Sanchez lowered himself into his desk chair, giving in to reality. "I still don't quite understand. There's this monstrosity brewing out there and yet it came out of the clear blue sky, literally."

Selma nodded. She pulled up a series of GOES images from the previous few hours and played them chronologically in a loop. The images were from outer space and time-lapsed. They showed a mass of weak and diffuse clouds gathering into a dense white knot and then forming, unusually quickly, into the rounded shape of a hurricane, complete with the eye in the center. She placed a finger to her lips as she considered it. "The first images in this sequence are already a few hours old now. Our data shows no anomalies for this period in time, no indications of a clear low forming or even an initial tropical depression. Nothing."

"Like I said—out of the blue," Sanchez grumbled.

"But that quickly?" Selma shot back, almost defiant.

"I can't explain it either!" he snapped. He took a deep breath. He needed to calm down and keep a clear head. "Let's try comparing this to Wilma. At the center of Wilma was the lowest atmospheric pressure ever measured in the Atlantic: 882 millibars. On top of that, Wilma intensified within only a few hours, from a tropical storm to a Category Five hurricane."

"The only thing missing here is that tropical low," Selma told him. "Like I said."

"I know, I know!" Sanchez glared at her.

He stared for a full minute at the monitor before pointing at the spiral-shaped cloud formation that kept growing as it headed toward the eastern coast of the United States. "I have no clue what's going on, but what I'm seeing says it all. I don't need more data for that. We're putting out a hurricane warning."

"Your decision."

"You're damn right it is." Sanchez went over to a table holding three old-fashioned push-button telephones from the 1970s. Each phone had a different color, and above the buttons of each someone had attached stickers with phone numbers and codes that were to be used for just such a situation. Sanchez picked up the receiver of the pink telephone. "I'm informing FEMA first this time."

"But protocol calls for—"

"I don't care. It's my responsibility to make sure that emergency procedures are in place for evacuating affected coastal areas at least thirty-six hours before possible landfall." He pointed at the blinking arrows on the NDBC monitor. "We still don't know the wind speed this hurricane coming at us has, but I do know that 41047 Northeast Bahamas is just five hundred nautical miles from Miami. That's too goddamn close. This hurricane is going to reach us much sooner than we'd like."

"Emily," Hafferman said.

"What's that?"

"The name for the fifth hurricane this year is Emily."

"Fine, whatever."

Selma looked at Sanchez inquiringly. "What category are we calling Emily?"

He scratched at the back of his head. It was a good question. The Saffir-Simpson scale used wind speeds for classification. The first category started at wind speeds of 74 miles per hour and the final one, Category Five, at 157 miles per hour and up. For most tropical cyclones, the higher wind speeds occurred in lower-lying areas, relatively close to the ocean surface. So the data buoys had proved highly valuable as an initial assessment. And yet, Sanchez just did not trust the buoys today. His only problem was that other, more reliable data wasn't available to him.

"I need a few minutes," he announced, then sat at his desk and did something he hadn't done for a very long time: he applied the Dvorak Technique to assess Emily's potential strength. He compared available satellite images of the cloud vortex and examined them for possible patterns—spiral bands, sheer patterns, and various cloud densities. He then compared infrared images and estimated the temperature difference between the storm's warm eye and the lower temperatures of the cloud tops. The greater this difference, the stronger the winds. Finally, he organized all of the patterns in relation to one another, which resulted in two key indicators—the T-number and the CI-number. He dropped these into a table and suddenly had an answer to Selma Cooper's question, or at least a rough guideline. He sighed, though. Categorizing this hurricane at all was playing a dangerous game, but he needed to come to a decision. He went back over to Selma Cooper and Zachary Haffernan. "Category Three."

She raised an eyebrow. "Are you sure?"

"According to Dvorak, anyway."

"Just Dvorak? Nothing else? What about the buoys?"

"I don't trust them."

"Fair enough, but—"

"Category Three!" He waved his calculations in the air for Selma to grab, then he made the long-overdue call to Amy Winter at FEMA, the U.S. Federal Emergency Management Agency.

Five minutes later, he slammed the receiver down and took a deep breath. Amy Winter was going to make big trouble for him, he could smell it already. But he'd just have to live with it.

"Selma, write up the hurricane report for me to sign when I get back," Sanchez ordered. "Haffernan, keep your eyes on those monitors every second. I want to be informed of any new development right away."

"Where are you heading?" Selma asked.

"Storm Surge Unit. I need to speak to Brandon LaHaye."

"Why not just call him? You think you should leave us here all alone right now? Amy Winter will want to know why we didn't see this hurricane coming earlier. Officials are going to bombard us with tons of questions I can't answer."

"I can't answer those questions any better than you," Sanchez told her. "Which is also why I'm unable to explain over the phone to Brandon that he needs to start mobilizing his whole unit as soon as possible."

He exited the HSU before Selma could test his nerves even more. Goddamn, this hurricane already getting him square in the gut. Emily, he recalled—so that was what they were calling the bitch, a name that would soon make headlines. As he rushed down the hallway passing photos of the last few decades' biggest and most powerful hurricanes on the bare concrete walls, he could already tell that a photo of Emily would soon be joining them. He wiped sweat from his brow. He suddenly felt an urgent need to grab a little fresh air.

He passed the Storm Surge Unit, reached the end of the hallway, pushed the door open, and stepped out. The parking lot stretched out before him, the asphalt shimmering in the midday sun. He shielded his eyes with a hand and looked up into the sky but still didn't see a single trace of that monstrosity closing in. And without knowing the exact speed of the storm system, it was impossible to determine how much time they had for evacuations. The Hurricane Hunters would get him the data. That would still take several hours. He thought of the millions of Americans living along the East Coast. Any hurricane, no matter the strength, always posed a serious threat to those people. Many lived in wood houses without foundations or even mobile homes made of aluminum. *Goddamn, it's hot out*, he thought before stepping back under the covered area near the door.

He suddenly remembered the special directive again. It had been issued from the highest levels and had taken them by surprise, but he'd nearly forgotten about it over time. Better to get it over with now, he realized, than confront someone blaming him later for hesitating.

He yanked out his smartphone, typed a short message. He then sent it to the specified email address, one that he never thought he would ever have to use.

27

WHEN LAURA RETURNED TO THE MEETING ROOM FROM Leinemann's office, she could tell just by looking at Daniel that he had discovered something. He bounded over to her before she even got the door shut.

"What did Leinemann want?" he asked.

"To know how I was coming along with Hardenberg's expenses."

"What did you tell him?"

"The truth—that I haven't found anything suspicious so far. And I'm guessing I won't find anything, either." She glanced at Leif. "How about you guys?"

"Direct hit," Leif told her.

"Xian Wang-Mei?"

He nodded and asked, "Where did you get that name, anyway?"

"From Hardenberg."

"Ah. Look here." He turned the laptop her way.

The portrait of a chubby-cheeked Chinese man filled the screen. His black hair was cut short, and he wore glasses with metal filigreed frames, his narrow eyes hidden behind them. He was gazing intently into the camera. His thick lips reminded Laura of a carp, and his thick neck barely fit inside his shirt collar.

"That's him?" she asked.

Daniel stepped next to her. "It is. Wang-Mei is an influential functionary in the Communist Party. He's not one of the big guns, but his name keeps popping up in various party resolutions. Not much about him on the Internet, but . . ." He patted Leif on the shoulder. "That's why we have the expert here."

Leif released a grunt, poured himself more Coke.

"It gets better," Daniel told her. "Wang-Mei has a pretty interesting position; the party assigned it to him for a period of three years." He gave Laura a triumphant look. "He is the Executive Director of the Chinese State Weather Modification Office."

Laura stared at the image of the fat man. He looked more like some peasant they'd plucked from the rice fields and stuffed into a suit than any politician. On the other hand, Hardenberg had always told her that you could never judge prominent Asians by their appearance—apart from the fact that Wang-Mei was much too fat to be a rice farmer.

She looked at Daniel. "I wonder if there's a connection between Wang-Mei's function as director of this agency and the Chenlong deal."

"You're kidding, right?" Leif stared at her as if she was from another planet. "Extreme weather events have been increasing for months, and now, thanks to your former boss, we have direct and traceable evidence of a Chinese agency conducting more weather modifications worldwide than all of the other nations put together. What more proof do you need?"

"Actually, Hardenberg only mentioned Wang-Mei in connection with Chenlong. Hardenberg never mentioned that he's director of their weather modification office. So maybe it doesn't play a role."

"Maybe because Hardenberg had no clue."

"It's not uncommon for a politician to be connected to a certain company and not talk about it publicly," Laura said. "Wang-Mei could be acting in a private capacity."

"Don't make me laugh," Leif said. "No one in his position operates in a private capacity, especially not in China. I'm telling you, Chenlong is somehow behind this—a planned terror attack. Possibly even with high-level political support."

"Don't be so sure," Laura said, crossing her arms over her chest. "Do you understand what that would mean?"

"The Americans would not be very happy about it," Daniel ventured.

Laura let out a bitter laugh. "If Chinese politicians were shown to be involved in an attack on the U.S.? It could lead to war."

"Presumably, yes."

"Which is exactly why I can't imagine the party being behind this."
She pointed at Wang-Mei's photo. "There must be something going
on behind the scenes that we don't know about."

Each of them briefly became lost in thought. Leif suddenly snatched
up his laptop and sat on the opposite side of the table.

"What are you doing?" Daniel said.

"Doesn't concern you," Leif replied without taking his eyes off the
monitor.

"You are not going to blog a single thing about what we found on
Wang-Mei. Is that clear?"

Leif didn't respond.

"I know you, Leif. Let it go."

"You can't tell me what I can and cannot do."

"Do you really want to risk getting busted?" Daniel said, clearly
aggravated now. "You really think these people aren't watching the
Internet all the time? There's too much happening for them to ignore
the online community. Remember Dobby? They've always had it in for
you, man. So don't even think about blogging about it. Are we clear?"

"Fuck," Leif barked and slapped his laptop shut in anger. He
grabbed the open bottle of Coke, drank it down in one chug.

Daniel turned away and went over to the window. He looked out
in silence.

"Who's Dobby?" Laura asked.

Leif shook his head.

She stepped over to Daniel at the window. "Where did you two get
all this info anyway? From your contact? The guy on the dark net?"

The two of them exchanged glances. Then Leif said, "That's the
problem. Rousseau, he's disappeared."

"Disappeared?"

"He's stopped checking in completely."

"Why?"

"How am I supposed to know?" Leif snapped. "Maybe someone
neutralized him."

"'Neutralized him'?" Laura could see Hardenberg's corpse again,
lying there before her. His wide-open eyes, staring motionless
into space.

"You heard me. Nothing surprises me anymore." Leif stuffed his
laptop under his arm, snatched up the power cable, and went to the
door. "I need to take a piss."

"What do you need your laptop for?" Daniel asked him warily.

"I never leave my baby unattended," he said, pointing at Laura. "Not as long as she's here." He flung the door open and stepped out into the hallway. A brief discussion ensued with the guard, who ended up escorting Leif to the restroom.

"What an idiot," Laura muttered.

Daniel sighed. "Diplomacy never was one of his strong points. But without him? I'd be up a creek."

"If you say so," she said, lost in her thoughts. "You think that this Rousseau, that someone ... killed him?"

"I just thought Leif meant that Rousseau couldn't access the dark net." Daniel shrugged. "We'll probably never know who this Rousseau is."

"If this guy really has been removed from the picture somehow, that means there's at least one person who knows his identity." Laura eyed the door. "The security guard is gone right now. What do you think about stretching our legs a little?"

"Why not?" Daniel said with a weary smile. "A little moving around never hurt."

They strolled the empty halls without a destination in mind, the building not exactly cheering them up with it so unoccupied. They entered the cafeteria with its stainless-steel counters, all silver shimmers under the dull emergency lighting, and eventually reached the long main corridor connecting the business offices with the production facility. They'd only advanced a few steps before a man came around the corner on the other end of the long hallway. He saw Laura and stopped in his tracks. His curly blond hair hung down in his face, messy like a California surfer just coming off the beach. He had sharp facial features and, most likely, a muscular body under his thick winter jacket.

Laura was absolutely certain that she'd never seen this man at Andra before. Her instincts told her that he didn't belong here. The way he looked at her gave her a fright, and she too had stopped in her tracks.

"What's wrong?" Daniel said, confused.

"I'm not sure." She kept staring at the man at the other end of the corridor. He started moving again, without taking his eyes off her. His gait was oddly springy.

Daniel's eyebrows rose. "Who is that?"

"No idea."

He was coming their way. He pulled down the zipper of his jacket with his left hand while sliding his right inside. Goosebumps covered Laura's arms. When the man pulled his hand back out, it was clamped around the grip of a pistol.

Her eyes widened.

Without slowing down, he extracted a silencer from his jacket and screwed it onto the weapon with practiced agility.

"What the hell?" blurted Daniel.

Then events took over. The men's restroom door in the middle of the corridor swung open, and Leif stepped out. With a look of contentment on his face, he dried his hands on his jeans, saw Daniel and Laura, and smirked. Laura briefly sensed something was different about him. But since a man was also approaching holding a gun, all she could think about was taking flight.

"Watch out!" shouted Daniel at Leif, indicating the man. But it was too late.

The man had reached Leif. He returned the gun inside his jacket in one smooth movement. Leif finally grasped that someone was behind him. He turned around.

The man grabbed hold of Leif's temples with both hands and brutally wrenched him sideways. The horrible cracking sound made it all the way to Laura and could only be Leif's neck breaking. Like a tree falling, he tipped over and hit the floor. His twisted-around head faced their direction, his dead eyes seeing nothing.

Laura wanted to scream, but nothing came out.

Leif's killer pulled out his gun again.

Daniel stared at his dead friend, paralyzed. Laura grabbed his arm and pulled him away with her. "Run!"

And they ran.

They quickly reached the end of the corridor they had come from and turned the corner. Concrete sprayed out from the wall behind them. Laura gasped—she hadn't even heard the shots.

The next corner was about fifty feet ahead. Laura's heart pounded so hard it ached. "Faster!"

They turned down another corridor, then rushed down the stairs to the ground floor. With some surprise Laura realized that Leif's killer wasn't very quick on his feet. It seemed that they had lost him. For now, anyway.

They ran into the lobby, passing the sofas and chairs they'd been lounging on just a few hours earlier while talking about the blizzard. They didn't find a soul in the entrance area. Laura went around the reception desk, checked the phone system. Not a single light was lit up or blinking. She held the receiver to her ear. Nothing. "The phone system is out."

"Shit. It's either the storm or that guy."

"Who is he?"

"No idea. We'll try to figure it out later. Right now we need to get out of here."

"Not outside we can't." Laura frantically considered their options. "We need to get to the production facility. It's confusing in there when you don't know your way around."

"Okay."

She rushed over to the stairs. "This way."

"No." Daniel caught up to her and held her arm back. "That guy's up there."

She shook off his hand. "He could just as well be somewhere down here by now. We have to risk it."

Glancing around warily, they headed back up to the second floor. Laura led the way. She turned another corner and halted abruptly. Just a few feet from them, in the middle of the corridor, lay Leif's lifeless body. She swallowed hard. The way to production was past his dead body.

When they reached him, Daniel knelt beside his dead friend and closed his eyelids. "Take care, nutjob."

Laura stared at Leif's hands, which he had been drying on his jeans after emerging from the restroom just a few minutes earlier. Suddenly she realized what was bothering her.

"Be right back," she said and headed for the men's restroom.

"Are you crazy? What for? We need to keep going!"

"Just one sec." She charged inside and looked around. In the back, through a rounded passageway, were the wall urinals, the stalls across from them. She was standing at a mirror, with a deeply distraught woman staring back at her, someone who had nothing in common with the happy young mother who just last weekend had been sitting on the edge of that fountain in such a great mood, waiting for a parade to begin. Underneath the mirror were sinks and a soap dispenser on a standing cabinet. Above that were two wall plugs. A black power unit was plugged into one, the cable leading inside the door of the cabinet, which happened to be open a crack. She knelt down and opened it.

"What the hell are you doing in here?" Daniel whispered loud from outside the door. "The guy could show up any second. We need to take off!"

She pulled out Leif's laptop. "Leif came in here right after you stopped him from going online. I didn't think much of him taking his laptop since he never let it out of his sight. But he came out of the restroom empty-handed, so it had to be here."

"Why would he leave it behind?" Daniel said, rumpling his brow. "That doesn't sound like him."

She yanked the power from the plug. "He was charging it."

"Leif never left his laptop unattended."

"I don't know either—"

"Doesn't matter." Daniel glanced back around frantically. "Let's just go! We're wasting too much time already."

"No, we aren't. Without the files on this laptop, no one is going to believe us."

"That's true," he said, nodding. "Good job."

They ran down the stretch of corridor where Leif's killer had come from. The door to one of the storerooms was ajar; it was where the cleaning crew kept their stuff. Laura spotted the soles of a pair of shoes standing upright. She flung the door open. The security guard sat with his eyes closed and his back against the wall, tossed into a corner like a bag of trash. The chest of his shirt and jacket were soaked with blood. Her lips started quivering.

"Come on," Daniel urged her.

They kept running and turned two more corners before reaching the security door leading to production. Through the door's observation window, they could make out the contours of machines and equipment in the dimly lit production hall. Laura held her company ID up to the security lock, the door unlocked with a click.

It smelled like oil and grease in the open hall, and it was bitterly cold. All the machines stood silent, and they didn't hear a sound. The few times Laura had been in here before, she had needed to wear earplugs. The door latched securely shut behind them. Laura took a deep breath, her breath steaming out.

"I'm calling the police." She pulled out her phone. "Shit. No service."

Daniel looked around. "What now?"

"That door will keep him at bay."

"We shouldn't assume that. What if he has a swipe card? We need to get out of sight."

"Okay. The production hall is huge. We'll find a good hiding spot."

"What I meant was, we need to get out of here, Laura. Out of this place completely—as far from Andra as possible."

Her eyes widened. "Into that blizzard?"

"I don't see any other way."

There was a knocking at the security door, against the observation window. They whipped around.

They could see Leif's killer through the glass. His outstretched hand held the gun, and his hardened face showed no expression. He fired several rounds their way in quick succession, the bullets pounding into the door. They struck the window and left circular patterns of splintering glass, gray at the center from the flowerlike shreds of ruptured metal.

Daniel gasped. "Let's get out of here, come on!"

They fled through the half-darkness between machines, conveyer belts, and bulky presses until they reached the opposite end of the hall. Next to a large loading door was a break room as well as locker rooms for the workers.

"Wait here." Laura handed Daniel the laptop and disappeared into a locker room. Thick work jackets hung next to the lockers. She pulled one on and brought one for Daniel.

A horrible banging came from the other end of the hall. The echoes of shattering glass bounced off the walls.

Laura pressed on the opener for the loading door. It rolled upward, the snow immediately drifting into the hall. Something clanked onto the floor somewhere behind them.

"He's coming," Daniel said.

They stepped outside. Thick freezing snowflakes whipped all around, smacking their faces.

"Which way to the parking lot?" Daniel shouted at her through the storm winds.

"This way."

They trudged off through the knee-high snow. Laura kept checking behind her, but she saw no one and nothing but the heavy driving snow.

Leif's pickup was not far from the main entrance. But like all the cars, it was covered with a thick blanket of snow, with icicles hanging from the bumpers and side mirrors. Laura could only frown. They just had to hope that the pickup's battery was in better shape than the one in her little VW Polo. If the thing didn't start, they were going to be trapped.

28

LAURA AND DANIEL QUICKLY CLEARED THE THICKEST snow off the windows using their forearms. Daniel opened the doors, and they climbed into the cab. The five-liter V8 started on the first try. Daniel gave the accelerator a few pumps, and the engine revved with hearty growls.

He put it in first gear and gave it gas. The tires spun a moment, then caught, and the truck jerked forward. They rolled slowly along the snow-covered parking lot toward the exit. The windshield was icy, the roadway blurred, the asphalt under the snow a sheet of ice. The pickup slid on the very first curve, and Daniel had to gently counter-steer.

They drove out of the business park without knowing if the roads were passable. The heavy snowfall swallowed the headlight beams after only twenty feet or so; the wipers scratched at ice. Laura only hoped that Daniel could see better than she could.

She glanced in the rearview mirror. "He doesn't seem to be following us."

Daniel pounded at the roof with his fist like a madman. "That fucker murdered Leif!" he shouted, shaking with rage. "Who was that bastard?"

"I don't know. But I'm fairly certain it's the same guy who murdered Hardenberg."

"Probably. So why would he show up at Andra?"

Laura shrugged. "No clue."

"Me, I don't think it's an accident. I noticed how he looked at you."

"Wait, what are you trying to say?"

Daniel hesitated. "He could have ... come there for you."

Laura gazed out the passenger window in silence. Deep down, she knew that Daniel was right. The ones pulling the strings must have gotten word that someone named Laura Wagner was in possession of Hardenberg's USB stick. But how was that possible? No one had seen her slip the flash drive into her pants pocket. She hadn't told Daniel about that part yet; she had decided to wait until they were safe. She nervously shifted back and forth on her seat. The idea that someone out there was running around trying to kill her was simply incomprehensible to her.

"What do we do now?" Daniel asked, a hint of resignation in his voice.

"We need to get to the police." She grabbed her phone. "Crap, still no service. Let's drive to the nearest station. I know where it is."

"All right, fine."

The cab was gradually warming up inside. Laura unzipped her grease-smeared work jacket and happened to feel something long and hard in the inside pocket, which turned out to be a screwdriver. She pulled off the jacket and laid it on the seat next to her.

They came to an intersection. Several cars were blocking the road, their warning blinkers flashing all over. Most of the cars were abandoned, but one had the motor running and inside sat a man wrapped in a thick Red Cross blanket. They exchanged glances. Laura waved to ask whether he needed a ride, but he only shook his head with a dejected expression on his face.

"Where to?" Daniel asked. "I don't know Hanover at all."

"There's a traffic circle up ahead—take the second exit."

They made slow progress. They kept having to go around cars left in the road, covered to their hoods in snowdrifts. The streetlights were out, and only a few houses had lights in the windows. Laura wondered if the heating had gone out along with the power. A city snowplow with orange blinking lights and chains on the tires approached, its plow scraping snow and ice from the asphalt and throwing loads of both to the sides in large arcs. The colossus thundered by them without reducing speed.

"We'll take the next exit," she told Daniel.

Laura could already see blue blinking lights up ahead at the base of the old round bunker standing in the middle of Deisterplatz, the snowpack on the hundred-foot-high tower piled up dangerously on its sharply pointed roof. They approached the traffic circle at a snail's pace. In front of the bunker were two police vehicles and an ambulance. A multiple pileup had occurred on the two-lane street, and the police and emergency services were attempting to gain control of the situation. Laura and Daniel slowly rolled by in the pickup. Through the open rear doors of the ambulance, she could see a paramedic trying to resuscitate a man, pumping breaths of steam into the ice-cold air. A second paramedic leaned his head out to a policeman and shook his head with a certainty that needed no explanation. Laura looked away in sorrow.

The next possible turnoff was blocked by a fallen traffic light. "With things this bad, it's best to drive across the Leine River and then take Bremer Damm," Laura said. "That'll get us into city center too."

Snow-covered trees now lined the two-lane road, and they glowed eerily in their headlights, the snow's weight bending their branches far downward.

Laura pointed up ahead. "Something's on the bridge."

A piercing honk rang out, and bright headlights glared from out of nowhere, blinding them. Laura shielded her eyes.

"Goddamn," Daniel said, fully hitting the brakes. It didn't help, and the pickup kept sliding forward.

The long honk magnified. Through her fingers Laura saw a semi-truck sliding toward them. Its front end was covered with slush; icicles hung from its bumper and side mirrors. She could see the driver behind the smeared windshield cranking the wheel and knew from her own experience how pointless it was. He must have started sliding and ended up in the opposite lane.

She clawed at her seat.

"Shit!" Daniel took his foot off the brake and yanked the wheel around.

The pickup bucked and swerved. They slid sideways past the big truck at the last second, their bumpers missing each other by an inch. Yet their relief didn't last long. The street forked up ahead, divided by a massive snowdrift looming before them.

"Hold on!" Daniel shouted.

The pickup rushed head-on into the snowdrift, smashing into the crash barrier hidden underneath. Laura's seatbelt dug into her abdomen. The engine died with a hiss; the wipers stopped halfway. She had a horrible feeling of déjà vu.

Silence reigned a moment.

"You okay?" Daniel said eventually, his hands still gripping the steering wheel.

"Yes. You?"

"I'm all right." He unfastened his belt. "Where in the hell did that truck come from?"

"All I know is, we need to find somewhere warm quick," she told him. Fresh snow was already starting to cover the windshield.

Daniel pulled up his collar. "You know this area?"

"I've driven through here before."

"So, not really."

She pulled on her jacket. "You ready?"

"Yes."

He grabbed the backpack with Leif's laptop off the back seat, and they climbed out. The freezing wind lashed snow into their faces. Daniel shielded his eyes and peered down the road. "Where did that truck go?"

"No idea, but we should get away from here." Laura looked around and faintly seemed to remember that there was a residential area beyond the little wooded parkland in front of them. She plodded onward.

There was no one else around apart from them, so they made their way down the middle of the road since the snow only reached their ankles there—a snowplow must have passed recently.

They came to a dense tree line, beyond which a park with leafy trees was barely visible in the pitch-dark night. Treading through the park took a lot of energy, the snow here also knee-deep. Laura's ankle boots weren't much help—her feet were soon damp and stung from the cold. To top it all off, their work jackets proved far less warm than their thick lining seemed to promise. She started to shiver.

A few minutes later, they found themselves underneath the bridge over the Leine River. Laura took a look around her. Nothing but trees all around them, and above stretched tons of concrete. What direction were they even going? She cursed under her breath and admitted to herself that she had lost her way.

"Are you sure we're going the right way?" Daniel asked, hugging himself for warmth.

"Let's try over there." She pointed at a clearing that revealed the silhouette of a low building.

"Looks abandoned," Daniel panted.

"There's no other option. Come on."

A little while later they were standing before an unadorned brick bungalow, the windows on either side of the front door blocked with green shutters. Snow had piled up on the roof; thick icicles hung from the gutters. Attached to the right of the bungalow was an elongated wooden shed. Above the front door was a sign: Hanover 1911 Rowing Club. Down the slope beyond, Laura could see the snow-covered banks of the Leine.

"There's no one here," Daniel said.

"I got it completely wrong," Laura admitted now, grinding her teeth. "We went the wrong direction. I'm sorry."

"How far is it from here to the next residential area?"

"In this weather? At least a half hour. Probably more." She looked at Daniel in despair. "But I won't make it, Daniel. I'm frozen stiff. I can't feel my toes anymore—"

"We're staying here," he told her. "Don't worry. We'll find a way inside."

She nodded.

Daniel looked around and then trudged over to the wooden shed. Laura followed. The shed door was secured with a simple padlock. Daniel hurled himself at it with full force and groaned in pain. The door hadn't given an inch. Laura suddenly remembered the screwdriver in her jacket. She could pry the door open. She placed the tip between the door and the frame next to the lock and drove it in as far as it would go. Then she leaned on it with all her might. The bolt bracket broke away from the rotten wood, and the door swung open. She shouted in triumph.

Daniel grinned. "Not bad."

The shed was pitch-dark inside and had a musty odor that mixed with the smell of turpentine. Daniel pulled out his phone and used it as a flashlight, directing its narrow beam around the room.

"Look what we have here," Laura said.

The wooden shed turned out to be storage for the club's rowboats and kayaks. Mounted on the walls were metal racks holding about twenty boats stacked on top of one another, with paddles and wooden oars standing upright in metal mesh boxes. A plastic cabinet took up the back wall along with shelving full of tools and cans of paint and lacquer. Two rowboats stood on jacks, apparently for repairs to be made during the winter months.

Daniel pulled out a paddle from the box and rammed the blade between the door and frame to secure it.

"Not exactly cozy," Laura said, "but it is dry, and we're protected from the storm." She looked around. "Shine some light over there," she told Daniel, then went over to another cabinet in the corner and opened its unlocked door. Neoprene suits, life vests, and rope fell out. On the bottom shelf she found a couple of wool blankets and a storm lantern with kerosene and matches next to it. She lit the lantern, replaced the protective glass, and the blazing little flame submerged the shed in a warm reddish-orange light. She got an idea.

"We could make beds using the kayaks," she said.

"Beds, huh?" Daniel gave her a questioning look but proceeded to follow her instructions. They moved the rowboats on jack stands to the side and spread the neoprene suits on the floor to block the cold from the earth. Then they removed two kayaks from the racks and placed them next to one another on top of the neoprene. They stood the storm lantern between the kayaks and laid out the wool blankets inside the seat and foot areas. Last but not least, they each climbed inside a kayak and wrapped their upper bodies in the rest of the blankets.

Daniel grinned. "Hard to believe, but I'm already getting warm. Wouldn't exactly call it comfortable, but I guess you can't have it all."

Laura was less ecstatic. The hard plastic seat kept her stiff and upright, and she wound the blanket all the way up around her ears. Still, her toes had begun to thaw out.

Exhaustion set in, and soon neither spoke a word.

"We should try sleeping a little," Daniel said eventually. "It'll be light in a few hours. We need to get our strength back."

"Sleep?" Laura snorted—a puff of steam shot out her nose, enveloping her head. "You're joking, right? I won't get one wink in here."

At that moment a heart-rending meow emanated from just outside the door.

They looked at each other, astounded. Without hesitation Daniel unwrapped himself from his blanket, with difficulty climbed out of his kayak, and opened the door a crack.

A red cat darted inside. Snow twinkled on his fur. He made his way to the kerosene lamp, shook himself, sat down, and began licking at his fur.

"Poor little guy," Laura said and stretched out a hand to him.

The cat ignored her.

Daniel wound himself back up in his wool blanket inside the kayak but left a little spot open. He nodded to the cat and said, "Well, come on up . . ."

The cat ran up to him and disappeared in the warm hollow. Soon Laura could hear it purring happily.

"His fur is freezing," Daniel said as he stroked it under the blanket. "I doubt he would've survived much longer out there."

Laura watched Daniel petting the cat inside his kayak. The flickering light of the kerosene lamp made the shadows dance on his face. "Tell me something," she said.

"What do you want to know?"

"Why was your show really cancelled?"

Daniel eyed her with surprise. "Okay . . ." He thought a moment. "My show wasn't cancelled. I was fired. The show is still on."

"I know. But without you, it's not the same."

He smiled.

"I liked the wacky parts you did," Laura said. "One time you had these poodles in little pink skirts, dancing on their hind legs to that song by the Weather Girls: 'It's raining men ... *Hallelujah!*'"

"Don't remind me of those mutts! They ended up peeing all over our studio."

They laughed, and for a moment Laura forgot where she was and the danger they were facing.

"I was even nominated for the German Television Award," Daniel said. His expression dimmed. "But soon after the nomination, my assistant, Jenny Kampers, went to the media saying that I had stolen the idea for the show from her."

"Stolen how?"

"It was a lie, but I had no way of disproving it, unfortunately. Yeah, well, that was basically it for me. It ended my career. A few weeks later, I found out that Jenny had been seeing my co-host, Karsten Gerlach, the whole time in secret, and—big surprise—he ended up taking over my show. It took me way too long to notice that they'd completely set me up."

"Why couldn't you dispute the claims of this Jenny Kampers?"

Daniel pulled a hand out from under the blanket and scratched his head. "We had something going, once. Jenny really had my head spinning. I was in love and didn't notice that she was only using me from the start. When she was at my place, she helped herself to my original show ideas, documents. I was such an idiot."

"But the burden of proof—"

"Forget it." Daniel shook his head. "In the media, I was the guilty one. There's nothing you can do about that. Even when everyone involved know that there is nothing to it. A scandal doesn't deliver the truth—it delivers ratings."

The wind was howling outside. Laura stared into space. Her thoughts had drifted elsewhere.

"What, you don't believe me?" Daniel asked. "You think I'm just shifting blame onto someone else?"

"No, I believe you," Laura said in a gentle voice. "And, I know all too well how you must have felt."

"Oh yeah?" he asked in surprise.

She stared into the darkest corners of the shed, where the flickers of the lantern could not penetrate, and realized she'd already said too much to back out now. She took a deep breath.

"I was fourteen years old. Thorsten, seventeen. He had one of those motocross motorbikes that everyone wanted back then. I was head over heels in love with him. He got me to go all the way after just three months. It was August—a barbecue. Behind my parents' garden shed, there on the wet grass, I lost my virginity." She sighed. "For weeks he'd been pressuring me and was threatening me more and more that he'd call it off if I didn't finally sleep with him. So that night I drank down two glasses of cheap champagne, for courage, lay on my back, and let him do it. Ten seconds, then it was over. What happened was what always happens—I got pregnant."

Daniel audibly took a breath.

"When that second line on the pregnancy test strip appeared, I went into a crying fit," she said in a monotone voice. "I didn't tell anyone about it. I was ashamed but also scared of my parents. I didn't know what I should do or who I could turn to. As the pregnancy progressed it got harder and harder to hide my stomach. At first, I'd just skip gym class. Later I stopped going to school altogether. I avoided my circle of friends and Thorsten as well."

"You didn't tell him?"

"No." She paused, thinking. "At least not right away. After several months, all the lying was wearing me down. He started pressuring me again. This time he wanted me to get an abortion. I refused, though I knew that I could have spared myself so much trouble that way. But my conscience wouldn't let me do it. Plus I would have needed my parents' consent."

"So, you didn't try?"

"Try what?"

"Talking to your parents about it."

She released a bitter laugh. "Oh, no."

"You never felt like you could confide in them?"

"Impossible." She shook her head hard at the thought. "My mother never would have spoken to me again, and my father probably would have just beaten me. Being fourteen, and so naïve, I came up with another plan altogether. Knowing what I know now, of course it never, ever could have worked."

"What was it?"

"I was going to give birth to the child in secret and give it up for adoption afterward. Please don't ask how I ever could have seen that actually happening because I have no clue." She stared into the lantern flame now, submerged in memory. She fell silent a while, and only the purring of the cat could be heard apart from the storm.

"What happened then?" Daniel asked.

"One day, near the end of my seventh month, I went to a department store. I needed bigger pants and blouses because nothing fit anymore. The changing room was stuffy. That's where it happened." She paused. "I can still see it so clearly. There was a stool in the corner. Someone had spilled Fanta on it—the crushed can was still lying there on the floor. I looked at myself in the mirror, my hands on my curved stomach, a black T-shirt of my father's stretched over it. Then, all of a sudden, these hellish pains hit me. As if someone was stabbing a knife into my belly." She closed her eyes. She made herself breathe calmly, evenly. "My stomach started cramping up tight. I screamed. Sticky, slimy blood ran down my thighs. My water broke, a stream of it splashed onto the floor. I threw up. At some point I sank down to the floor, into the pool of blood and vomit and amniotic fluid. I will never forget that smell."

"You don't have to tell me," Daniel said gently. The empathy on his face spoke volumes.

"By that point, I was of course pretty well versed in how pregnancy worked," she continued. "It was immediately clear to me what had happened. Panic took hold of me. I had this insane fear I was going to die." She took a deep breath. "An employee at the department store heard me moaning and crying and eventually broke the door open. By that point, the birth couldn't be halted." She freed her arms from the wool blanket, to push back the hair that had fallen into her face. "I gave birth to my child in the goddamn changing room of a shitty department store. Can you imagine how that made me feel? It was humiliating. EMTs and a young paramedic doctor came eventually. They strapped me to a gurney, placed Robin in a mobile incubator, and rolled us right through the middle of the store to the exit, all surrounded by dozens of rubberneckers, and loaded us into the ambulance." She released a bitter laugh. "Of course the story spread like wildfire through my town. The local paper reported on it in every detail, and one TV network even showed up at the hospital to do a report on me." Her voice strained to get out the rest. "Suddenly I was the town's biggest slut. No one wanted anything more to do with me."

Daniel looked at her sympathetically.

"But you know what?" Her voice regained confidence. "The next day, when Robin was lying in my own arms for the first time, it was clear to me immediately that I would never give him up for adoption. The decision changed my life. I was thrown into the adult world at barely fifteen. Without wanting to be or knowing any of its rules. Luckily, I had my Uncle Martin. He stood by me, helped me."

"How did it go with you and your parents?"

"We're not in contact anymore. Robin and I don't exist as far as they're concerned."

"I'm sorry to hear that."

"I got over it long ago."

"What about Robin's father?"

"He took off soon after Robin was born. I don't know what's become of him, and I don't want to know. Robin and me, we get along just fine."

Daniel nodded.

Laura felt even more exhausted from telling it all, but also a little relieved. For the first time in years, she'd talked to someone about the darkest time in her life. The memories still stung, yet she also felt that Daniel for some reason understood her and accepted her.

"I think I'm going to close my eyes for a while," she said eventually and slid farther down into her kayak.

"Good idea," he said gently.

Right before Laura dozed off, she could see Daniel pulling Leif's laptop from the pack. Then the last few days finally took their toll, and she fell into a deep and dreamless sleep.

29

FRED BISHOP'S CLOTHES WEREN'T EXACTLY SUITED TO this kind of weather. The wind blew through his jacket down to his T-shirt. Sharp ice crystals pricked at his face as he propped himself against the metal gate blocking access to the narrow bridge. His hands wanted to stick to the icy steel, and it took a lot of strength to slide open the gate. Panting, he went back to his rented Audi and dropped into the heated driver's seat. He let the car slowly roll over the bridge, the snow crunching under the tires as the beams of the xenon headlights crept across the vast godforsaken grounds that once belonged to a tire factory. Moving along at a crawl, he neared the large complex of brick buildings with their arched windows. Every one of them had been smashed over the years, by kids or drunks, and graffiti covered the ground floor façade. The sight reminded Bishop of his old neighborhood in Brooklyn. He hated the building already. Yet it provided the best option for a few hours of uninterrupted sleep.

After his mission at Andra failed, he had driven around a while to put a little distance between himself and the crime scene. Bile rose up his throat like scorching lava just thinking about it. Some idiot had blown the whole operation by showing up in that hallway at the worst possible moment. Bishop always tried to avoid collateral damage, but this time he was left with no other option but to take that dumbshit out for good. All because of him, the operation had changed from a routine job to a highly complex situation—the target was now on high alert. He had been planning on having breakfast at home under his own roof, but it would just have to wait.

Bishop coasted along the long building until the headlight beams revealed a wide opening in the wall, where the remains of a demolished garage door hung down. He put on the brakes and looked around. A wide tower rose into the sky nearby, covered all the way around with graffiti close to the ground, and in the middle of it was a rusted sign bearing the word *Conti*.

Bishop figured the abandoned garage had once been used for loading tires onto delivery trucks, He immediately steered his vehicle inside.

He was condemned to waiting things out for as long as the blizzard raged on. On top of that, his body needed a rest after over thirty-two hours without sleep. That created two issues. Going on the assumption that Laura Wagner would be a quick and easy job, he had not bothered packing any gear that would let him change his appearance—apart from the blond wig he was still wearing since it kept his naked head warm. He could have slapped himself for such carelessness, because it meant it was now too risky to find an inn or a hotel at this hour. So he would have to sleep in the car. And public parking spots were out of the question, since he needed to keep the motor running so that he wouldn't freeze to death while sleeping, and he also couldn't risk a patrol cop taking notice of him. The same went for parking garages, where a running motor would always attract attention. This abandoned old ruin of a factory was perfect. He had certainly slept in far worse places.

The rear side garage wall had collapsed, Bishop now saw. He carefully maneuvered the Audi through until he reached the inside of the main building, then swung the wheel around. The front of the car should always point to the exit so that he could speed back out right away if any danger arose. The Audi's headlight beams slowly traveled over the graffiti-covered walls and—found a man's face.

Bishop stepped on the brake.

In front of him, in a corner of the large hall, slept a bum. The lower half of his body was wrapped in a grimy sleeping bag, his torso in a ragged overcoat. A plastic tarp covered his head and shoulders and protected him from the water that was dripping down. Next to him stood a Bunsen burner, a spoon next to that. Bishop didn't need to know more. Ten feet farther down lay another man, buried under several blankets on a filthy mattress. His eyes were closed, his face white as snow against the brick wall.

Two junkies. Bishop stared at them. Usually he could care less about them, but seeing them like this, here in this setting, it propelled him back many years into the past. He felt at his stump through his pants. That old phantom limb pain crept back, and the old memories flared up along with it.

After he returned from Afghanistan and spent the next few months in that injury rehab clinic, where it took so much pain and effort to learn how to walk again, he had finally returned to his old life. Except that life didn't exist anymore. His fiancée had left him, he had no job or future prospects, and he was pumped full of opiates. He sank into a depression. He didn't leave his room for weeks. Nightmares stalked him every night—images of dying buddies, body parts ripped off, intestines hanging out. But there were also those images of children dying—either shot or mutilated beyond recognition by mines or mortar fire.

Bishop squeezed the steering wheel so tightly that his knuckles cracked. He'd always dreamed of returning from the war a hero, but instead they shipped him back home a cripple. He was so naïve he'd expected Uncle Sam to honor him for his service and his patriotism. Instead, the military covered up the disaster that was Operation Python for years. The only form of recognition he ever got was a ridiculously small check for his lost leg. He had stared for hours at the envelope holding the check. They had even gotten his name wrong— *Bishopp*, it read. He couldn't believe it. He had sacrificed his leg for his country, and in thanks that country hadn't even taken the trouble to get his fucking name right.

They'd shown the deepest contempt for a man who, in a dusty and rocky desert in the butt end of nowhere, had sacrificed, along with that leg, his very soul believing in a good and just cause. It was the final straw. The realization had given him a cleansing feeling of catharsis, and like the phoenix, he had risen from the ashes—but this time driven by pure hatred for Uncle Sam.

Bishop came back to the present. He was still staring at the two junkies, he realized. He was having trouble breathing, and a cold sweat coated his skin. He still got flashbacks like this, but they were hitting him less often. In that moment, he made the decision to let the junkies live, even though he doubted that he would be doing them much of a favor.

He turned off the headlights, lowered the seat back, and closed his eyes. In three hours, he would renew his hunt for Laura Wagner. This time he'd handle things differently, and he knew exactly how. In this one respect at least, his client had provided him with useful and current background info. He let out a deep breath, hoping he could get to sleep right away. His body was ready, but his soul was not—not by a mile.

30

LAURA WOKE WITH A START. A SOUND HAD WOKEN HER. The kerosene storm lamp was out, and a bright strip of moonlight beamed through a small window next to the front door. The storm appeared to be over; the howling wind was now silent. Daniel was sleeping in his kayak, bent to one side, all muffled up in his wool blanket. The cat was nowhere to be seen. Laura sat up straight, her muscles tight, every movement making her stiff neck and shoulders twinge. Another sound made her start. It was at the door. A figure darted by the window. She was fully awake now.

"Daniel," she whispered. "Wake up!"

He didn't respond. She unwound her blanket, stepped out of the kayak, and shook him awake. "There's someone outside."

He let out a yawn. "What?"

"Outside, there's—"

Someone pounded hard on the door.

The rusty hinges separated from rotting wood, and the door sprang open. Two figures bounded into the shed. Bright flashlights glared, blinding them.

"Hands over your heads!" a male voice ordered.

"All right," Daniel said. He raised his hands, and Laura copied him.

"Leif Gundarsson?" the voice asked.

"Come again?" Daniel sounded confused, which was understandable. Laura wasn't doing any better.

"Are you Leif Gundarsson?" the man repeated.

He sounded as if he might be English or American.

"Uh, no. Leif, he ... he's not here."

"Where is he?" It was a female voice. To Laura it sounded like sandpaper dragged over a rusty saw. She had the same accent as the man.

"What do you want with Leif?" Daniel said. "What makes you think he's here?"

"Answer the question."

"My name is Daniel Bender. The woman next to me here is Laura Wagner."

"You're Daniel Bender?" The woman's voice revealed her surprise. She stepped in front of Daniel, still hunkered inside his kayak, and looked him over. "Could be Bender."

"Would you please tell me what's going on here?" Daniel asked.

The man and woman exchanged glances. They finally lowered their flashlights. Laura suddenly noticed that they were also carrying handguns, which they now holstered.

"You can put your hands down now and stand up," the woman told them.

Laura eyed the two strangers. The woman was in her mid-thirties, with a harsh face and pasty skin. Her burgundy red hair was cut in a long bob, which lent a softer note to her slightly masculine appearance. She wore a dark pantsuit. The man was somewhat older. He was tall, with short black hair, his eyebrows meeting above his nose. He too wore a dark suit.

"Are you looking for Leif?" Daniel asked.

"Not exactly," the woman said. "Leif Gundarsson is of secondary interest. We've actually been searching for the two of you."

Laura and Daniel gaped at each other in confusion.

"We'll explain it all to you," the man said. "Inside our van is better. It's warm in there, and there's hot coffee."

"How do we know we can trust you?" Laura asked him.

"You can't," the man said.

The woman intervened. "It's in your own interest. We can protect you."

"Protect us? From whom?"

"From the man who's been after you."

"How do you know about him? Who was that man?"

The woman took a deep breath. "A certain Fred Bishop, but—"

"We'll answer all your questions when the time comes," the man cut in. "Now, please come along."

Laura took another look at the two. Neither gave the impression they would take no for an answer. She glanced over at Daniel. He didn't look at all convinced either, but what choice did they have? If the man responsible for killing Leif was still after them, they were still in danger. They needed to accept any help they could get.

The man checked his wristwatch. "Well?"

Laura nodded. "We'll come."

Daniel didn't object.

They followed the man outside through the broken shed door. The blizzard really had subsided. The air was fresh and clean, and a few stars shone in the sky.

Reaching the van, the man pointed at the side door. "Please, get in."

Another man in a dark suit sat at the wheel. His expression didn't change as they entered the back and took a seat. The woman slid the door shut, gave the driver a signal, and the van started moving. The warm interior felt nice.

"Where are we going?" Daniel asked and glanced at Laura sharply, as if it were her fault these people had gotten ahold of them.

"To the airport," the man said, pouring coffee into four paper cups from a thermos.

"Who are you? Who do you work for?" Laura asked, taking a steaming cup, the hot liquid warming up her freezing hands.

"My name is Fenton Link," the man said. "This is my colleague, Jennifer West. We work for the United States government."

Laura and Daniel exchanged incredulous glances. "What are you planning to do with us?" Laura asked.

"Don't worry," said the man who had introduced himself as Fenton Link. "You are safe and secure with us."

"I'm not getting into any airplane," Daniel told them.

Both Fenton Link and Jennifer West ignored the comment. Link rose and made his way up to the driver while his colleague studied her smartphone. It was becoming clear to Laura and Daniel that they wouldn't be getting any answers anytime soon. Laura looked at Daniel, but he only stared out the window looking grumpy.

A full blanket of snow still covered the streets, but the van had no problem with it. Dawn was breaking, and the first vehicles were already heading out despite the early hour, mostly snowplows back at work. Abandoned and snow-covered cars dominated the cityscape.

Laura tried getting her bearings. They were on the A2 autobahn now and, sure enough, soon they were taking the A352 toward the airport, where they passed all three of the terminals. She figured they would exit the airport again, but the driver turned and stopped at a gate. He entered a code on a keypad, and the gate slid open. They drove into a fenced compound, passing containers covered by gray plastic tarps, and slowed down in front of the nondescript entrance to a plain building. Prominently displayed on its facade was a large and dark letter D.

"Terminal D?" Laura asked, puzzled now.

"What about it?" Daniel said.

"It hasn't been a passenger terminal for years now, not officially." She thought for a moment. "The British still use it, I think. As a base for the Royal Air Force."

Daniel turned to Jennifer West. "That true?"

She didn't answer.

The van stopped. Fenton Link got out and slid open the van's door from the outside.

The two American officials led Laura and Daniel over to the building at a quick pace. Inside, they walked down brightly lit corridors. They stopped at a door.

Link turned to Laura. "Wait in here," he said and opened the door.

The ocher-colored room held only a table with two chairs. A ceiling lamp hung over it. An uneasy feeling was spreading through Laura's gut. She turned and watched Jennifer West guide Daniel farther down the corridor.

"I have to ask you to hand over your phone," Link said. "You'll get it back as soon as I return."

Laura hesitated, but deep down she knew there was no point in resisting. She pulled her phone out of her jacket pocket. Link took it and left, closing the door behind him.

A wave of panic hit Laura. No one knew where she was. What if these people weren't who they said they were? What if they wanted to make her and Daniel disappear for some reason?

She bounded over to the door and pushed down on the door handle. It was locked.

31

THE WAIT TOOK AN AGONIZINGLY LONG TIME. LAURA was starting to think they'd forgotten all about her when the door finally opened. Fenton Link entered. She noticed that he'd changed his suit and was now wearing a perfectly knotted tie. His black shoes shined as if just polished. His brown eyes fixed on her. Deep creases ran around the corners of his mouth, and a thick scar ran down the side of his neck from under his right ear.

Link unfastened the top button of his jacket and sat down. "Please, have a seat."

"Where is Daniel?" Laura asked.

"You can see Mr. Bender right after this. I have a few questions first."

Laura sat, reluctantly. "What would you like to know?"

"We found you with Mr. Bender. How did you end up with him?"

Laura kept it short, summarizing the events that led her and Daniel to the boathouse shed. Once she finished, she sat back and folded her hands on the tabletop.

"Tell me about the Diamond series."

Laura swallowed hard. She tried being evasive. "How do you mean?"

"Don't play dumb. You worked with Herr Hardenberg. We know that he sold the Diamond series prototype to a company named Chenlong Industries. What do you know about it?"

Laura nervously bit at her lower lip. She thought about the USB stick, still in her pants pocket. Should she tell them? Hardenberg's instructions to her were to give the flash drive to no one but Lars Windrup. She decided not to mention it for now.

"Well?" Link said.

"Any transaction between Andra and Chenlong was done using the strictest security. So I'm not aware of any details."

Link eyed her. "All right, fine. What do you know about the Diamond prototype?"

"Not much," she said, telling the truth. "The Diamond device itself was some kind of high-performance gyrotron. It was developed from a previous series, currently used by the Wendelstein 7-X project, in Greifswald."

"Go on," Link told her.

"Diamond is far more powerful than any other device on the market."

"We already know all of this."

Laura shrugged. "Well, that's all I know."

Link looked at her a moment, then stood up. "Follow me."

They walked down a long hallway and entered a room at the end that was just as plainly furnished as the one she had just spent the last hour inside. Daniel sat at the table, staring at the corrugated paper cup steaming before him, deep in thought. Jennifer West stood in the far corner, her back resting against the wall. Fenton Link closed the door.

When Daniel saw Laura, he leaped up and went over to her. "You holding up all right?"

She nodded. "Do you know what's going on here?"

He pulled her to the side. "These two are from a U.S. federal agency—NOAA, the National Oceanic and Atmospheric Administration."

Laura glanced at the American agents. "What do they want from us?"

"They're tracking some highly abnormal weather nearing the U.S. East Coast right at this moment. They're looking for my expert opinion." Daniel scratched behind an ear. "I have no idea what they might want from you."

"So why you?"

"No idea either, but there must be a good reason, and I'm definitely curious to learn more about what the hell this is all about."

Agent Fenton Link came up to them. "So, what's your decision, Mr. Bender? Will you come with us?"

"Where are these people taking you?" Laura asked Daniel.

"You can come along to Frankfurt as well if you like, Frau Wagner. Your presence just got authorized a few minutes ago."

"Frankfurt? What's in Frankfurt?"

Agent Link eyed her sternly. "You'll get your answers. But time is short."

Daniel placed a hand on her arm. "I would feel better if you came along." He added a look that wasn't easy to interpret—as if he wanted to tell her something, but not in front of the two Americans.

She alternated glances between Agents Link and Jennifer West. It was tough judging the two of them. But if they had wanted to harm her and Daniel, they would've tried it long ago.

"All right," she said finally and turned to Agent Link. "I'll come too. But I have to insist on one thing."

Agent Link stared, waiting for more.

She stretched out her hand. "My phone. I need to tell my boy, Robin. He's in the hospital. I was actually supposed to pick him up yesterday . . ."

Agent Link eyed her a moment, then took her phone from his pants pocket and placed it in her hand. "Make it quick."

She dialed the number for Robin's room. The phone network seemed to be working again, at least for the moment. She had to wait a long time for a nurse to answer. The nurse told her that Robin was not in his room because he was getting a diagnostic exam. Laura said she'd call back later, then hung up. She briefly wondered when they had started doing tests so early in the morning but suppressed the thought.

"We head out in fifteen minutes," Agent Link announced. He gave his fellow agent a wave, and together they left the room.

As soon as they were alone, Laura asked Daniel, "Do you really believe that these people are from an environmental agency?"

He frowned. "I'm guessing they're doing work for NOAA, at least."

"How were they able to find us?"

Daniel nodded as if he'd been wondering the same thing. "Last night, when Leif and I were sitting there together, watching that storm brewing, he explained a few things to me."

"What kind of things?"

"Leif claimed that someone had been watching him, for weeks now. I didn't believe him." Daniel reached for his paper cup and drank down the rest of his coffee. "Leif also told me that someone was trying to infiltrate his network with a Trojan horse. He did say that he'd quickly rendered the Trojan harmless, but now I'm doubting that."

"Why?"

"My guess is, that Trojan dropper malware was just a diversionary tactic. While Leif was busy with that, someone could have planted a surveillance tool inside his network."

A light went off in Laura's head. "You were using the laptop in the boat shed—it must have been transmitting some kind of signal."

"Exactly. By the way, I now realize that Leif was blogging about the deal with Chenlong right from Andra—even though I told him not to."

"From the toilet! That idiot."

Daniel nodded.

Right then Laura's phone vibrated, from a text coming in. She looked at the screen. The message was from Robin. Laura read it and shook her head, not comprehending. "Is this supposed to be a joke?"

"What's wrong?" Daniel said.

Laura ignored him and dialed Robin's number, her face hardening. Just what was he thinking? Did he think this was funny somehow?

The other end picked up.

"You got my text," said a deep male voice, in English.

Laura started, her head spun, and she sank into the nearest chair. "Who are you? Where is Robin?"

"Your son is doing fine."

"Are you a doctor? I need to speak with Robin, now." She tried to sound assertive, but her hand that held the phone was shaking, and probably her voice as well.

"You have something that I would like to have. As soon as you give me Hardenberg's recording, you'll get your little scaredy-cat back."

Laura's heart raced. Nausea rose up from her gut. The text was no joke.

"I have to know that Robin is okay. I need to hear his voice!"

The connection made a rustling sound, then she heard, from a far distance: "Mom?"

"Robin! Honey, are you doing okay?" Tears streamed out of Laura's eyes.

"That's enough," the man said. "You're going to delete all existing copies of that voice memo. I'll give you one hour. After that, I'll contact you again and name a time and place where you can hand over the original. Once that's done, you'll get your son back."

"You are the one who killed Leif," Laura said.

"One hour."

"You'll get everything you demand, Mr. Bishop. Just don't harm my son."

There was a silence on the other end of the line. Laura could hear the man breathing. "How do you know that name?" he said.

Laura stiffened. Icy chills ran down her spine. She realized her mistake. "I . . ." Her voice broke.

"How?" he growled.

She couldn't think of anything that sounded like a plausible explanation. Tears ran down her cheeks. She pressed the phone to her ear, in a daze, waiting for him to reply.

The connection broke off.

Laura let her phone drop to the floor and slapped her hands over her face. What had she done?

Daniel knelt down next to her, eyeing her with worry. "My God, Laura, who was that? What's wrong?"

"That was Leif's killer." She could barely get out a whisper. "He kidnapped Robin from the hospital. And if he harms him somehow, it's all my fault."

32

THE NHC'S SMALL MEDIA ROOM WAS BURSTING AT the seams. Emilio Sanchez stood at the podium. Before him sat approximately fifty people in eight rows of chairs so close to each other that they touched, the glass-walled room divided into the usual English- and Spanish-speaking groups. The tension showed on both the faces of the NHC staff and the invited journalists, and absolute silence reigned. Selma Cooper, knowing what he had to tell them, stood behind the last row and gave him an encouraging nod. Brandon LaHaye of the Storm Surge Unit and Amy Winter from FEMA sat directly in front, eyeing him with anticipation.

"Ladies and gentlemen," Sanchez began finally. "A few minutes ago, Hurricane Emily reached Category Five on the Saffir-Simpson scale with wind speeds of 160 miles per hour. We're receiving the data from the Hurricane Hunters' airdrop buoys, and it's all verified. Another unit of Hunters is in the air at this very moment, taking exact measurements from inside the hurricane. But that's not all . . ."

Sanchez gave everyone in the room a grave look. He tugged at his shirt, which stuck to his back. He made eye contact with Amy Winter, sitting with her legs and arms crossed and dissecting him with her stare. She wore her black hair combed back, secured with a bulky hairpin, and had no makeup on, her high cheekbones bulging on her narrow face. Her baggy jeans and too-large blouse only emphasized her gaunt figure. But Sanchez wasn't fooled by her fragile exterior. Amy Winter could make some real trouble for him.

"Are you going to come out with it, or we supposed to guess what's next?" Winter barked at him. "Clock's ticking."

"I'm sorry to pull you out of a family gathering, Ms. Winter," Sanchez said, his blood now boiling. He reserved the right to contact the head of Emergency Management at any time of day or night. Hell, it was actually his goddamn duty when the lives of thousands of people were at stake.

Her eyes flared in anger. "Get to the point, Sanchez. After what I've seen and heard so far, we're looking at a real time crunch in regard to potential evacuations. I'm eager to hear your explanation of why the NHC didn't sound the alarm sooner."

He swallowed a comeback and then started a computer animation that combined complex calculations from various satellite images with images and data provided by the Hurricane Hunters and NDBC buoys. The large screen on the wall behind him showed a GOES satellite image of the massive, swirling white cloud constantly rotating toward Florida from the southeastern Atlantic.

"As I mentioned, Emily has developed into a Category Five hurricane over the last few hours," Sanchez told them. "The center is still over the Atlantic. In about five hours, though, Emily will sweep across the Turks and Caicos Islands with full force. Emily will bring exceptionally heavy rains. It's our concern that this could result in major flooding and destruction."

Winter came at him again. "In only five hours' time?"

Sanchez scratched at his chest. "Well, look, this storm system is moving at wind speeds that are quite exceptional, so that's one reason why we have so little time. Typically, Atlantic hurricanes between the 20th and 30th parallels move about nine or ten miles per hour. But that's just a statistical average. We do see much higher speeds every now and then."

"Just get to the point," Winter pointed at the satellite image. "How fast is that hurricane coming at us?"

"Currently, Emily is approaching the U.S. coast at a speed of forty-six miles per hour."

Murmurs traveled around the room.

Winter furrowed her brow. "That's pretty goddamn fast."

Sanchez nodded. "Especially when you keep in mind that such speeds usually only occur when a hurricane is veering off, heading north for the central latitudes. And even up there they only reach such high speeds under certain circumstances, like when influenced by upper low pressure." He took a deep breath. "Forty-six miles per hour at these latitudes is not something we ever see. This hurricane, it's a goddamn Ferrari."

Winter shifted restlessly on her chair. "Continue, please."

"Let's take a look at the expected path over the next five days."

Sanchez pressed a button on the remote control in his hand. A satellite image appeared with Florida in the middle and a graphic resembling multicolored raindrops superimposed on it. The current position of the storm's center, with its extremely high wind speeds, was displayed in purple. Its likely path turned from red to yellow and then to dark and light green, each respective color signifying declining wind speeds. A layer of red blanketed nearly the entire eastern coast of Florida. More murmurs passed through the room.

Brandon spoke up. "Emily is certain to make landfall based on this scenario, is that correct?"

"It's unavoidable, I'm afraid. My team has prepared a second computer simulation that should give you a better idea." On the screen, the white swirling mass was replaced by a remarkably authentic rotating graphic—the animation of the hurricane swept over the Turks and Caicos, its edges traversing Cuba in the south and the Bahamas in the north, all while making directly for South Florida. Shortly before the Florida Keys, Sanchez stopped the simulation.

"The probability of Emily passing over the Keys is over 90 percent. Ladies and gentlemen, we're now facing the first Category Five hurricane to make landfall there since Irma in 2017. We need to prepare for the worst."

"What are the chances of the storm weakening beforehand?" Brandon asked.

"Practically zero."

"How much time do we have until landfall?" Winter said.

Sanchez took a deep breath. Here came the sensitive part. "If its speed remains the same, about thirteen hours."

Anxious murmurs spread down the rows of seats. Winter shot up. "Thirteen hours? How am I supposed to get seventy thousand residents off those islands in such a short time?" Her voice was cracking. "That means the first ridge of the storm could hit Key West just about any time. Not much you can do then."

The murmurs died out. It was deathly silent in the NHC media room. Everyone present knew that evacuating under such constraints was an impossible task. Amy Winter of FEMA had good reason to be concerned.

The veins on Winter's neck throbbed. "There will be repercussions, Sanchez," she said, giving him a withering glare, and left the room. Outside, she stopped and pulled out her phone.

Sanchez knew the procedure. Winter would first inform the mayors of all larger towns in the Keys, after that the fire departments, police, and military. Then came hospitals, schools, power utilities, and various governmental agencies.

Sanchez kept eyeing Winter out of the corner of his eye while he answered the journalists' questions. Her calls were brief. There was no explaining, just instructions. With the essential calls now made, the evacuation of the Keys would get underway according to plan. First, the residents of Key West and other southerly islands would be advised to leave their homes. The central islands were up next, a few hours later, then the northerly Upper Keys right after that. Sanchez could only hope the evacuations transpired in a peaceful and orderly manner. If residents all tried reaching the mainland at once, the roads would jam up instantly. The Overseas Highway would take the brunt of it since it was the only route connecting the Keys to the mainland, and all major island-to-island traffic traveled it. If a single car broke down or if there was an accident, everything would grind to a halt. Thousands of people would be exposed to Emily's wrath out in the open and unprotected, especially those unlucky enough to get caught on the Keys' miles-long bridges spanning the sea. It was a nightmare scenario that Sanchez preferred not to think about.

As Winter continued going down her call list, checking off her boxes, Sanchez stopped taking questions and headed back into the HSU.

Selma handed him the latest forecasts. As he scanned the data, he kept scratching at his chest, lost in thought. He poured himself a cup of coffee from the hotplate, took a sip, and frowned in disgust. Lukewarm. It made him wince to think of downing mugs of this swill to stay awake over the next forty-eight hours—the storm's most critical phase.

Brandon and Winter joined him. Winter put her phone away. "The most important contacts have been informed. The machinery is now in motion."

"Good. Coffee?"

"Black."

Brandon waved no thanks.

"It's going to be a long night," Sanchez said. "I'm assuming that you all will stay. I've already had them set up a sleeping area next door."

"My husband is just going to love that."

"Yeah, well, luckily it doesn't happen too often."

"Sanchez, do you have any idea what it feels like to constantly catch hell from all sides?" Winter stared off into the distance for a moment. "The decision to evacuate is no easy one to make. You know how many irate calls my office will get in the next few hours? Plenty of islanders think that abandoning their homes is taking it too far. Many stick around, to save what there is to save. Hard to believe, but I even get cussed out by mayors."

"You'd think people would finally have learned their lesson after Irma hit," Sanchez said, trying to maintain a conciliatory tone.

"The problem is the false alarms," Winter explained. "Ten thousand people leave their homes, make their way to the mainland, hunker down in overcrowded emergency shelters, and then ... nothing happens. Remember 2004 and 2005?"

Sanchez nodded. "I wasn't at this office yet, luckily."

"I was." Winter took another sip of her coffee and set the half-empty paper cup down. "We kept demanding that people leave their homes, yet nothing ever happened. Can you imagine how much flak I was taking from all sides?"

"And then Hurricane Wilma comes—and a sixteen-foot tidal wave along with it," Sanchez said.

"Exactly. Because of previous false alarms, only 10 percent of the Keys' population ended up leaving. Six people died, thousands of homes and cars destroyed. We had to set up accommodation containers."

"I do admit, you have a tougher job than the both of us." Sanchez put on a smile.

Winter's expression didn't change. "If you had done your job correctly, my job would not be so tough."

Sanchez's smile dropped.

"May I interrupt a second?" Selma asked. "You need to see this, Emilio."

Sanchez was happy to get called away. He spent the next half hour on the latest data and forgot his troubles with FEMA almost immediately. He now had far greater worries.

"Ladies and gentlemen, can I please have your attention?" he announced shortly thereafter at the top of his voice after they had all gathered in the media room again. The journalists' agitated conversations hushed at once. "We have some new information. Contrary to our initial assessments, which, I'd like to point out, were based on extremely vague data, we now know that Emily is not the usual Cape Verde–type hurricane. Instead, it's likely that we're dealing with a Bahama Buster. For the reporters in the room, that's a hurricane that intensifies over warm Gulf Stream waters. This may be one reason why it's traveling at such high speed. That doesn't explain it all, not in the least, but this fact does give us a slightly adjusted forecast for its direction." He turned to one of the GOES satellite images and tapped a finger on Miami. "Urban areas will not be spared. Landfall will first occur in the Keys. Then Emily will pass over Dade and Broward Counties, including Miami and Fort Lauderdale. From there Emily will work her way up the East Coast, and . . ." He hesitated. "Then, something extremely rare could happen. Hurricanes usually turn back toward the ocean as soon as they reach mainland. Not this one. Emily could head north, and pass over Orlando."

"Mickey and Minnie won't like that," Brandon LaHaye muttered.

Winter rubbed at her forehead as if fighting off another headache. "If your forecast is correct, Sanchez, we'll need to close Disney World and the other parks for at least two days."

"Report from Key West," Zachary Haffernan shouted from the back. "The storm's beginning to reach the islands. Parts of the coast and some streets are already flooded. Police are reporting minor accidents and traffic jams on the main roads."

Sanchez looked at Winter, and their eyes met. "Game on," he muttered.

33

Frankfurt, Germany

THE BOMBARDIER DHC-6 TOUCHED DOWN AT Frankfurt Airport and rumbled along the tarmac. Laura rubbed at her tear-stained face and eyes, impatiently waiting for her phone to reconnect to the network. She wondered when Robin's kidnapper would make contact again. Would he even try calling? Over two hours had passed since he had hung up. She bit at her lower lip until it hurt. Why did she call Bishop by his name? How could she have been so stupid?

Daniel sat next to her. He tried squeezing her hand for reassurance. She pulled it away and pointed toward the front. Agents Link and West were coming through the cabin to them. No one else was on board the roughly fifty-foot-long turbo-prop plane.

"Anything new?" Laura asked them immediately.

Agent West was carrying a dark leather briefcase. She sat on the armrest of the chair facing Laura. "I made a few calls during the flight, as I promised. There's no news about your son's whereabouts. We did learn, though, that a man pretending to be a doctor took Robin from his room. This person told the nurse on duty Robin needed a brief exam that couldn't wait. We're assuming this supposed doctor was Fred Bishop. We're currently going through surveillance camera video, which could tell us more."

The Bombardier kept jolting along toward its park position.

Laura looked Agent Link with an urgent expression. "I shouldn't have flown here. I should have gone to the police."

Agent Link shook his head. "Fred Bishop is not your usual criminal, Frau Wagner. The police wouldn't have been any help."

"I need to delete that voice memo on my computer. He demanded that I do it, that I—"

"Believe me," Agent Link said. "Bishop isn't interested in Hardenberg's voice memo. That's just an excuse. It's you that Bishop is after, Frau Wagner."

"But why?"

"We're going to find that out," he said.

"You have to trust us," Agent West said. "We're good at what we do."

"But this isn't just about me." Laura's feelings were threatening to overwhelm her, and her voice sounded harsher than she had intended. "This is about my son. His name is Robin!"

Agent West's expression softened a bit. "Believe me, we're doing everything in our power to help you."

Laura eyed them. "Yeah? How exactly is an environmental agency from the United States supposed to fix all this?"

Agent West looked to Agent Link for help. He slowly yet firmly shook his head. "Just be patient a little longer."

He turned around and went back to the cockpit. Agent West gave Laura an encouraging nod, then followed him back.

The Bombardier jerked to a stop. Laura checked her phone, saw five bars in the upper left corner—she had a connection. The only thing missing was Bishop making contact, and the thought of him possibly harming Robin tormented her.

The doors opened. A drizzle hit them as they exited the plane. There was still snow alongside the tarmac, but the sizeable puddles revealed that it had all started melting. A black van exactly like the one in Hanover was waiting at the edge of the tarmac, and they climbed in.

They passed hangars and according to a sign were heading for Cargo City South, the larger of the two shipping centers at Frankfurt Airport. After traveling between spacious warehouses and office buildings, they eventually halted in front of an inconspicuous door at the far end of one of the warehouses. *Aero Contractors* read a sign with fading letters. Agent Link got out and disappeared inside. He was back less than two minutes later. They continued on their way.

They exited Cargo City South through a gate and took a road leading into a stretch of woods until they reached a gravel lane that sent them even deeper into the forest. They rumbled along the uneven road, passing through deep puddles at a crawl, then came to a large clearing. Lining it was a barbed wire fence, and Laura peered inside the compound from her rain-covered window. She spotted two olive-drab U.S. military vehicles next to a low mound, where she thought she could make out a door. Her first thought: a bunker.

They stopped at a gate guarded by two soldiers wearing black armbands with white letters: *MP*.

"U.S. Military Police," Daniel whispered to her.

"Where are we?"

"Looks like a military site."

Agent Link gestured at one of the sentries, and the gate opened. Inside the fenced-off grounds, the roadway was paved again. As they drove up to the low and windowless block of concrete, Laura noticed the antennas and radar domes standing out on the snow-covered lawn. She thought it odd that an American military facility was operating just a few miles from Germany's biggest airport.

"What are the antennas for?" Daniel asked.

"No idea. You'll have to ask the tour guide," Agent Link told him.

They halted at the windowless block of concrete and climbed out. Agent Link directed his face at a monitor. A green laser scanned him, and the door opened.

Laura looked around. "What is this place?"

"You have set foot in the Egelsbach Transmitter Facility," Agent Link said without hesitating. "This post is under the command of U.S. ground forces Europe HQ in Wiesbaden."

"Why are we here?'

"That takes some explaining. But you'll find out in a few minutes. Please, follow me."

The four of them entered a hallway with an elevator at the end. Agent Link pressed a button, and the elevator opened. He took them three floors underground, to a brightly lit corridor with more corridors branching off at regular intervals. Surveillance cameras were mounted everywhere. Air vents appeared in the ceiling every twenty feet or so, pumping in fresh air. The facility seemed amazingly vast but also deserted. Laura wondered just how far this bunker maze stretched out below the fenced-off compound above.

Soon they entered a state-of-the-art conference room with a long table running down the middle surrounded by a dozen leather executive chairs. A headset lay on the table before every armchair, and in the center stood bottles of various beverages, coffee pots, glasses, and cups. In one corner of the room was a water cooler, and in the other stood the flag of the United States of America. The walls were covered with flatscreens, the back wall with a single massive screen. It was currently black but prominently displayed a round seal with a bald eagle head and a white shield bearing a compass rose on a blue background rimmed with gold. The words above the eagle sent a chill down Laura's spine: CENTRAL INTELLIGENCE AGENCY.

"National oceanic authorities, my ass," she whispered to Daniel. "What now?"

"They want something from us," he said. "Our Mr. Link will finally have to let the cat out of the bag."

Agent Link had gone over to the long table, and they followed.

They were expected.

A slender man in a perfectly fitting suit bounded up to them full of energy. His face shone as if freshly shaved, and his narrow slanting eyebrows looked recently plucked. He held out an impeccably manicured hand to Laura, and fragrant aftershave wafted their way.

"Special Agent Lance Deckard. Thank you for coming." His handshake was as firm as his gaze, his German nearly free of accent.

Daniel pointed at the CIA seal. "Have to admit, now I'm even more curious than before."

"You pledged your absolute secrecy," Special Agent Deckard told him. "I return you were promised an explanation, and you're going to receive one."

"I was also promised that you'd get my son back," Laura said.

Deckard nodded. "Which we will." He pointed at the conference table. "There's tea, coffee."

Laura and Daniel took a seat. Agents Fenton Link and Jennifer West sat across from them, and Deckard sat on the end.

"Let's get right to the point," Deckard said, checking his watch. "We belong to one of the lesser-known organizations inside the CIA. For the most part, we concern ourselves with the consequences of climate change to national security and whatever challenges that may result."

"The Climate Engineering Center," Daniel said with a knowing nod.

Deckard turned to Agent Link. "I told you he was our man."

Link stared back blankly.

Daniel leaned back in his chair. "Your organization isn't exactly a huge secret among us meteorologists."

"Because we make no secret of it," Deckard replied. "Then again, we're not exactly shouting it from the rooftops."

"Your group was officially disbanded in 2012. Why put out false information?"

"We had our reasons."

"Can someone please explain?" Laura said. "What exactly do you do, Agent Deckard?"

"We monitor, research, and analyze changes in climate across the globe," he explained, smoothing his tie flat. "Based on that, we develop various scenarios that could arise from such changes."

"Meaning what, exactly?"

"We ask ourselves, for example, what impact would increasingly pronounced droughts in the Middle East have on political stability in that region as well as any water and food shortages that may ensue." He gestured with his hands as he spoke. "What implications would any changes in a given power structure have for the United States? Which of our political allies might lose power, and would it be the right time for forming new alliances? Those are the kinds of issues we're facing."

"But not today," Daniel said.

"No. Not today."

Deckard's phone vibrated. "One second." He turned away and took the call.

Daniel bent toward Laura and whispered, "Just so you know what they're really about. The National Academy of Sciences, for instance, oversees studies in climate engineering having to do with technology and the effects of changing weather, climate. It's all financed by the CIA."

"How do you know such things?"

Daniel shrugged. "Leif."

"Of course."

"Climate researcher Alan Robock revealed a while back that he'd been contacted by the CIA. They wanted Robock to tell them if it was possible to know if, and how, a given country was manipulating and controlling the weather in a targeted manner."

"I thought those weather centers the Chinese have aren't a secret to anyone."

"This is about more than that." Daniel glanced over, making sure Deckard was still on the phone. "The CIA is obviously interested in lots more than climate change and how to fight it. They aim to expand their climate research into manipulating the weather for military applications. The other thing Robock revealed was that he had been asked if it was possible to deploy geo-engineering and weather manipulation against foreign governments." He gave her a stern look. "So we should be careful about what we tell Deckard."

"You're the expert. I'll gladly leave that to you."

Deckard ended his call. "Now, where were we?"

Daniel looked around the table. "Why did you contact me?"

Deckard took a folded page out of his pants pocket, fished reading glasses from inside his jacket and flipped them open with a deft flick of the wrist. He unfolded the page, and read: "Modern Methods for Impacting Weather in the Ionosphere Using Pulsed Electromagnetic Waves on the Lower Shortwave Spectrum."

He eyed Daniel from over the top of his glasses. "Sound familiar?"

Daniel's eyebrows contracted. "Where did you get that?"

"You once had an agency publish the ebook of your dissertation in the archives of the German National Library," Deckard replied. "Anyone who's interested can easily find your doctoral work on the Internet."

Daniel glared at Deckard, and Laura saw Daniel wringing his hands under the table. "So why would you be interested?" he said.

Deckard's phone buzzed again. He took the call.

Laura made the most of it. "You have a PhD?"

"No. My dissertation was rejected. I wanted to publish the work anyway because I think it's good."

"It was rejected?"

Daniel hesitated. "Yes."

"Why?"

He stared up at the ceiling as if memories from long ago were hovering there. "It's a long story . . ."

Deckard ended his call and cleared his throat. It didn't escape Laura that his timing was pretty convenient for Daniel, considering.

"That was Langley," Deckard told them. "The situation is escalating. The way it's looking, we have less time than we thought. I'm now going to tell you about certain events occurring off the East Coast of the United States. We welcome your expert opinion, Mr. Bender."

Daniel looked around cautiously. He pointed at a sign on the wall that read *MIC*. "Are you recording all this?"

"Not at the moment. Only when the sign's lit." Deckard stood up and went around the conference table. "A few hours ago, the head of the National Hurricane Center in Miami, Emilio Sanchez, reported an unusual incident about six hundred miles southeast of the U.S. coastline. Data buoys started acting crazy for no apparent reason, transmitting figures that made no sense. At first, NHC assumed a technical defect. But this was no defect."

He signaled to Agent Link, who swiped at a tablet on the table and the CIA symbol on the big screen faded to a satellite image showing a white swirling cloud mass over the northern Caribbean Sea. "Hurricane Emily formed in just a few hours, in an area where the weather pattern had been stable. It's currently moving at an exceptionally fast speed toward the eastern coast of Florida. At the moment, the NHC in Miami finds itself incapable of issuing an exact forecast for the storm's path, since the internal volatility of this storm system is apparently too high to deliver a dependable prediction."

Daniel peered at the screen. "You just say that this hurricane formed within a few hours?"

Deckard nodded. "That's not all. Emily appears to ignore basic laws of physics. Meteorologists worldwide are already having heated and divisive debates about its features. We've prepared an overview, Mr. Bender. It pulls together all the data and facts we find relevant."

Taking that as his cue, Agent Link pushed a folder across the table to Daniel. The blue cover had the CIA seal with the word *Confidential* underneath. Daniel stood without taking a look inside the folder. He stepped up to the big screen and considered the satellite image, his forehead wrinkling up. "Date and time correct?"

"Of course," Deckard said. "Why do you ask?'

Daniel ignored him. He asked for an animation of all still images coming from the GOES satellite over the previous forty-eight hours. He needed to see the hurricane come into being with his own eyes.

Deckard glanced at his watch. "Is that necessary?"

"Hard to say without seeing it."

"We're joining a video conference in ten minutes." Deckard pointed at the folder. "Till then, I suggest you get acquainted with the facts we compiled for you."

Agent Link looked up in surprise. "Ten minutes? I thought we still had two hours."

"Langley just told me about the change," Deckard said. "Events are happening too fast. We need to act. Now."

"What kind of video conference?" Daniel asked.

"A discussion among experts."

"What sort of experts?"

"Certain persons have deliberated your dissertation and its thesis in great detail, Mr. Bender." With his narrow eyes, Deckard resembled a raptor about to swoop down and snatch prey. "We didn't search for you all over Germany and bring you here just on a whim."

Daniel took a deep breath but didn't comment.

Laura had been left watching them the whole time and was increasingly feeling like a fifth wheel. But she wasn't naïve. There must be some good reason for her to be present in this room. She would find that out once it was the right time.

"Start the animation of the last forty-eight hours," Deckard ordered.

A GOES satellite image appeared on the big screen. It showed a cloudless sky over the western Atlantic as well as over the Caribbean Sea. Then the image changed. Clouds formed. At first they resembled delicate wisps of cotton candy passing over the sea, but then they drew together and consolidated into an impenetrable ball. Soon they could make out a cloud formation characteristic of a hurricane, complete with eye in the center. From its southeasterly position, the storm system began rotating with the clear aim of heading toward Florida. The animation stopped shortly before the storm reached the Florida Keys, then it began back at the beginning.

Daniel watched the endless loop a few times. He returned to his chair. He picked up the folder but didn't open it. "Agent Deckard, do you have any proof that this hurricane did not happen naturally?"

Deckard nodded, slowly.

Daniel gave Laura a telling glance, then turned back to Deckard. "I'm going to need to know more."

The CIA agent smoothed his tie again and pursed his lips. He seemed to be weighing whether he could trust Daniel or not.

"Three more minutes until we're patched into the conference," Agent Link told Deckard.

"You're completely correct in your assumption," Deckard admitted to Daniel. "Certain covertly acquired intelligence does give us reasonable suspicion that Emily was artificially created and, on top of that, is intentionally being controlled with the goal of destroying the East Coast of the U.S." He fixed his eyes on Daniel. "It's one of the scenarios that you yourself describe in your dissertation, Mr. Bender."

Laura stared at Deckard and then at Daniel, her mouth hanging open. She could hardly believe what she was hearing.

"I knew it," Daniel blurted. "It is possible." He gazed up at the ceiling. "You hear that, Leif? We were right, buddy."

"Who's responsible?" Laura asked.

"It's like I told you," Daniel said, turning to her. "There are loads of interested parties hoping to control the weather for their own ends. I should also add that I wasn't the first to consider the subject of waging war with weather control in a scholarly way. The U.S. Air Force commissioned a study back in 1996 that explored this exact kind of military application. It talks of ordering up thunderstorms as well as lightning strikes." Daniel turned back to Deckard and pointed at the satellite image. "They also had a scenario in that study where they put South American drug cartels out of business by using tropical storms."

Deckard propped his elbows on the table and placed his fingertips together. "That may be. But it was your very own dissertation, Mr. Bender, that gave everyone new food for thought. You weren't content just to put your theories on paper. You went so far as to describe the technological means for implementing your theories."

"*Imagined* technological means," Daniel told him. "I was simply providing purely hypothetical circumstances and calculations. Not to mention that the technological criteria for a project of this magnitude did not exist eight years ago."

"That has all changed, apparently."

"Thirty seconds until linkup," Agent Link announced.

Deckard sat up straight, adjusted his tie, and checked the part in his hair. "From here on out, speak only if I ask you a question. At this moment, the United States is being attacked in an act of war. We're facing billions in damages. The lives of thousands are in danger. In light of this situation, the people you'll be engaging with any second are not in the mood for jokes."

"Put on your headsets," Agent Link said.

And the sign reading *MIC* lit up.

34

THE REAR WALL OF THE CONFERENCE ROOM CAME TO
life, its ceiling-high screen separating into six square windows. Four
of them showed the faces of Caucasian men, a fifth a black woman,
and the last window remained dark. The lower edge of each image
showed each person's name and the organization they represented. All
the participants stared into their webcams with pinched expressions.
An older man with flabby cheeks, bushy eyebrows, and thin hair
looked familiar to Laura. She caught her breath as she read his name:
Carl S. Hudson.

"That's the Secretary of Defense," she whispered to Daniel.

Daniel noticed too. It made him gulp.

"The group is all here except for one participant," Deckard began.
He was speaking English now, but in her headset Laura heard the
crystal-clear German voice of a simultaneous interpreter. "Professor
De la Vega will give us his take just as soon as he's connected."

"Ramon De la Vega?" Daniel released a low whistle through his
teeth.

"You know him?"

"Not personally. He is *the* eminent authority in the field of
computerized weather simulation."

The deep voice of the Secretary of Defense filled the speakers. "Let's
get right to the point. Agent Deckard, what's the latest?"

"First," Deckard replied, "I should inform you that the President is
bestowing my agency with all authority necessary to solve our...problem."

"The U.S. military will support and give you whatever you need," a general named "Norman Williamson" informed the group. With his haircut of gray stubble and haggard expression, he looked exactly like Laura's idea of a general. She counted four stars on his shoulder insignia.

"It's extremely vital to national security that as little as possible gets mentioned publicly of the events as they occur." This came from a middle-aged man with angular features—his name was Evan Wilcox and the title under his name was Acting Director of Homeland Security. He sat behind a desk holding a can of Sprite. "The quicker we resolve this issue, the better."

"Your concerns are justified, as is the urgency," Deckard concurred. "That said, I'd first like to introduce the expert from Germany we've called in. Here with me is Daniel Bender, the author of the work on weather manipulation that you've all been given. We're assuming that substantial excerpts could have been used ... or, at least could have provided the inspiration for those now attacking us."

A tiny camera in the ceiling aimed on Daniel.

"So you're the one we have to thank for this," thundered Hudson.

Daniel gave Deckard a hesitant look.

"No one's trying to pin the blame on you," Deckard countered immediately. A thin smile curled his lips. "If that were the case, you wouldn't be sitting here at this table."

He turned back to the camera. "We believe that Mr. Bender can be of use to us. That's why I authorized him to participate here today."

"Who's the woman?" Wilcox asked.

"This is Laura Wagner. She is our connection to Andra. But more about that later."

Laura's eyes widened at Deckard. Why had he told them that? What sort of connection did he mean? Her stomach tightened. All at once, it became clear to her why Agent Fenton Link had tried so hard back in Hanover to convince her to come here—even after they learned of Robin's abduction. They sensed that there was more to her role. People like that didn't offer their help for nothing. But what did they want from her? Now she was the one wringing her hands nervously under the table.

Of her presence, Wilcox remarked, "That's your call, Agent Deckard, and your responsibility as well."

A brief discussion flared up over the jurisdictions of various agencies.

Laura stopped following their war of words and observed the fourth man of the group—Calvin Sutherfield of NASA. He had not said a word yet. He looked short and stocky, and his unruly brown bangs covered his forehead. The sole woman was named Ophelia Barnes. Her straightened, glossy black hair had strands colored cherry-red, and reading glasses were balanced on the tip of her nose. She represented the NOAA.

"Gentlemen!" General Williamson's forceful voice instantly silenced the group. "Let's stick to the vital issues at hand. Who is responsible for this hurricane? I have special units ready to go. All I need is a target."

Agent Deckard adjusted his tie and cleared his throat. "Six months ago, the CIA came into possession of several documents indicating that our country has become the target of a political faction that was previously unknown to us. There was concrete evidence of a terrorist attack planned to take place on November 22nd of this year."

"On Thanksgiving," Hudson said.

"Exactly. The most important holiday of the year after Christmas."

"So why are these sons of bitches hitting us now?" Hudson asked.

Deckard frowned. "It might be that the ones behind this feared that they would get caught before they could strike. But we can only speculate."

Hudson muttered something incomprehensible, then waved for Deckard to continue.

"We face a wholly new type of threat," Deckard said. "These people are deploying the latest methods of weather control. Maybe our German expert has something to add?"

Daniel looked up in surprise. "Uh, sure." He thought for a moment. "In the past, people have attempted to manipulate the ionosphere using a variety of methods. Injecting chemical vapors, using heat or charges of electromagnetic radiation or particle beams. All involved influencing the upper atmosphere, and some of them proved quite successful in experiments. These included vertical as well as indirect high-frequency heating, microwave heating, and magnetospheric manipulation. Also, pulsed radio waves."

"Can you put that into terms we understand?" Hudson grumbled.

"In short, you're heating up the ionosphere, usually for research purposes. The goal is to shape this layer of the atmosphere in a certain way, which isn't exactly simple because the character of the ionosphere is constantly changing. Your country, Mr. Hudson, took a leading role in all this years ago with HAARP in Alaska."

"This is all too abstract," the Secretary of Defense said. "Why is it being done? What do they expect to gain from this?"

"Perhaps you'd like to direct your question to General Williamson?" Daniel replied.

Hudson glared in annoyance, but to Laura's surprise he did turn to the surly-looking Williamson.

"Well, General?"

"A significant military application of this technology provides us with global communications between various units by way of extremely low-frequency radio waves," Williamson explained. "We achieve this by creating an artificial ionosphere in the form of a parabolic mirror. This puts us in a position to communicate with our submarines even during severe solar storms or other breakdowns in communications."

"You turn the ionosphere into a mirror?" Wilcox asked with interest, as he absently played with his Sprite can in his hand.

"We're talking about an area of a couple square miles. But, yes, apart from civilian research, this is the goal of facilities such as HAARP."

Deckard cut in. "Back to Emily. There are two crucial questions: one, who is responsible for this hurricane occurring; and, two, what was the technology used to create it? We are only able to take countermeasures once we know how Emily was created in the first place. Now, since Professor De la Vega has not been patched in yet, we'll go ahead and address the first point."

The monitors on the side walls displayed the black-and-white photo of a man, evidently Chinese. His age was tough to make out. Laura placed him in his early forties.

"This is Huang Zhen," Deckard said. "He's the suspected head of this operation. Zhen runs the secret police for the Chinese province of Anhui, which makes him directly subordinate to the Chinese Ministry of State Security. Not much is known about Zhen. He's the son of a former Chinese ambassador to Switzerland, where as a boy he spent several years in boarding school. Zhen is married and has two sons, both minors."

"Do we know anything about the motive?" Hudson asked.

"Not so far. Zhen is a Maoist of the old school," Deckard continued. "Over the years he's gathered a small, elite political faction around him that shares his ideals and aims. We're assuming that Zhen is acting on his own initiative, though he can rely on the backing of several high-ranking politicians in the Communist Party."

Hudson leaned forward. "Do you mean to say that the Chinese government has a hand in all this?"

"No, I don't. At least not at the highest levels."

"We'll need to get assurances of that," General Williamson said. "If we're facing a declaration of war on the part of the Chinese, however indirect, then we need to respond accordingly."

"Just hold on," countered Acting Director of Homeland Security Wilcox. "This is a highly sensitive foreign policy situation we're talking about here, so we can't just rush into anything."

Williamson turned red. "We're being attacked, and you're preaching *diplomacy*?"

"Before I act I prefer proof, not supposition."

"Proof?" Williamson shouted. "There is no proof! This is exactly what waging war with weather manipulation is all about. A country doesn't even notice that it's being attacked. Much less, by whom."

"There actually is proof," Deckard objected, "which is exactly why we should not go jumping to conclusions."

Wilcox offered, "Agent Deckard, you say that intelligence was leaked to your agency mentioning an attack being planned."

"That is correct."

"Where does this intel come from?"

Deckard exchanged a quick glance with Agent Link. "From a reliable source."

"Naturally." Wilcox's arrogant smirk revealed that he only had to make a call and the intelligence was his.

Deckard stood, went over to the water cooler, and filled a paper cup with water. "As I said, we're operating on the assumption that we're dealing with a political splinter group acting on its own. Possibly with support of certain sympathizers. Now, direct your attention to an important ally of Huang Zhen's."

The image of Zhen was replaced by that of an overweight Chinese man. Laura and Daniel exchanged glances. Thanks to Leif's Internet sleuthing, they already knew about him.

"We know for certain," Deckard continued, "that a certain Xian Wang-Mei, director of the Chinese State Weather Modification Office, is working closely with Zhen. The two are second cousins. In contrast to Zhen, we have a comprehensive dossier on Wang-Mei, which we provided to you beforehand."

"I don't have time for that," growled Secretary of Defense Hudson. "Please cut to the chase."

"Wang-Mei comes from a respected family, whose members all hold high office. He is married, which never stops him from squandering the family's fortune on cars, jewelry, and prostitutes. He gambles too much and supposedly has an alcohol problem." Deckard glimpsed at the dossier before him. "Two years ago, a little scandal arose involving Wang-Mei's addiction to gambling. He lost practically everything he owned. We're presuming that he was only able to keep his post with the help of his cousin, Zhen. According to our sources, his cousin made the whole thing go away."

"So this Wang-Mei might owe Zhen," Wilcox surmised. "That could explain his taking part in this."

"It's possible. Which now brings us to how they're financing it all."

Another photo appeared. Laura took a look at the pale, gaunt man wearing a tweed jacket and a checkered cravat. The ruler-straight part in his hair and haughty expression made him look younger than he probably was.

"Charles St. Adams, forty years old, English, descended from minor nobility," Deckard recited from a second dossier. "The accidental death of his parents nine years ago left him the sole heir to a considerable fortune."

"Enough to support Zhen?" Wilcox asked.

"More than enough. *Forbes* estimates St. Adams to be worth four hundred million pounds. We're still in the process of probing his intricate investment assets. One interesting thing, though, is his relationship with a woman some thirty years older: a Lady Marian Wilshire. Like St. Adams, she moves in the highest circles of English society."

Secretary Hudson scratched at an ear. "What's the connection between a filthy rich English nobleman and the head of the Chinese secret police?"

Deckard nodded. "Both of them, St. Adams and Zhen, spent several years together at the same elite boarding school in Switzerland."

"What do we know about St. Adams's motives?" asked Acting Director Wilcox. "Why would anyone back an extremist like this Zhen?"

"We're still in the dark about that."

"Find out," Wilcox told Deckard.

"We're working on it."

"We're running out of time."

"I am thoroughly aware of that." Deckard took another glance at the dossier. "We do have one clue. On May 13th, 2013, the Chinese sent a rocket into space from Xichang Space Center. Perhaps Mr. Sutherfield from NASA has something to contribute on that topic?"

Sutherfield still hadn't said a word. He nervously whisked his bangs from his forehead. "Well, in this one instance, we're looking at a ballistic flight over six thousand miles in altitude. The rocket then landed in the Indian Ocean. NASA recorded the launch of the rocket and tracked the flight course in coordination with the relevant agencies."

"Do we know anything about the goal of this mission?" Wilcox asked.

"China responded to our requests by calling it a failed satellite test, but we didn't believe that for a second. We looked at the complete path and duration of the flight and couldn't identify a single object that could have been sent into orbit."

"The military takes a different view," General Williamson countered. "It's our belief that the Chinese sent a new spy satellite into orbit."

Wilcox raised his eyebrows. "Yet NASA tracked nothing of the sort?"

"Our data is conclusive," protested Sutherfield from NASA. "No object was released into orbit."

"Gentlemen," intervened Deckard. "Before we start tearing each other apart, maybe we should first hear about the intel that was leaked to us. Agent Link?"

Agent Link cleared his throat. "Our source has evidence that the true goal on the part of the Chinese was to carry out their first active experiment in the ionosphere. During the flight, on-site measurements were taken for analyzing the vertical distribution of the surrounding space. For that purpose, an atomizer introduced two pounds of barium powder into the ionosphere at an altitude of about 125 miles. A Langmuir probe for taking measurements was also on board."

"What's all that supposed to mean?"

"The purpose of a probe like that," Sutherfield explained, "can be to determine the density and temperature of electrons as well as any potential plasma present."

"What were the Chinese after?" barked Hudson.

"We don't know for sure," Deckard said. "It's conceivable that they're taking a different approach to altering the ionosphere than the ones we've been monitoring. The main point is, this rocket was developed with the help of a company called Chenlong Industries. Behind the scenes, Zhen and St. Adams are the ones pulling the strings."

Laura caught her breath. Did Hardenberg know all this before he went in on the deal?

As if reading her thoughts, Deckard turned to her and said, "There's another connection to St. Adams—through the Germany company Andra. Andra developed the gyrotron, the prototype of a new series, as mentioned."

Deckard glanced at Laura before continuing: "The Diamond series represents a revolutionary new generation of gyrotron. We're talking about an entirely updated type of microwave oscillator, one capable of reaching an enormous output."

"What are these gyrotrons all about?" Wilcox asked, clearly oblivious.

Sutherfield spoke up. "Gyrotrons are very complicated and sensitive instruments, with a complex array of dozens of mirrors and special water-cooled windows made of synthetic diamond. They're used, for instance, at Wendelstein 7-X, a nuclear fusion facility in Germany operated by the Max Planck Institute of Plasma Physics. The aim is to generate energy by means of nuclear fusion, like the sun does. To give you a sense of what we're talking about: to achieve nuclear fusion, plasma must be heated to a hundred million degrees Celsius."

"A hundred million degrees?" Wilcox blurted in disbelief.

Sutherfield nodded. "Correct. It's not even that hot on the sun. But such temperatures are required in order to fuse hydrogen isotopes into helium. That's how we make the sun's energy technically feasible for us here on earth."

"What does any of this have to do with the Andra prototype?" Hudson asked, growing impatient.

"To reach these temperatures," Sutherfield told them, "Wendelstein 7-X actually deploys ten high-performance gyrotrons, which heat up the plasma using extremely strong microwave radiation. This heating phase only lasts anywhere from fifty to a hundred seconds. Which gives you a clue as to the power of a gyrotron."

"The gyrotrons at Wendelstein 7-X were developed and built by Andra," Deckard added. "They were the first gyrotrons to maintain that level of performance for a full half hour at a time. Diamond takes things much further by delivering substantially more performance and over a remarkably longer timeframe."

"I keep asking myself," Hudson snarled, "what any of this has to do with controlling the weather. This device hardly seems capable of making a hurricane appear all on its own."

Daniel spoke up. "Definitely not. Though Diamond could be a crucial component for doing so."

The Secretary of Defense stared at Daniel as if trying to remember just who this German guy was again. "To what extent?" he said finally.

"Well, the principle of a gyrotron is similar in certain ways to that of a microwave we all have at home. Only Diamond doesn't heat up your food for you. The device would vaporize a frozen meal from your freezer in a matter of seconds."

Hudson stared, his face blank. "Go on."

"My guess," Daniel said, "is that the Diamond gyrotron could heat up the ocean and make water vaporize. That's a critical requirement for the formation of a hurricane."

"I don't see that as possible," countered Sutherfield from NASA. "The gyrotron would have to be positioned right over the spot where the hurricane forms—over the middle of the Atlantic. And at not too great of a height, on top of that, so that the microwave radiation can have the most effect over such a large area. I can't imagine how that is supposed to work."

"Ask General Williamson," Daniel offered, "about the range of the U.S. Army's ADS weapons. The general can confirm that large distances don't pose a problem for those types of high-tech ray guns anymore."

Williamson cleared his throat. "Our Active Denial Systems do emit electromagnetic rays close to the speed of light. They can affect the uppermost layer of a person's skin from a distance of 550 yards."

"Five hundred and fifty yards," Sutherfield said. "Okay, that sounds plausible. The Diamond gyrotron would still have to be situated at a height of several miles in order to radiate such a large area and vaporize water at the same time—"

"One moment, please," interrupted Agent Link before looking to Deckard. "Professor De la Vega is now connected. Should I patch him in?"

Deckard spun around. "Of course. We've been expecting the good professor for hours." He adjusted his tie again. "Hopefully the professor's assessment and prognosis will provide us with a clearer picture of the situation."

"I've added him," Agent Link announced.

The only empty screen came to life. The bearded face of a tanned man with shoulder-length, salt-and-pepper hair appeared. He was probably around sixty but looked younger.

"Please excuse my tardiness," the professor said, "but I was waiting for the results of our latest simulation."

"In that case," Deckard said, "I suggest you bring us up to date on the situation, Professor."

"Of course." Professor De la Vega looked down and they heard the rustle of pages shuffling. "Using the latest data sent over by the NHC, my team and I have created a new intensity forecast for Emily as well as calculated the anticipated path. That is, at least according to how things look right this second."

"Define 'right this second,'" Deckard said.

"It's like it's jinxed. We've run all the data through the computer five times now, and every time we get a completely different result."

"How can that be?" Hudson asked.

De la Vega looked up from his papers and stared into the camera. "Let me start by restating what some of you may already know: we build IT-based hurricane forecasts using the HWRF model here at the Environmental Modeling Center in Camp Springs. Huge amounts of data are needed for us to process the kinds of complex calculations that we do." De la Vega looked baffled again. "Unfortunately, this hurricane contradicts all laws of math and meteorology. I'm sorry, but Emily is simply not something that can be predicted."

"Are you telling us," Wilcox said, "that your institute cannot provide us with a forecast of what's coming our way?"

"At the moment, we can't do much more than calculate a simple average from all our simulations. That only gives us a crudely probable scenario."

Wilcox said nothing. He took one last drink from his dented Sprite can instead, and his disparaging look made it clear what he thought of De la Vega and his work.

"The data is continually changing," De la Vega said defensively. "The NHC keeps sending us new inputs."

"We can only furnish data that's been transmitted by our satellites and data buoys," said Ophelia Barnes; it was the first time the director of NOAA had spoken. "I know the data. It really is disturbing. My people in Miami don't know what to think. Right this minute, another of our storm planes is approaching Emily. The data buoys that my boys drop inside the hurricane should provide us with more dependable data."

"I'm skeptical," said Daniel.

All eyes turned to him.

"That so? And why's that?" Ophelia Barnes asked.

"The readings are constantly changing because they do not conform to the rules of nature—because they are being manipulated." Daniel looked them all in the eye. "Emily is, by its very nature, *unpredictable*. That's the whole idea behind this type of weapon."

"But there must be something we can do," Hudson blurted in anger.

"There is definitely one thing." Daniel took a deep breath. "Evacuate as many people from the East Coast as you can. And do it fast."

35

The fan whirred above the crooked flap of the ceiling vent. It was the only sound Robin had heard for hours in the shabby little room. His head hurt, and he felt like he had a fever. He was still wearing the Spiderman pajamas his mom had brought to the hospital the day after the hailstorm. He sat at the head of the bed, his hands wrapped around his knees. The mattress was stained and sagging, and the blanket smelled like a damp cellar.

The bed was the only furniture in the room. No table, no chair, no closet. Nothing apart from a metal pail that Robin guessed he was supposed to use if he needed to go. The bare concrete floor was dusty, and the walls were covered with greenish spots. The door was locked. Robin knew that because he'd tried pushing and tugging on it right after he'd woken up, but it wouldn't budge. He wondered how long he could have been sleeping. The last thing he remembered was the sandwich they brought him for dinner at the hospital. He must have fallen deep asleep after that. Then someone had brought him here.

At least it wasn't cold. He wondered why the air was so warm in here, and yet the floor itself was cold. Who brought him here, and why? Did they abduct him to demand a ransom? Though his mother didn't like him to, he'd seen enough action films to know how these things worked. Or maybe they even meant to harm him? His eyes filled with tears. Where was his mom? He missed her really bad and swore to always be a good boy in future and to always listen to her, if only she would come very soon and get him out of here.

He licked at his raw lips and tried gathering saliva, but he couldn't. His tongue stuck to the roof of his mouth, which felt dry, as if someone had filled it with wood shavings. Still, he refused to touch the white porcelain pitcher on the floor next to the bed. The liquid inside did look like water, but it smelled funny—like iron. That wasn't drinking water, Robin was sure of it.

Suddenly the door cracked open.

It startled Robin. He had been so lost in thought that he had not heard the key turning in the lock. The door opened some more.

Outside, in the faintly lit hallway, a shadow moved. For one terrible moment, Robin was convinced that it was a shadow demon coming to get him. He slid all the way to the end of the bed and hugged his knees tighter. His heart raced.

The shadow demon entered the room and in the dim light transformed into a Chinese man walking stooped in a black velvet robe. At least Robin took him to be Chinese, since he had slanted eyes and a long, thin goatee. His white hair was braided and ran down his back. He held something in his hand.

He slowly approached Robin.

Robin pressed himself into the corner of the bed, as far back as he could.

36

In the conference room three floors below ground, everyone in the video conference kept their eyes glued on Daniel. His hands were out on the table, and he spoke quickly. "Hurricanes form at a water temperature of 79.7 degrees Fahrenheit. Water evaporates in huge quantities and then rises. Large clouds are created by the condensation. This condensation releases enormous amounts of energy. The rotational movement of the earth then causes the entire system to start rotating. There are two other requirements: You can't have any major vertical wind shear. If an upper wind blows in from another direction or is much stronger than the surface wind, then the emerging hurricane gets dispersed and can't develop. Also, every storm requires some kind of start mechanism."

Secretary of State Hudson pounded on his desk. "Get to the point. You're the expert. How in the hell did the Chinese create this hurricane?"

Daniel stroked at his chin nervously. "My guess is with a facility like HAARP, only with a much higher capacity. By bombarding the ionosphere with pulsed electromagnetic waves in a highly targeted way. This would create a massive low-pressure system over the Caribbean Sea. At the same time, it redirected the Jet Stream so that as few wind shears as possible appear."

"That explanation seems too simple to me," Professor De la Vega objected. "The amounts of energy that you'd require—"

"...would be enormous," Daniel elaborated for him. "That's correct. I'm not claiming that the Chinese were actually doing it this way. I'm only saying that it would be possible."

"How, exactly?" asked Acting Director of Homeland Security Wilcox.

"Well, to be able to create a low-pressure system, the facility we're talking about would need to be many times larger than HAARP and with significantly higher capacity."

Laura noticed that Deckard and Agent Link kept exchanging secretive glances. "So that's it?" Wilcox said with surprise. "Just a few more antennas?"

Daniel shook his head. "You'd still need one other crucial component."

"Which is?"

"As I said, large amounts of seawater would have to be heated and evaporated to give the hurricane its fuel."

"The Diamond gyrotron," Deckard blurted.

Daniel nodded. "The gyrotron heats up the surface of the ocean using extremely strong, targeted microwave radiation, which then causes the uppermost layer of water to evaporate." He looked at Laura now. "This would also explain some of the weather phenomena we've been seeing over the last few months. For example, in Eastern Russia and in Australia. Unusually high extreme temperatures have been recorded all over. Those could have been test runs."

"Let's assume your theory is correct," Hudson said. "How, in your opinion, could a hurricane be steered?"

Daniel had his answer ready. "In 2005, Ross N. Hoffmann looked at whether a complex storm system could be manipulated. Using Hurricane Iniki as an example, Hoffmann recreated the hurricane in an elaborate computer simulation and found that only slight changes were needed at the start of the hurricane forming for its expected path to be redirected into a previously defined target area."

"What sort of changes?" Deckard asked.

"Primarily higher temperatures, but also humidity at specific locations."

"So what does that tell us in concrete terms?"

"Simply put, you only need to heat the air slightly at specific, precisely calculated spots in the approaching storm system to divert a hurricane, which is precisely something that this latest gyrotron from Andra could achieve for you."

"But how is Huang Zhen doing it?" Wilcox asked the group. "How is that son of a bitch radiating specific parts of the earth's surface? Did he use a satellite to shoot the gyrotron into orbit near earth? Chenlong is capable of that, as we have learned."

"Not possible," Sutherfield from NASA told them. "For a satellite to maintain a constant position above a precisely defined point on earth, it must be brought into a geostationary orbit. That's roughly twenty-two thousand miles up, which is far too removed from the surface of the ocean for microwave radiation to have any such effect."

"True," Daniel told him. "What about low-flying satellites?"

Sutherfield gave him a slight smile. "Even those are about a hundred miles up."

"Still much too high," Daniel muttered.

Deckard's face lit up. "What if Chenlong could bring Diamond into the target area using an unmanned aircraft?"

"Like a drone?" General Williamson said.

Deckard gave Agent Link a signal, and photographed documents soon appeared on one of the wall monitors. "Fifteen months ago, a subsidiary of Chenlong named Shangdi Incorporated bought an MQ-4 Triton on the Asian black market. These documents show that the Triton was fully operational."

Wilcox brought his fist down on his desk, making his empty Sprite can wobble around. "Why am I only hearing about this now?"

"There was no reason to inform Homeland Security. At that point in time, there was no acute danger posed to the sovereign territory of the United States."

Laura could tell by looking at Wilcox that he wasn't convinced. He started to reply, but the Secretary of Defense beat him to it. "Why a drone?"

"The Triton is comparable to the Global Hawk," General Williamson explained, "but was specially developed for the Navy as part of a reconnaissance program. The Triton can bear loads up to three thousand pounds. So it could transport the gyrotron no problem—and would be able to fly at a desired altitude for up to forty hours at a time. If the Chinese have upgraded it, which I'm assuming they have, it could stay in the air for practically a week with the help of a refueling drone."

"The Triton also has a robust fuselage that can withstand hail and lightning strikes with no problem," Sutherfield added. "And its operator wouldn't have any trouble steering it, not even if it was flown directly into the hurricane."

Deckard nodded. "So let's assume that the gyrotron is now being used by a drone, likely at an altitude of seven to ten miles, somewhere above Emily in a radius of sixty miles tops from the eye of the hurricane."

"That's a large area," General Williamson growled. "I'll shoot out instructions for AWACS air surveillance to search the entire airspace above the western North Atlantic."

"We need to find the location of Zhen's control center," Deckard continued. "Once we gain control of the Triton, we can put an end to this nightmare. Do you agree with me on that, Mr. Bender?"

Daniel thought about it. "It would at least be possible for us to better influence the path of Emily that way."

"Goddamn slant-eyes," said Wilcox.

Agent Link spoke up. "This Charles St. Adams would know where the control center is. If our assumption is correct, he's where all the dots connect. We need to track him down at all costs."

"The search is already on for him," Deckard said.

For a while now Laura had had something to contribute. She bit uncertainly at her lip. She finally pulled herself together, sat up straight, and cleared her throat. "Even if you do find the control center," she said, "you are still going to need someone who's familiar with how the gyrotron is programmed."

"You mean, someone who's able to reprogram it," Deckard said.

Laura frowned. She didn't know who had programmed the Diamond software. Lars Windrup was a likely candidate, but it could have been one of a number of employees.

"Maybe, instead, you could save yourselves a ton of work," she said.

"How do you mean?" Deckard said.

Laura looked at them all, took a deep breath, then pulled the USB stick from her pants pocket and placed it on the table.

Deckard's eyebrows scrunched together. "What is that?"

"There's a virus on this stick that will immobilize the software."

Deckard sprang up. "Where did you get that?"

"Herr Hardenberg had the stick sent to me before he died."

Deckard grabbed the stick off the table.

"If you have any questions," Laura continued, "contact someone at Andra named Lars Windrup. I was supposed to give the stick to him."

Deckard exchanged yet another quick glance with Agent Link. He then announced to all of them, "We are aware of Lars Windrup. Windrup went by the pseudonym 'Rousseau' and actively engaged in chatroom discussions with Leif Gundarsson. A few weeks ago, while monitoring Gundarsson's activities on the Net, we were able to gain access to a hidden chatroom in the dark net. There Windrup drew Gundarsson's attention to, among other matters, Andra."

Wilcox couldn't help smirking. "So that's your reliable source. What was Windrup hoping to get out of all this?"

"That's what we were all asking ourselves," Deckard said. "Windrup is a loner, lives alone. He uses a second pseudonym for one of those blogs highly critical of the establishment and so forth, though it doesn't have the reach Leif Gundarsson had with his Viking blog. Windrup was involved in the development of the gyrotron from the beginning. He must have foreseen the dangers."

"I'm not sure if this originated with Windrup," Laura interjected. "I think it's more that Hardenberg had pressured Windrup into it—as a precautionary measure, since Hardenberg was increasingly having doubts about Chenlong."

"Either way," Deckard said, handing Agent Jennifer West the USB stick. "See what our people can do with this."

Agent West nodded and disappeared out the door.

Laura leaned over to Daniel and whispered, "So that means Windrup knew about November 22. He learned it from Hardenberg."

"Right," Daniel said. "Hardenberg probably got a message to him after coming back from Beijing. And Windrup, acting as Rousseau, then let Leif know."

"That could also explain why Rousseau has vanished from the face of the earth," Laura said. "Because he's scared."

Daniel nodded.

Sutherfield from NASA spoke up. "I hate to spoil the party, but the virus alone isn't going to help us very much. Communications between the Chinese base station and the drone have to run through a satellite. Our hands are tied if we don't know which satellite to contact. And even if we did reach the satellite from our command center, we'd still need its access code."

"Our expects can crack the code," Deckard told him.

"Don't be so sure," Sutherfield said, pushing his unruly bangs off his forehead again. "Satellites are extremely well protected against unauthorized access. Plus, we only have a very limited time frame in which we'd be able to transmit."

"Goddamn it," Deckard cursed. "We need to track down Zhen's location. We'll blow the whole facility sky high if we have to."

"In both cases, Charles St. Adams would be the key to solving our problem," Agent Link reminded the group. "He has the exact know-how, and he knows where Zhen is."

"Why don't we have access to this bastard?" Wilcox asked.

Deckard grimaced. "His trail went cold in Istanbul. If he has left Turkey, then it was on a false passport."

"If he's left the country by sea," Agent Link added, "he could be anywhere by now."

"So we don't have a single actionable lead?" thundered Wilcox.

Deckard shook his head.

Wilcox crushed his empty Sprite can. "Goddammit!"

Laura took a good look at the photo of the Englishman, which was still on one of the screens. She recalled something that Special Agent Deckard had said a few minutes earlier. It was a slight detail, and she'd given it little importance at the time, but it made some sense considering what they now knew. It had to do with that restaurant receipt totaling over 687 euros for two people that she'd found in Hardenberg's files. Hardenberg's calendar for that afternoon had been blocked out under the rubric "Personal Time." Yet a few weeks later he submitted a meal receipt for that very time. The bill was exorbitant, but Laura also recalled that Hardenberg wrote it down by hand, which he very rarely did. Six hundred and eighty seven euros, for a business meal for two, in a fashionable yacht club in Hamburg. She remembered more than just the bill, though—Hardenberg had also specified the name of the person dining with him. Her pulse raced.

She raised a hand for everyone's attention.

"Maybe I can help," she said, feeling all of their eyes on her. "I think I have an idea where this Charles St. Adams might be."

37

Off the Coast of Malta

CHARLES ST. ADAMS STOOD ON THE HIGHEST OF HIS yacht's four decks and gazed around the bay. *Lady Marian of the Sea* had been anchored here since the late morning, and the view was breathtaking despite the captain's faint praise for an anchorage he'd chosen from many such spots around the islands of Malta. Directly in front of them, the rocky coast plunged down to the shimmering dark blue sea as spectacular cliffs. Cresting waves glittered from the sun, practically blinding St. Adams. He put on his sunglasses and nipped at the Pimm's No. 1 and ginger ale the steward had mixed for him, the ice cubes clinking, the cocktail going down nicely. A little refreshment always did him good. Soon he would have to return to his air-conditioned suite one deck below. Before he did so, though, he hoped to get up to speed on the latest developments in the Emily matter. He pressed a remote control, and a flat screen lowered from the partially covered Skydeck.

"You're curious, aren't you?" said Lady Marian Wilshire. She was taking in the sun's rays out on the circular sunpad next to the Jacuzzi. The wrinkles and age spots covering her skin showed all the years she'd spent exposing herself to the sun, but that didn't bother St. Adams any more than their difference in age. Thirty years—what was thirty years to a man who viewed life as a brief interlude between two eternities?

"Of course I'm curious, my dear."

He'd tuned in at just the right time. On the BBC a starched presenter was interviewing an obese meteorologist for a special broadcast. The studio backdrop showed satellite images of the hurricane.

"...all this points to a storm that could develop into one of the most devastating hurricanes ever to hit the United States," the meteorologist stated to conclude his report.

"Thanks very much for your assessment, Professor Thornton." The presenter looked into the camera. "At this moment, Hurricane Emily is beginning to hit Key West, causing flooding and its first damage to buildings. Residents along the entire gulf coast of Florida and Georgia are preparing for the hurricane's arrival. Many are fleeing inland. Those attempting to defy the storm are stocking up on water and provisions and barricading their windows. The NHC in Miami calls it the biggest challenge in decades. Next, we'll have an interview with Amy Winter of the U.S. disaster management agency FEMA. She's raising serious allegations against the NHC and its head, Emilio Sanchez. Stay tuned for that—"

St. Adams turned off the television.

"Happy?" Lady Marian Wilshire asked him.

He smiled. "Emily looks first-rate."

"I'm impressed, Charles."

He sauntered up to her. "To be honest, I'd always had my doubts whether it would actually work as planned."

"I assume you never mentioned any such doubts to that Zhen fellow."

"How could I? Huang and I do enjoy a certain friendship, but his tolerance for failure is rather low." St. Adams thought of Xian Wang-Mei a moment—Huang Zhen would have chopped off his own cousin's head at the slightest mistake. Zhen's unpredictability was the main reason St. Adams returned to Europe as soon as Heilongjiang had started pulsing. If his calculations had proven false, and Operation Black Dragon had backfired because of it, it was far better for his health to put as much distance as possible between him and Huang Zhen.

On the sunpad, Lady Wilshire flipped onto her back, adding a blissful sigh. "Lovely, this."

"You like it here? The Mediterranean does not get any bluer."

"That may be so. Though Valletta used to be more chic, as I recall." She showed her face to the sun. "The town harbor stinks like the London docks."

"As if you've ever set foot on the docks, my dear."

She smiled. "I have many facets, Charles."

"Is that so?" He tipped his drink back and flung himself down next to her. "I'd certainly wish to learn more about some of those facets."

A small two-seat helicopter flew over them. St. Adams raised his head and watched it continue on until landing on a mega yacht anchored at the other side of the bay.

"Let's go below deck," he told her. "It's too hot in the sun."

"My dear Charles, you obviously have forgotten that I've been spending the last three months in London. I like the warmth. You'll just have to be patient."

The helicopter was coming back.

"It's like an airport around here," he muttered.

She snickered.

The helicopter was flying high enough. No one could see them on the sunpad from that height.

The helicopter had not flown past. It hovered high above the yacht now. St. Adams couldn't make out details in the sunlight, not even with sunglasses on. He had noticed one thing, though: the helicopter was far too large for a standard shipboard model.

He grabbed Marian's wrist and yanked at her hand as he jumped up. "We have to get below right now."

"What's wrong with you, Charles?"

The helicopter started its descent.

"No time to explain." He pulled her up and rushed them to the elevator. "We need to get into the panic room at once."

"Why do we need to... There's a panic room onboard?"

"Of course." He pounded on the elevator button, shooting glances at the helicopter. It was aiming right for the Skydeck. The turbine noise was deafening, as the wind from the rotors fluttered the solar sail violently and threatened to rip it away. Lines dropped from the helicopter's open sides. Helmeted men in black combat gear appeared, hooked onto the lines.

"Where's the fucking lift?" St. Adams hammered on the button.

The men above pushed off the chopper's landing skids and shot downward at alarming speed.

St. Adams cursed the elevator and pushed Lady Marian over to the spiral staircase leading below. They rushed down the narrow teakwood stairs. His darling fell as they reached the bottom, but he couldn't help that. He just needed to get to the panic room. His pursuers couldn't that know it existed—he had instructed the shipyard to leave the hidden chamber out of the official blueprints, so that one could only find it if one knew where to look.

"Stop where you are!" he heard from above.

The men stood at the top of the stairs aiming short-barreled machine guns. Lady Wilshire halted as ordered and raised her hands, her face filled with shock. St. Adams did regret not being able to help her.

He dove under part of the roof and out of the line of fire as bullets obliterated the teakwood in the exact spot where he'd just been standing. He crashed into a life preserver on the wall and sprinted down a long passageway.

St. Adams pushed open the door to his private quarters and ran for the section of paneling hiding the panic room. He tapped his foot on an inconspicuous bulge at the floor, and the invisible waist-high door silently slid open. He darted through the gap, crawled into the chamber and hammered on a red button inside. The steel-plated door slid shut without a sound.

He slumped against the wall. He was panting, and his heart was pumping. But he had made it. The soundproof room was designed for pirate attacks, and they would never find him in here. He could hold out for a whole week if he had to—maybe even ten days if he rationed his store of provisions and water.

He pulled off his drenched shirt, used it to wipe the sweat from his face, and tossed it into the corner.

"Don't move!"

St. Adams recoiled in shock.

The door had silently slid open. A commando masked in black stuck his upper body into the opening and aimed a pistol at him.

The blood drained from St. Adam's face. He stared at the intruder, speechless. How was this possible? No one but the yacht builder had known of this room, and he had died of a heart attack over a year ago.

Keeping the pistol trained on St. Adams, the commando crawled into the chamber and planted himself in front of him. He placed a large hand on St. Adams's shoulder and pushed him toward the door. "Out. Now."

St. Adams faced more masked men outside the panic room, and combat divers, their special suits still dripping. He counted seven weapons aiming at him.

He raised his chin. "I wish to speak to my lawyer."

The commando laughed from deep in his throat and brought his masked face within a couple of inches of St. Adams. "Where you're going, there aren't any lawyers."

38

THE SILENCE WAS DOING LAURA SOME GOOD. SHE HAD closed her eyes and was massaging her tight neck. The conference room was empty apart from herself, Daniel, and Agent Jennifer West, who was speaking on the phone off to the side with her voice lowered. The screens were dark now except for the main one, which kept showing Emily's eerie swirling mass as seen from space. Agent Lance Deckard had halted the video conference so that he could follow up on Laura's tip as to the whereabouts of Charles St. Adams.

"More coffee?" Daniel asked her.

She opened her eyes. He was waving a thermos in front of her face. "No, thanks. If I drink any more my eyes will pop out of my sockets like that General Williamson's."

He smiled. He sat with her. "Now can you please explain to me how you knew about that yacht? I mean, what gave you the idea? Not even the CIA knew of a yacht called *Lady Marian of the Sea*."

Laura shrugged. "I didn't know either. But when Deckard mentioned St. Adams together with a Lady Marian Wilshire while you all kept mentioning the sea, it made me think of boats, too, and it just clicked somehow. Back at Andra I had to go through Hardenberg's expenses, remember?"

He nodded.

"Hardenberg was expensing a bill from some sinfully expensive restaurant. He named the other diner as a 'Maria von der See,' but she did not show up in either Andra's database or in any of Hardenberg's other reports." Laura thought a moment. "A leopard can't change his spots—despite pocketing loads of kickbacks from the Chinese, he still felt that he had to expense his meals for meeting St. Adams at the yacht club. I was just guessing, a shot in the dark."

"A really good shot." Daniel gave her a weary smile.

"If Hardenberg didn't have such a skewed sense of humor, the CIA never would have stumbled onto that trust of St. Adams's in Panama held by Lady Wilshire."

"Definitely not as quickly," Daniel said.

Laura stood up and pressed at her lower back. "All my muscles ache from spending that night in a kayak."

"You're telling me. I'm totally tight."

She eyed Daniel a moment. "Why was your dissertation rejected, anyway? It's obvious you knew the topic inside and out."

He sighed. "I turned in my dissertation, and soon after that my doctoral supervisor distanced himself from me. I'm guessing that his fellow professors led him to do it, since they were all dismissing my thesis as the work of a crank—something I only found out later."

"Yet now here we are. All because you were right."

"Yeah, well . . ."

Right then Agent West ended her call and came over to them. "We're on to Bishop," she told them.

Laura stepped closer to her. "You have a solid lead?"

"We're currently pursuing several solid leads."

"Can you tell me anything about this man?"

"I'm sorry. That's highly confidential."

Laura pointed at the sign reading *MIC*. It had stopped glowing after they'd paused. "We're the only three in the room."

Agent West didn't reply.

"Please," Laura begged. "He has my son."

The agent sighed. "Wait here," she told Daniel. She placed a hand on Laura's shoulder and led her out of the conference room.

"Where are we going?"

Agent West gave her a tired smile. "I need a cigarette."

They took the elevator up in silence and stepped outside of the bunker. Dusk was falling. Clouds still filled the sky, but it had stopped raining, and the snow had melted down to individual white islands on the open ground, the sodden grass resembling marshland.

Agent West lit a cigarette and eagerly inhaled the smoke. "I'm going to tell you a couple things about Fred Bishop. If you ever tell anyone, even one word of it—"

Laura held up a hand to calm her.

Agent West nodded. "Fred Bishop was an NCO in Delta Force. He had a promising career ahead of him—before he stepped on a landmine in Afghanistan. This was in 2002. He lost his leg. He now wears a prosthesis."

"That's why he walked strangely. But he moves pretty fast on it."

"Modern prosthetics are marvels of technology." Agent West sucked on her cigarette, making it glow red. "After his incident, Bishop battled depression and post-traumatic stress disorder. Something happened during injury rehab, but no one knows what. At some point he fell off the radar."

The screech of an owl sounded in the nearby woods. Laura was shivering, and she wrapped her arms around herself. "When did he show up again?"

"I really can't talk about exact context. We do know that Bishop spent several months of 2005 in the Middle East, where he was trained in an Al-Qaeda camp."

Laura closed her eyes and tried to keep her tears in check. It was almost unbearable thinking of Robin being held by such a man.

"We're on to him. I told you," Agent West assured her.

"How close are you?"

"We're talking about a few hours before we can strike."

"My son might not have that much time."

"Bishop's psychological profile indicates that he wouldn't harm a child."

"Small comfort."

Agent West took one last drag of her cigarette, dropped the butt and ground it out with the heel of her shoe. She gave Laura a terse but understanding smile. "In situations such as these, small comfort is the best we have to offer." Then she pointed at the bunker entrance. "We need to get back downstairs."

Gradually, the screens returned to life. Secretary of Defense Hudson was the last one patched in, and the sign reading *MIC* lit up.

"We have St. Adams," Deckard told the group. "He's already on his way to us. We're looking at an ETA of about three hours."

"We're running out of time," said Acting Director of Homeland Security Wilcox. "What if the son of a bitch doesn't tell us anything?"

Hudson slapped at his desk. "We'll need another option."

"I once heard about a project called 'Storm Fury,'" Wilcox said, "though I can't remember the details—"

"Forget it," said Ophelia Barnes from NOAA, quick on the trigger. "Project Storm Fury was intended to weaken hurricanes. We tried it for years, sprayed loads of silver iodide deep inside hurricanes. Not one single hurricane got any weaker. So we halted the project."

Wilcox cursed and swept his empty Sprite can off his desk. "Sounds like only a miracle can save us now."

Deckard waved Agent West over to him and whispered something in her ear. She nodded and rushed out of the room. Deckard then cleared his throat. "We had an expert like Mr. Bender brought here for good reason." He turned to Daniel. "Tell us about your theory, please."

Daniel gave him a questioning stare. "You mean, my dissertation?"

"Yes."

Daniel thought a moment. "Well, in theory, you could try fighting Huang Zhen with his own weapons, but for that you'd need a facility such as HAARP in Alaska, yet with more power. Much more power."

"Go on," Deckard told him.

Daniel shrugged. "I would try using such a facility to create a massive high-pressure system off the East Coast. Emily might then turn away back toward the Atlantic. In the colder northern waters, Emily then ends up contracting back into a harmless storm."

"How in the world can you create a high-pressure system?" Professor De la Vega asked.

"By using the jet stream," Daniel replied. "With extremely strong, targeted radiation, you might be able to change its path. It might be our best shot, since jet streams play the most decisive role in distributing atmospheric pressure around earth."

De la Vega shook his head. "I doubt your theory would work in practice."

"We don't have the right kind of facility available anyway," Daniel said, sitting back in his chair, "so we won't ever get to find out."

Deckard nervously tapped his fingers on the conference table, staring at the satellite image.

Laura stared at each participant's helpless expression, both inside the room and on the screens. The veins on General Williamson's neck pulsed—he seemed to realize, despite the military might at his disposal, just how helpless he was against the strike about to hit his country.

Agent West entered the room. She stepped next to Deckard and whispered something into his ear. Laura overheard the words "top priority" and "clearance."

Deckard nodded, took a deep breath, pushed back his chair and slowly stood up. "You want a miracle, Director Wilcox?" He smoothed his tie and fixed his eyes on Daniel. "Then that's exactly what you're going to get."

39

ROBIN WOKE WITH A START. AT FIRST HE WASN'T SURE where he was, but then his eyes landed on the old Chinese man in the black robe standing at his bed and staring at him. Robin scrambled back to the far corner of his bed in panic.

How long was the Chinese man going to keep standing there staring at him? Robin was mad at himself. He was the one who'd fallen asleep. That was his mistake. He needed to stay awake.

The old man placed a tray next to the bed bearing white bread and a mug of water. The man had brought him the same thing yesterday. Robin wasn't about to touch it today either. Even though his head was still hurting and his lips quivered with fear, he pulled himself together and spoke to the Chinese man. "Please, I want my mom."

The Chinese man's expression didn't change.

Robin resigned himself to being left alone again, but right then the old man slid his wrinkly hand into a slit running down the side of his robe. Robin could see the old man's hand moving under the thin fabric. What was he doing there?

The Chinese man slowly pulled his hand back out. His gnarled fingers held a bar of chocolate.

The old man stretched out his hand and nodded with encouragement. Robin hesitated. Maybe it was a trap?

The old man nodded again at Robin, this time more forcefully. Robin cautiously shifted forward on the bed, snapped up the bar of chocolate and then scurried back into his corner.

The Chinese man smiled, almost imperceptibly. He placed a finger to his lips and watched Robin eagerly.

Understanding, Robin nodded. "I won't tell anyone."

The old man looked satisfied. He shuffled away and left the room.

Once Robin heard the door being locked from outside, he immediately devoted himself to the chocolate bar in his hand. He carefully opened the wrapper. His eyes lit up. He wasn't mistaken. The old Chinese man really had brought him chocolate.

His mouth watered. Maybe this man wasn't so evil, he thought, and started feeling something like hope as he bit off a piece of the chocolate and savored it. Never in his life had chocolate tasted so good to him.

40

LANCE DECKARD STRODE AROUND THE CONFERENCE table and stepped up to one of the few wall screens that was still blank. He gave Agent Link a signal, and a satellite image appeared. It showed a gray-brown rocky desert, the left side of the screen dotted with dark green spots.

"The desert of El Paso County, Colorado," Deckard explained. "On the left you can see the Cheyenne Mountains."

"NORAD is located in Colorado Springs," General Williamson said. "I'm really hoping, for your sake, Agent Deckard, that you aren't involving our main command center for air defense and early warning systems in a CIA operation without my knowledge."

"Wait for it . . ."

The picture gradually zoomed in closer to earth. The forested mountains at the edge of the screen receded, replaced by a large square gray field in the middle of the desert. Not far away, Laura could make out a smaller area with several buildings.

"Here we see Schriever Air Force Base, about ten miles from NORAD," Deckard told them. "As you know, General Williamson, Department of Defense satellites as well as worldwide GPS are monitored and controlled from there. Next door, the Air Force Space Battlelab develops and tests weapons for possible operations in space."

"I fail to see," Williamson said, "what any of this has to do with Emily."

Deckard raised a hand and started counting off fingers. "A secluded desert and available military infrastructure and, on top of that, seasoned experts with loads of know-how... What could be a better setting for establishing HAARP 2? Far away from curious onlookers."

"No way," Daniel whispered. He stared at the monitor, eyes wide.

"HAARP 2?" Wilcox said. "Why here? What about HAARP in Alaska?"

"Someone blew the facility sky high," Deckard explained to the group. "A few days ago. A soldier from Fort Wainwright, Private First Class Brad Ellison, lost his life. It was an unfortunate incident that didn't cause much real damage apart from PFC Ellison. That's because we, as I mentioned, now have HAARP 2—the logical extension of a great idea." Deckard gave Daniel a meaningful glance. "Now do you see, Mr. Bender, why we had to have you and you alone sitting here?"

"What's he talking about?" Laura asked.

Daniel shook his head in disbelief, almost as if in a daze. Laura looked back up at the satellite image zooming in. Black dots now started appearing at regular intervals inside the gray area. Bit by bit, they started taking the shape of antennas. Dozens of them. Hundreds. Thousands.

"How many antennas are there, anyway?" she asked softly.

"Fifty thousand," Daniel muttered without hesitation.

She looked at him in amazement. "Where did you get that figure?"

He kept shaking his head, very slowly. "This is pure madness. Fifty thousand antennas, plus another five areas holding ten thousand antennas each surrounding the main facility at a distance of about sixty miles, all of them connected together."

"How do you know all that?" she asked, dumbfounded.

Daniel kept staring at the monitor, his upper lip twitching. "Because I was the one who designed this facility."

The zoom stopped. The picture showed a single antenna with a strangely bent end resembling a large S. A helmeted technician holding a clipboard stood next to it, his shadow stretching far along the dusty desert floor. Judging from the man's size, Laura guessed the antenna's height to be about 70 feet.

Deckard returned to the conference table. "HAARP 2 consists of six fields of active phased array antennas. In the main field are fifty thousand crossed dipole antennas, and the other five fields along the perimeter hold ten thousand antennas each. HAARP 2 is by far the largest facility of its kind in the world."

"Why am I only now hearing about this?" blurted the Secretary of Defense.

"Primarily, Mr. Secretary, because this doesn't fall into your area of responsibility. There wasn't any reason to burden you with the knowledge until today."

"Two words: plausible deniability," added Agent Link.

"HAARP 2 replaces the facility in Alaska," Deckard continued. "The latter had been hopelessly outdated for some time, not to mention that it was receiving far too much attention from certain conspiracy theories."

"Leif among them," Laura muttered.

Daniel nodded.

"That's the only reason why we never dismantled those antennas in Alaska," Agent Link explained. "We wanted to divert attention from the construction of HAARP 2. The destruction of HAARP 1 was a pointless endeavor on the part of our enemies, and it only confirms that our strategy was correct."

Deckard planted his hands on his hips, clearly pleased with their gambit. "The main facility at HAARP 2 is capable of sending out pulsed radio waves on any part of the spectrum we choose. Every station can either measure returning radio signals with special receivers or, when necessary, couple them so as to amplify accordingly." He let the group ponder that a moment. "Without going into too much detail, HAARP 2 is a thousand times more powerful than its predecessor. I have just received clearance to put Mr. Bender's theory into practice. At full capacity, if necessary."

"So, have you ever used this facility?" asked Professor De la Vega.

"Where did you get the funds?" added Secretary Hudson. "Congress didn't approve this. I'd know."

Deckard again smoothed his tie. "The Institute for Climate Engineering has more than enough funds at its disposal for these types of projects. You don't need to know any more, and you wouldn't want to."

"With all due respect, Mr. Secretary," said Acting Director Wilcox, "the only question at the moment is whether HAARP 2 can help us. What's your take, Mr. Bender?"

All eyes turned to Daniel.

He didn't say anything for a long time. Then he turned to Lance Deckard and whispered, "You based this facility on my ideas."

"That's correct," Deckard told him without batting an eyelash.

"You stole my ideas, my plans!"

"Like I said, Mr. Bender—certain people have devoted themselves to your dissertation in great detail."

"But that's just—"

"Just what?" Deckard gave him a dismissive look. He turned away and strode back to his chair. "We have no room for error now. There's only time for one attempt. For that, I need each and every professional assessment I can get. And you, Mr. Bender, are now the intellectual father of HAARP 2." He looked at his watch. "Agent Link, get us a connection to Schriever Air Force Base and to Professor Ferenc."

Agent Link nodded. "Right away."

"Professor Ferenc is the Managing Director of HAARP 2," Deckard explained. "He's been briefed and is waiting on our command to start."

Laura placed a hand on Daniel's forearm. He was shaking.

"They have no idea what they're attempting," he whispered. "The principle of trying to redirect a storm system to specific parameters is like poking an elephant in the ass with a needle. He might just run off, sure. But he could always charge you first."

Laura was about to say something when she spotted Agent West coming her way. Enveloped in the odor of cold smoke, Agent West leaned down to her. "We have more on Fred Bishop."

Laura's heart skipped a beat. "What about Robin?"

"Not here. Come with me."

Laura sprang up and followed Agent West to the door. A thousand thoughts raced through her head, her legs seemed to lose strength with every step and threatened to buckle, and she couldn't tell from watching Agent West whether the news was good or bad. Before the door to the conference room closed after her, she heard Agent Link say, "We're connected to Professor Ferenc. Time to get started."

41

AGENT WEST LED LAURA DOWN A MAZE OF CORRIDORS and into a small and surprisingly messy office. One side of the room consisted of an open rolling cabinet with sloppy stacks of files and books. The decrepit, pale wooden desk was actually bowing under the weight of the files piled on top of it. There was a smell of yellowed papers. The fan of a PC whirred below the desk, and along the back wall stood a narrow cot.

"Close the door," Agent West said.

"What about Robin?"

"We have new information about Bishop's probable whereabouts."

Laura stepped closer. "Where is he? Is Robin with him? Is my son doing all right?"

Agent West held up a hand to calm her. "We need to confirm the tip first. It's from Charles St. Adams."

"St. Adams? How did you get that?"

"The man is smart enough to know when to make a deal. Bishop's whereabouts were just the start, tossing us a breadcrumb—signaling his goodwill, so to speak."

"So where is Bishop supposed to be?"

"On Alderney."

Laura's gaze betrayed no comprehension.

"A small island in the English Channel," Agent West told her. "St. Adams has an estate there that, like the *Lady Marian of the Sea,* is held in trust via a shell company in Panama. We weren't clued into it until now."

Laura's thoughts raced. This whole time she'd always assumed that Robin was in Germany, probably somewhere near Hanover. Knowing that he was so far away only added to her worries.

"St. Adams, by the way, shares our assessment that Robin is not in any direct danger from Bishop," Agent West continued after Laura fell silent. "The only thing driving Bishop is his hatred for the United States. The way he sees it, his own country denied him the recognition he deserved for his military service. He's an embittered patriot, not a psychopath."

Laura recalled how cold-bloodedly Bishop had broken Leif's neck. And even if Bishop wasn't supposed to be a typical psychopath—didn't men like him resort to any means possible when cornered? She let out a shaky sigh, asking herself yet again how she could possibly have gotten mixed up in all of this.

For a moment, the only sound was the whirring of the PC fan.

"Can you tell me why the CIA had Leif under surveillance?" she asked eventually.

"What makes you think we did?

"Come off it." Laura glared at Agent West. "When you stormed that boat shed? You and Agent Link thought you were going to find Leif there."

"Well, like Agent Deckard already said, we knew from our source that Leif Gundarsson and Daniel Bender had recently been acting on leads. The boat shed was a shot in the dark. We had no choice, what with time running out. We needed to find Daniel Bender at all costs and bring him here. You now know why that was."

Laura nodded. "But one thing I still don't understand is how Bishop knew that Hardenberg had given me that USB stick with the virus on it. Bishop showed up at Andra just a few hours later. How is that possible?"

"We can only speculate. We discovered a log note on the Andra intranet left by a man named Marc Bauer from the IT department. This Bauer person reported that you came to see him and asked him to upload suspicious files without authorization, ones that had to do with the Diamond gyrotron software. We're guessing that the Chinese intercepted that note and put two and two together. We do know that Chenlong had access to your intranet."

Laura thought a moment. "Bauer was wary. That's true. I'm guessing he wanted to cover his bases so that no one could try and blame him later."

Agent West observed Laura for a moment. Then she said, "You look tired," and for once her sandpaper voice almost sounded gentle. "You should get some rest. Nothing is likely to happen over the next few hours. You can stay here." She pointed at the narrow cot. "I'll wake you if anything happens."

"How am I supposed to sleep now?"

"I think sooner or later you're going to collapse. You're not helping your son that way. Trust me."

Laura stood there frozen, unable to decide. She didn't want to sleep now. She didn't want to miss the moment that the news about Bishop and Robin came in, not for anything in the world. But Agent West was right. Having some kind of breakdown wasn't going to help her or Robin any. "All right. But, please, promise me one thing . . ."

"What's that?"

Laura looked straight into Agent West's eyes. "I want to be there when you catch Bishop."

"Impossible."

"You were able to track down St. Adams thanks to me," Laura reminded her. "Plus, I gave you the virus for the Diamond gyrotron. Please, do me this one favor."

Agent West hesitated a moment. Then she said, "Do you know what you are asking of me?"

Laura stared, her expression unchanging.

Eventually, Agent West turned to go. "I'll see what I can do."

42

BESIDE HIMSELF WITH RAGE, HUANG ZHEN STORMED into the control room of the Heilongjiang facility. Two hapless-looking engineers huddling over a clipboard jumped out of the way in fright and bowed in awe as Zhen, taking no notice of them, bounded over to his cousin. Xian Wang-Mei sat on the supervisor's platform above the control panels wearing a headset. He was immersed in an animated debate with a scrawny scientist who kept tapping on a tablet with a pen. Seeing Zhen approaching, Wang-Mei sent the scientist away.

"How do you explain this?" Zhen snarled at him before he was even halfway there. He pointed at the main monitor. It showed the Black Dragon heading back into the Atlantic.

All conversation in the control room died.

"We're analyzing possible factors that might have led to this," Wang-Mei said. "Our systems are working flawlessly, Diamond among them."

Zhen stepped onto the platform and glared down at Wang-Mei, whose full girth barely fit between the chair's armrests. "You're the head of this operation. What do you intend to do?"

Wang-Mei's beady eyes twitched behind his metal-rim glasses. "It deeply pains me to deliver the message to you, honorable cousin, but I'm starting to wonder whether we still have sole control of the Black Dragon."

"What is that supposed to mean?"

"Everything points to an outside actor."

"Go on."

"Our satellites are reading unusual electromagnetic activity over the southwestern United States," Wang-Mei explained. "It almost looks as if the Americans are fighting back with our very same weapon."

"They're pulsing too?"

"Everything points to it."

"We sent Bishop to Alaska to avoid just that. Did we miss something?" Zhen stroked his mustache with thumb and forefinger, now deep in thought. "Is it conceivable that these fiends are operating a second facility that we did not know about?"

"That is the most probable explanation." Wang-Mei pulled a handkerchief from his pants pocket and dabbed at the thin film of sweat on his forehead.

Zhen slammed his fist on Wang-Mei's desk. A spoon jumped from an empty tea cup next to the keyboard and rattled away. "Why didn't we know about this?"

"Apparently, your good friend Charles had no idea either," Wang-Mei said in his defense.

Zhen did not reply. He looked into the face of every scientist and engineer in the room, each of whom quickly lowered their head as soon as his eyes found them. He knew they were waiting for his instructions. But the situation was tricky. They had not been able to reach Charles for several hours, and he knew more about the technology behind Heilongjiang than anybody. Zhen could only speculate as to why he had not been in contact. It was decidedly not out of negligence. His old friend had been an ardent champion of this project and would surely have watched events transpire from wherever he was. And he would have attempted contact a long time ago under normal circumstances—Zhen was convinced of it. Which could only mean one thing: someone was preventing Charles from making contact. Zhen could not fathom how the tables had turned so quickly, so unexpectedly. Yet he still had an ace up his sleeve.

"We're currently pulsing at what capacity?" he asked.

Wang-Mei glanced at his display. "Heilongjiang capacity remains at a steady 80 percent."

"We're going to 100 percent."

"Full capacity?" The color drained from Wang-Mei's plump face. "Honorable cousin, we've never tested that. We can't predict what effect it will—"

"Increase to 100 percent!" Zhen barked. Spit flew from his mouth, landing on Wang-Mei's glasses.

Wang-Mei's plump lips quivered. "As you wish . . ."

"The Americans will soon learn what it means to stand in the way of the Black Dragon," Zhen hissed, and a chilling smile stretched across his face. "For he who blows at fire is sure to get sparks in his eyes."

43

THE WAITING ROOM IN THE BUNKER DEEP UNDERNEATH the Egelsbach Transmitter Facility was modeled after an airport lounge: club chairs of imitation brown leather, glass coffee tables, a counter with glasses waiting upside down and a bowl full of crackers. A stocked fridge hummed away behind the counter, while surprisingly true-to-life artificial plants in the corners provided a homey touch. Laura sat cross-legged in one of the club chairs and watched the men in suits celebrating in the opposite corner. They were standing around the counter cracking jokes, laughing and toasting their success. No alcohol flowed down here, though, so it was all soft drinks and water instead of champagne. The agents were in such high spirits because they had just defeated "that Chinese bitch," as one of the men put it.

About an hour earlier, Emily had actually changed course and had been turning back ever since, back out over the Atlantic, away from Key West, away from the coast of Florida. Everyone had been in a festive mood ever since. Everyone but Laura.

She stood up and left the room. She couldn't stand all the jokes and big talk any longer. There was still no news about Robin even though she knew that he must now be in more danger than ever. As soon as Bishop learned the operation wasn't proceeding according to plan, he would start asking questions. Her only hope was that he didn't arrive at certain answers.

Daniel, Jennifer West, and Lance Deckard were coming down the hallway toward her.

"Laura!" Daniel ran up to her beaming. "We did it."

"I heard."

"Our plan is working." His eyes sparkled. "We were able to create strong enough high pressure over Florida to push Emily back out over the Atlantic. The whole storm system turned away and moved north along the jet stream."

"Emily will start breaking up out there," added Deckard, clearly relieved. "A few minutes ago, the NHC in Miami confirmed the latest developments. Apart from some minor damages to the Keys, we saved our skins once again."

"That's great." She tried a smile. But the thought of Robin nearly brought tears to her eyes. She felt guilty. She knew he trusted her, that he was putting all his hope in her. And what was she doing? Sitting around here watching strangers party.

"We will find Robin," Deckard said, reading her thoughts. "Nothing is going to happen to him."

Laura ignored him. She was trying to make eye contact with Agent West. But Agent West was avoiding her.

Deckard patted Daniel on the shoulder as if he were a long-lost pal of his. Then he and Agent West entered the waiting room, where loud cheers rang out.

"This means your idea worked," Laura said.

Daniel shrugged. "It could just as well have turned out differently."

"'An elephant with a needle.' Right? You poked the elephant, and it took off. It didn't charge at you."

"There was a fifty-fifty chance."

It was just them here now. They fell silent a while.

"What happens next?" Laura said eventually.

"No idea. I'm guessing we wait and see if Emily sticks to its new path."

Laura looked around. "Where is Agent Link?"

"I haven't seen him since after you gave Deckard that flash drive."

"Where did he go?"

"No clue."

Laura sighed. She noticed that her barrette had gotten all crooked. She unclamped it, pushed her hair back, and fastened it in place again. Then she pointed at the elevator door at the end of the hallway. "Want to come with me?"

"Where to?"

"I have to get out of here."

44

EMILIO SANCHEZ SAT AT HIS DESK, RUBBING AT HIS RED eyes. His long night and trying day were now behind him, and gentle sunshine was finally streaming through the small windows of his office. The storm clouds that had just chased away Emily were moving along with the hurricane off into the North Atlantic. Sanchez reached for the paper cup in front of him, staring into the black brew that had gone cold hours earlier. They'd ridden it out. They'd been spared complete mayhem. Apart from a few traffic pileups, no significant destruction or injuries had occurred. The Keys of course had some flooded streets and homes as well as temporary power outages, but no major damage was being reported. It could have been so much worse.

All around Sanchez, staffers were getting ready to leave, packing up their stuff and clearing their desks of empty plates, bottles, and crumpled candy wrappers. Two cots serving as temporary beds were being dismantled. No one spoke more than necessary.

Everyone was relieved, but without sleep no one had the energy for talking big or cracking the usual jokes. The creases around Brandon LaHaye's mouth and nose had dug in a little deeper, and Selma Cooper's eyes sported dark rings. Sanchez couldn't wait to get back home and fall into bed.

Amy Winter approached him. Her eyes looked tired as well. Her hair was coming undone, and strands of it hung in her face. "Well, that's it. Looks like Emily won't get any closer to the East Coast."

"From your lips to God's ears," said Sanchez, rapping his desktop. "This hurricane was different. It was not predictable."

"That's not what I want to hear from you. It's your job to predict hurricanes."

"You're accusing the NHC of failing," he told her. "You think we were sleeping on the job and discovered Emily too late."

"Do we need to keep arguing this? The investigation will show which of us is right."

"Sure."

"It is clear to you, Sanchez, that you were more lucky than smart on this one?"

He yawned. "Let's bury the hatchet, all right? At least until the assessment is completed."

"You have my number if you need me." Winter shouldered her handbag and marched off.

Sanchez glared at her leaving. If he ever did try calling that fire-breathing dragon, he'd only get his fingers burned. The only time he'd be needing her was when the next hurricane was heading their way, and not a second sooner.

Selma came up to him carrying a backpack. "I'm just *done*. I'll see you tomorrow."

"You held up well," Sanchez said, mustering a smile.

"It's not like I had a choice."

"True. But now it's the late shift's turn for once. That is until we—"

A harsh tone blared, a familiar alarm that they had all grown to loathe.

Sanchez let out a groan. "What is it now?"

Selma scowled. "Another buoy?"

"Could someone turn off that goddamn alarm?" Sanchez bellowed across the room.

"Uh, boss . . ." Zachary Haffernan was huddled around his monitor at the other end of the HSU. He turned and looked to Sanchez, his face ashen.

"Fuck, not again!" Sanchez abruptly stood up, knocking his chair back, and stomped across the room. One look at the satellite image on Haffernan's monitor told him why the alarm had gone off—an arrow symbol in the Atlantic was blinking red: NDBC Buoy 41002 South Hatteras.

Haffernan nodded. "That buoy is not far from the center of Emily."

"And it's gone out completely?"

"If only." Haffernan directed Sanchez to the data under the satellite image. "Atmospheric pressure decrease over the last hour, down 41 millibars to 856. Average wind speed, 197 miles an hour over the course of at least one minute, with gusts of up to 255 miles an hour at peak."

"Impossible," Sanchez said. "No measurements like that have ever been recorded from a hurricane. Not even close. That buoy must be faulty."

Selma, who had followed him over, placed her backpack on a chair. "What's the current speed of the storm?"

"We're registering strong upper low-pressure zones," Haffernan told her. "Emily is gaining speed. Right now that beast is tearing across the ocean at 65 miles an hour."

"Do we have any other buoys in the area?"

"Not right there, but 41424 East Charleston is in its path. One sec, I'll check the figures."

Sanchez was awash in conflicting emotions. He was only just telling Amy Winter how different this hurricane had behaved from all the other tropical storms he'd ever analyzed in his career with the NHC. Now the realization hit him that Emily had even more nasty surprises in store for him and his team.

"414424 East Charleston also reporting a rapid drop in atmospheric pressure, now at 870 millibars," Haffernan told them. "Average wind speed 180 miles an hour, gusts peaking at 231."

"That can't be." Sanchez shook his head. "The center is much too far away to make this buoy produce anything even close to those figures."

"Hold on." Selma found the nearest empty seat and slid closer to the monitor. "Let's assume for the moment that the data is correct. At first we thought those other buoys had been faulty too. But we were wrong. So, what's the next step?"

Sanchez felt the blood draining from his head. He had to sit down.

"What's the matter?"

"I'm fine."

Selma pointed at the monitor. "Look! 41424 East Charleston just went out too. Last data transmitted—gusts of 263 miles per hour!"

Sanchez took a look at the latest GOES satellite image just then appearing on the main monitor. "Contrary to everything we know to be true, Emily is now gaining energy and mass. The whole storm system won't stop growing. No need to check the data. Jesus, you can see it with your naked eye."

Haffernan nodded. "The Hurricane Hunters are confirming exactly that. Flight crew is reporting they've never experienced such heavy turbulence in the eyewall."

"When's the next mission?"

"The plane's currently being serviced and fueled. The next flight leaves Biloxi in three hours."

Sanchez glanced at his watch. "That works. Contact the Hunters. They should redirect to MacDill Air Force Base in Tampa and wait for me there. I'm on my way. I'll be flying with them."

Haffernan looked at him with surprise a moment before picking up the phone.

Selma took Sanchez to the side and lowered her voice. "Listen. I really can understand that you want to see this monster of a storm with your own eyes, Emilio. But you need to remain here. If Amy Winter finds out that you're up there getting your thrills at such a critical moment, you'll lose your job."

"'Thrills'? This is about the farthest thing from getting my thrills."

"You know what I mean."

"Let me worry about Winter. Go on home now. You need some sleep."

"You're making a huge mistake." Selma gave him an angry glance, hauled her pack onto a shoulder, and stomped out of the office.

Sanchez watched her leave. Selma was as smart as she was attractive. Of course he shouldn't be leaving the NHC at a time like this. It probably would cost him his job. Yet that deep unease brewing inside him gave him no choice. He fixed his gaze back on the spiraling white vortex cloud, its dimensions dwarfing anything he had ever seen. He couldn't deny being fascinated. Over the last forty-eight hours, many theories and schools of thought about tropical storm systems had proved inadequate, and that thing moving out there in the Atlantic could not be explained with conventional methods and analyses. Of course he was intrigued. He secretly admired the unrelenting power of this monster and needed to witness it with his own eyes. A chance like this would not come again.

"The Hunters have confirmed you for the next flight," Haffernan told him.

"Good." Sanchez scanned the latest data once more. The figures blew the doors off any readings ever taken. Two days ago, he would have laughed out loud at someone telling him measurements like this were being recorded on earth. So he made a decision. "Before I head out, let's put out a new announcement."

Haffernan grabbed his notepad and a pen. "I'm listening."

"Emily is the first hurricane to clearly and continuously surpass Category Five on the Saffir-Simpson Scale. It's now a Category Six."

Haffernan stopped writing. "Come again?"

"Don't look so stunned. I know there's officially no Category Six." Sanchez tossed his printout of the latest data across the desk to Haffernan. "The reason it doesn't exist is because we never could have imagined a storm developing this much power, not on the face of this earth."

"That may be, but—"

"They were already looking at expanding the scale back at the end of 2013 after Super Typhoon Haiyan hit," Sanchez told him. "Haffernan, look, with climates continuing to warm up on earth, El Niño style events are going to influence weather systems more and more often. That means hurricanes will be fed more and more thermal energy. In fifteen to twenty years? Hurricanes could grow even stronger, wreaking even more destruction than Irma in 2017 or Emily today. By then no one's going to question a sixth category. It'll be the norm."

"We still have a few years before that," Haffernan said.

"Just make the goddamn announcement." Sanchez turned without adding another word, grabbed his car keys off his desk, and left the building. In Tampa, a good four hours away, the Hurricane Hunters would be waiting for him. And out there in the Atlantic, five hundred miles off the East Coast, Emily was waiting, the first Category Six hurricane in the history of meteorology.

45

IT WAS WELL PAST MIDNIGHT. THE EVENING'S THICK blanket of clouds had dispersed, and the moon shined brightly. The nighttime ban on flights out of Frankfurt Airport provided something like peaceful silence out on the secluded grounds of the Egelsbach Transmitter Facility. It was cool out, with the smell of damp grass. Laura hugged herself for warmth and felt grateful for the down vest one of the bunker guards had given her as she and Daniel strolled the open field in the middle of the fenced-off compound. The ground was slushy. She gave Daniel a lot of credit for coming up here with her instead of huddling in front of all those screens several stories underground. He had to be dying to know what the hurricane was doing now. They'd exchanged only a few trivial words the last half hour, keeping well clear of the topic of Robin and Bishop.

She tilted her head back and breathed in fresh air—a real blessing after the recycled and temperature-controlled ventilation down in the bunker. Suddenly Daniel nudged her. He pointed toward the bunker entrance. An open jeep was coming from across the field with its headlights on.

"Something must have happened," he said.

All of a sudden Laura's legs felt heavy as lead. She thought of Robin, and her mouth went dry.

The driver of the jeep raced right up and stopped a few feet from them, the tires sliding on the wet grass and leaving ruts. A young CIA agent leaned out of the side. "Deckard needs to see both of you. It's urgent."

"Bad news," Lance Deckard told them back down in the conference room. Agent West stood next to him, her expression tense. Agent Link was still nowhere to be seen.

"What has happened?" Laura said as they entered.

Deckard gave them a grave look. "Emily is back."

Daniel's eyebrows contracted. "How could that happen?"

"Something's not right. We've been pulsing nonstop, and even so... I just don't understand."

They stepped in front of the main monitor and watched the satellite image of the hurricane.

"This image is up to date?" Daniel asked.

"Came in eight minutes ago."

Daniel stared at the white vortex cloud. "My God. Emily is growing again. I've never seen such a gigantic storm system. Its diameter must be over six hundred miles by now."

"There's more." Deckard picked up a tablet and ran a finger over the screen, causing a red line to travel across the satellite image. "This represents the most up-to-date projected path of Emily. Professor De la Vega calculated it a few minutes ago."

Daniel gasped. "You can't be serious."

"We couldn't believe it at first either, but here we are. Emily is racing on a direct course for the East Coast. And fast, too. Really goddamn fast."

Daniel traced a finger along the red line until it reached Emily's probable landfall according to the latest calculations. He drew a loud breath. "New York?"

"Judging from Emily's full diameter," Deckard told him, "the metro areas of both New York and Philadelphia are lying right in its path. Further south, Baltimore and the Washington, D.C., area will take a big hit as well. We're talking about an area affecting more than thirty million Americans."

Goosebumps ran down Laura's arms. No one had expected this. An even greater catastrophe followed their supposed triumph over Emily. Those agents in the waiting room had all been cheering too soon.

"What do you think?" Deckard asked Daniel. "HAARP 2 is still pulsing away nonstop, still trying to push Emily back into the Atlantic. Any idea what else we could be doing?"

Daniel went over to the water cooler and filled up a cup. "Maybe," he said, "that's exactly the problem."

"I'm not following you."

"Well, HAARP 2 is pulsing, and the Chinese are pulsing, and the Diamond gyrotron on top of that, presumably still working away to heat up the ocean's surface . . ." He drank a sip and looked at each of them, shaking his head. "It's all too much. Far too much. We're manipulating the forces of nature without fully understanding them. Maybe we need to give nature time to regulate itself." He went over to the table and sat down.

"That's your suggestion?" Deckard stepped over to him and pressed his hands to the tabletop, his tie swinging. "Just switch off HAARP 2 and *wait for the whole thing to regulate itself?* Allow the destruction of several major cities and the deaths of possibly thousands of Americans? Is that really what you're suggesting?"

Daniel pursed his lips, then took a deep breath. "All I'm saying is, we might be making things even worse by continuing to pulse. We are now seeing the result of where all this escalation can lead."

"It's pure speculation," Deckard said.

Daniel pointed at the main monitor. "Does that look like pure speculation?"

"You know what *I* see?" Deckard raised his voice at Daniel. "I see New York reduced to rubble within a few hours. The Hurricane Hunters squadron is now reporting wind speeds peaking at over 280 miles an hour."

Daniel rose, stepped before the monitor and pointed at the thick ring of clouds around the eye of the hurricane that had formed over the last hour and was growing steadily. "See that there, Agent Deckard? That is a new cyclical eyewall generating. What that does is strengthen the outer rainbands and forms a second ring of stronger storms inside the hurricane."

"What are you getting at?"

"This second eyewall is traveling toward the center until it reaches the eye and replaces the original eyewall." He gave Deckard an urgent stare. "Once that happens, the hurricane will only intensify even more."

"Are you trying to tell me that Emily will grow *stronger?*"

Daniel kept looking him in the eye. "Emily will hit New York like the Last Judgment."

Deckard gritted his teeth. Then he kicked at one of the chairs, sending it across the floor squealing.

Daniel stepped before Deckard, tried again. "You have to believe me, Agent Deckard. HAARP 2 is only making things worse. You have to switch it off. Stop pulsing. With every second you keep pulsing, Emily's gaining fresh new energy. The figures speak for themselves."

Deckard gave Daniel a hard shove. "We're not switching off HAARP 2!" His face was all red, his jaw muscles twitching. "As long as the Chinese are pulsing, we're going to hit them with everything we've got."

Grim despair filled Daniel's face. "Don't you see? You're achieving the exact opposite."

"We're done discussing this." Deckard turned away.

It was suddenly silent. Deckard marched over to the serving cart, grabbed a tuna sandwich and angrily bit into it. Daniel dropped into a chair with resignation.

Laura spoke up. "Why couldn't HAARP 2 generate the same high-pressure area near New York that it had off Florida?"

"It's not like pressing a remote," Daniel explained with a shake of his head. "We've diverted the jet stream once already—you can't make it turn back again in such a short time, switching these kinds of global atmospheric occurrences on and off again. The biggest problem is that they're too unpredictable, as we're now seeing." He looked back up at the satellite image. "It's highly possible, yes, that Emily would swing back out over the Atlantic if the Chinese switched off their facility along with the Diamond gyrotron. But that is not likely to happen."

"Don't be so sure," Deckard told him, still chewing away nervously. "How much time do we have left until Emily hits New York?"

"If this data is correct? About nine hours."

Deckard looked at his watch. "It's going to be close."

"What's going to be close?"

Deckard ignored Daniel.

"So what now?" Daniel asked after a while.

"We wait." Deckard took another bite of his sandwich. "There's not much more we can do at the moment."

"But what exactly are we waiting for?" Laura asked.

Deckard's expression darkened, and he tossed the rest of his sandwich into the garbage can. "For our final hope."

46

The Atlantic Ocean, 580 Miles Southeast of New York

THE HURRICANE HUNTERS' LOCKHEED WP-3D ORION flew under a cloudless sky at an altitude of just over 6,500 feet, heading directly for the hurricane. It still felt to Emilio Sanchez as if they were drifting along weightlessly, but he wasn't deluding himself. In a few short minutes this cramped cockpit was going to get extremely uncomfortable. He stood behind the pilots of the four-engine propeller plane and looked out the front windshield at the horizon, where the storm system's massive gray clouds had been looming for some time. His pulse quickened. He grasped at the seat in front of him with both hands.

"Nervous?" asked the pilot, Larry Dunn.

"No."

Dunn's mouth stretched into a grin below the reflective lens of his aviators. "Your first flight with the Hunters?"

"No."

Co-pilot Pete Novack turned to Sanchez. "It's completely all right to be nervous. But I can assure you, man, you can always rely on Kermit the Frog to get you through in one piece."

Not for the first time, Sanchez wondered why they gave these planes such dumb names. "At least we're not flying in Miss Piggy," he grumbled.

"Don't worry," Novack said. "The WP-3D was specially developed for flying into the eye. This baby can take a lot, even when we're getting spun around close to the eyewall like it's a washing machine."

"You're scaring him worse." Dunn grinned again. "Listen, Sanchez, we'll climb a few thousand feet to avoid the worst of it. It's usually calmer there, in our experience."

"I'm going to go make sure everything's okay in the back," Sanchez said and pushed and pulled himself back through the passageway crammed with measuring equipment.

"Relax!" yelled Novack after him merrily. "Since 1946 we've only lost four planes."

Sanchez knew the statistics. But this comedian up in the cockpit didn't have the foggiest idea what was awaiting them inside Emily. The crew had gotten their usual pre-flight briefing on the hurricane's specific properties, but they obviously weren't taking the whole thing seriously enough. Still, he also figured that a Hurricane Hunter needed to possess a certain mentality to keep any fears from creeping in.

Reaching the rear of the plane, Sanchez bumped his stomach against the launching device for the dropsonde probes and cursed.

"Careful," warned one of the crew as they performed their various duties. They were seated in front of instruments giving them continuous meteorological data. The centerpiece of the Lockheed, apart from its huge Doppler radar device, was the launcher for the fifteen-inch-long probes that delivered the onboard instruments various data from diverse layers of a hurricane, such as barometric pressure, humidity, and temperature as well as wind speed and direction. The plane then transmitted the data to the NHC in Miami every thirty seconds. Sanchez could hardly wait for the latest results. He looked out of one of the side windows, saw the black-gray walls of clouds getting closer. As he expected, his office was already attracting harsh criticism just three hours after he had instructed Zachary Haffernan to send out the announcement that Emily was being upgraded to Category Six. Some experts were charging him with exceeding his authority, sowing panic, possibly craving recognition, and there were voices demanding he resign. Yet every time those absurdly high wind speeds broke another record, Sanchez felt all the more justified in the way he had handled it. Emily was no usual hurricane, and it couldn't be evaluated as one.

The first vibrations hit the plane. The experienced crew strapped themselves into their seats without a word. Sanchez went back to the cockpit and dropped into his seat directly behind the pilots.

"About time," pilot Dunn said before operating a series of toggle switches on the instrument panel. "Buckle up! Right now."

Sanchez obeyed and looked ahead. His jaw dropped. Emily's dimensions truly were gigantic. The enormous gray walls of clouds were towering all around and seemed to stretch on forever. Then the sun disappeared behind the clouds, and all at once everything grew dark. They had reached the periphery of the hurricane.

The Lockheed vibrated harder now. Far below them, the white crests of massive waves crashed and foamed on the turbulent sea, the once deep-blue water now a fluid lead gray color. Sanchez's breathing picked up.

"Hold on," Dunn ordered. "Here we go."

Sanchez nodded and tried a brave smile.

"We're passing through the eye four times on this mission," pilot Novack said. "You will never forget the view, I guarantee you that."

Right as he stopped talking, the first truly serious gusts of wind shook the plane. Sanchez jolted back against his seat, clawed at the leather armrests. Seconds later the first rain drops splashed at the windshield glass—and from then on they were in the middle of it.

Torrential rains battered the Lockheed. The windshield wipers were completely overwhelmed, visibility decreased to near zero. Vertical hurricane gusts hurled the plane upward, only to send it hurtling back downward with twice the force. Hail and sleet hammered away at the fuselage. The closer they got to the eye, Sanchez rapidly got jolted from side to side with more and more force, as his safety belt cut into him. He wondered how the men at the rear of the plane were able to work under these conditions, let alone drop the probes.

The plane plummeted suddenly, a thousand-foot drop. Sanchez's knuckles turned white from gripping the armrests so tight. Stomach acid rose up his esophagus. He worried he was going to vomit onto the back of pilot Dunn's neck any moment, but then the pilot got the plane under control and stabilized their course.

"Everything all right back there?" Dunn asked. "This happens sometimes."

"All good," Sanchez uttered through clenched teeth. His heart raced.

"Great, then prepare yourself for an hour of this rollercoaster."

"Pretty intense storm," Novack added, not sounding as loose as he had a few minutes earlier. "And we're not even near the eye yet."

"Yep," Dunn said, "those vertical gusts sure are intense."

"No one ever listens to me," Sanchez grumbled.

Another gust hurled them sideways, and Sanchez's belt pressed into him again.

The propeller plane penetrated deeper and deeper into the hurricane. Sanchez looked out the side windows with growing concern as the wings bowed from the turbulence as if they were made of balsa wood. He knew of course that the WP-3D was specifically constructed for flights like this, that the fuselage and wings could tolerate enormous force. But did that also hold true for Emily?

Rain and hail lashed harder and harder at the windows. Their surroundings darkened even more, something Sanchez would not have thought possible. And then, in the blink of an eye, they broke through the eyewall, and all grew calm. Suddenly there was not even the slightest vibration. Absolute peace. They were inside the eye.

Sanchez took a deep breath and looked out. They found themselves inside a gigantic chimney lined with curtains of thick, heavy clouds. They experienced no wind at all. The sun in the blue sky above sent its rays down through the circular eye, while below them the sea looked so tranquil it resembled a goldfish pond more than the Atlantic Ocean. Sanchez had never seen anything more beautiful.

Breathtaking, he thought. He became conscious of how small and vulnerable people on earth compared to such a spectacle of nature. Among all the calm, he congratulated himself for deciding to fly with the Hunters. He was so taken by the thought that he forgot all else.

He was jerked back to reality a few minutes later. They broke through the eyewall on the opposite side of the eye. Suddenly all hell broke loose on them all over again, rain, hail, hurricane gusts, with the propeller craft tossed around like a paper plane. Sanchez couldn't imagine enduring this procedure three more times. Then, like a blast of scalding water, a thought struck him.

"We approached Emily from behind," he shouted at Dunn, who had his hands full getting the plane under control. "That true?"

"It is, yes," Dunn yelled back.

"That means we're now in the front-most quarter?"

"Yes, so you better hang on. It's gonna get really rough now."

Sanchez cursed and clawed at his armrests again. No one needed to say what everyone on board knew: they were now in what was known as the most dangerous quarter, where the winds and gusts were at their strongest and most lethal. They were promptly flung upward by a violent vertical gust. Sanchez's stomach protested. He shut his eyes.

Suddenly there was a grinding sound that shocked Sanchez to his core.

"Shit!" Dunn yelled.

"What was that?" shouted Novack.

Sanchez looked out a side window, his eyes widening. A section of the left wing had buckled. Its tip pointed upward at a crooked angle, fluttering in the storm. "Good Lord," he muttered.

The plane was losing altitude fast, plunging down toward the ocean surface.

Novack and Dunn tried to regain control and shouted orders at each other, but nothing worked. Sanchez retched. It all came up a second later, and he vomited onto his shirt. For a moment Dunn got the plane under control. But another gust ripped off the tip of the damaged wing, and seconds later they started plummeting again.

"Shit!" Dunn shouted.

They heard a bang at the rear of the plane, followed by panicked screaming.

God help us, Sanchez thought. The hurricane was tearing the plane into pieces.

Dunn and Novack lost control for good. They went into a spin. Sanchez's head buzzed; he couldn't tell up from down anymore. For a moment he caught a glimpse through the front windshield. They were plunging downward and couldn't be stopped, down toward the slate gray ocean churning up massive breakers. Dirty-white crests of foam streaked the water in long thin shreds. Only seconds to go until impact.

Sanchez closed his eyes. He thought about Selma Cooper advising him against getting on this plane. He thought of his ex-wife, who, the way it was looking, was going to get the house after all. His final thought was of Emily, a force of nature as wonderful as she was deadly, her unimaginably perfect form nothing less than a work of art. He took one last moment to regard, in full amazement, the singular beauty of that chimney tower of clouds rising straight up into the sky from inside the eye and all of the grandeur and awe he'd felt witnessing such a wonder. Then the plane smashed into the surface of the sea.

47

THE HEAVY SCENT OF INCENSE FILLED HUANG ZHEN'S meditation chamber at the Heilongjiang facility. As he always did when performing his daily Neigong exercises, he devoted a portion to cleansing and strengthening his qi, his life force. He had fastened the golden buttons of his white Zhongshan suit up to his neck and stood on a straw mat rotating his outstretched arms in a wide circle in order to rotate his shoulder joints as fully as possible. He was halfway through when an explosion outside the walls rudely jolted him from his meditative state.

He stormed out of the room and passed through the neighboring office to the balcony, bracing himself on the railing with both hands. The sight left him speechless. Huge flames were shooting up at the edge of the woods where the far rows of antennas ran along the high-voltage fence. Zhen couldn't see how many antennas were affected through all the heavy billowing smoke. He squinted harder, as if trying to disperse the smoke through sheer will, when a second explosion shook the antenna field, this one much closer to the main building. At the same time, about a dozen of the stork-legged antennas burst into flame. It was immediately clear to Zhen that this was no technical failure. It was sabotage.

He cursed and resolved to head to the control room when more demolitions went off, this time just a hundred feet below his balcony.

A wall of flame rose up and died out right in front of the railing. Zhen felt the heat on his face, automatically pulling back.

From the corner of his eye, he spotted movement out on the antenna field—he could make out several men in black combat gear crouching as they ran between those antennas that were still standing. They were heading for the control room. Zhen pounded with fury on the balcony railing. Then glass shattered on the right side of the building below him. He bounded over to the other side of the balcony and looked down. A second team of helmeted attackers in black were coming in from the right flank. They threw flash and smoke grenades into the building through a smashed window. Zhen cursed again. These were pros. Of course they were.

A gun battle commenced at the far end of the control room. He heard the Chinese military-issue Norinco Type 95 assault rifles of his Heilongjiang security forces clattering and echoing through the valley as they exchanged salvos with the attackers.

Four stories below him, the main entrance doors flew open and many of his staff ran into the open air. They scattered in all directions, screaming pathetically like so many scared children. Zhen was not surprised. When the tree fell, all the monkeys scattered. It has always been so.

He rushed into his office. He was no monkey. He was a tiger, and he would fight. He threw open the top drawer of his desk and stared at the empty space, furiously remembering that he had given his vintage Shansi Arsenal 45 mm to weapons staff for maintenance.

Another explosion, this one inside the building, shook the floor beneath Zhen's feet. Shots and screams echoed up the stairway. The attackers were getting closer.

He looked around, saw the two dao sabers on the wall, and yanked them down from their brackets. With a saber in each hand, he planted himself in the middle of the room with his feet wide, eyeing the door. It would take more than a few armed men to take him out now.

He heard loud shouts coming from the top of the stairwell and the stomping of boots. He tensed his muscles, ready to strike down each one coming through the door with a single chop of his saber.

Another brief exchange of fire, a cry, hectic commotion out in the hallway, then the door flew open. Zhen bared his teeth and raised a saber for the first swing.

An obese man staggered into the room. He panted heavily and could barely stay on his feet. Behind him, in the hallway, two of Zhen's security guards were holding off the attackers with sustained fire. Interrupting his first lunge with the saber, Zhen stared at his cousin, who was currently gasping for breath.

"How many came after you?" Zhen asked.

Xian Wang-Mei gagged, seeking sufficient air. "They're shooting everyone who doesn't surrender."

The stomping boots got closer. Shots rang out. One of the two guards outside was hurled against a wall and slumped to the floor, dead.

"Give me your gun," Zhen barked at his cousin. "You don't know how to use it anyway."

Wang-Mei bent forward, propping himself on his thighs, still panting. "I lost it in all the commotion."

"You're worthless!" Zhen lunged forward and swung his saber, slicing his cousin's head off his neck in a single blow. Wang-Mei's head banged on the floor and rolled a few yards over to the TV. His headless body stood upright for a few seconds as a fountain of blood sprayed from his neck. Suddenly the body collapsed, and a thick pool of blood formed around the gaping neck wound.

Outside in the hallway, the last guard fell in a hail of bullets. The attackers ceased firing. Zhen could hear more assault rifles firing outside the building, along with explosions. Quietly and nimbly, like a jungle cat in pursuit of prey, he rushed behind one of the open double doors and stood motionless.

Heavy footsteps came down the hallway and stopped in front of his room. He closed his eyes and focused. He could hear the intruders' labored breathing from behind the door and discerned the breathing patterns of three individuals. He gripped the sabers' grips more tightly.

The men carefully entered the room.

"Shit," blurted one. "What the hell happened to the fat guy?"

"Be careful," warned a second. "That bastard we're looking for has to be here some—"

Zhen leaped from behind the door and lunged at the two men with his sabers. He hacked off the first soldier's forearm with a forceful swing before he was able turn his gun on Zhen. The soldier cried out and went down on one knee. His comrade pivoted lightning fast and got a shot off. The bullet whizzed by Zhen's chest, missing by a hair. He would not fire a second round, as Zhen drove the tip of the saber directly into the soldier's larynx, right between his bulletproof vest and helmet strap. The soldier fell to the ground, gurgling.

Zhen turned around. Whimpering, The first attacker knelt next to Wang-Mei's headless body and tried to stanch his heavily bleeding arm stump with plastic handcuffs. Zhen gave him the final blow, driving the blade of his saber into the man's stomach below his bulletproof vest. He jerked the blade 180 degrees, then pulled it back out with a squishing sound and a section of his intestines along with it. The soldier fell over.

"Don't move!" ordered a deep voice. "Put down your weapons!"

Zhen turned slowly around, gripping both sabers. He wasn't about to drop them. About fifteen feet away stood a colossus in black combat gear aiming a 9 mm Glock. A thick scar ran down the side of his neck from below his right ear and continued under his bulletproof vest.

"Huang Zhen," the colossus said. "Drop your weapons, get on your knees, and place your hands behind your head. I am Special Agent Fenton Link. Follow my instructions, and you will remain among the living."

"Why would I do such a thing?" Zhen replied. "Remain among the living, only to betray my country?"

"You will appear before a regular court of law in the United States and be held accountable for a terrorist attack."

"A *regular court of law*?" Zhen's eyes flashed with rage. "You will never allow the world to learn of Heilongjiang. No, I am only accountable to my own people."

"I'm telling you one last time: drop your weapons."

"Charles told you about this place, didn't he? He betrayed the coordinates of Heilongjiang."

"That doesn't matter now." The colossus took a step toward Zhen. "It's over. Accept it, and start cooperating."

Zhen calculated the distance between them. He only needed one step closer to achieve a swift blow that the CIA agent would never see coming.

"I am going to count to three. If you do not drop your weapons by then, I'm going to shoot."

Zhen sized up the colossus. "Two tigers cannot live atop one mountain together. You and I, we are both tigers. Without question. But all of this, Special Agent, is *my* mountain." He lunged at the colossus, swinging his saber.

Agent Link pulled the trigger.

Zhen was thrown back and crashed to the floor. A hot, piercing pain burned in his gut. Blood seeped through his white shirt. He'd lost one saber, but his left hand still clutched the grip of the second.

Agent Link stepped closer, still aiming the barrel of his gun. "I knew you'd try it, asshole. Thanks for giving me a reason to fire."

Zhen's body began twitching uncontrollably. He wanted to say something, but all that came out of his mouth was a bubbling gush of blood. Using his last ounce of strength, he raised the saber.

The colossus fired again.

Huang Zhen's head exploded.

48

THE TIME PASSED MORE SLOWLY THAN EVER. LAURA AND
Daniel sat in the bunker waiting room, silently watching the satellite
images transmitted on two of the screens. Agents Lance Deckard and
Jennifer West had not shown themselves for hours—or at least that
was the way it seemed to Laura, who had tried to get some sleep in
one of the club chairs without success.

Daniel didn't seem to consider sleeping an option. They only grew
more nervous watching the satellite images.

"Something's changing," Daniel muttered.

Laura sat up in her chair. "How do you mean?"

"It's Emily. I wouldn't swear on it, but I think Emily is changing
course again."

"Away from New York?"

He nodded. "It's not as if anyone here Is telling us anything, but I
think, yeah, the hurricane is actually turning away, back toward the
Atlantic."

"But that's great."

He ignored her.

"What?" she asked. "What's the problem?"

"I don't know, I just have a bad feeling."

"What for?"

He frowned. "The problem is—"

Right then the door to the waiting room opened, and a man in a
suit looked in.

"Mr. Bender, Ms. Wagner?" he said to them. "Agent Deckard would like to speak with you."

Laura and Daniel reached the conference room at the same time as Agent West, who was coming from the opposite end of the corridor. She entered at a brisk pace with a smile on her lips and marched up to Deckard, who sat in his shirt sleeves. He looked exhausted.

"Agent Link just reported in," she told him. "Operation Stormbreaker was successful."

"Excellent!" Deckard balled his fists and shut his eyes a moment, as if giving silent thanks to whatever deity it was he prayed to. "Any losses?"

"Two men dead, two injured. The team has already flown out."

"Status?"

"The Heilongjiang facility was taken and destroyed. The virus was uploaded to the Diamond gyrotron software beforehand via satellite."

"Perfect."

"Zhen and Wang-Mei?"

"Both dead."

Deckard rose, adjusted his tie, and took his jacket off the back of the chair. "I'll inform Washington."

"Then you can also prepare your superiors," Daniel said, "for the fact that the second eyewall is now fusing with the original eyewall, meaning that Emily is gaining strength and intensity all over again. I tried to tell you that this would happen."

"That's your opinion, as far as I'm concerned," Deckard replied, seemingly unmoved. He patted a few imaginary specks of dust off his jacket. "In any case, we don't need to worry. The Chinese are not able to pulse anymore, and Diamond is now only so much scrap metal. Meanwhile, Emily is heading out over the Atlantic."

"That's good," Daniel said. "So HAARP 2 can finally stop pulsing."

The two CIA agents exchanged a look, then Deckard cleared his throat. "On the advice of Professor De la Vega, HAARP 2 is not being switched off for now."

Daniel's eyes widened. "It's what? Don't you get it? The longer you pulse, the more power you're feeding the hurricane. You're only making it worse."

Deckard pulled on his jacket, the very picture of calm. "That is just a theory, for which there's not the slightest evidence."

"What about that second eyewall? It's a clear sign that the storm system is intensifying."

"That kind of thing has happened before. It's not specific to Emily. You've admitted as much yourself."

"Sure, but—"

Deckard raised a hand. "My first priority is to protect my country. First and foremost, I'm responsible for keeping this fucking hurricane away from our coastline. And if that means using HAARP 2, then those goddamn antennas can pulse away until they're glowing red as far as I'm concerned. We'll keep it up until we stop seeing any danger."

"I wouldn't call that responsible," Laura blurted.

Deckard gave her a thin smile. "Of course it is. From where I'm standing, anything else would be irresponsible. It just depends on your perspective."

"I can't wait to see what Europe has to say about this," Daniel snapped. "I highly doubt that anyone here will show much understanding for your acting this way."

"I'm afraid I'm not following, Mr. Bender."

Daniel pointed at the satellite image. "I've been watching Emily's pattern of movement very closely. I think I'm beginning to understand a few connections that weren't clear to me before." He spread out his arms. "Emily has double the power of any hurricane ever known. So I can assure you, Agent Deckard, that if you keep HAARP 2 pulsing, this hurricane will not dissipate over the North Atlantic."

Laura's eyes widened at Daniel. "Are you saying that Emily will reach Europe?"

Daniel nodded. "If HAARP 2 keeps pulsing, that is the logical consequence."

Deckard exchanged another glance with Agent West, fiddled with his sleeves, and fastened the top button of his jacket. "I will make note of your concern. As soon as we see no further threat to the United States, we will shut off HAARP 2. You'll have to excuse me now. Washington is waiting for my report."

"Fuck . . ." Daniel followed him. "You at least need to inform the European authorities what's coming their way."

"We will, once we find it necessary to do so," Deckard told him.

Daniel rushed in front of him, blocking his way. "Meteorologists have no clue what Emily's capable of. All will assume that the storm system over North Atlantic is forming back into a low-pressure system. No one apart from us knows that Emily is no usual hurricane and isn't exactly behaving like one, either."

"Like I said, I'm making note of your concerns." Deckard shoved Daniel aside and disappeared out the door.

"At its current speed," Daniel shouted after him, "Emily will already start reaching European coastlines by early tomorrow morning. People here are not prepared for any sort of major evacuation. You *must* warn the authorities!"

But Deckard was already long gone.

Daniel whipped around and kicked a chair. He looked to Agent West, who observed him without expression from across the room. He then turned to Laura and stepped closer. "We need to get out of here," he whispered to her.

"Where can we go?"

"Doesn't matter. Anywhere but here. We need to warn the authorities."

"And you think that anyone will believe you?"

He hesitated. "Maybe not me personally. But I still have my contacts."

"Maybe you're right," she said. "You have to at least try."

"'You' as in just me?" He gave her a quizzical stare. "What's up with you?"

Laura sighed. "Bishop is still holding Robin. I can't leave, Daniel. Not until Robin is safe." She gave him a pitiable look. "Please understand."

Daniel expression showed that he did. "Would you rather I stay here with you?"

"You can't do anything for Robin by staying here." She pointed toward the doorway. "But out there? Maybe you can help save people's lives." He nodded.

They walked over to Agent West. She was standing at the door now and blocking their exit, but it was hard to tell if it was intentional.

"Take me back to the airport," Daniel demanded.

"I'm sorry, but I can't do that."

"Why can't you?"

"I have instructions to escort you both to the waiting room."

"Why?" Daniel said. "Our help obviously isn't required anymore."

Agent West started to answer, but her phone rang. She looked at the screen and took the call.

Laura's pulse raced. Something told her that the call was about Robin.

"Understood," Agent West said after a moment and looked at her watch. "Put a team together. We go before dawn, at zero five-hundred hours local time. You'll have operational approval by then. Agent Deckard will authorize." She ended the call.

"Anything new about my son?" Laura asked immediately.

"Yes. Come with me. Both of you."

They followed Agent West through the underground network of corridors. After they'd walked a while, a door twenty feet or so ahead of them suddenly opened. Three men stepped out. The men on either side wore dark suits, the man in the middle tan overalls. He had trouble breathing and needed to be held up. He was handcuffed, his greasy hair hung in his eyes, and his pale face looked doughy in the artificial fluorescent light. Laura noticed dried, crusty blood under his nose.

The three neared them. The slender chest of the prisoner kept rising and falling as the two dragged him along. Laura, Daniel, and Agent West pressed themselves against the wall to give the men room, as the prisoner stared straight ahead. Laura recognized him from the photos Deckard had put up on one of the monitors not long ago, and a tingling sensation shot through her. The CIA was now leading Charles St. Adams himself into the conference room.

Laura and Daniel followed Agent Jennifer West into the waiting room.

Laura was all out of patience. "What's going on with Robin?"

Agent West turned to her, straightening her jacket. "We tracked down Bishop. St. Adams gave us the correct info. We've checked the estates on Alderney and detected evidence of Bishop's presence."

"And Robin?"

"Our France station has not mentioned him. If he's there too, we will find him. I'll proceed to Alderney immediately." She turned to leave.

"Take me with you!"

Agent West let out a gentle sigh. "Laura, listen—"

Laura blocked the agent's way. "Right this moment, Charles St. Adams is sitting in your conference room just a few feet from here. Because of me, the CIA was able to catch him on his yacht the way they did. You owe me for that."

The two women stared each other down. Agent West looked away first. She rubbed at her temples. "I'm going to get in huge trouble for this."

"You're doing the right thing," Laura assured her.

Daniel cleared his throat for them to listen up.

"Alderney is right in Emily's path," he said. "The way things stand now? You and your team will end up in the middle of the storm. You'll need someone who knows his way around extreme weather."

Agent West eyed him a moment, deep in thought. Then she went over to a club chair, sat down, slipped off her shoes and massaged her feet. "Are you truly convinced this hurricane will make its way across the pond?"

"I am. Emily has been absorbing more than enough power for some time now in the form of water vapor," Daniel explained. "Complicating matters further is the fact that we've diverted the jet stream. That was a big help to us at first, but now it's turned into a type of boomerang, unfortunately—that very same jet stream is exactly what is speeding Emily across the Atlantic in record time." He gave Agent West a grave look. "You are going to need me."

Agent West sighed and slipped her shoes back on. "All right, fine. I'll talk to Deckard." She passed by Laura on the way to the door. "At 5:30 a.m., a helicopter will take us to Ramstein Air Base. We head out from there. Both of you wait here. I'll come get you."

49

ABOVE THE MATTRESS, RIGHT IN FRONT OF ROBIN'S nose, hovered Silver Man.

"Can you get us out of here, Silver Man?" Robin asked him.

The superhero nodded. "Normally I would smash this door down with a single blow of my fist, but the villain possesses a magic substance that has robbed me of my powers."

"What kind of a substance?"

"It's an artifact." Silver Man hovered back and forth restlessly. "It comes from a faraway planet."

"Like Kryptonite?"

"Something like that, yes," Silver Man said. "As long as this artifact remains hidden somewhere in this labyrinth, I am powerless."

"We have to find it," Robin said and sprang out of bed, its iron frame squeaking.

The concrete floor under Robin's bare feet was ice cold. He sighed, his shoulders slumping, and climbed back onto the stained mattress. He laid Silver Man next to him. He'd made him out of the tinfoil from the chocolate. Pretending to have a strong protector by his side had been comforting for a while, but now harsh reality was winning out over his wishful games. At least his head wasn't pounding as bad as it had been the last two days.

He lay there a long time, losing track of time. Suddenly the old Chinese man in the black robe appeared in the doorway. Robin still felt uncomfortable in his presence, but he'd stopped being scared. The man stepped up to the bed, stooping. He held a mug of fresh water in one hand, a bar of chocolate in the other.

This time Robin grabbed it without hesitating. "Thank you."

The Chinese man's expression revealed something like a smile. He set down the mug and gave Robin an encouraging nod.

"Why do I have to be here?" Robin said in a firm voice. "I want to be with my mom. She has to be really worried about me. Can't you take me to her? Please?"

The Chinese man stared blankly. Suddenly something moved behind him, and a dark shadow came closer. The old Chinese man heard the footsteps and turned around, giving Robin full view of a large and gloomy-looking man.

For a moment Robin thought he was looking at a villain from one of his comics. The man had muscles like the Hulk and wore an olive-green T-shirt and shorts. But he only had one leg. In the place where the other leg was supposed to be was a shiny tube with an artificial foot at the end. *A being that is half-man, half-machine*, ran through Robin's head.

The man-machine grabbed the old man by the collar of his robe, pulled him close, and barked at him in a language Robin didn't understand. He struck the Chinese man's face hard with the back of his hand. The old man flew up against the wall. Blood ran down his nose.

"Stop. Please," Robin begged, fighting back tears.

The man-machine sent Robin's minder out the door with a kick and then followed him. Seeing the artificial leg bending and extending like that scared Robin stiff. The man-machine had stopped in the doorway. He turned his head Robin's way and gave him a strange look. Then he turned and slammed the door shut behind him.

Robin slumped down and started crying. His hopes of being saved had burst like a soap bubble.

He picked up Silver Man and made him float back and forth before his puffy, tear-stained eyes. "Please, Silver Man, can you find a way to protect me from that man?"

"I'm not sure how," said Silver Man.

50

THE SIKORSKY HH-60G PAVE HAWK APPROACHED Alderney flying 180 miles per hour at the required minimum altitude of 490 feet. The booming hum of the rotors droned dully in their ears despite the protective earmuffs Agent West had handed them. Laura sat next to Daniel on a barely padded bench looking at the six men tasked with taking out Fred Bishop and liberating Robin. They wore black combat gear reinforced with Kevlar, and their helmets and short-barreled machine guns hung above them in nets. Agent West said that they belonged to Delta Force—the CIA relied on U.S. Army Special Forces when a secret mission involved fighting terrorism or freeing hostages. They would locate Robin and deliver him back to Laura—Agent West was certain of it. Laura really wanted to share the CIA agent's optimism, but her worries and fears that they might be too late were starting to overwhelm her.

They had flown over the French-German border near Saarbrücken before heading toward Normandy south of the low Walloon mountain range that stretched across southern Belgium. The clouds were becoming much thicker, the wind stronger. They had felt the first turbulence near Reims, about an hour after liftoff. At first only brief jerks and shudders made the Sikorsky vibrate. Then the rain set in, slapping at the windows.

Daniel gestured at Laura to push back her protective earmuffs. The booming rotors practically bored into her brain.

"We're seeing the first signs of Emily," he shouted into her ear. "It's going to get worse."

Agent West leaned over to them. "Don't worry. The Pave Hawk can handle any kind of weather. Even when it's part of a hurricane."

"How much more time?" asked Laura.

"We're flying at top speed. That requires a lot of fuel. We'll need to refuel in Le Havre."

Laura was growing impatient and had no interest in mechanical details. "How long till Alderney?" she asked.

Agent West looked at her watch, calculating in her head. "Still about two hours, including refueling."

Laura closed her eyes and tried to think of something to calm her nerves. She wasn't able to.

The turbulence grew stronger as they neared Le Havre airport. The pilot chose to fly right over the city center for some reason, and they passed through the south end of Le Havre. Daniel nudged Laura and pointed out the window. Since they were flying very low, they could see most everything below in spite of the bad weather.

The Seine River, which flowed into the ocean near Le Havre, had overflowed both its banks for miles from the wind and churning sea relentlessly pumping more and more water into the river. Large-scale flooding had submerged the southern parts of Le Havre, and waves washed over the port facilities and the neighboring streets. Residents were fleeing the city in cars, on bicycles, and on foot—the streams of people were clearly identifiable from the air. The whole thing resembled a panicked exodus more than any orderly evacuation since no one had been prepared for what they would encounter. Daniel's appeal to Deckard had obviously come to nothing.

They flew lower, neared the airport, and made a rough landing. While the Sikorsky was being refueled, Laura saw that the airfield around them was all but abandoned because of the storm.

"You think Emily will hit Germany just as bad?" she asked Daniel.

"I don't even want to think about how far the North Sea is going to push inland," he told her, his expression somber. "One thing I do know: for people on the coast, this will become a matter of life and death."

51

Fred Bishop was cursing everyone and everything. He cursed St. Adams, and he cursed Huang Zhen, spitting out his words. Those fucking bastards. What the hell had gone wrong? The USA was supposed to have been the target, not Europe, and definitely not Alderney, which according to the latest news now lay right in the hurricane's path.

Bishop certainly wasn't going to barricade himself in. He hadn't been able to reach St. Adams or Huang Zhen for hours, so he had to assume the worst—either they had been taken out or they were in confinement somewhere. Both scenarios presented the very real possibility that the CIA had learned of his whereabouts. So he packed as many guns and ammo into his gym bag as he could carry. He didn't have much time. He needed to leave Alderney while the weather would let him.

He left the house with the heavy gym bag in one hand and a briefcase in the other. The briefcase held his emergency kit for such situations— four fake passports and twenty thousand dollars in various currencies. The wind and rain whipped at him, and for the first time in a long while he had to concentrate on his every step. Once he reached the two-man Schweizer 300C helicopter sitting on the lawn a short distance from the guest house, he tossed the gym bag and briefcase onto the co-pilot's seat and returned to the main house. There was one thing he still needed to do, and he wasn't happy about it.

He went down into the cellar, grabbed a padlock and iron chain from the storeroom, and hung them over his shoulder. Then he turned down one of the dimly lit halls and unlocked a door.

The boy sat on the bed with his knees pulled all the way up, staring at him in fear. This was the part Bishop did not like. It wasn't in the original plan, but he couldn't change things now. When the boy's mother blurted his name out on the phone, it became clear that the boy wasn't worth much to him. He should have eliminated the kid first thing, but he'd needed a more than good reason to kill a child. So he'd put off the moment of decision for as long as he could.

"You can thank your mother for this," he snarled. He yanked the boy off the bed and dragged him along with him. The scaredy-cat was crying, jabbering in German. But one harsh look from him shut the kid up.

Bishop made his way to the Chinese man's room holding the boy by one hand. The old man hadn't been well suited for keeping an eye on the boy, something Bishop had suspected from the start. But the old man had been sent by Zhen, so what was he supposed to do? Bishop couldn't allow him or the boy to live now. If the CIA showed up, they could not find anyone who might talk.

He entered the old man's room and pulled out his gun. "Come with me!"

The three of them left the main house. They fought their way through the storm across the grass, all the way to the Finnish-style log cabin sauna perched at the edge of the steep bluff. It was part of a wellness retreat, with cold pool, hydrotherapy facilities, swimming pool. Bishop had wasted valuable minutes wondering how to eliminate the boy without having to kill him with his own hands. The log cabin was perfect, he could see. The hurricane would demolish it like a house of cards by evening at the latest, sending it and all occupants over the cliffs.

He waved his gun at the Chinese man to open the double door of the cabin. He obeyed. Bishop gave him a shove, sending him inside, then dragged the boy in behind him. He flung the doors shut, wrapped the iron chain around the two handles, and secured it all with the padlock. He made sure that the chain was holding, then marched back toward the helicopter.

The hurricane was gaining even more strength. It was time to clear out.

52

THE SIKORSKY FINISHED REFUELING, AND THE PILOT GAVE it thrust. The engines roared; the sound was deafening. Laura put on her protective earmuffs. The rotors started spinning, and soon they lifted off and swung around Le Havre toward the English Channel.

Black clouds hovered over the ocean with a density and force Laura had never witnessed. Hurricane winds gave the Sikorsky a thorough shaking, the Delta Force's equipment vibrating and clattering up in the cargo nets. Daniel's hand found Laura's, squeezed it gently, and he smiled to give her courage. She was grateful to have it.

Massive white-capped breakers pushed through the English Channel far below them, and chunks of sea foam shot into the air with every cresting wave. They saw a container ship listing as it struggled to make it through the breakers. A huge wave had struck it from the side, and several containers had already slid off the foredeck into the sea.

"Emily's speed must have picked up even more in the last few hours," Daniel told her. "This isn't just the edge of the storm anymore. It's coming faster than I feared. We'll soon be right in the middle of it."

Laura shut her eyes.

About twenty minutes later they were flying over the northernmost tip of Normandy, passing the peninsula of Cotentin and the harbor city of Cherbourg. The harbor jetties had long ceased to provide any protection against the deluge of water, and the rolling sea flooded into the city's docks and port areas, which also happened to harbor some of the French Navy.

Pleasure boats torn from their moorings drifted around inside the harbor, while others were driven onto land by the foaming breakers. Sailboats rocked about in the waves, their masts and rigs hooking onto each other and buckling. The Sikorsky stayed on course, heading for its target. Not far from the coastline, a fishing cutter was trying to reach the supposed protection of the harbor. But the effort was in vain. A monster wave caught it and dragged it under. When it surfaced again, it drifted with its hull facing upward.

The island of Alderney soon materialized in the distance, barely visible in the rain, all dark cliffs against a black sky.

"Ten minutes to landing," the pilot told them.

53

FRED BISHOP SAT AT THE HELM OF THE LITTLE SCHWEIZER 300C helicopter on the lawn and could see the Pave Hawk approaching through his curved window. He reached under the seat and pulled out his binoculars. His eyes were not deceiving him. They actually had sent the fucking Delta Force—his own former buddies. For an instant he wasn't sure if he should laugh or cry.

He tossed the binocs on the co-pilot seat. His decision was made. There would never be a better opportunity to show them all the damage he could do despite his missing leg.

He climbed out of the helicopter, the rain pelting down on him. He put on a baseball cap and hauled out his gym bag. Trying to flee with the tiny chopper would have been pointless anyway, he knew—the Pave Hawk would shoot him out of the sky before he could even get close enough to show them his middle finger. He looked inside his gym bag and couldn't help but grin. He was going to send them all straight to hell.

He marched through the wind and rain to a cluster of tall cypress trees, going over the plan forming in his head. He estimated about five minutes before the Pave Hawk touched down. The Delta Force outnumbered him in troop strength and armament, so he needed to exploit his knowledge of the terrain and use it to his advantage. And he already knew how.

He reached the cypresses bending back and forth in the storm, dropped his bag on muddy earth, and got to work. He was going to need every second now.

Three minutes later, dripping wet, Bishop stopped to consider his work and felt satisfied, given the time constraints. He shoved his Beretta M9 into his waistband and grabbed the HK MP7, a short-barreled submachine gun with the penetration power of an assault rifle. Its small-caliber cartridges could pierce his former buddies' Kevlar vests at a distance of over two hundred yards, plus the MP7 didn't weigh much. He could fire it one-handed while keeping the other hand free. He shoved ammo into all the pockets he had, then ran as fast as his prosthesis let him to the cliffs at the opposite end of the yard. The log cabin was still holding up in the storm, he saw. That offered him another option.

Bishop reached the cabin, aimed the MP7 at the chain and padlock and tore them open with a short burst, sending wood chips flying. He pushed open the door and looked into the boy's frightened face as he crouched below the cabin's cliffside window. Bishop pulled him up. The scaredy-cat screamed and flailed around. Bishop held the barrel of his gun under the boy's chin and glared at him in warning. The boy shut up instantly. Tears ran down his cheeks. All of which was good. Nobody liked firing at an armed man holding a hostage, not even all those U.S. Army snipers with ice in their veins. Even the hardcore Delta Force guys started sweating when an innocent child was in the way—as a live human shield.

Bishop heard a battle cry.

The Chinese man charged him, his face contorted with rage. A few rounds from his MP7 sent the old codger hurtling against the wall, leaving red streaks on the wood as he slowly sank to the floor, his eyes wide open.

The boy was frozen from shock, so Bishop took a moment to launch his smartphone app with the icon of a telescopic sight. He was going to remotely control the sniper rifle he had concealed among the cypress trees. The virtual gunsight showed him area temperature, wind, air pressure, and gradient. He had only to wait for his target, get it in its sights, and select it with one tap.

It would soon be time. The Pave Hawk was coming in to land.

Bishop used the app's virtual crosshairs to select the helicopter as his primary target. He could now fire remotely once any of them showed themselves outside the craft. Before all the fun started, he also remembered to turn on the video function. He could already see himself sitting in front of the fireplace with a glass of red wine, celebrating the death of his former buddies on the big screen, complete with sound. A surge of adrenalin charged through him. He hadn't felt this alive in a long, long time.

54

THE HELICOPTER TOUCHED DOWN WITH A JOLT. LAURA unclamped her fingers from the grab handles above her head, her heart beating faster now. In a few minutes, she'd be able to take Robin in her arms—she fervently hoped so, at least.

"Get ready!" Agent West ordered her Delta Force team.

The men got started. They put on the rest of their gear with practiced efficiency and checked their weapons one last time.

Agent West bent down to Laura and Daniel. "Do not move from this spot, either of you. Do you understand?" She directed her question at Daniel especially. "You will remain hunkered down right here on your butt until I personally give the all-clear."

"Understood," Daniel said.

Laura nodded.

Agent West fastened her protective vest tight and checked her pistol. She turned to one of the helicopter crew, a skinny young man sitting before a wall of monitors, instruments, and switches. "What's infrared telling us?"

"We got a weak heat source a little over a hundred yards north of the main house." The soldier pointed at a bright spot on the upper edge of the green monochrome screen. "Could be one person, maybe two. Otherwise, nothing else in the surrounding five hundred feet."

Agent West looked out the window and pointed between the pilot and co-pilot. "That little house over there?"

"Probably, but remember, this heavy rain can disrupt the sensors on our thermal imaging camera."

"Okay." Agent West waved the signal for the doors to open. Six Delta Force men leaped out both sides of the helicopter and secured the immediate area, then Agent West glanced at Laura one last time and disappeared into the rain after them. A few seconds later Laura heard the rattle of machine-gun fire—for the first time in her life. Then she heard screams that froze the blood in her veins. She shuddered. So this was what people dying sounded like.

The seconds turned to minutes as the gun battle raged on. Laura and Daniel kept glancing at each other with fright, neither knowing what was happening outside the helicopter's protective metal hull. One last shot sounded, a final scream, and then suddenly all was calm. The howling wind and pelting rain filled their ears again.

Someone outside the Sikorsky groaned. A hand covered in blood appeared in the doorway, clawing at a grab handle. Laura gasped. It was a woman's hand and could only belong to one person.

She didn't hesitate. She jumped out of the helicopter. Agent West was squatting on the ground pressing a hand to her stomach, her face contorted with pain. Dark blood gushed out between her fingers, mixing with the raindrops splashing on her hand.

"Help me," she wheezed.

"Oh my God . . ." Laura wrapped her arms around Agent West and held her up as Daniel appeared in the doorway with the soldiers who had stayed behind. They worked together to haul the injured agent into the chopper and lay her out on the floor. Agent West was as white as a sheet, her wet hair sticking to her face. She shivered.

"We need a first-aid kit," Laura shouted at the young soldier.

He turned and came back with one immediately. While Daniel carefully peeled away Agent West's protective vest, Laura went through the kit and pulled out compress bandages, gauze, scissors. She ripped open the packaging.

"No," Agent West blurted, "do XStat first—"

"'XStat'? What is that?" Laura said.

"Injection ... stops bleeding."

Laura grabbed the kit again. She pulled out two curious syringes holding what looked like chunky white pellets. She stuffed one of the syringes into her pants pocket and held the other up to the dim light inside the cabin.

"How does it work?" Daniel said.

Laura scanned the directions on the packaging. "Says here, the syringe holds little blood-absorbing sponges you inject directly into gunshot wounds. Do it right, the little sponges swell up in contact with blood and seal the wound within seconds."

"Fine, but what about the bullet?" Daniel looked like he might vomit at any moment. "Shouldn't we get the bullet out first?"

"Probably." Laura started going through the first-aid kit again. "But how? Don't see any forceps or something similar in here."

"Do it," Agent West wheezed. "Now!"

Laura nodded, took a deep breath. Her hand shook as she inserted the syringe into the blood-drenched bullet hole. She slowly forced the pellets out. Agent West groaned.

Laura pulled the syringe back out and placed a compress over the wound. Daniel handed her a gauze bandage, and Laura applied a temporary dressing.

"Let's hope that does the job," she said. "A doctor will have to remove the bullet."

Agent West's hand found Laura's. "That fucking bastard, he tricked us."

"What happened out there?"

"Ambush. Three men are dead. But everything points to Bishop acting alone. We haven't been able to pinpoint his location—"

"I don't understand," Daniel said.

"Remote-controlled ... sniper rifle..."

"Don't talk." Laura pushed wet hair off Agent West's face.

"What now?" Daniel asked.

Laura stood, pulled a barrette from her pants, and clamped her hair down.

"What are you going to do?"

"You stay with her, and make sure that bandage doesn't come off."

"Don't be stupid, Laura."

"I need to get to Robin." She took a look outside. About 150 feet away, three soldiers lay motionless on the muddy ground. The rain pelted down on their dead bodies, mixing with their blood.

"There are six of them—three are still going after Bishop," Daniel added.

"Daniel, you don't understand."

The pilot spoke up. "Because of this hurricane I have instructions to clear out of here in thirty minutes, tops." He gave Laura a hard stare. "Your decision. If you are not back by then . . ."

"You go out there," Agent West whispered faintly to Laura, "and he will kill you."

"I'll be back in a half hour," Laura told the pilot. "With Robin."

"We will not wait," the pilot confirmed.

"Don't do it," Daniel told her.

Laura glanced at him one last time, then jumped out of the helicopter.

55

THE RAIN BATTERED LAURA'S FACE AS SHE RAN TO THE dead soldiers, the soggy grass squelching with every step. She knelt down next to one of the dead, saw that his protective vest was riddled with bullet holes. She took the pistol from his holster and found the weapon surprisingly heavy.

She stuffed it in the back of her waistband. Then she ran onward.

She reached the end of the vast lawn, completely soaked now. It connected to a little park area with leafy trees and cypresses bending violently in the strong winds as leaves and clumps of earth swirled around. Between two of the cypress trees, Laura spotted a rifle on a swiveling bipod—this had to be the remote-controlled rifle Agent West told them about. She gave the bipod a swift kick to knock it over. Now the gun couldn't do any more harm.

Right then she heard shots in the distance.

She crossed the park, went around a wing of the estate, and suddenly faced a low brick wall. Beyond, steep cliffs plunged down to giant waves smashing against jagged rocks, the crashing of the breakers making its way up to her only as muffled thumps. She could see a small island in the distance, out in the churning sea, and the remains of an old fort there. A lone seagull hovered, fighting the wind.

Again she heard shots, this time closer. She leaned over the wall and looked down. She caught her breath. Robin!

Fred Bishop was pulling her son along a coastal road. She scanned the route and realized what the psychopath had in mind. Her stomach tightened. Where the hell was Delta Force? Then she spotted two soldiers a several hundred feet behind Bishop and Robin—they were rushing down a footpath that twisted down to the coastal road from the estate. Where was the third soldier? She headed out for the terrain below her.

The footpath was steep, treacherous. She kept slipping on the wet gravel. As she managed a turn in the path she came upon the third soldier. A bullet had shredded the left half of his face. No one could help him now.

Laura reached the end of the footpath and stepped onto the paved road that wound along the rocky coast like a black ribbon. Churning waves burst at the rocks, and their spray and foam spilled onto the road, leaving large puddles on the asphalt. Laura ran until she reached the causeway leading out to the island. The island was just off the coast, the causeway about twelve feet wide and five hundred feet long. A sign reading *Fort Clonque* clattered in the wind; below it a second sign warned against using the causeway path in the event of flooding. Then she spotted Bishop and Robin out in the middle of the causeway. Bishop was clearly trying to reach the partially ruined fort on the island. The two soldiers followed him but weren't nearly as fast as she hoped. Soon they even had to stop because a three-foot-high wave washed over the causeway right in front of them. Laura swallowed hard. If she was going to reach Robin, she was going to have to cross over that.

She saw to her relief that Bishop and Robin were just then clearing the end of the causeway path, safe from those lethal waves. From there it led uphill to the fort. The two soldiers were still in the middle of the causeway, the waves bursting all around them with full force. Foamy spray blocked her view again. When it returned, she could see a big breaker coming. It kept rising, rolling toward the soldiers. They spotted the foaming, cresting monster. They froze. The wall of water crashed over them and pulled back seconds later, and Laura saw the two mercilessly dragged out to open sea by the current.

She trembled—from the cold, from the horror. She stared at the narrow causeway.

She had no chance of saving Robin if she didn't try.

"Laura!"

It was Daniel. She whipped around. "What are you doing here?"

Daniel pushed his soaked hair off his face. "Come on! The helicopter isn't going to wait much longer," he shouted into the blustering wind. With that he sprinted past her and out onto the causeway.

Laura gathered all her courage and followed. The wet path was slippery, and her ankle boots could get no traction.

Daniel held out a hand. "Give me your hand!"

Hand in hand they ventured forward, step by slippery step. The farther they got from the coast, the bigger the waves crashing against the bank of the causeway and submerging everything in whitewater and foam. Another huge breaker rolled over the path about 150 feet ahead of them, the water washing back foaming and gurgling only to return seconds later. Laura and Daniel looked at each other. They both understood that the next wave of that magnitude would spell certain death.

They fought their way forward. Lightning flickered in the sky behind them, bringing ear-splitting thunder a moment later. Another bolt of lightning shot downward right after.

"Not a good sign," Daniel shouted. "It's getting worse. Hurricane lightning strikes relate to wind speed. The more electrical discharges come down, the stronger the gusts."

"Keep going!" Laura shouted, focused solely on not slipping now. In a few minutes Fort Clonque would likely be cut off from the world for hours, maybe days. The mere thought of Robin alone with the psychopath just about drove her mad.

A few feet before they reached the end of the causeway, a deep rumble made them turn around. The stormy sea had released a huge breaker out of nowhere.

"Come on!" she shouted.

They ran along the final stretch of causeway as fast as they could, still hand in hand. The rushing wall of water neared, threatening to break at any moment. They dared a huge leap onto the island and found cover behind a boulder mere instants before the breaker washed over the causeway.

"That was close," Daniel panted.

Laura's heart raced. She looked up at the fort looming above them all cold and gray. "Let's keep moving!"

They ran up the cobblestone path. When they reached the top, Laura glanced back; she could barely make out the causeway anymore—the sea had swallowed it. She didn't bother worrying about what that meant for finding a way back.

She faced the fort. She saw a wide door of heavy wood next to a tower with arrow slits—the only way into the fort, as far as she could tell. The door had a red metal sign: *Please Respect the Privacy of Our Guests*.

Laura pushed the door open, and they entered the fort.

They found themselves on a small inner courtyard. The surrounding structures were built from rubble stone and provided them with good cover. A door to the left led into the tower with the arrow slits. Laura turned the knob, but the door was locked. Daniel peered into one of the windows. He saw a double bed with a metal frame and an antique chest of drawers, true to the image of a Victorian fort.

"Is this a hotel or something?" he asked.

"Definitely looks like it."

"I'm guessing the guests were evacuated."

"We need to search every corner of this place. Robin has to be here somewhere. I'll start on the right, you look over there."

"No, we stay together."

"But it'll go faster if we—"

Daniel's face darkened. "Have you given any thought to what you're going to do once you find this guy?" He eyed her gun skeptically.

She ignored him.

"He's a professional killer, Laura."

She raised the pistol. "I'm ready for whatever."

Daniel took a deep breath, then nodded. "All right, fine, but we're staying together."

He looked around, and Laura saw what he was looking at. Down along the broad main wall, a path led to more buildings and towers.

"I'm going first," he told her, stepping out into the open. "Let's—"

A shot rang out, echoing off the stone walls.

Daniel cried out and fell to his knees. He grabbed at his left wrist. It took a second for Laura to comprehend what had happened. She then bounded over to him, grabbed him under his armpits, and dragged him back to the cover of the inner courtyard.

She leaned him down against the wall and pushed the hair out of his eyes. Splatters of blood covered his cheeks. He whimpered.

"Show me," Laura said.

He held his hand up, his face contorted with pain. She stared at the blood-smeared lump of flesh that had been Daniel's hand just moments before. His middle and ring fingers were missing. Pulsing blood squirted from an artery.

Laura frantically searched her pockets for a cloth, a tissue—anything she could use to constrict the blood. In her back pocket, she found the extra syringe for stanching blood. Thanks to Agent West, She knew exactly what to do.

She looked at Daniel. He gritted his teeth and nodded for her to go ahead.

Laura carefully inserted the syringe into the bloody flesh and slowly depressed it to implant the pellets. Daniel groaned and automatically tried to pull his hand away, but she grasped his wrist with her other hand until she had injected all of the syringe into the wound.

"All over," she said and tossed the syringe away. "Daniel?"

He didn't answer. His eyes were shut. For a moment, Laura feared the worst. Then she saw his chest rising and falling. He had passed out.

She couldn't do anything more for him at the moment. She took out her pistol and cautiously stood up. She had no idea where Bishop was hiding, but he'd just had a clear shot a moment ago. She wondered why he hadn't fired at Daniel again once he'd put him on the ground, then figured he must have retreated to another part of the fort.

She sprinted back into the open, out in the storm, headed for the opposite wall and took cover there. The fear of taking a bullet like Daniel made her adrenalin spike. She crept along the wall, crouching. The ground rose slightly, up a hill—Bishop must have fired from up there. Lightning was now flashing over the ocean practically nonstop. A broken branch flew by, missing her head by inches.

She rounded a turret, went around a rusty cannon, and soon came to an open yard overgrown with weeds; it was about the size of a soccer field. It looked to be the center of the whole fort. In the middle of the yard, a flagpole wobbled in the wind, its now-ragged Union Jack flapping away. It was a long and steep way down beyond the surrounding outer walls. To the right was a little chapel. There stood Fred Bishop, wearing olive-green camo fatigues and a baseball cap, hammering on the padlock of the chapel's double gate with the butt of his gun.

Next to him stood Robin.

56

LAURA'S HEART POUNDED, BUT SHE DIDN'T HESITATE FOR a second. She raised her gun and slowly advanced toward them. Bishop was still working on the lock. It suddenly sprang open. Robin glanced Laura's way at the same time. His eyes widened.

"Mom!" he shouted. He tried running to her, but Bishop was quicker. He grabbed him by the collar and held him back.

Laura aimed her pistol at Bishop, who now held Robin by the hip, using him as a human shield. His other hand was aiming his gun at Robin.

"If you fire, your son dies," he shouted into the storm.

"Let Robin go!" She stepped forward, undeterred.

"What are you going to do, shoot at me? You'll hit your kid."

About thirty feet separated them now. Laura halted. Her mind was racing. Why had he used the grip of the gun to break open that lock? And why hadn't he fired at her? He could have long ago.

All at once, she realized why.

"You don't have any more ammo. That's why you only fired one shot before. It was your last bullet." She raised her gun a little higher, aiming at his face. "Let my son go—now."

Lightning flashed repeatedly right off the island, followed by thunder strikes sounding like cannons.

"One step closer, and I'll break the kid's neck." Bishop pulled Robin even closer. The boy screamed.

"I'm counting to three," Laura shouted.

As Bishop eyed her, his face contorted into a grin. "Your hand is shaking."

Laura grasped the gun's grip with both hands. "One."

"You won't pull the trigger," Bishop said calmly.

"I wouldn't bet on that. Two."

He grinned again, but to Laura's surprise he suddenly let Robin go.

Robin ran up to her, threw himself up against her, wrapped his arms around her stomach. "Mom!" Tears ran down his cheeks.

Bishop slowly moved her way. "Did you really think you could win?"

Laura pulled back in fear. Robin clung to her, clawing at her. "Stay where you are!"

He came closer. "Like I said. You aren't going to shoot."

Only ten feet separated them now.

Laura's hand shook more than ever. She knew she'd have to fire to save herself and Robin. Yet something inside her would not let her finger pull the trigger. She tightened her grip on the gun. "Don't make me do it."

Bishop spread out his arms. He lunged at her.

Laura pulled the trigger.

Nothing happened. She tried again, but the trigger wouldn't budge.

Bishop closed on her and ripped the gun from her hand in one quick motion. "Seems that I underestimated you. Unfortunately, you forgot to press this little lever here—it releases the safety." He turned the pistol to show her. "Rookie mistake."

She wrapped her arms around Robin, stepping back. A single thought shot through her: *It's all over.*

Bishop leveled the gun at them.

A branch broke off a tree next to the chapel and hit the ground. Bishop glanced up at the sky, and low black clouds started dumping rain full force. "It's time. Say goodbye." He pointed the barrel at Laura's head.

A light brighter than a thousand suns stung Laura's eyes. A crash of thunder rang out right next to her, like a jet fighter breaking the sound barrier. The blast wave hit her, ripping Robin from her arms. She flew several feet through the air, landing on her back in the mud. She couldn't draw breath, and her head felt like it was boiling. She couldn't see or hear, and her muscles quivered beyond her control.

She tried to move, but her body wouldn't obey. Had Bishop shot her? Was this what it felt like to die? But she was still alive. *Wasn't she?*

She lay there like that a while. Then she started to feel the rain falling on her face. The tightening in her chest eased. A blurry image appeared in front of her eyes. *Fire.* Something was burning.

She worked to pull herself up. She could see better now, though the whistling sound in her ears would not go away. In the middle of the yard lay the top of the flagpole, roughly six feet long. It had broken off. The remains of the tattered flag were ablaze. The rain quickly doused the flames, leaving only black wisps of smoke.

Laura peered around frantically.

She first spotted Bishop lying on the other side of the yard on his stomach. He wasn't moving. Then she saw Robin. He too lay motionless, out in the middle of the yard. She ran over to him.

Robin lay on his back. His eyes were closed. Laura knelt next to him and shook him by the shoulder. "Honey, wake up!"

He didn't respond. His left arm lay across his chest. It limply slid off onto the ground. Panic overcame Laura. She shook him as hard as she could. "Wake up!" she screamed. It didn't help. She stared at his chest, and suddenly all the blood drained from her face. Robin wasn't breathing! She felt his neck for a pulse.

Nothing.

Robin was dead.

57

A DARK ABYSS OPENED BEFORE LAURA AND THREATENED to consume her. The howling wind, the crashing surf, the thunder, even the whistling in her ears—all sounds around her seemed to fall away. Her hands were shaking so badly that she couldn't even manage to stroke Robin's cheek. She stared numbly at the lifeless body of her son and yet could hardly see him.

A figure stood next to her all of a sudden. *Daniel.* His face showed pure horror. He was pleading with her and gesturing wildly, but she couldn't understand him. He ended up crouching next to Robin. He leaned over Robin's face, straightened up, then leaned over again. Laura began to comprehend what was happening. Daniel was artificially respirating Robin. He was attempting to bring her son back to life.

All her senses returned at once.

"How can I help?" she said.

Daniel saw her, his face contorted with pain. "He needs cardiac massage. I can't, not with my hand. Press down hard thirty times, then I'll give him air twice. Got it?"

"Yes."

"Go!"

Laura squatted next to her son, set the balls of her hands on his chest, and started pressing down with a quick and steady rhythm. Then she let go and watched Daniel respirate him. Then it was her turn again.

Laura had no idea how many times they traded off. Suddenly Robin twitched underneath her and gasped for air. She let out a hysterical shriek of joy.

Daniel raised Robin's upper body. "Hey, buddy, you back?"

"Robin!" Laura stroked his wet cheeks. "Honey, say something! Mommy's right here."

He slowly opened his eyes. "Where ... am I?"

Laura couldn't speak. Her throat heaved with sobs. She slapped her hands over her mouth and let her tears of joy roll down her face.

"Lightning struck the flagpole," Daniel said. "You guys were pretty close, so you really got it good. A few feet closer, and it would not have ended too well."

Laura hugged Robin, kissed him on the forehead, and rocked him gently. "How did you know," she asked Daniel, "that we could bring Robin back?"

"People who are too close to a lightning strike often suffer cardiac arrest." He looked around. "We have to get out of here before it strikes again."

"The chapel," suggested Laura.

Together they helped Robin to his feet.

"Not so fast," said a voice behind them.

They turned around.

Fred Bishop stood facing them, his feet planted far apart, aiming the gun he'd taken from Laura.

Bishop's fatigues were all muddy, and his pant leg was torn open, revealing the gleaming carbon frame of his prosthesis. His face shined all red and raw. He'd obviously suffered burns. He wobbled slightly.

"A touching scene, really," he said, "but we're still going to end this right here and now."

Daniel turned to Laura and gave her Robin's hand. Their eyes met for a moment. There was a mournful finality to the way that he looked at her. Suddenly he whipped around, charged at the thoroughly surprised Bishop, and rammed a shoulder into his ribs. The impact sent them to the ground. They landed in mud. Bishop lost his gun. Daniel sat on his chest and punched him with his unharmed hand. "Lock yourselves in the chapel!" he shouted at Laura. He had caught Bishop off guard, but Bishop soon recovered. He repelled Daniel's blows with his forearms, reared up and threw Daniel off him.

"Can you walk on your own?" Laura asked Robin.

He nodded.

"Go hide in the chapel. I'll be right behind you."

Robin hesitated.

"Get going!" Laura turned him toward the chapel, and the boy staggered off.

Bishop had gotten the upper hand. He hurled Daniel into the mud headfirst and bent over him; his hands found Daniel's throat. "Going to break your neck, you piece of shit."

Laura ran over and jumped on Bishop from behind. He released Daniel and whirled around in rage, shaking Laura off.

Daniel was able to free his legs. He kicked Bishop hard in the chest.

Bishop reeled backward a few steps.

Daniel sprang up and again charged Bishop, whose movements since the lightning strike seemed wooden and clumsy. Coiled together, they slammed against the ground. Laura watched the two men rolling in the mud, her fear growing. Bishop might have been weakened by lightning, but he was still an ex-Marine with full command of many lethal moves. She had to help Daniel somehow.

The pistol grip was sticking out of the mud a few feet away. She picked up the gun and pointed it at the men. But their tussle had turned them into an inseparable knot. She gradually stepped closer. She watched helplessly as Bishop gave Daniel a punch to the temple, knocking him out. Bishop bared his teeth. His powerful hands were wrapped around Daniel's neck.

Laura stepped behind him, aiming the gun. Bishop whirled around and struck her hard in the face with the back of his hand. The gun flew high in the air. Stars filled Laura's eyes, and she tasted blood. Bishop turned back to Daniel and kept squeezing on his windpipe.

A strong lightning strike over Alderney lit up the scene for an extended moment, the light bouncing off of an object in the grass behind Laura. She bent down and picked up the broken tip of the flagpole. The metal rod was heavy, the fractured end jagged and razor-sharp. She focused on Bishop, still crouched over Daniel with his back to her. She took a deep breath. Then she charged.

She rammed the broken end of the flagpole into his back with all the force she had.

The sharp edges bored through his flesh and exited his gut smeared with blood. Bishop let out a scream. He stared, dumbfounded, at the metal sticking out of his body.

Laura let go, panting, and took a step back.

Bishop screamed again in rage and pain. He tried to stand up but did not quite succeed. He retched and spat blood. He stared at Laura one last time, his eyes full of hatred, and then toppled to the side with the metal rod still through him.

For a moment Laura stood there, frozen. Her breathing came in spurts and ached, her heart thumping. She planted her hands on her thighs and waited for her breathing to return to normal. Then she went over to Daniel.

She knelt next to him and gave his face two hard slaps.

Daniel coughed, opening his eyes. "Oh, damn," he croaked, rubbing at his neck. "What happened to Bishop?"

She pointed behind her. "Dead."

She helped Daniel to his feet and hurried into the chapel, where Robin waited, fearing the worst. Laura shut the door. It took a moment for her eyes to adjust to the darkness. Soaked through and freezing, covered in mud and fully spent, they sat on the pew in front of the plain stone altar. Laura held Robin in her lap and kissed him on the forehead as he buried his head in her arms in thanks. He was trembling. The hurricane shook the door, and the wooden beams of the roof creaked precariously.

"We have a long night ahead of us," Daniel told them. He stared at his severely wounded hand, his face contorting again with pain.

"Is there anything I can do for you?"

He shook his head. "It'll be all right."

It thundered again outside the chapel.

"Do you think it's safe to be in here?" Laura said.

Daniel looked around. "These walls are pretty massive, and they've seen their share of storms."

"But never a hurricane like this one."

A meow echoed through the chapel, then a spotted gray-and-white cat came slinking out from behind the altar. It headed straight for Daniel and rubbed against his legs. Daniel scratched it between the ears. "It's all going to be okay now. See, Robin? This cat's not scared, and cats can always sense danger."

Robin reluctantly reached out to the cat.

Right then the hurricane blew rows of wooden shingles from the roof with an infernal screech. Heavy gusts blew into the chapel, and a puddle quickly formed below the hole in the roof. A partially rotted wooden beam loosened, broke away from its brittle bracket, and came crashing down on the altar right in front of them. The cat leaped away and ran off.

"Cats make mistakes too, I'm afraid," Laura said as she bent over to shield her son. "This might be a good time to pray."

Epilogue

THE WINTER SUN SHONE THROUGH THE LIVING ROOM window, transforming the simple room with the old sofa and cheap shelving into a much more comfortable and pleasant space. Robin knelt on the round carpet in his sweat suit, stroking the cat they had brought back from Alderney.

"Who would have thought?" Daniel said chuckling as he sat at the kitchen table and watched Robin and Sammy playing through the open door.

"They're inseparable, those two," Laura said smiling as she set a pitcher of homemade lemonade on the table. She sat next to Daniel, poured two glasses, and held one out for him. "Three months ago, to the day. Things weren't so cozy then."

Daniel grabbed the glass with his deformed hand. "No, that they were not."

Her smile faded. "How are you coming along?"

He took a look at the scar-covered skin where two of his fingers used to be. "Well, if I ever get married, the ring will have to go on the other hand. So there's that. But I've had enough adventure for the moment, not to mention storms. Here's to that chapel crypt."

They toasted and drank.

"I can't believe you found us shelter in that crypt. If you hadn't spotted the entrance behind the altar, we would not be sitting here today."

"Total fluke."

"It sure was." Laura could still see herself climbing up the stairs of the crypt the morning after the hurricane, holding Robin as she tried to reenter the chapel. Emily had destroyed the roof during the night before knocking the entire chapel to its foundations. That morning they had made their way through the mess of downed rafters and wood shingles and stepped through deep puddles to eventually emerge in the open air.

"The latest estimates are out on the damage Emily caused to Europe's coastlines," Daniel told her. "Insurance companies and reinsurers are now talking more than a hundred billion euros. Just in Europe alone."

"A lot of money. No one talks about the forty-eight dead anymore."

"I will, though—tomorrow on my show."

"That's good." Laura nodded. "Robin's recovering well. He was suffering from nightmares those first few days after the lightning strike, in that hospital in Cherbourg. But it's all subsided." She watched Robin playing with the cat. "Sammy's good for him."

"That's great." Daniel smiled.

Laura eyed him, deep in thought. "We got really lucky, you know. Imagine if that microchip in Bishop's artificial knee hadn't malfunctioned from the lightning strike . . ."

That was the reason that Bishop's movements had been so odd. Under normal conditions they wouldn't have had a chance against him—as Laura knew all too well.

"So, how are you doing?" Daniel asked her.

She looked out the window. "I'm fine." Two weeks before, she had confessed to him that she sometimes suffered from anxiety since Alderney. He didn't press her on the subject. Knowing when to refrain from talking was just one of his many character traits that she had come to appreciate.

"How's it going with your new boss?" he said.

"Not bad. He's more relaxed than Hardenberg."

"Luckily Leinemann didn't have anything to do with the scandal."

Laura nodded. "True. Despite Leif's suspicions, Leinemann had only ever been worried about his company's reputation."

Daniel had changed, she saw. Not much was left of the cocky on-air talent who used to smirk into the camera—even though he had all the more reason to be proud these days.

"So, the new show starts tomorrow," she said. "Nervous?"

Daniel smiled. "Who, me?"

"Now you can show everyone how right you were all along with your theories about controlling the weather. I heard your old university is finally going to accept your dissertation."

He waved away the thought. "Sure, but I'm not interested. Other things are more important at present, as you know."

Laura nodded. "Who do you think is responsible for what's happening in China right now?"

Daniel shrugged. "There's currently only one facility capable of manipulating the weather like that. HAARP 2. We just don't have proof, unfortunately."

"And Charles St. Adams is now working for the CIA?"

"That's just my suspicion. But I assume he was ready to share what he knew with them."

"Of his own free will?"

"I think Lance Deckard found a way to motivate him. Say, a suspended sentence or light house arrest instead of 856 years in solitary, something along those lines."

"That makes sense," Laura said, "considering the name St. Adams never appeared in any official news reports."

"Exactly."

She sipped at her lemonade. "You know what I've been wondering for days now? When will the Chinese respond? And how? It's not a normal situation to be in."

"Hard to say if they're even able to respond."

"How do you mean?"

"I have this theory." Daniel leaned back and rotated his glass back and forth. "It's been raining in northern China for over two weeks now, almost constantly. Devastating storms have already caused flooding in large parts of what's called the Chinese breadbasket and destroyed lots of crops. If it continues, China is facing widespread famine."

"That's what I don't get—why they're not trying to thwart it somehow," Laura said. "They obviously have the means."

"Heilongjiang was destroyed," Daniel reminded her, "and all WetTec facilities were closed until further notice under pressure from the international community."

"But why would the Americans make it rain in China? Wouldn't drought be the logical way to destroy crops?"

Daniel shook his head. "Drought can be overcome with rain. The Chinese are still capable of deploying silver iodide seeding. But they can't fight a monsoon."

"So, the Americans turned the tables and hit China's weak spot," Laura said. "They're now making China pay a bitter price for Emily."

Daniel stood up, stepped to the window, and looked out, lost in thought. "It's looking like the U.S. military has finally attained the goal it's been after for more than twenty years. They're controlling the weather."

They fell silent. Daniel suddenly glanced at the clock and grabbed his jacket from the back of the chair. "I have to go. Final prep for the show." He told Robin goodbye, and Laura walked him to the door.

"After Emily, people should now know better," Laura said. "That hurricane was a warning shot. It could have have turned out far worse."

Daniel nodded. "That's exactly why what's happening in China cannot be swept under the rug."

"So you're planning to tell the truth about it on your show?" She placed a hand on his forearm. She didn't want to let him go. "Deckard won't like you divulging certain things."

Daniel shrugged. "The worst that can happen is they make me look like a crank, a conspiracy theorist. It wouldn't be the first time."

He added a smile, and those pleasant little wrinkles returned to the corners of his eyes, which Laura had liked from the moment she met Daniel. "I think I know what I'm doing," he said.

"I sure hope so," she told him.

Afterword

CHANGING THE WEATHER TO SUIT ONE'S OWN NEEDS IS one of the oldest dreams of mankind, and Daniel Bender in *Storm* was far from the first to consider it. Around 360 BC, the Greek philosopher Plato credited the people of Atlantis with the ability to pull in two harvests a year just by manipulating rainfall. In the Bible, too, we see many examples of weather's lethal power, all caused by divine manipulation. Consider the ten plagues that befell Egypt, or the Deluge—the mother of all weather disasters.

Today, manipulating the weather is no longer a mere intellectual pursuit. Modern science and technology have long taken an active role and have nothing to do with various crank theories about weather control and HAARP that can unfortunately be found all over the Internet. There, on obscure blogs and arcane forums and social networks, people speak of chemtrails all over the globe, of artificially triggered earthquakes, and of thought and mind control through electromagnetic radiation, to mention only a few examples. If anything, modern weather manipulation is quite the opposite of what conspiracy theories claim.

Manipulating the weather has long been a regular occurrence. Humans interfere with natural weather thousands of times a year worldwide, and it is fully legal and official. Since 2002, the Chinese State Weather Modification Office alone has carried out more than five hundred thousand such alterations. The weather also gets manipulated dozens of times every day in the United States, Russia,

Australia, and Thailand specifically, but it's mostly in China. All across the globe, hundreds of companies earn big money by delivering rain to the countryside or preventing potentially dangerous rainfall.

It goes without saying that private interests form only a part of the picture. The potential military applications are manifold and extremely worrisome—the Planning Office of the German Bundeswehr came to the same conclusion in its analysis of late 2012.

My idea for *Storm* was triggered by a U.S. military study from 1996 bearing the title "Owning the Weather in 2025." It provides scenarios of weather manipulation in support of military operations. It also proposes the idea of putting South American drug cartels out of action by directing tropical storms at their strongholds.

One could argue that none of these scenarios have ever been realized. But how could we know? And how could it be proved otherwise? In *Storm*, General Williamson is correct in dismissing any evidence: "There is no proof! This is exactly what waging war with weather manipulation is all about. A country doesn't even notice that it's being attacked. Much less, by whom." The U.S. military has not pumped billions of dollars into this branch of research since the 1960s for no reason. Today, agencies like DARPA are the ones financing projects such as Nimbus, mentioned in this book, which was why Daniel Bender could well have chosen to reword that famous quote from Mark Twain to: "Everyone's doing something about the weather, but nobody talks about it."

Storm is a novel. It is a work of fiction. I invented the names of the protagonists and companies, though some are based on real persons and companies. Equally fictitious are the Heilongjiang and HAARP 2 facilities. The idea for HAARP 2 derives from a project called EISCAT 3D, which was constructed to begin operations in 2020 near Tromsø, Norway. The final stage of this project involves a total of 100,000 antennas at various Scandinavian locations, all linked to one another, radiating pulsed electromagnetic waves into the ionosphere. What's more, dozens of facilities similar to HAARP have been operating worldwide for years. Officially, their intended purpose is always stated as some form of "basic atmospheric research." That can mean anything and rules out nothing.

Also fictitious is the scenario I created combining an "ionosphere heater" with the Diamond gyrotron. While a modern, high-performance gyroscope is capable of the incredible output described in relation to the Wendelstein 7-X nuclear fusion project, the science is still not there yet, as of this writing, for heating the surface of the sea on a large scale. It's my opinion, though, that it's only a matter of time before the technology catches up with my fictional scenario.

Apart from these liberties that I take as an author to provide you, dear readers, with an engaging and thrilling story, all the other agencies and institutions mentioned in this book have existed along with various studies, trials, and projects—there's the CIA's center for climate change as well as HAARP, DARPA, and various patents, even the Egelsbach Transmitter Facility. Plenty of rumors surround that sealed-off compound in the heart of Germany, and no one knows for certain just how vast its underground bunker system truly is or what purpose its many antennas and radomes actually serve. Even the air ionizers deployed in certain regions of the Arabian Peninsula for rainmaking exist; the technology is not quite developed enough, but results so far look promising. All that is thought to be known about the Chinese State Weather Manipulation Office has been confirmed by fact, as are the natural catastrophes described as well as certain inexplicable weather phenomena. It remains to be seen whether any causal links actually exist such as the ones I establish in *Storm*. But we can't rule them out either.

Correspondingly, all the failed weather experiments I describe are proven to have occurred, as have the repercussions. Some of the stories were only confirmed by official bodies some fifty years after the fact, as was the case with the Lynmouth disaster in England. I'm convinced that we are still being left in the dark about many other episodes. The only ones that were fully the products of my imagination were the city of Yakutsk sinking into thawing permafrost soil and Lake Alexandria in Australia drying up.

Every year, thousands of alterations to the earth's atmospheric circulation are carried out worldwide. The idea that a butterfly flapping its wings in Beijing could cause a hurricane to hit New York is the simplified version of the branch of mathematics known as chaos theory, which takes weather as its prime example—if you manipulate the weather at a certain spot, the side effects could be unpredictable. As the theory goes, a brief rainstorm caused by silver iodide cloud seeding might lead to a dangerous snowstorm at a different location (see Beijing in 2009). So if a single alteration is not without certain consequences, then what might be the overall effect of a steady accumulation of such manipulations?

I don't mean to paint too bleak of a picture. Any scenario like we see in *Storm* would only come in the distant future, if ever. No one on our planet will rise to become ruler of our weather anytime soon. My fear, however, is that many countries are working toward this very goal right at this moment.

PS: For further information and links about this topic, come visit my website:

www.uwelaub.de

Feel free to contact me there as well with any feedback. I'm looking forward to it!

Acknowledgments

IN WRITING A NOVEL, AN AUTHOR ALWAYS RELIES ON certain people for valuable help and support during various stages of the writing process; *Storm* would never be what it is without such individuals. I would therefore like to express my warmest thanks to the following people:

Florian Sellmaier and Bernadette Jung from the German Aerospace Center in Oberpfaffenhofen near Munich for highly interesting discussions about the technologies and processes involved in satellite missions as well as the opportunity to peek behind the scenes.

Dennis Feltgen and John Cangialosi from the National Hurricane Center in Miami for their exciting and illuminating insights into predicting, analyzing, and monitoring tropical storm systems as well as for their knowledge of evacuation processes and Hurricane Hunters missions.

Michael Nonnengäßer from Nonnengäßer & Tebbi orthopedic technologies for their remarkable insights about modern leg prostheses. Any errors involving technology or science that found their way into *Storm* are due to me alone.

I would also like to thank:

Tim Müller from the Heyne publishing house and Heiko Arntz for their critical and extremely keen editing as well as valuable advice on storytelling.

Markus Naegele and the entire Heyne team for all the expert work required to create a published book.

Markus Michalek from AVA International literary agency for his enthusiasm for *Storm* as well as for his tireless commitment and always sympathetic ear.

Roman Hocke and the entire AVA International team for their outstanding support and professionalism.

Rainer Wekwerth, who went through the story and plot with me and always had valuable comments and suggestions.

The ladies from my office, who always had my back and freed up my workload so that I could find the spare time to write: Andrea, Katrin, Simone, Conny, Anita, and Anni—I appreciate it all very much.

My friends from the "Fat Poets Society" (Club der fetten Dichter), who always provided a sounding board as well as valuable tips. The ouzo always tastes best there with you at Perry's place.

I thank you, dear readers, for choosing *Storm* from so many wonderful books out there. I hope I was able to provide you with a compelling read.

My greatest thanks, though, go to my family—to my wife, Marion, above all, for her valuable comments and advice on the manuscript but especially for her love, patience, and support, particularly when things weren't exactly going as I'd imagined. I'd also like to thank my daughter, Amélie, as well as my parents, who have always shown such wonderful understanding, are always there for me, and allow me the freedom to write. I love you all!

—Uwe Laub

About the Author

Uwe Laub was born in Romania in 1971 and returned to Germany with his family at the age of two. Laub worked for several years in pharmaceutical sales before starting his own company in 2010. His main passion is writing. He spent years researching the techno-thriller *Storm*.

www.uwelaub.de

About the Translator

Steve Anderson is a translator, an editor, and a novelist. His latest novel is Lost Kin. He was a Fulbright Fellow in Munich, Germany, and lives in Portland, Oregon.

www.stephenfanderson.com